The horrors he bring...
horrors...

A dark figure emerged from the mists.

Opening their eyes wide, the guards made to stop him, stepping in his way and crossing their silver-tipped spears, but one look from the night-clad man and they cringed back. He didn't have to speak—the chilling resolve that surrounded him said enough. It didn't even occur to them to ask his name or his business, for they knew they would soon find out. They weren't sure, however, that they wanted to.

The man called Walker strode calmly past the silent, nervous guards without a second glance, carrying a small bundle wrapped in rough leather. His pace was relaxed and his strides were great.

He had one task: an ultimatum to issue. A warning.

Erik Scott de Bie spins a haunting tale of revenge, honor, love, and hate, all bound within a dark man whose indomitable spirit marks him as one of

FORGOTTEN REALMS®

THE FIGHTERS

Master of Chains
Jess Lebow

Ghostwalker
Erik Scott de Bie

Son of Thunder
Murray J. D. Leeder

Bladesinger
Keith Francis Strohm

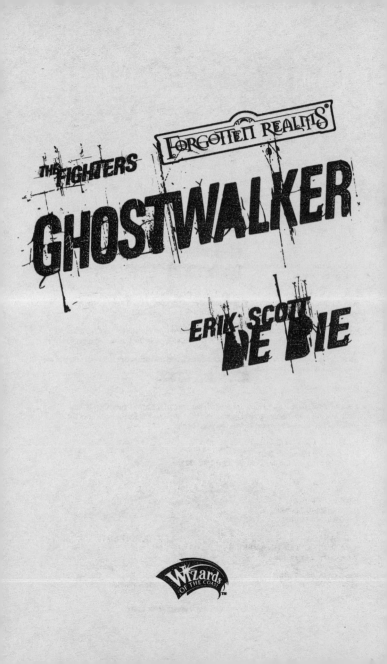

THE FIGHTERS

FORGOTTEN REALMS

GHOSTWALKER

ERIK SCOTT DE BIE

Wizards
OF THE COAST

The Fighters
Ghostwalker

©2005 Wizards of the Coast, Inc.

Cover art by Raymond Swanland
First Printing: December 2005
Library of Congress Catalog Card Number: 2005932832

9 8 7 6 5 4 3 2

ISBN-10: 0-7869-3962-1
ISBN-13: 978-0-7869-3962-6
620-95602740-001-EN

U.S., CANADA,
ASIA, PACIFIC, & LATIN AMERICA
Wizards of the Coast, Inc.
P.O. Box 707
Renton, WA 98057-0707
+1-800-324-6496

EUROPEAN HEADQUARTERS
Hasbro UK Ltd
Caswell Way
Newport, Gwent NP9 0YH
GREAT BRITAIN
Save this address for your records.

Visit our web site at **www.wizards.com**

Dedication

To Shelley, my perfect melody.
If I could sing of her forever, it might be enough.

Acknowledgements

My heroes who inspire,
My family who support,
My friends who cheer,
My editors who guide,
And my readers who enjoy;
All I would acknowledge.

30 Tarsakh, the Year of the Serpent
(1359 DR)

He ran through the woods, jumping at every snapping twig, every moving shadow. The height of the moon told him it was midnight, but the youth cared little. His clothes had been torn to ribbons in his desperate flight, and his flesh had been scratched brutally by the shrubs, branches, and rocks.

The youth would do anything to avoid his pursuers.

Cruel faces, real and imagined, greeted him at every turn, and sometimes a fist lashed out and sent him sprawling. He always got up again, his head ringing and his vision swimming, only to run on, mocking laughter echoing behind him. They were playing with him, as a cat toys with its prey, allowing him to run and to think he might escape, but ultimately wearing down his nerves—and his fragile resolve—to nothing.

"Oh, Ri-in," a voice came, "here little Rhyn!"

Startled, Rhyn Thardeyn stumbled, tripped, and fell with a cry down a rocky hill into muddy water. He struggled to rise and squeaked despite himself when fiery pain shot through his right leg, and he collapsed again. He heard their voices steadily approaching and was nearly petrified with doubt and uncertainty, unsure of which direction to run—or even if running had any purpose.

The youth was thinking about how to drag his twelve-year-old body along when he heard footsteps among the trees. He froze.

"Why do you run, lovely boy?" a sharp voice called sweetly. "Come—come dance with me. I'll teach you how."

"Ugly little goblin's get," a gruff voice joined the first. "Come an' face us like a man. We won't hurt ye ... much."

He cowered, hiding deep in the shallows, coated in mud. He saw two forms run by—the two men who had shouted. They seemed oblivious to his presence.

Fighting to calm his breathing, Rhyn hummed a merry tune over and over again in his head. Everything would be all right. Everything ...

Rhyn heard a splash in the stream behind him. Slowly, he turned to look.

A young boy with curly ebony hair waded there, dressed in rich silks.

Rhyn looked, pleading, into the boy's eyes, and saw there unwillingness, even sympathy. The boy was not to blame for the sins of the father.

"I've found him!" shouted the boy. It was a condemnation.

Then they were upon him, rough hands clutching at his arms and his broken leg. He screamed and cried for his mother, but it was no use.

They threw him down in the circle of trees and lay into him with hobnailed boots. The kicks broke ribs, arms, and his uninjured leg, and when he tried to rise, the pain drove him back before the brutal men could punch him down once more.

Finally, the beating stopped. Rhyn looked up with bleary, red-filled eyes.

"You're going to die now, boy," a thick, slurred voice said. A huge man with a heavy wood axe loomed over him, patting the massive weapon.

"No, no, let him dance with me first," the thin man said. A rapier gleamed in his hand, and he whisked it through the air. "I will enjoy tracing his red trail, watching his broken moves. Come dance with me, boy—I'll be the last thing you ever see."

"If any o' us gets him, it'll be me!" said a bearlike man with a wicked grin. "I'll grind his bones an' tear his flesh with me teeth!"

Moaning, Rhyn tried to curl into a ball, away from them, away from the world of pain.

"Now, now, gentlemen," said the leader in a sonorous voice. He was the one Rhyn feared the most—the one behind this, the one who commanded the others. Rhyn just wanted to get away from him, the man he had once wanted to become.

"Please . . . please m-my Lord Greyt. . . ." he managed through cracking lips. His voice was broken and slurred with pain.

His pleas went ignored. The man bent low over Rhyn and slipped a silver ring onto his finger.

"We have a job to do, and we shall do it." He flipped his rapier idly in the moonlight. "One blow at a time. Don't worry about killing him—'tis *my* ring. Death won't spoil our fun, or his pain. Let us hear him sing."

Mocking, lyrical words. . . .

"Aye," said the woodsman, "me first."

The axe came down and Rhyn screamed as it cut into his shoulder.

"Then me," the thin man said before the bearlike one could speak. The rapier pierced Rhyn's arm, bringing with it razor-sharp pain.

"My turn!" the bear man spat.

The boy prayed he was far enough gone that he would not

know pain, but when the spiked ball of the man's weapon slammed into his chest, he felt every shattering rib.

Rhyn moaned as darkness closed in. Blood trickled from his mouth.

"Good work," the leader said. Somehow, Rhyn could still hear. A rapier gleamed golden in the moonlight. "Now, let us teach him a new song."

The boy stood over Rhyn, his eyes filled with fire. Anger? Rage? Indignation? Rhyn had thought there was softness there....

Then he passed out, whether for a moment or an eternity, he did not know. He felt someone reach down and pull the silver ring from his finger—the ring whose magic had kept him alive through this torture.

"A horde of good it will do you now," said a soft voice.

Arguing broke out in the darkness. Lord Greyt was angry. "That was never our bargain!"

Whispers.

"Damned if you will have this boy!" Rhyn heard someone shout.

A cold finger ran down his cheek—the touch of death.

Then a sharp pang ran through his chest, a blade pierced his throat, and he started back into the world of misery.

"Let's hear you sing now," the soft voice said.

Rhyn opened his lips, as though to oblige, and only a bloody rattle emerged.

Angry shouts erupted and a scuffle ensued. Something small and metal, like a tear, fell against his left cheek and rested next to his eye.

"Whether you will it or no," whispered another voice in his ear.

The world went black.

CHAPTER 1

24 Tarsakh, The Year of Lightning Storms
(1374 DR)

Shivering, the courier pulled her cloak tight around herself, warding off the chill of the Moonwood night. At least the stinging drops no longer slapped down on her—the forest canopy caught much of the rain. She rode slowly down the road to Quaervarr so her mare could avoid stumbling on unforeseen rocks and sticks. Her parents told her spring was coming, but it was definitely taking its time. Chandra Stardown couldn't stand the cold, and she prayed to Mielikki and Chauntea that the warmth would come soon.

She clutched the leather case strapped around her stomach protectively, just to reassure herself it was there. This was not Chandra's first assignment, so negligence or jitters would not be excused. Grand Commander Alathar had said this message was important, so it wouldn't do to lose it en route. If she wanted a promotion, perhaps even membership in the famous Knights in Silver, she could not fail.

As she rode deeper into the shadowtops and firs of the Moonwood, the storm passed. The cold, however, grew no gentler. Chandra longed for the Whistling Stag, where she could order a room and a long, hot bath with the silver her father had loaned her.

Abruptly, Songbird, Chandra's mare, neighed and tossed her mane. She stopped all forward motion and pranced in a circle.

"What is it, girl?" Chandra asked, running a soothing hand along Songbird's mane. "Did you see something?"

Chandra looked around, but didn't see anyone. The trees loomed forbiddingly beside the trail like towering mountains hiding unseen dangers in their heights. She looked up, wary of an ambush by gnolls or even elves, and clutched her silver short spear tightly. Even though the real threat of the Moonwood—the People of the Black Blood, a cult of werebeasts—had been chased away months before, Chandra's father had wanted her to be prepared. The courier was far from a capable fighter, but any werewolf would think twice before it charged onto a silver spearhead.

There was something out there, something that had frightened Songbird, but Chandra didn't see anything out of the ordinary. The forest was peaceful.

Somehow it seemed almost *too* peaceful. The birds had stopped chirping, and there were no sounds of rustling leaves or lonely crickets. Absolute silence reigned.

The hair on the back of her neck rose and Chandra had the unnerving sensation she was being watched. Was she being hunted? Surely no werebeast would dare....

Another cold sensation ran through her—this one very different. She was suddenly intensely conscious of the blood pumping through her veins and the breath passing through her lungs—more so than she had ever been before. Trembling, she became aware of a ghostly presence, one that touched her soul with tenuous fingers and probed at the vibrancy within her, seeking, perhaps, to explore.

Or to feast.

She had heard legends about a ghost who haunted these woods, but she had always dismissed them as mere fancy, as children's stories told by young men who wanted to weasel their way into awed young ladies' beds.

Until now.

"Chandra..." the wind seemed to whisper.

Chandra dug her spurs into Songbird's side and the mare gave a fierce neigh as they burst into a gallop. Chandra no longer cared about the rocks and twigs—Songbird could handle herself. Indeed, the mare seemed just as terrified as she was. All Chandra cared about was getting away from that awful feeling, that ghostly chill that had come upon her. She flicked the reins and shouted to Songbird, urging her on to Quaervarr.

As such, she hardly even registered the click of the crossbow until a bolt sprouted in her right shoulder.

Gasping in surprise and pain, Chandra jerked in the saddle, slamming her head into a low-hanging tree branch. The impact hurled her off Songbird's back, and she landed with jarring force on the ground. Fortunately, the trail lay muddy with rain—else, her back might have snapped from the impact.

As it was, Chandra sat stunned for a moment. Then a ringing broke out in her head, an ache tore her backside, and the sucking pain of the bolt in her shoulder cried for attention. Her leg was twisted as well. Hot blood flowed into her eyes, and the world was cast in crimson. She wiped at her face, clearing the sticky stuff as best she could, but more oozed from the cut on her forehead.

Then she remembered Songbird, galloping on ahead of her.

"Wait!" she tried to cry out, but the choked sound that came from her throat was more a gurgle than a word. Chandra tried to push herself to her feet, but horrible pain lanced through her and she collapsed to the ground again with a short scream. Dragging her broken leg behind her and wincing from the darkwood shaft in her shoulder, she crawled along the trail after Songbird.

Right up to a pair of black boots.

Chandra looked up at the man standing over her. Cloaked with a cowl that covered his face, he seemed a pillar of black. A sheathed sword hung from one hip.

"A-ah," Chandra started to choke out. "H-help . . . m-me . . . P-please. . . ."

The man may have smiled at her, but she could not see through the black hood pulled low. He bent down and ran one cold finger down her cheek.

She thought she could hear her name on the wind.

Few heard Chandra's scream, except for unthinking animals, and even they recoiled.

❖ ❖ ❖ ❖ ❖

It was a cold evening after the rain passed—the last great chill of winter—but the darkness was warm with cheer.

Hundreds had crowded into the plaza of Quaervarr for the largest gathering in months. Children huddled with their mothers, trying to pull as much of themselves into the warmth of their parents' cloaks as they could. Fathers and unmarried men mulled around in the town square, working to light the fires before dusk, trading hearty jokes and even more raucous laughter. Even the grumpy ones could hardly keep smiles off their faces. Fine, fey eyes twinkled and a scattering of elf faces seemed to glow in the falling light of the setting sun. The men finally got the fires lit, and flames danced up, hissing and crackling. Children laughed and squirmed, escaping possessive mothers.

Tonight would mark the beginning of the Greengrass festival which would end with the dawn of spring seven days hence. Cruel winter would leave behind the frontier town of Quaervarr, and the rebirth of all growing things would see the people of the Moonwood in higher spirits. True, the winter frost would not actually leave until summer, but there was a noticeable difference between winter's cold and spring's cool.

Lord Dharan Greyt had always preferred the spring.

Gold-haired, clad in a rich crimson doublet, and wrapped in a violet cloak with gold lining, the Lord Singer of the Silver Marches cut a dashing figure as he stepped onto the wooden stage in the square. A one-eyed wolf, his family seal, grinned from the velvet of his cloak. At once the crowd went silent, waiting to hear him speak, but he merely looked out at them, a sea of blank faces.

All of them looked expectant. All expect one: the handsome, dusky face of Meris, framed with ebony curls and sitting atop his white-cloaked body. Meris looked on in bemused contempt. Greyt suppressed a smile. Much of the rabble was hopelessly bewitched at the sight of the Lord Singer, but not Meris. He was greater than any of them.

Greyt was pleased. He expected nothing less from his favorite—and only living—son.

Straight-faced, he tossed back his cloak and drew forth his gleaming golden rapier with a flourish. The crowd was stunned and drew back in awe.

"Well met, my friends!" His voice was rich and melodious, as though he sang a tune with every word. "Spring is coming—let's come to an accord!" Greyt spun his sword once with dazzling finesse and stabbed it into the planks at his feet where it stood, quivering. The audience gasped. "To live by art instead of the sword!"

Greyt smiled as he pulled his golden wood yarting from beneath his cloak. He strummed a perfect chord on the gilded instrument.

The crowd erupted into cheering as the Lord Singer began a raucous and comical story about a wandering lady, a dimwitted squire, and the dragon he had lost. The lewder adventures drew shocked gasps from the younger ladies, roaring laughter from the men, and giggles from more than a few older women. Mothers, stifling guffaws, remembered themselves and covered their children's ears.

Greyt saw two of his closest friends—Drex Redgill and Bilgren Bladefist—in the back of the crowd, roaring drunk, alternately shouting challenges to young rangers in the square and making lecherous comments to serving wenches. Just like in their adventuring days, Greyt mused.

The Lord Singer saw Bilgren shove one man down and steal his sweetheart—or strumpet, as the case may have been. Greyt decided it was time to change key.

The song took on an epic tone as he began a ballad of battles. Greyt sang of Quaervarr's victory against Fierce Eye's giants in the Year of Moonsfall, 1344: he sang of the glorious defense and of the heroic Raven Claw band—his own adventuring group.

Meanwhile, he plied his bardic magic through the music, creating curtains of flame and illusions of brave knights, fierce giants, and dancing dragons to amaze the crowd. Drex and Bilgren calmed and joined in the singing, lending their slurred voices to the cacophony. Even the sneering half-elf Torlic, the only other surviving member of the Raven Claw band, watched from the edge of the crowd. The people cheered, enraptured. Greyt almost enjoyed it.

He sang a third ballad, this one again about Quaervarr: the well-known legend of the Ghostly Lady who haunted the Dark Woods to the west. It had started one night over a century ago—a night of fire and death woven by a beautiful angel of fury. The druids of the Oak House—an order recently established at that time—had fought her and ended the threat with her death, but the town thrived on stories that called her alive and well, or perhaps undead and well, haunting the woods. More than a few children—and some who were older than children—shivered at Greyt's tale and smiled all the wider for it.

There was a moment of silence. The yarting fell still, and the people grew silent. After allowing the tension to build, Greyt began the story of Gharask Child-killer, the mad lord, his own father, and the tragic disappearances fifteen years before, when nine of the town's children had fallen to the mad hand of—

Greyt's fingers faltered and his voice cracked for the first time in thirty years as a bard.

A cloud uncovered the moon and he saw a figure clad all in black watching his performance as it walked over the crest of the hill at the edge of town. The figure wasn't just watching him, though—it was staring right through him. Even at a distance of nearly a quarter of a mile, Greyt could feel that gaze, palpable and fierce, boring into him, seeing through his art, and searching his very soul.

"A ghost that walks. . . ." he breathed. The legend of Walker of the woods had long been the subject of hunters' whispers and boys' blustering—but it was just a ghost story. Nothing more than foolish child's play.

He blinked, and the dark figure was gone as though it had never been.

The Lord Singer realized he had paused for a full breath at his father's name, and the villagers were looking at him in shock. He gave a little shrug and tried to begin again, but he had lost the note. He flashed a dazzling smile, bowed, and proceeded to hurry off the stage to uncertain applause. Meris was there, smirking, and near him the sharp-eyed Torlic, but Greyt skulked past. Speaker Geth Stonar, mopping his thick forehead, moved to stop him, but the bard stormed on.

His mind reeled. He wanted to dismiss the incident as a mere trick of the light, or the result of too much wine, but those had never broken his song before. Perhaps he was just getting old.

It began to rain, a bitter, cold cloudburst, and Lord Dharan Greyt shivered.

❂ ❂ ❂ ❂ ❂

The streets emptied soon after the rain began. The few hundred citizens of Quaervarr dispersed into the town's several common rooms to celebrate with ales and friends or scurried back to their homes, where they might celebrate in a more private, intimate fashion.

For Drex Redgill, the latter was the case. Roaring drunk, the man bid farewell to his friend Bilgren and staggered home with his squire and servants, eagerly seeking his room and the half-elf lass hired for the occasion. His was a large house in the south part of town, girded on every corner by watchtowers and guards.

The stranger knew this because he watched it all from the shadows.

Walker considered the scale of this duel. Guards didn't make for a fair confrontation. Of course, once Walker penetrated the house, the scales would tip in the other direction. Did two inequalities make equality? He did not care. Fairness seemed like something his father would scold him about. If Tarm could speak, that was.

As for how to get in . . . There was only one way in.

"Cold as winter," he whispered. His voice was a deep rasp.

❧ ❧ ❧ ❧ ❧

The guards started when a man dressed in black melted from the shadows a short distance away and took a step toward them. A sweeping, tattered cloak fanned out behind him. Dark, rain-slick hair that might have been brown fell to his shoulders in a ragged mass. His collar was pulled up high, obscuring his mouth. But more than anything else, he wore resolution around him like a mantle. The intensity of his deep blue eyes was chilling. This man seemed a demon in flesh.

"Oi, where did ye come from?" the scarred one asked. "Ye don't be no friend o' Jarthon, do ye?" The second, much younger guard shook himself from his stupor and hefted his halberd.

The phantom man planted a fist in the first man's face. Blood burst from the guard's nose and he staggered back. The young man let the halberd fall from his cold fingers in surprise. The weapon clattered to the ground with a loud rattle and he grabbed for it with an oath.

The scarred guard yanked out a sword and thrust, but the phantom slapped the blade away and punched the guard hard in the stomach. The older man went down to his knees.

"Gods be curs—" the guard managed. Then a foot met his face and ended his obscenities.

The younger guard, eyes wild with terror, managed to draw his short sword. As if he had sensed the blade, the dark man turned toward the guard, throwing his cloak out wide.

Shaking, the guard thrust blindly into the shadow.

To his surprise, the blade sank home, drawing blood, and the phantom staggered and fell to the ground. The guard's blade went with it, red fluid leaking around the sharp steel.

The clouds chose that moment to release their rain.

It took the younger guard twenty breaths to steady himself. He was too terrified to be ashamed, shaking like a goblin before a dragon.

The other guard, recovered from the stranger's attack, slapped him on the side of the head. "Oaf!" he shouted at the boy. "Ye didn't 'ave to kill him! How're we going to explain this? A drunk wanders up after the party an' ye spit him? Are ye stupid?"

"But . . ." the youth stammered as his scarred companion knelt to examine the body. He had never killed a man before. "I didn't mean—"

"Oh, 'tis sure ye didn't *mean*," the older guard mocked. He felt at the dark man's throat. "Damn. 'E be dead." He reached out and punched the youth's thigh. "Idiot! At least help me dispose o' the poor bastard, aye?"

Together, they hoisted the dark figure up and dragged him to the alley near Drex's house, where they unceremoniously dumped the body. The youth started off, shaking, but remembered and reclaimed his short sword, yanking it from the dark man's belly. The blade made a sickly squishing sound coming out of the flesh. The youth wiped it on the dead man's cloak.

Not much blood. The man didn't seem to bleed much, now that he was dead.

The older guard drew the man's silvery sword and stuck it in the hole in his side. The handle was bitterly cold, and the blade seemed almost translucent in the moonlight, prompting both guards to make the warding gesture of Silvanus.

An accident, a passerby would think, with Tymora's blessing. Lord Singer Greyt would be another matter, but he need not know.

"C'mon." The scarred guardsman spat at the youth. "Come, afore someone be seein' us."

They left the body slumped in the alleyway and hurried away.

The rain chilled to the bone.

❂ ❂ ❂ ❂ ❂

Walker waited until they were gone before opening his eyes. The sword—his sword—in his side hurt, but Walker was used to pain. He grasped the sword hilt and pulled the weapon out. The wound began to mend, thanks to his ring. He rubbed the silver wolf's head with its single sapphire eye and empty socket. At least the guards had not noticed the shine of silver and taken the ring from his cold, "dead" finger.

"Still as death," Walker said quietly as he sheathed his sword.

He had almost achieved his goal. The wall of the house of Drex was not an arm's length away.

Closing his eyes and laying his hands upon the stones, Walker allowed himself to slip into the Ethereal, where he existed but could barely feel his body. Only the heat of his hate differentiated him from the icy darkness. The world became dusky, shapes and objects mere blurry masses, and the moonlight turned into a soft, muddy radiance. He let his body relax, felt his weight lighten, and he could feel a gentle tug, the pull toward somewhere else. . . .

Walker tapped into powers few could understand and even fewer dared touch and walked into the wall.

And through the wall.

In a heartbeat, he was inside Drex's mansion. He let the ghostly power slide from him but maintained his focus. His body became heavier and he could feel the air around him. He sensed the warmth radiating from a distant hearth, where a fire still smoldered. He was tempted to move toward that heat, but he put the ache aside.

He would not fail in this. He could not fail.

He moved through the hallways as a black fish moves through a dark stream. Two servants passed, carrying a basket of woolens and a platter of empty plates and tankards respectively, and Walker did not hinder them, hiding against the wall with ease.

As Walker turned a corner, a guardsman carrying a candle almost ran into him. "Wha—" the man started.

Walker's sword was out, darting for the guard's life. Light from the spilling candle flashed along its mithral surface, dazzling the guard. The man stumbled back and set a hand on his own weapon, but before he could draw he stopped, shuddered, and slumped down, gagging. The dying guard glimpsed the dagger standing out of his throat then stared at the gleam of Walker's mithral blade, still distracting him even after the real attack had come.

Walker whispered an apology over the body—the guard had not been his target. He knelt and recovered his knife with a quick jerk. Blood splashed on his cloak but did not discolor the black.

Black absorbs blood, Walker mused wryly. Black covers all things and hides all hurts.

Drex's bedchamber stood within half a dozen paces. Though he had no foreknowledge of the house, he could recognize the grunting and yelping sounds coming from behind the door easily enough. With a dismissive shake of his head, he turned the handle, silently opened the door, and slipped into the warm room.

Drex was in bed, and he was not alone. Walker averted his eyes and drifted silently over to an axe on the mantelpiece.

Rain pounded on the wooden roof overhead and on the shutters. A fire was sputtering and dying on the hearth, and he could feel the enticing heat as he neared it. Walker had known so little warmth that he found it succulent, fulfilling, and altogether intoxicating. He could have forgotten his purpose and just sat, watching the fading flames spark and flicker. They called to him....

But the voices he heard were those of spirits rather than flames, hissing whispers of unwanted memories of pain and hatred. The fragments of words cut like knives.

He stood, tall and slim, and pulled his cloak around him. Lightning flashed and thunder growled outside. He waited, motionless and prepared. It fell to his enemy to make the first move. Drex would notice his presence when he was no longer distracted.

Soon enough, Drex's eye happened to wander the room and alight on Walker. Or, rather, his looming shadow on the wall.

"Who's there?" Drex stuttered, shoving the lass away.

Walker didn't answer. He merely stood, blending in with the surrounding dark, but Drex met his terrible gaze and the rest of the world seemed to slide away.

Drex sat bolt upright in bed, startling his courtesan. "Who in the Nine Hells are you?" he roared, now angry. The older man was from the south, by his accent. Walker remembered that.

And more.

A memory washed over him: *Pain, blood. Drex's laughter. Swords...death....*

"I am tears on the mountain," Walker said. His voice was a rasp, a deep, throaty whisper. "I am the chill in the night. I hunt with the spirits, and I walk with the dead ... as will you." He put his hand on his sword hilt. "Soon."

Drex shivered at the intensity of that glare, but he sprang from bed all the same. He yanked the blanket with him, revealing the cowering woman, who screamed and curled into a ball. He wound it around himself to cover his nakedness.

In truth, Walker did not care. He kept his arms crossed and his gaze level.

"Pretty speech," Drex chuckled. His hair was gray now. Different. "One of Greyt's 'prentices, eh?"

Walker felt a flicker of irony, but the feeling passed. His neutral frown was hidden behind the twin flaps of his high collar. Lightning flashed again. Drex was approaching fifty now, almost double Walker's age. They stalked around each other.

"Sounds like something out of the Singer's songs, lad," Drex said. "So what, you barge into my room in the night to tell me a children's rhyme? You think I'm in the mood?" He laughed and gestured to the terrified woman.

"Apparently not," Walker replied in a monotone. He remembered the axe, the blood running down his chest and arms, the murderers standing over him. . . .

"Then speak, boy." Drex's voice became irate. "Speak quickly. As you can see, I'm occupied at the moment." The woman had rolled off the bed and was hiding beside it. "What is it you want?" he demanded.

"Your life," Walker replied.

Drex froze, staring at the ghostwalker in outright shock. His expression turned to one of anger, then disdain, then contempt.

"I have no time for the games of Dharan Greyt or that bastard son of his," said Drex. He spat at Walker's feet, then reached over and hefted the great woodsman's axe from the mantelpiece. "Now get out, or I'll send you out . . . in several small bundles."

"No," Walker said. "You will not."

Drex slashed his axe at him in reply, his shout slurred with too much ale.

Walker sidestepped and brought his arm around with a snap as though embracing Drex, allowing the axe to swipe past and the drunken lord's momentum to carry him staggering toward the opposite wall. The heel of Walker's hand darted for Drex's back and should have put him down, but the lord dived, rolled, and came up, his axe slashing across in a blur. Walker fell back, and the blade tore a long gash through his cloak.

Drex kept up the assault, egged on by the ripping of fabric, and reversed his slash.

Dark cloak trailing, Walker leaped horizontally over the flashing steel and rolled away from the deadly side chop—even when half-drunk, Drex was fast—and the steel burst wood chips from the side of a desk. Walker came up with his hand on his sword hilt and his knees bent. His hard eyes cut into Drex's watery ones. The lord was growing sober.

"You move like Torlic," growled Drex as he pulled the axe free, splintering the hardwood desk. "All jumping an' twirlin' like a lass."

"Torlic," repeated Walker, the name crashing against his mind like a wave. Torlic. . . .

Seeing his opponent distracted, Drex slashed low.

Walker leaped, his black boots clearing the glittering steel by a hair's breadth, and turned in the air, lashing out with one foot. He caught Drex on the chin and sent him staggering back a few steps. Walker landed with a creak of wood even as Drex crashed backward into a nightstand, spilling several tankards and a pouch of coins to the floor.

The woodsman felt at the blood coming from his split lip and looked at Walker in surprise. Then his face twisted in outrage. "You're going to die now, boy!" Drex growled.

Walker shuddered, a memory flooding through him: Drex's face, red with blood that wasn't his, laughing at those same words. Walker's eyes narrowed. The world slowed as a dead calm flooded his limbs.

You're going to die now, boy!

"I remember you," he pronounced, as though intoning an elegy. "Standing over me. . . ."

"As I will be in a moment," Drex growled. His words spoke of confidence, but his eyes held doubt.

Walker drew his sword, letting the mithral glow with silver fire. The weapon seemed ghostly, almost translucent, though surely it was a trick of the light.

"The time has come for a reckoning, Drex Redgill," Walker said softly. A familiar bleak power filled him—a terrible emptiness in which nothing existed.

Nothing but vengeance.

The axe darted, but Walker flowed out of the way. It missed cutting through his floating cloak by a breath. Drex reversed the blow, but Walker almost lazily swept his long sword down, catching the axe and throwing it back as though Drex were a child. The lord roared in frustration and slashed at him again and again, but Walker turned it aside each time.

Each time, he felt the pain of those first blows, struck so long ago....

After the fifth chop, Walker countered, his movement casual but blindingly fast. The sword seemed to snap into his left hand, startling Drex so that he missed the parry. Walker's blade slashed a line across Drex's naked torso.

Pained, the lord grunted and slashed, but Walker easily parried and countered, stabbing Drex in the thigh.

The warrior slashed again, hit nothing, took a third cut to his belly, and roared.

Drex chopped high to low with his axe. Walker parried it high and the blades locked. Drex punched Walker's shoulder, but the dark man shrugged off the blow, shifted the sword to his right hand, and answered with a left hook to Drex's jaw. The lord staggered back, Walker chopped at Drex's weapon, and the mithral blade cut through it like paper, laying the axe blade in two.

Drex looked as though he would have said something, but Walker sliced open his throat. Blood splattered the half-elf courtesan's face. Without a word, Drex slumped onto his belly.

Lightning crackled and thunder roiled. The man in black stood over him and reached a tentative hand up to touch his own shoulder.

The woman whimpered. After a heartbeat, Walker regarded her.

Then he vanished as lightning struck.

CHAPTER 2

25 Tarsakh

The day was born stormy, brooding in a shifting downpour that grew in intensity and slackened off unpredictably. The weather seemed unable to decide whether to rage viciously or merely to simmer with mocking drizzles.

For Lord Singer Dharan Greyt, on the other hand, there was no such ambivalence: This was not a pleasant morning.

The capricious weather spoiled any chance of decent hunting. He had a terrible headache such that even being awake was a trial. Meris was nowhere to be found. And, finally, the man Greyt liked least in the Silver Marches had come to call.

"Why Speaker, what a pleasant surprise," he said to the large man in his sitting room. Then he muttered sarcastically under his breath, "I was just hoping for banality at sunrise."

With one meaty hand, Speaker Geth Stonar smoothed his bountiful moustache. "Well met to you, too," the lord said with a note of weariness in his voice.

"Won't you sit down? Can I offer you some wine—Cormyrean red? I have a bottle of feywine, but I'm saving that for a special occasion."

From his expression, it was clear the gruff Lord Speaker had missed the subtle barb.

Greyt sighed. Typically oblivious.

The sitting room was large and lavish, as was the rest of Greyt's home. In a town where every building had at least five—and usually eight or more—residents, Dharan Greyt and three others lived in an expansive house that could have held thirty or forty comfortably. It was a frontier manor, and Greyt had decorated the interior appropriately, with tapestries depicting epic battles, monsters, and legends. He kept it, he said, in the style of Waterdhavian high society. The trinkets and treasures he had won in his adventuring days were scattered around the mansion—many were cheap imitations, but starry-eyed youth rarely knew the difference. A trip to Greyt Manor was a journey into the castles of old, like walking into a dragon's chamber.

"If you'll just look over these papers and documents, I'll deliver them to Alustriel in Silverymoon," Stonar said brusquely. He declined the drink but took a seat. "She's calling a council of the league within the month, and several matters need to be handled before I can give her my report."

"Matters such as getting the hunters to stop talking about the mythical silver pheasant?" Greyt asked. "Or perhaps redecorating the Whistling Stag? Indeed, I have no doubt those are tasks for Alustriel's personal attention." Then, softly: "The hag."

Stonar frowned. "Of course not," he said. "Matters of real importance—matters relevant to the survival of our city!"

Almost rolling his eyes, Greyt looked at the Speaker askance. Stonar wore a rich green baldric with a rearing stag, the symbol of Quaervarr, emblazoned on his thick chest. Greyt found it distasteful.

Stonar wasn't exactly fat, but he was quite sturdy—a life of smithy work had made him that way. Greyt expected that the last few years in his authority role, lodging in Quaervarr's second largest house, and Stonar's recent diet of more rothé and potatoes than roots and venison, hadn't hurt the process either. He was a dull man without a mind for politics who relied more on his hands than his head. Of course, leadership like that carried much weight in uncivilized frontier towns such as Quaervarr.

"What matters?" Greyt asked. He absentmindedly plucked at the strings of his yarting and eased himself back in his gilded chair. "As though we have matters of interest to deal with in Quaervarr. At the very height of danger, we are." The unintentional rhyme brought a smile to his face. He was a natural.

"Matters such as getting the hunters and rangers to stop bickering over territory and hunting rights. They all get commissions in the Whistling Stag, but there are only so many travelers who come through and more than enough rangers to go around! Matters such as the giants Goodman Revnir saw two days past, or the orc war party your own son caught! So many monsters shouldn't be wandering the Moonwood this time of year. Winter's not over and we're already seeing migrations. Ever since the Black Blood died out—"

"Revnir's half-blind, and not because he lost an eye thirty winters ago," Greyt said dismissively. "Couldn't win that lass he wanted before he grew a beard, so he tries to be a hero."

"Greyt, Revnir's not much older than you," Stonar countered.

"Do you see me pretending to be a ranger?"

Stonar conceded the point with a grunt.

"As for Meris, it wasn't much of a war party he encountered," Greyt continued. "Four orcs, lost and wandering the woods—he was just in the right place at the right time."

"Your boy does like wandering those woods," Stonar admitted. "Quite the ranger."

"Ah, Meris, my proud boy. My only joy," Greyt said flatly. In truth, he was proud his son had vanquished four orcs single-handedly, even if it had been through ambush, not heroism. He had to smile though—at least Meris wasn't that stupid.

"As for the rangers, what do we do to decrease the bickering, the competition for commissions?" Stonar asked. "Thank Torm no blood has been spilled yet, but this is getting out of—"

"Not every boy or wench who picks up a sword or bow in this town is cut out to be a ranger," Greyt replied, interrupting the lord. "You can, you know, see and speak. Encourage the strong, not the weak." His rhyme was mocking.

"Speak for yourself, Greyt!" Stonar rumbled. "And speak like a man, not all that poetry. You're the one they all look up to, you and your stories—your songs about heroes. Even the one about Drizzit, or whatever his name is! A dark elf ranger? Rubbish!"

"Drizzt Do'Urden, hero of Icewind Dale? Who fought an orc army by himself? Is that the name you're looking for?" Greyt had dropped the witty poetry; epic verse was wasted on men of Stonar's caliber.

Stonar looked as though he bit back a curse. The Singer shook his head. A mewling, uncouth dog changed little, even when he was dressed up.

"And couriers are disappearing!" Stonar continued. "Something has been stopping more than a few on the path to Silverymoon, and their horses return without riders. Who could be doing such a thing?"

The Lord Singer sighed. "Why bother me with all these things?" Greyt asked. "You're the Speaker. Call Unddreth if you want to keep things in order—that is, after all, the job of the watch. What do you want me to do? I'm a bard; I sing."

"You're the hero of Quaervarr," Stonar replied in an incredulous tone. "Dharan 'Quickwid'—er—'Quickfinger' Greyt, hero of the blade and yarting. All the young men want to be you, all the young women want to chase off Lyetha...."

Greyt smiled at the mention of Lyetha. The most beautiful woman in the town, she had been his wife for fifteen winters, much longer than any woman before her. No children, but he hadn't needed more. The last of the children he'd had from previous women, Meris, was the only one he needed—it was only too convenient the others had died early in life.

His smile faded remembering that Stonar had almost used his less-than-complimentary nickname "Quickwidower," playing on his foul luck with women before his marriage to Lyetha.

"You worry too much, Lord Speaker," Greyt said, flipping idly through the papers. The papers reiterated what Stonar had just told him but in a much longer, very wordy format. That was what happened when one turned a blacksmith into a lord—redundancy. Or gruffness. It was certainly not the elegance upon which Greyt prided himself. "Look on the lighter side. At least Jarthon haven't resurfaced, after those adventurers dealt with the Black Blood. There hasn't been a murder in six months, and none of the guards have reported sighting any of the Malarites. Maybe Jarthon finally got what he deserved."

"Maybe he ran afoul of the Ghostly Lady," agreed Stonar.

Greyt's face turned stony and annoyance flashed across his face before he gave Stonar a bemused smile. "Please, Ston—Lord Speaker. The Ghostly Lady? 'Tis a fairytale, nothing more." He sipped his wine. "I have been all over the Moonwood, and I've never encountered this 'golden spirit.' You sound as naïve as the rest of the simpletons who live here."

Stonar looked flustered, but he laughed nevertheless. "They may be naïve, but as long as you are their hero, they are in good hands, Greyt," he said. He rose and gathered up his cape. "I'm leaving you in charge of Quaervarr during my absence. See that you protect the people while I am away in Silverymoon. I shall be back before Greengrass, seven days hence, I expect."

Whatever difference your absence makes, Greyt mused silently. Instead, he offered a winning smile. "Of course, my lord," he sighed. "Consider them safe."

When Stonar opened the door to leave, Greyt stopped him with a soft call. "Stonar?"

"Aye?"

"What do Clearwater and Unddreth have to say about this?" he asked.

"Why, nothing," Stonar said. "I was elected to represent these people, I make the decisions. I trust Unddreth to do his job; he always does. As for Amra Clearwater ... well, the Silvanites have a festival to prepare for. If you even see her, I'd be surprised." With that, Speaker Geth Stonar passed out the inlaid doors of Greyt's lavish sitting room.

Greyt nodded, smiling. The appointment of the task was unexpected, but the trust Stonar exhibited amused him. Particularly since Greyt could easily use the position to undermine the Speaker's authority. Perhaps now was the time to set long overdue plans in motion.

He looked out the window and saw that the rain was clearing outside. It was turning out not to be such a bad morning after all. There would be no hunting, but at least it wouldn't look so dismal outside. The fading drizzle on the rooftop was pleasant.

He began singing to himself, a tale of Thadax Graywolf, a mighty warlord of the north and an ancestor of his, as he considered what he would ask the servant to bring him for a noon meal.

◈ ◈ ◈ ◈ ◈

Quaervarr was a simple frontier town in the southern depths of the untamed Moonwood. A crude wall of felled trees encircled no more than fifty buildings. The cobbled main street—the greatest thoroughfare of the town—ran from the single gate straight to the plaza. The side streets were narrow and twisting, giving Quaervarr the feeling of a larger city, but rarely cobbled, as in Silverymoon or Everlund, maintaining the rustic atmosphere. Moon elves lived in the southern fringes of the Moonwood and existed in a state of benevolent neutrality with the human town, allowing it to stand as a symbol of peace and cooperation between the races.

In the recent past, Quaervarr had been a fort, plagued by the werebeasts of the Black Blood, but no more, not since adventurers and soldiers of the Argent Legion had driven the cultists out. These days, travelers could always find a welcoming smile, a warm bed, and a hearty mug of ale at Quaervarr's renowned inn, the Whistling Stag.

With the Greengrass festival fast approaching, however, room vacancies were at a premium. The end of winter and the beginning of spring demanded celebration, and excitement was in the air. Hundreds of men and woman scurried every which way, making preparations.

The three Knights in Silver were acutely aware of the unusually bustling activity in the peaceful town, and the leader hoped they might find any room at all.

Heroes by appearance alone, the knights attracted smiles and shouts from running children, who hopped alongside the horses as fast as they could. The lead knight, slim of build, looked down at each one with a smile barely hidden behind a silver-inlaid helmet. A lance stood up from the rear of the saddle, and a fine Everlundian long sword hung next to it. A shield with a star and nightingale was on the knight's arm. The two others—much less elegant in poise and carriage—rode approximately level with one another, exchanging bemused glances. They were engaged in quiet banter, as always.

"I say, Bars, that didn't seem very wise to me," one of the knights, a slender man in mail, said to the other. An ornate long sword hung from his saddle, but he looked too small of stature to have much use for such a heavy blade.

"Eh?" his companion, a hulking man in plate, replied. His voice was a growl.

"The watch at the gate," the slender man said. "They let us through unchallenged. What if we'd been monsters in disguise, or brigands, or Malarites, or Zhents, or lycanthropes, or, worse, Sembians?" He shuddered. "They could be allowing truly dangerous men freely into their town. You'd better hide that voice, or you'll be mistaken for a werebear for sure."

"Derst," the burly knight rumbled. Two light, flanged maces hung from his saddle, and his hand rested on one. "You're going to have to watch your tongue. No right-minded citizen of the Silver Marches would mistake you for a werebear, but your shape is right for a wererat."

"What does that have to do with my speech, pray tell, Sir Hartwine?" Derst asked.

"You're being quite flippant, Sir Goldtook, and only a fool would be flippant, and a wererat would be a fool to wander into Quaervarr, disguised as a Knight in Silver," Bars said. "Since you are being flippant, you are definitely a fool, ergo, you might be a wererat."

"Ah, but could I not be a thief disguised as a Knight in Silver?" Derst asked. "As you often remind me, brother paladin, I am quite the rogue. Besides, you used a lot of words there that you probably shouldn't—dangerous 'logic,' too. After all, what if some suspicious citizen overheard and questioned you, or reported you to the watch for 'thinking?' I would have a difficult time explaining all that back hair you seem to cultivate—"

"When did we lose the right to be logical?" Bars asked. He glared at Derst. "And leave the hair alone."

Derst grinned behind his silver faceplate. "More to the point, when did we lose the right to be flippant?" he asked. "My life would be a complete waste of air if I found myself without that right. I mean, I wouldn't be able to speak at *all*—"

"Bless the Morning Lord," the burly knight bellowed. "Were it ever so!"

Derst glowered at him for a moment, but perked up when they entered Quaervarr's main plaza. "Ah, the Whistling Stag," he said as they approached the inn. "At least, so I would assume, by yon hanging, which bears a striking resemblance to Quaervarr's pennant."

The Whistling Stag was a plain but sturdy building of fir and pine, a great hunting lodge that had become a gathering place for travelers and locals alike. The knights heard laughter, jesting, and the clacking of tankards through the windows. Clearly, they had come to the right place for merry-making.

They dismounted and Bars turned to address the third member of their party. "Sir Venkyr, if you would be so good as to go in with me and reserve rooms, Sir Goldtook will take our noble steeds to the stables."

"The horses?" Derst interjected with a look of disgust. "Why me?"

"Less chance of you swindling the innkeeper that way," Bars explained.

Derst started a retort, stopped, then nodded.

The stout knight turned to their silent companion. "Please, allow me to do the negotiations. You must be tired from our long journey. Pray, get some rest. One of your distincti—"

The knight laughed, a high, musical sound, and reached up to loosen the helmet's straps. "Excuse me?" came the melodious voice. "Being a noble, Bars, does not make me helpless." The helmet came off, and the knight shook out a long mane of dark auburn hair. Gray eyes sparkled above her smile and sunlight danced across her smooth, lightly tanned face. Arya Venkyr was a songbird clad in steel feathers. More than a few passersby caught their breath. "Nor does being a noble lady."

"Of course not, lass—I mean, Lady *Sir* Arya," Bars stammered. "I said nothing of the sort."

"Were you going to say one of those things, perhaps?" She put her hands on her hips and raised one crimson-dashed eyebrow. There was that fiery passion—the defiance well known in Everlund and the reason she was here, in a knight's armor, rather than at home in a study hall, garden, or drawing room.

Cursing the demands of chivalry, Bars felt his face becoming a similar burning shade. "You may do all the diplomacy you like, Lady Sir," he managed, after clearing his throat.

"I've asked you not to call me that," Arya replied with a roll of her eyes that belied her anger.

"Yes, Lady Sir." Bars flinched at his accidental use of the title.

Arya sighed. She stroked her chestnut mare, Swiftfall.

"But since you've been so kind as to offer," Arya said, her face amused, "I won't refuse. Lead the way, *Sir* Hartwine, if it please you. And draw your coin purse. Sir Goldtook? The horses."

"Forth the Nightingale," the two men said together, without meaning to. It was their battle cry, which referred to Arya's coat of arms. The synchronization drew a laugh from Arya.

Grumbling and half-smiling, Bars escorted her into the Whistling Stag. Grumbling and not smiling, Derst escorted the three horses to the stable.

The Whistling Stag was surprisingly roomy, and the dark atmosphere typical of an inn, with its choking smoke, was absent. Instead, thanks to the open windows, the knights found themselves able to breathe easy and free. Excepting the heads that turned as she entered, Arya admired everything about the common room.

Tables and long benches, each carved from single shadow-top trunks, were laid out with enough walking space for two people. Stuffed heads of animals, orc and goblin weapons, spears, axes, and broken arrows adorned the room. A glorious tapestry depicting elves hunting deer graced the north wall. Barmaids flitted about, hurrying to clear tables for guests and to set down wide trays of ale tankards. The common room was stuffed with patrons and celebrants who had gathered to observe the coming of spring.

Arya pushed herself up to the counter next to a loud man who was bragging about his lewd exploits in a slurred voice.

"Excuse me," Arya said to the innkeeper, a burly man she gathered from the noise was named Garion. "We are looking for rooms for a tenday or two, and stables for our steeds."

"Stables are open," Garion said as he wiped a tankard clean. "But Greengrass's got us all full. I'd love to help ye, Lady Knight, but we got no empty rooms."

"Wha?" sounded a voice to her left.

The man who had grunted—not spoken, exactly—saw Arya and grinned lasciviously. Brown hair fell to his shoulders and he wore a half beard—a goatee, they called it in Waterdeep.

He was dressed exquisitely, with a long feather in his hat and a rapier and main gauche at his belt. He was clearly the foppish sort, and was just as clearly drunk.

"Ye kin stay in me own room, lassie," the man slurred. "Me bed's not too wide, but that needn't bother us. . . ."

"How romantic," Arya murmured.

"Shut up, Morgan," Garion said. He turned to Arya. "Decent enough fella, him, but when he gets in his cups—"

"Who axed ye, Garion?" scolded Morgan. "I was jes' havin' a chat with this comely wench 'ere—"

"My thanks," said Arya, smiling politely, "but no." Then she ignored Morgan and turned back. "Are you quite certain? Do you know of any other rooms in town?"

"Hey!" Morgan snapped, reaching for Arya. "I was talkin' to ye, flipskirt!"

A dagger appeared, quivering in the wooden surface of the bar a hair's breadth from Morgan's fingers.

"Sorry, sorry," said Derst with a cough. "Must have slipped out of my hand."

"Ye almost hit me!" shouted Morgan, following his exclamation with a string of curses that made Arya and even the innkeeper blush faintly.

"I say, Bars," Derst said from behind Arya. "Quite a mouth on that knave."

"Indeed," replied the burly knight, standing to Derst's right. "A knave indeed, to speak in such a manner in the presence of a lady. I fear I must ask him to desist."

Arya looked at them sidelong, rolled her eyes, and slid out of the way. The two moved up to Morgan, Bars to his left and Derst to his right.

"Ye gots a problem, ye fat orc?" the drunk asked.

Bars's face colored deeply and his hands clenched into fists. Morgan laughed at the spectacle and took a pull from his tankard.

"Uh-oh, he insulted the weight," observed Derst. "Only I get to do that."

"Bars, Derst—let it alone," Arya warned.

"Too late, lass," rumbled Bars as he fingered the twin maces at his belt.

"He's very sensitive about his Beshaba-cursed figure," explained Derst. "You shouldn't have said that, Sir Inebriate."

Morgan shoved his stool back and drained the last of his ale. "I'll hear none o' thy insults, mangy goblin!" he shouted as he yanked his rapier free of its scabbard.

Arya saw Derst wince and shook her head. "He shouldn't have said that either," she observed to Garion.

The barkeep nodded. "I'd stop them, but I have a feeling that'd just make it worse."

Arya agreed silently.

" 'Ave at ye!" Morgan shouted as he lunged, sword first, at Bars.

The big knight's maces were out in a blur and he swatted the blade to the right, harmlessly wide, into the bar. The drunk drew the blade back and thrust again, this time at Derst. The roguish knight had already drawn his curious weapon—a dagger with a foot-long chain trailing from the grip—with which he parried, even as he spun the chain around in an underhand motion inside his arm. Morgan's eyes grew confused. As the rapier slid past, Derst threw the chain up and struck Morgan on the chin with a resounding thump.

The rake staggered back clutching at his goatee, where a trickle of blood seeped between his fingers. Bars held two light maces, one overhand and one underhand, crossed before him. At the burly knight's side, Derst absently spun the chain around, inside and outside his arm, alternating with a flick of his wrist.

Morgan's eyes clouded over with rage and drink. Screaming, he drew his left-hand dagger and lunged again. His movements were graceless, but he carried with him a ferocity born of pure anger.

Derst parried at the last moment and whirled the chain around the rapier's blade. With a flick and twist of his wrist, he tore the weapon free of Morgan's grasp and sent both it and his chain-dagger clattering to the floor. Morgan, however, did not hesitate to stab out with his main-gauche, thinking to catch the knight unarmed and helpless.

A light mace darted in like lightning and smashed down on Morgan's hand. The dagger clattered to the floor even as Bars's other mace shot around and caught Morgan on the back of the head. Without even realizing what had happened, the rake toppled limply to the floor.

Bars reached down and scooped him up over one shoulder. He disentangled the chain from the rapier and handed the chain-dagger back to Derst. The roguish knight accepted it with a smile and twirled it around his wrist, where it hung like a bracelet. Then he turned to Garion.

"I think he's had enough," said Derst. "What's his tab?"

Garion looked at the knight curiously then spoke. "Four silver an' five copper," he said.

Scowling at the price, Derst nodded nonetheless. He took a small purse from his belt and started counting coins out into his hand.

Garion eyed him sidelong. "Right courteous, seeing as how ye just caved his head in," he said.

"Well, a knight is always courteous," said Derst. He patted Morgan's backside as Bars carried him past.

"How hard did you hit him?" Arya asked Bars as he carried Morgan to the door.

"Hard enough," Bars replied without hesitation.

"Don't worry, he's still breathing. I think," Derst reassured her. Arya raised an eyebrow. "Pretty sure." The eyebrow went higher. Derst shrugged. "Mayhap."

The barkeep Garion looked to Derst again. "Well, I don't take fight starters under my roof, but you didn't start the fight—he did," he said. "Excellent throw, by the way." He indicated the dagger.

"My thanks," replied Derst, retrieving the blade with some effort. "Oh, sorry about the damage, too." He reached for his pouch again, but Garion waved away payment.

Bars returned from throwing Morgan into the street.

"You three can have his room," Garion said. He held up the key to one of the rooms upstairs. "Fox room. Upstairs, second on the right—look for the etching on the door. Basin, copper tub. I'll send hot water up. Only one bed, though."

"That won't be a problem," said Arya. "These two wool-heads will take the floor, of course." Bars and Derst both looked at Arya sidelong, but Arya just smiled sweetly and stretched road-weary muscles. "A bath. I can't wait." She took her leave, humming lightly as she went.

Bars and Derst looked at one another, then at the innkeeper.

"Lasses," Derst said to Garion. "Always in distress, and always ungrateful."

Bars laughed.

CHAPTER 3

26 Tarsakh

The dawn rose cold the following morning and dark clouds choked the pale skies. A chill and a light blanket of snow had settled over the western Moonwood, what local legend called the Dark Woods—a patch of deep forest where even the elves of the Moonwood would not venture. The guardsmen at the gate of Quaervarr, near the road south to Silverymoon, stood easy, however. There were no visitors that morning and the road seemed deserted.

Deserted, at least, until a dark figure emerged from the mists.

Opening their eyes wide, the guards made to stop him, stepping in his way and crossing their silver-tipped spears, but one look from the night-clad man and they cringed back. He didn't have to speak—the chilling resolve that surrounded him said enough. It didn't even occur to them to ask his name or his business, for they knew they would soon find out. They weren't sure, however, that they wanted to.

The man called Walker strode calmly past the silent, nervous guards without a second glance, carrying a small bundle wrapped in rough leather. His pace was relaxed and his strides were great.

He had one task: an ultimatum to issue. A warning.

Children in the streets ceased their play and crowded under the snow-covered eaves to watch as the man in black strode by. "Walker, Walker, Walker," they whispered to each other in excited, hushed tones. "Silent, not a talker!"

Stillness reigned in Quaervarr where he walked. It spread up the street, causing children's games to fall silent, adults to cut off conversations and watch, and even the barking of dogs and the neighing of horses to cease. When a pail slipped the notice of a stable boy and fell clattering to the ground, those nearby cringed in surprise.

Walker did not slow or pause. Carrying his bundle, he walked through the main street of Quaervarr toward the mansion of Lord Singer Dharan Greyt.

❧ ❧ ❧ ❧ ❧

Reading a romance by Alin the Mad, a Cormyrean writer of great skill who had a talent for description, even if that description ran to the fantastical, Greyt had just finished swallowing the last bit of venison and had lifted the vintage to his lips when the doors to his dining hall banged open. He looked up in annoyance, but he didn't need to. He knew who it would be.

"Stonar's gone?" the young man asked. "Now at least you can relax, with that oaf out of the way. At least for a while."

"Dearest son, won't you join me? I'm almost finished with my lunch," he said.

Meris, frost caked on his white cloak, grinned and smoothed his jet-black hair with a brush of his hand. He had a couple of men with him at the door—the Greyt family rangers were little more than hired thugs and disconsolate woodsmen—but the Lord Singer hardly noticed. Meris took all his attention.

Meris was armed with a sword and a hand axe, the weapons of hara-sakal, the specialized high axe, low sword style imported from the barbarians of Rashemen, and his dusky skin was rosy from the frosty morning. While Greyt admired the pale sheen of his own face, he found Meris's slightly darker features, aesthetically, to be more than decent. Greyt had made a good choice with Meris's Amnian mother, gods rest her soul. He tried to remember how she had died, but the exact details escaped him. No matter.

"Thank you, no, father. I've already eaten," Meris said. His voice was rich and full but carried a sinister undercurrent, a twist to the tone that hinted that everything he said was slightly mocking. "I'm afraid I have some bad news."

"That it's terrible out and there's nothing to hunt?" Greyt yawned. He swirled the wine in his goblet and pointed to the window, where it was still dark outside, even though the sun had risen some time ago. "I already noticed the lack of sun."

"Something else," Meris replied.

Their manner was always curt, which was fine by Greyt. He didn't like Meris so much as he approved of him. The dusky youth reminded him of himself. He suspected his illegitimate son had killed his siblings to clear his own path to inheritance. Ruthlessness ran in the Greyt family like blood.

"Aye?"

"A death that occurred two nights past. Well, two deaths, actually," Meris said.

"A drunken brawl?" Greyt asked. "Tell me Unddreth finally had an accident—"

"No," Meris replied. "Deaths at the house of Sir Drex Redgill, your longtime friend."

"Drex got a little hot under the collar and took it out on a couple servants again, eh?" Greyt waved dismissively and took a sip of his wine. "Not my concern."

"Unless he took it out on himself, something else happened," Meris said. "Drex was killed two nights past, along with one of his guards."

The Lord Singer squeezed the goblet so hard it shattered in his hand. "What?" he asked, wincing as the shards sank into his flesh. A healing potion was brought quickly, and he quaffed it to stifle the pain.

"Drex was slain." The guards at the door—Greyt family rangers, loyal servants all of them—looked at Meris expectantly, and he added, "Oh yes. And the guard had a family ... apparently."

"Drex is dead?" Greyt asked, ignoring the news of the guard. He was beginning to take an interest in the discussion. He halfheartedly made the sign of Milil, his supposed patron. As they spoke, he delicately picked shards of glass out of his flesh, which healed as he removed the glass, thanks to the potion. "What happened?"

"Single slash to the throat, found naked in his bedroom, his guard dead in similar fashion, though he was armed and armored," Meris said. "Dagger wounds, runs my thinking."

"Why did you not come to me yesterday?" asked Greyt, narrowing his eyes, but he already knew the answer. Meris had wanted to solve the mystery himself—not to win his father's favor but to demonstrate his own superiority. He only came to Greyt because he had failed.

The grimace on Meris's face told him his suspicions were correct. The fool.

"Suspects?" Greyt asked. He felt irritation and more than a little anger. Accidental death, if Drex had fallen from a window and broken his neck, was one thing, but murder was quite another. "Goodwife Redgill has been dead these past ten winters, so she's out of the question. One of his guards?"

"His flipskirt, I wager," another, deeper voice called.

Bilgren, wild black mane flowing around his shoulders, huge gyrspike on his back, and rage on his face, dragged in a struggling half-elf maid who was clad only in a torn shift. Her face was bruised and spattered with congealed blood, some of it her own.

Bilgren threw the half-elf down and spat on her. The maid cringed.

"Th' wench was caught fleeing from 'is house in th' middle o' the night. No knife, but bloodied up."

With a flourish of his scarlet cape, Torlic glided in behind Bilgren. He disdained to touch the barbarian, and weaved a path around him, heading to the wall. He leaned against it. Greyt supposed he should have expected Torlic to appear—he, Bilgren, and the late Drex, in addition to Greyt himself, had once been members of the Raven Claw band.

"She didn't put up much of a fight." Torlic sneered and ran his hand over the handle of the rapier sheathed at his belt. "Typical, for a wench."

The half-elf knelt before Greyt's chair and table and looked up with teary eyes. While her condition no doubt had been poor the night in question—Greyt knew well the late Drex's propensity for violence coupled with pleasure—he was sure she hadn't been caught in quite this poor a condition. Greyt was certain his son or perhaps Bilgren had interrogated her in his own way; another reason for the troublesome delay in information.

The Lord Singer rose and unfurled his violet cape, which trailed from his shoulders. "Leave us," he said to the guards and Bilgren. "Meris, you may stay."

Bilgren shot him a look. His azure eyes were burning with dim-witted anger. "What about me, Greyt?" he spat. "Let me help ye 'persuade' this little . . ."

Greyt did not flinch as he looked up at the Uthgardt barbarian, who was a foot taller and almost twice his weight. Even Bilgren's gyrspike—a wicked sword with a flail on the end that was about the size of Greyt's head—did not move the Lord Singer.

"Begone," Greyt said without blinking. Cutting off any objection, Greyt added, "It wouldn't do for you to be seen here after this incident. People might suspect."

"Drex was me friend, don't ye forget!" Bilgren bellowed. He took the opportunity to shoot the half-elf woman another angry glare and to take a menacing step toward her. "An' just ye wait, little flipskirt—" She cringed and tried to fold herself into a tighter ball. Then Bilgren stormed out. From the way the girl's face relaxed when Bilgren left, Greyt could tell his guess had been correct.

"What about you?" Greyt asked Torlic, who had been standing impassively.

Torlic squinted bright blue eyes and gave a shrug. "Drex was swine. At least, I always thought so." He turned abruptly on his heel and followed Bilgren.

The half-elf woman was noticeably less nervous. Apparently, Meris hadn't touched her, or she would have scurried away from him as well. That helped. Greyt removed a rich crimson blanket from the back of his chair and draped it around her shivering shoulders. "Have no fear, child. You are quite safe."

She looked up at Greyt through blurry eyes and a smile spread across her face. "Oh, good Lord Singer!" she stammered, her voice broken with sobs. "Th-those men—"

"I know, I know," Greyt replied. He reached down to help her up. "Have no fear, they will be dealt with. They are servants of Sir Drex. They're a bit unhappy, eh? Don't worry—you're safe now." Most of that was a lie, but Dharan Greyt had always been glib and persuasive.

"Thank you, oh, thank you!" she said. She took his hand and kissed it several times. "I was so afraid."

"There is no need for you to fear, fair lady," he said silkily, lifting her gently by the hand. His words sounded almost lyrical. "But I am afraid, maid—"

"Tillee," she said quickly, filling in the gap his words left.

"Maid Tillee," Greyt repeated. "I'm afraid you will have to help me. You see, I need to know what happened that night. The faster you tell me, the safer you will be."

Tillee paled, but she managed to speak. She unfolded

the story as she had seen it, about the man appearing out of the shadows, the vicious fight, and the bloody outcome of the duel. She even described, in detail, the rasping of the ghostly warrior's voice, so filled with darkness and hate. By the end of her story, she was shuddering with remembered fear.

Greyt shook his head. Such a feat as she described would take a powerful wizard, and he knew without a doubt that no wizards had been active in Quaervarr that night. Neither had he heard of a wizard who possessed such blade skill.

Greyt walked to Meris. "What do you think?" he asked softly. No affectionate name. No "son." Not even "boy."

Meris shrugged. "Maybe she really is an innocent victim of circumstance."

"Or a whore trying to save her neck," Greyt said. "Who else is there? Jarthon hasn't sent any killers into Quaervarr in a long while, and this kind of murder isn't like him anyway."

"The killing wounds are too precise for a woman suffering Drex's attentions," Meris said. "The attacks must have come from a trained hand, perhaps someone like the assassin she describes. And there's something else besides—"

"You said you were convinced it was her," Greyt argued. "Bilgren certainly thought so."

"That was in front of the men," Meris replied. "And Bilgren's skills don't exactly run to thinking. It wouldn't do to share my real suspicions in the hearing of possibly disloyal ears, and all the remaining ears in this mansion are yours." He gestured toward the tapestry behind Greyt, where both knew of a secret passage perfect for just such spying.

With a disarming smile, Greyt nodded. How little Meris knew about his "ears."

"I think she speaks the truth," said Meris.

Greyt raised an eyebrow. "Go on," he invited.

"Two of Drex's guards mentioned a man in black," Meris said. "Who swept out of the shadows and attacked them at their posts. They killed him on instinct, but decided afterward that he had been just a drunk. We examined the alley where they swore they had dumped the body, but there was nothing there. An assassin, perhaps?"

"A man in black." Greyt stopped. A flash of memory came to him, but he pushed it aside. "Ludicrous. If those guards killed a man, his body would still be there. And there are no assassins in Quaervarr. Whose death is worth the expense?" He shrugged dismissively. "Pay it no mind."

"They said he was a demon," Meris said. His voice was calm but his tone was intent.

"I said to pay it no mind," Greyt said again. "I'll not have you chasing after a shadow or a dream, like all the other young fools in the Marches."

The youth shrugged. "As you say." The look on his face, though, told Greyt that Meris was not so pleased.

Let the boy fume for a while—it would teach him proper respect.

At that moment, there was a knock at the door. Meris's hand dropped to his sword hilt, but Greyt waved at him. "Enter," he called.

The Greyt family steward—a gaunt man by the name of Claudir—entered with a neutral expression on his face. Greyt was unsurprised and from his son's scowl, he reasoned that Meris was wondering how he had known the knock would be Claudir.

Greyt smiled.

"Your niece, the Lady Knight Arya Venkyr of Everlund, begs an audience with your lordship," the steward said. "With her are her two companions, Sirs Bars Hartwine and Derst Goldtook of the Knights in Silver. Shall I show them in, Lord Singer?"

His niece? A knight? Greyt had not been in contact with Rom Venkyr of Everlund, his brother-in-law, for some time. Rom's daughter?

"A moment, please," Greyt said. "I shall receive them in the sitting room."

Claudir offered a half-bow and left without a word.

Meris and Greyt regarded one another, silently. The only

sound was the half-elf Tillee's sobs. Finally, the Lord Singer spoke.

"Aught else?" Greyt prompted.

Meris nodded and shrugged noncommittally.

It was the only answer Greyt needed.

The Lord Singer clapped his hands and turned back to Tillee. "Well, since you seem so insistent, it might well be truth. We'll send you to the Oak House and set you before Amra Clearwater. Let her tell us if you speak true." With a smile, he took the crimson blanket back. "I'm sure, since you sound so passionate and honest, you must be telling the truth. Besides, a good maid such as yourself would not lie, eh? Meris will take you there."

The ranger couldn't hide his smirk.

"Oh, thank you, Lord Singer!" the half-elf woman replied with a wide smile. She reached for his legs to embrace him. Despite his half-hearted effort to dodge, she caught him. She kissed his gold ring, the one with his family seal. "You really are a hero!"

He put on a fake smile, rolled his eyes, and pulled his cape from her grasp. Then he started toward the door, rubbing at the gold wolf ring. On the way, he caught Meris by the arm and dipped his head toward his son's ear. "Do you want her?" he asked.

Meris's nose wrinkled.

Greyt smiled. He would have responded the same way.

"Bilgren will be disappointed, but he'll get over it," Greyt said.

Then, as he was leaving, he paused. "Oh, and see that you leave no stain," he said. "I've just had the carpet re-laid. It is red, but still ... It is also new."

Shrugging, Meris turned away. His sword scraped out of its sheath.

As Greyt closed the doors behind him, he heard Tillee's surprised gasp. Meris hadn't allowed her to scream.

CHAPTER 4

26 Tarsakh

In Greyt's waiting room, Arya was tapping her fingers on the oak table and chewing on the edge of her lip.

It was a spacious room, with elegant windows and real glass. There were three lavish couches, upholstered with varying colors of fur and leather, ranging from the tanned flesh of caribou to what the steward Claudir claimed was tundra yeti. Arya's nose always turned up at the thought of harvesting furs. Her distaste was not, however, shared by her two companions. On the middle couch, they lounged on feather pillows and shared laughs—Derst's witty snickers and Bars's rumbles—over something or other. Too nervous to join them, Arya lingered near the cold fireplace, running her fingers along the stems and petals of the flowers Greyt's servants had collected for display.

Winter lilies and frost roses stood in bright array among emerald stems and leaves, curled into bunches along a golden banister. The flowers might have been picked that morning; they were so soft and vibrant. The ones that gave the trick away, however, were the stunning fire-dragons—snapdragons so red the people of the north claimed they were slain dragons reborn. The burning petals sparkled with dew, but Arya knew they only bloomed in the warmth of Flamerule. There was no way Greyt could have had them gathered that morning.

"Admiring the blooms, Lady Sir Venkyr?" Derst asked. "Pretty this time of year, eh?"

Arya smiled wryly. "Oh, indeed, Sir Goldtook," she replied. "As you can see, they're quite lovely." She inhaled a fire-dragon deeply, wondering about the fragrance, but there was nothing. The flower was stale and had obviously been dead for some time. Magic.

Appearances, in Greyt's house, were everything.

The door clicked and three pairs of eyes turned as Greyt's steward Claudir entered. "The Lord Singer of the Silver Marches, Dharan Greyt," he said. The three knights started at the odd title, but quickly composed themselves.

At that announcement, Greyt swept into the room. Trailing his rich violet cape behind him and clad in his finest black doublet, the man was resplendent in his noble attire. His dark blond hair was swept back and his blue eyes sparkled. A rapier with a golden basket hilt hung from a beautifully embroidered and stitched belt around his hips. If the knights didn't know better, they would have thought him the lord of Quaervarr, if not the lord of Silverymoon itself. He was smiling as though it was habitual. He paused, ducked into a low bow, and folded his hands in front of him.

"Well met, Uncle," Arya said with a slight curtsy, even though she was wearing a man's leggings and not a skirt. Arya was not much for dresses.

"Ah, my beloved niece, what a pleasant surprise," Greyt said with a grin as he took Arya's fingers. He bent and kissed the young woman's hand with an exaggerated bow, then stepped back to examine her. He gazed at the star and nightingale design on her tunic, the arms of House Venkyr. "Nightingale of Everlund, you would teach nymphs beauty."

Arya blushed, though she could have sworn she had read that particular bit of poesy somewhere before. Ignoring Bars's and Derst's bemused looks, Arya forced a neutral smile. She knew this contrived manner—the style of court—and could play at it if necessary.

"Speak plainly, please, Uncle," Arya said. "I lack your training in such poetry."

Greyt bowed his head a little. "You have grown into quite the young woman, niece. When I last saw you—what was it, a dozen years ago?—you were only half as tall and not nearly as . . . full-bodied." His grin was waxy and his eyes glittered. He turned away, went to the side table, and poured two glasses of a sparkling red wine.

Arya felt her face growing warm—again—and could hear her companions' snickers from behind her. She would have shot a glance back at the two young knights, but it would only have made them laugh louder. "My thanks, Uncle," she said. "Time has been kind to you as well."

Greyt inclined his head.

Composing herself with a brief repetition of the knight's code, she met his gaze levelly. "Allow me to introduce my companions, Sir Bars Hartwine and Sir Derst Goldtook, of the Knights in Silver."

The Lord Singer bowed and proceeded to ignore them. The knights shifted uncomfortably but said nothing. Greyt indicated the couch with one glass, but Arya made no move to sit. He shrugged indifferently.

"I must admit, your arrival comes as a bit of a surprise," he said as he handed the wine glass to Arya. She accepted it gracefully and inhaled the aroma but did not drink. Leaning against the sideboard, Greyt continued. "I had thought you at court in Everlund, waiting on your father, Lord Rom, and that you were to be schooled in letters, poetry, and the sorts of things that—that, well, noblewomen do. And yet here you are, clothed in an adventurer's garb and companioned by knights." He looked at the pendant of Silverymoon hanging over her blue tunic. His smile broadened. "I see you take after my sister."

"She is my step-mother, Uncle," Arya reminded him lightly. "You and I are not related by blood. She merely married my father."

"Of course." Greyt smiled and gave a little laugh. He rubbed the gold ring with a wolf's head around the fourth finger of his left hand—a nervous habit. The pause was an awkward one.

"You must be wondering why I have come," Arya prompted, raising the wine to her lips.

"Ah, and direct, I see," Greyt replied, driving into a new subject. "You do indeed show the Greyt spirit, though the Illuskan coloration doesn't fit us." He brushed her auburn hair with his fingers. "A product of that dull, pretty knight who stole my sister."

Arya didn't know how to reply.

"But please, speak. I am anxious to hear your tale." He finally sat, flinging his cape across the fur-covered couch. Then he raised the glass to his lips and smiled. "I do so love tales."

Arya opened her mouth to speak, but the doors slammed open and a white-garbed young man walked through the portal. A naked sword was in his hands.

Bars and Derst leaped to their feet, the roguish knight's hand going to a belt dagger, but Arya stopped them with a raised hand. The dusky-skinned man was also carrying a kerchief. He paused and his stance shifted to a defensive posture, from which he eyed the two men.

"Ah, Meris," Lord Greyt said from the couch. "Allow me to introduce my niece, Lady Arya Venkyr of Everlund. And, ah—well, her companions." He gestured to the dark-haired man. "My son—your step-cousin—Meris Wayfarer."

Arya noted the strange surname. Meris was not a legitimate son.

Meris sniffed, measuring and dismissing the two knights in a glance, then shifted his gaze to Arya. There his eyes stopped and rested. Taking his sword in one hand, he knelt and took her hand. "Charmed, cousin," he said. He kissed the back of her hand, and when his eyes met hers, they smoldered. "Passionately charmed."

Bars took a step forward, but Derst caught his shoulder and stopped him.

Arya bowed to Meris and turned her attention back to Greyt. Seeing her lack of interest, Meris's smile fell into an irritated frown. He slunk back and threw himself onto the couch opposite Greyt, where he drew a whetstone across his blade with a scraping snicker. The tone of the meeting changed entirely because of that little sound.

"But you were beginning your tale," Greyt said. "Please, do go on."

The doors swung open again and this time the gaunt steward Claudir glided in. "Lord Greyt, sir," Claudir said in his haughty tin voice. He stretched out the last word.

"What is it now?" Greyt snapped. He almost splashed wine on his leather-wrapped couch as he waved in annoyance.

"There appears to be a visitor at your door who will not identify himself and who says little." The steward sniffed. "Much of Quaervarr has turned out to see him and appears stricken dumb. Will you see him, my lord?"

Arya furrowed her brow, and she reached for the sword at her hip but did not draw it. Her companions had risen as well. Meris was oblivious, still sharpening his sword.

Greyt rolled his eyes and rubbed at his temples. "Must I be saddled with unceasing interruptions?" he asked with venom. "Meris, go see who in the Hells is stirring up trouble out there, won't you?"

Frowning, the dusky scout got to his feet, his sword still out. As he followed the steward out, he let it slide back into his scabbard with a clink of steel. The doors closed behind them.

As soon as they were gone, Greyt's gracious manner returned, along with his grin. "Pardon my outburst, Niece," he said. "As the lor—er, *hero* of Quaervarr, I'm constantly dealing with these odd occurrences, which always seem to occur at the least convenient of times. Ah, the perils of living on the frontier. The wild can cause a man to . . . crack, as it were. I'm sure our visitor is just another crazed ranger, mad youth, or broken adventurer. Pay it no mind."

"Aren't you a bit concerned, Uncle?" Arya asked, shifting uncertainly. "The Cult of the Black Blood is rebuilding, according to the rumors my father has heard at court. Could this not be one of their men? Or perhaps even their leader, this—"

"Jarthon," Greyt said. "And no. I doubt even the People of the Black Blood would be so stupid as to attack in public. The Beast Lord's foul spawn seem to have left us for good." He shuddered but quickly composed himself. He sank back into the couch and swirled his wine. "But, if, as I hope, some triviality will not interrupt us again, do continue your tale."

Perturbed but determined not to show it, Arya kept the false smile on her face—even as it pained her—and took a sip of her wine.

❧   ❧   ❧   ❧   ❧

Meris suppressed a sigh of disgust as he followed Claudir through the halls of Greyt's manor. Hunting trophies, tapestries, statues, and treasures—from adventuring, supposedly—adorned the place, gaudy and mostly fake. Meris could tell at a glance.

The old man's power and charm impressed him, but he did not allow it to reduce him to a simpering moron like the rest of the people of Quaervarr. He could see right through the old Singer, with the penetrating eye only a wayward son can acquire.

Meris was always honest with those around him—he didn't put on a pleasant face or a charming façade to impress the pitiful fools who surrounded him.

Still, Meris respected the old man's success, a success won through deceit and charisma. And he did like the Greyt fortune. Besides, as much as it pained him to admit it, he held a sort of subtle tolerance of his aging father. Perhaps it was because he could see so many similarities between Dharan Greyt and himself.

Claudir reached the front door and opened it for him. Hand on his sword hilt—a comfort to him—Meris stepped out into the sun.

Or, at least, what should have been sun.

Meris blinked, but not from the dazzling light. Instead, the sun and clearing skies he had seen not long ago had hidden behind dark, foreboding clouds. Lightning split the black haze and thunder growled. From what curse had this storm come? Magic, mayhap. Meris detested magic.

Then he caught sight of a lone black figure staring at him from behind a high collar that was laced over his mouth and nose, concealing his face. The man stood in the main road before the Greyt family manor. Meris felt colder upon seeing the dark figure, but the tingle creeping down his spine only ignited a flare of anger. Rain poured down.

"You there," Meris called. In the near silence after the thunder's clap, it sounded like an ear-splitting shout.

If the man heard, he gave no sign. He merely held out a dark bundle and allowed it to fall from his hands onto the muddy ground.

Meris was already walking toward him, sword ready to be drawn.

The dark figure turned and walked away.

"Wait," Meris called. "Stand and face me, boy!"

The figure continued to walk away.

Rushing after him, Meris vaulted the plain wood fence, but the man was already half a block away. When he came down, landing smoothly on his feet, mud splattered up, staining his snowy cloak. He paid it no mind. Neither did he stoop to see the package the man had left.

"Coward!" he called as he ran.

Meris was almost on top of him when the silent figure ducked into an alleyway, one Meris knew ended in a wall. The white-clad scout jumped after him, but when he entered the darkened alley, there was nothing to be seen. The shadows of the two thatch-covered houses were deep, but they hid nothing but air. The man had vanished.

With a frustrated curse, Meris furrowed his brow and sniffed at the air. He didn't smell the usual scent of ozone or feel the pressure change that usually indicated magic had been spent, but the storm might be the reason. Meris cursed the strange weather but did not let it distract him from his search. Still, the falling water had done its work. He looked for tracks in the muddy ground and found none—had the man left any, they must have been washed away in the storm. There was no trace of even a horse's passing, much less a man's presence.

The man in black had simply vanished, as though he'd melted into the shadows, or had never been there in the first place.

But Meris knew it hadn't been an illusion or a dream. The man in black had been real, was real. Meris did not remember ever feeling so cold, so hateful when he had looked upon anyone, and yet something was familiar about that haunted gaze, that thin posture....

Ignoring the crowd that had formed around him in the street, Meris started back to Greyt's manor.

❧ ❧ ❧ ❧ ❧

When Claudir returned, Arya had just finished her tale.

"And I suppose your father has nothing to say about your gallivanting around the Marches with a sword instead of keeping track of the family fortune and studying your letters like a proper girl?" Greyt took a drink. He had drained the rest of his second glass and was now working on a third. "Does he approve of your stay in Quaervarr, I wonder?"

"He doesn't say anything about it, since he doesn't know I'm here," Arya explained. She was still working on her first glass—Arya had never been fond of strong drink. "You and he are estranged—he'd never think to look for me here. And Quaervarr is remote, even if it is only a full day's ride from Silverymoon. I was wintering there, and he'll expect me to have gone farther out of his reach, not run to an uncle I hardly know and my father hardly tolerates."

"You are very candid," Greyt said with a little frown. Then he smiled. "I like that. Reminds me of me, in my fiery youth." He reached over and took his golden yarting from the sideboard—clearly, it had been placed purposefully—and strummed a chord. "Now I'm just an old man who likes music. I want none of your father's rash anger or politicking, but I am a doting uncle. You're free to stay here in Quaervarr as long as you like, but if Everlund's knights come knocking, my doors I won't be locking." It was a musical line.

Arya bowed. "I understand," she said. "Thank you, Uncle. I ask for nothing more."

"And that you shall have," Greyt said, amused at his own wit. He stood with a flourish. "But please accept my invitation to dine here tonight. Claudir . . . set an extra place, if you would."

The steward piped up. "But sir, I have not prepared—"

"Ah, three extra places," Bars corrected.

"Don't you mean four, Sir Hartpaunch?" Derst countered. "You'll need two."

Claudir blanched. "But sir," he said, "I have only enough in the storerooms—"

"Do not trouble yourself, Goodman Claudir," Arya said. "We must decline your generous offer. We have business at the Whistling Stag, and if we're to keep a low profile, we shouldn't dine in such luxury as your, ah, beautiful home." She wasn't sure those last words were true, but she said them for the sake of etiquette.

Greyt inclined his head. "Quite acceptable," he said. "I wish you a good night."

Bars and Derst rose to leave and Arya turned away. "As soon as we pay Speaker Stonar a visit, and ask him to keep our presence a secret—" she said.

"Oh, that's a shame," Greyt said. "He's just gone to Silverymoon—he left yesterday. You must have passed him on the road."

Arya's face fell, but only for a moment. Then her smile was back and she shrugged. "Well, I suppose that saves me a visit, doesn't it? Well met."

"Sweet wine and light jests, until next we might meet," replied Greyt.

It was a version of the traditional elf farewell, but it struck Arya as inexplicably unnerving.

The three moved toward the door Claudir had opened for them. Greyt sank back onto the couch, seemingly lost in thought. The knights, pleased to be free of the tense situation, made their way out.

"Oh, Arya, niece," Greyt called.

Arya was startled despite herself. "Yes?" she asked, turning and looking between the shoulders of her two companions.

"The Stag, did you say?" Greyt asked. He looked like he was making notes in his head. "Excellent choice. Good food, better wine, and excellent company and service. Known all over the Marches. However, it's not the best place for keeping your head below ground."

"What choice do we have?" Arya asked rhetorically.

Greyt laughed, a musical sound. "Quite true, quite true," he said. "In a town such as this, small as it is, the best inn is the only inn. How silly of me." He waved them on and turned his attention back to his wine.

Arya smiled, nodded, and turned away. Somehow, she felt uneasy telling him where they were staying. She dismissed the feeling, though, and left the room.

❂ ❂ ❂ ❂ ❂

As the door was closing, Greyt's grin slipped into a considering frown.

He saw right through Arya's act. Though it was probably true her father was looking for her, she was hardly the directionless runaway. So Silverymoon had sent some of her own to converse with Speaker Stonar. He vaguely remembered Stonar mentioning something about missing couriers.

What was Taern Hornblade playing at? Or Lady Alustriel herself? Had they discovered the magical barrier? Or was this a battle at home? Could Stonar be raising support against the Lord Singer? Greyt didn't know the nature of Arya's visit, but he intended to find out.

Hers was a tantalizing situation, and one that could be used to his advantage, if he could only decide how....

"Unwise...." a voice whispered in his ear, but Greyt dismissed it with a tsking sound.

He beckoned to Claudir with a surreptitious wave.

A pair of invisible eyes watched impartially.

❧ ❧ ❧ ❧ ❧

"You know your way out, I imagine," Claudir said in his stuffy voice. Arya nodded. The steward cleared his throat and went back into the sitting room, shutting the doors behind him.

The knights were silent for a moment.

"You almost gave it away," Derst said. "He may suspect our true intentions."

"Hmm?" Arya wasn't paying attention.

"You didn't tell him about the missing couriers," Bars observed. "Stonar never would have gone to Alustriel for help if Silverymoon had still been able to contact—"

Arya perked up. "What?" she asked, feigning distraction. "I'm sure I don't know what you're talking about."

Bars took the hint.

Derst didn't.

"You remember, the couriers?" he prompted. "The real reason we're here?"

Arya slapped Derst lightly on the side of the head. "The real reason is to hide from father," she hissed. "There just happen to be two real reasons. Who told you about the couriers?"

"The same person who told you," Derst replied indignantly, though he had the sense to keep his voice low. "Alus—Ow!" He shook his foot where Bars had stomped on it.

"Let us adjourn, and go to dinner," Arya said, her voice at normal speaking volume. Then she added, in a terse whisper. "Where certain ears that do not need to hear certain things will not, right, Sir Goldtook?"

Derst furrowed his brow but then shrugged. "Indeed, Lady Sir Venkyr," he said. "I am famished myself. I heard they were cooking some excellent venison at the Stag this eve. Shall we?" He put out his arm for Arya to take.

"Famished, eh?" Bars asked. "That's what happens when you don't eat for a month and become a stick." He shoved Derst away and put out his thick arm for Arya to take.

"Only because you ate all the month's rations, bulbous rothé," Derst pushed Bars aside and put his own arm back out.

Arya threw her hands up with a sigh and stomped off toward the door by herself, leaving the two casting angry looks and flashing obscene gestures at one another. She threw open the door and almost stumbled into a frowning Meris.

As it was, Arya barely avoided falling, but she still ran bodily into him. A package wrapped in water-stained leather fell to his feet. The two staggered for a breath, and Meris's strong hands grasped Arya by the shoulders. He righted her and pushed her away, none-too-gently, with a low growl.

His frown disappeared when he caught sight of her face. "Cousin," Meris said, as though recognizing her for the first time. "Anya, wasn't it?" He scrutinized her closely. His former angry expression had become cool and calculating.

There was an edge there—something about the gleam in his eye—that unnerved Arya more than any frown would have.

"Arya, if it please you, Cousin Meris," the young woman said with an awkward bow.

"Whatever it was," Meris said dismissively. He was eyeing her up and down.

Arya stifled a twinge of irritation. "I'm sorry for startling you, sir," she said. Meris's eyes flickered back to her face. There was fire in those eyes. Arya did not care to think where they might have lingered before. "And for colliding with you."

"Apology accepted," Meris said. "And I'm no knight, lass. I wouldn't address me by a title that matters nothing to me. I might take offense."

Arya was appalled. The lady knight made it a point not to stand on ceremony, but Meris's complete discourtesy made her gape.

Derst stepped up beside Arya. "Have a care how you address the good lady knight, Goodman," he said. His words were civil, but when spoken with that whiplike tongue they carried a thinly veiled threat. "She might take offense at your uncultured tongue."

Meris's smoldering eyes shot to the rapier-thin knight. His nose turned up. "Silence, boy," he said, even though Derst had clearly seen a couple more winters than had Meris. Greyt's son was probably about the same age as Arya. "Can't you see the wench and I were having a conversation?"

All three started.

Meris continued speaking to Derst. "Your face displeases me. Begone, before I have to show you out myself."

"That is no way to talk to a knight," Bars growled. He looked at Derst and shrugged. "Well, I can see the argument, but he is a knight, after all, and that's no way to speak in front of a lady." Meris lifted his brow.

"Aye, so apologize, orc-spawn," Derst snapped.

Meris looked at him incredulously for a moment,

blinked, and laid him low with a right hook. The thin knight staggered back, stunned. Bars lumbered in with a swinging left, but Meris ducked and slammed an elbow into the big man's great belly.

Bars gave a great "Oof!" and staggered, bending over Meris, who had dropped low.

Meris had his foot behind the big man's ankle and stood up abruptly, throwing Bars to the ground. Next to him, Arya had disappeared, and a charging Derst was in her place. The wiry knight threw a left hook feint, which Meris ignored, and a right fist thrust, which he ducked. Meris bent, put his shoulder into Derst's stomach, and threw the thin man over him.

"Bastard," Derst gasped as he landed in a roll and reached for a knife.

"You called?" Meris mocked. In response, the thin man's face scrunched.

Bars rose, but Meris shoved him down with his left hand, keeping his eyes on the thin man. Meris's hand went to his sword hilt.

There, it found the point of a long sword hovering at his groin.

Putting his hands out wide, Meris slowly turned. Arya had drawn her sword and was standing just within slashing range.

"Enough of this," she said. Her eyes were deadly. "Cousin, I was truly sorry to have offended you, but I take back my apology now."

Meris rolled his eyes at the sword pointing at his belly and looked up at her with a sarcastic frown. "You can't be serious, Cousin," he said contemptuously. "You side with these fools? They are no better than stupid sheep, and that makes you no better than a shepherdess."

"At least a shepherdess has some dignity," Arya snapped back. "Unlike you, Cousin."

"Until one takes it from her," Meris said without missing a beat. Ignoring Arya's sword, he wiped himself free of invisible dust and brushed past her. The two knights gave him angry stares as he strode away, his white cape swirling behind him, driven up by the haste of his walk.

They watched him slam the inner door behind his heels.

"Well," Derst said, wiping the blood from his nose. "At least you don't take after that side of the family, Arya."

Under any other circumstances, Arya might have replied wryly that she wasn't even related to that side of the family, but the encounter with Meris had unnerved her.

That cold hatred, pent up behind walls of calm. . . .

Arya had faced many enemies, but none who frightened her so. She saw through his every movement, heard the bitterness in his voice, and knew that he was utterly cold-blooded. Meris was the personification of the injustice the Knights in Silver stood against.

"Arya?" a voice said behind her, startling her from her reverie. "Are you well?"

"Aye?" She turned and looked into Bars's concerned eyes. As she did so, she realized with a flash that passing such a judgment was unfair. She did not, after all, know Meris. Perhaps he was just temperamental, or abrasive. It hardly justified labeling him. . . .

"I'm sorry, you were saying?" she forced herself to ask.

He smiled weakly. "Let us be gone," he said, rubbing his solid belly with a slight wince. "That bastard's hit made me stomach queasy. And when the demons stop playing in there, I'm going to be hungry."

"You shouldn't have had so much wine, mayhap then you wouldn't whine so much," Derst quipped with a wry grin.

"If we don't get moving, maybe I'll just have to eat you," Bars said.

Arya smiled and was about to add to that, but Derst was already nowhere to be seen.

CHAPTER 5

26 Tarsakh

Legs crossed and body stripped to the waist, Walker sat peacefully in the forest glade singing the last, bittersweet lines of a song. His ruined voice—like blood flowing through broken glass—mingled with the warm breezes blowing north.

A chilly brook swirled and danced by his feet, flowing from a waterfall that poured over a fallen shadowtop. The sun was setting, painting the forest canopy with emerald light and seeming to set the reddish bark of the firs afire. The snow had melted from the trees already, and not just because of the druidic charm that kept the grove warm. Spring was approaching, and while the snow would not completely disappear until the summer months, the air was warm.

Walker hardly noticed. He did not see the beauty either, for his eyes did not see the world around him.

The shadowy world he walked in his mind was one of ghosts. Colors were so dim that the world seemed painted in shades of gray, and outlines were indistinct. It was difficult for even an experienced ghostwalker to judge where the ground ended and the trees began. A normal mortal would be completely lost, disoriented, and terrified. On the border of material existence, he walked slowly, taking his time and watching. He saw memories of the past as easily as the present. At times, he could not even tell them apart.

He lay on his back, blood spurting from his mouth with every labored breath. Laughing faces ... cruel faces hovered above him. Some faces he recognized, and some he did not.

Walker remembered his first visits to the ghost world, when he had been young—one of the first memories he could recall. He had been terrified and had shone so brightly that he had been swarmed with ghosts. His guide had warned him it would happen, but that had not been preparation enough. He would never forget his terror.

Since then, his glow had dulled, even as the shock of entry faded. Now, Walker was coolly accustomed to the bleak landscape of the Ethereal and the Shadow beyond it. It was dark, true, but the ghost world had never held evil: only peace, and his task.

Face calm as it blurred in the Ethereal, Walker took a taste of the peace that surrounded him. Today, almost fifteen years after his first visit, the ghost world was more familiar to him than the living world.

He sensed a presence and turned. A hulking warrior raised its axe to slash at him.

Drex spat upon him. His woodsman's axe gleamed. His growl was that of a beast.

Walker shook his head. Drex was dead. A glimpse of his spirit, that was all he saw.

Ghosts hovered all around him, spirits of those who had passed away: rangers, humanoid creatures who had wandered into the forest and died, and adventurers slain by the forest's dangers. The souls, barely aware and wandering, were the remnants of humans and all those races akin to them—orcs, goblins, and even dwarves. Some spirits, pleasant and dancing around, were those of elves and the fey, rare and joyous things that took comfort in their perpetual, ethereal existence. Many were servants of the Seldarine, but a few tragic ones, the only ones to whom Walker paid any mind, wandered around, unsure of their purpose and without a patron.

The strength of a spirit's passion dictated the vibrancy of its shade, and some seemed truly alive before him. He could only tell they were dead because they lacked the telltale glow of life. Some—the younger and more confused spirits—reached out supplicating hands to him, begging for help, reassurance, or comfort, but Walker did not reply.

There was only one spirit who never talked to him, and Walker only spoke to that one.

"Father," he said softly. "Tarm, my father."

As if in reply, the spirit of the middle-aged man turned to him. Dark, wavy hair fell to his shoulders and soft brown eyes peered at Walker. Tarm was dressed as he had died, in the priestly vestments of Tyr, the deity of justice he had served. As always, the spirit was silent, allowing Walker to speak to himself, to allow his thoughts to reflect back in his own ears.

"Father, I have slain one of them, one of our murderers," said Walker. "Justice has been done at long last."

Tarm's spirit only looked at him with that same sad expression. Then, as though unhappy with Walker, the spirit turned away and disappeared into the trees.

Walker might have felt wounded, except that he knew this feeling all too well. His father never approved of the deaths he inflicted, even those that were necessary. He was always there, except when Walker killed. At those times, Tarm would leave to walk on his invisible path, toward what, the ghostwalker did not know.

Walker turned back to the spirits crowding around him, begging for his attention. Another memory came then, unbidden—a flash of the past Walker could not decipher. *A spectral laugh, that of the shadows themselves.*

As always, though, Walker ignored their pleas. Many of the weaker spirits did not even see him as distinct—his life-force was so in touch with the ethereal. He was, as in material life, merely an observer, existing on the fringes of the world. He could not have accepted or met those pleas even had he tried and he could not fully join in the ghost world, because something held him back, something that was fiercely material and could only be satisfied in the world of the living.

Vengeance.

He had a thirst to punish those who had wronged him—who still wronged him. He lived for his revenge. It was his task, the task that was his only purpose. And when that task was done....

Blurred memories—a laughing face, covered with his blood, looming over him. Drex ... the warrior with the woodsman's axe. Other faces ... other men, four others beside Drex. He did not know their names yet, but he would find out....

A smile gleamed in the moonlight above him.

No, that wasn't true. He did not have to find them all anew.

That mocking smile. Those lips that had spoken such kind words leveled a curse at him instead as he lay panting for breath on the grass. "Now, let us teach him how to sing," it said.

He knew one without seeing his face, the one he would kill last.

The thought and sight of his ghostly enemy pulled him from the ghost world. Before he returned to his body, though, there was one more vision, just a flash.

The boy ... the boy with the dark eyes and ebony curls ...

There was something significant about that boy ... there was pain in those eyes.

No matter, though. Walker had to complete his vengeance—his thirst would permit no less. It was all that had driven him for as long as he could remember.

Then Walker opened his eyes in the Material world.

"Well met, my lady," Walker said in perfect Elvish.

"Well met," a rich, sonorous voice replied in kind. There was a bit of laughter in its tone. "How did you know I was here?"

"I am at peace," Walker said. "And I am always at peace when you are near." He looked.

Standing before him was a diminutive woman with sparkling gold skin and gleaming hair that flowed to her waist. Her eyes glittered a majestic hazel with crimson motes and her lips were brushed with the slightest touch of frost. Resplendent in her partial gown of leaves—leaf-shaped pieces of leather stitched in intricate patterns and wound around her slim frame in a manner as wild as it was beautiful—she crossed her arms over her breast and smiled.

Gylther'yel, the Ghostly Lady of legend.

She smiled thinly. "That does not mean I cannot attempt to catch you unawares," Gylther'yel said. "Your abilities grow stronger by the day."

"Abilities you taught me."

Gylther'yel accepted the compliment without a twitch.

"You are not ready," she said. Walker felt a stab of irritation.

"We have spoken of this before," he rasped, his tone flat in warning. "You tell me the same thing every year—that I am not ready."

"I am not about to question your methods, or even your need for revenge," Gylther'yel said. "I only question your timing. Perhaps another year of training—"

"My training is complete. I have struck the first blow," Walker said. "I have delivered my warning. My task is a matter of speed now, and I cannot stop."

"I understand, but why now, of all seasons?" Gylther'yel asked, her voice tranquil. "The snows are falling away and the sun is returning, but Auril still holds sway. The winter is not over."

"All the more fitting for my vengeance," said Walker. "Let them feel fear colder than the snows around them. I am at my strongest when a chill wind blows."

"And I am at my weakest," Gylther'yel countered. Indeed, Walker knew that the ghost druid was most powerful with her fire magic. "The cold is anathema to my powers."

"My deathday approaches—less than a tenday," Walker said. "It is a fitting time."

She continued despite his reply. "You are my guardian, my champion—what if they were to follow you back here? I have not raised you to bring danger to my doorstep. . . ."

Walker smiled. "I did not realize you were so humorous, Gylther'yel," he rasped. Walker had watched the Ghostly Lady hurl fire and call down lightning to smite adventurers who strayed from the paths. He turned away. "Anyone foolish enough to challenge you deserves to feed the earth with his ashes."

Gylther'yel did not nod, but a hint of a smile crossed her golden face. "Still, I warn you against allowing your vendetta to harm my woods." Her face grew stormy. "If you fight here, you will be on your own, and if you fall, so be it. I will not interfere with the will of nature—"

"The strongest and fittest will survive, I know," Walker said. "But fear not. Even the fiercest wolf leads the wild boar away from its den—and family."

His silver wolf ring gleamed as he stood. Its single sapphire eye radiated a calm but dangerous light. It was silent, stoic, and resolute; like Walker himself.

"You speak true," the sun elf said. "Only your timing—"

He rounded on her. "I saw him, Gylther'yel!" he shouted, suddenly speaking in the Common tongue. His voice shattered and broke in his ears. "I saw the boy! He is important, I know it!"

With that, Walker sank to his knees, his hands over his face, racked by unknown tremors. His cloak billowed in the strong breeze and all was silent.

Gylther'yel moved as though to comfort him, but stopped, her attention turned to another face. Tarm, priest of the Justicar, appeared out of the shadows as though drawn to Walker's grief, trying to speak. She hissed at Tarm and the spirit retreated. His father had always feared Gylther'yel, the only mother Walker had ever known.

The ghost druid stepped back and folded her arms over her breast. "I am sorry, Walker," she said. "I remembered for a moment your sweet voice, wafting on the breezes that breathed through this place, before. . . ." She trailed off.

His blue eyes opened. "Do not remind me of days that are gone," he said, speaking Elvish again. His ragged voice was bitter. "I remember the sword that silenced my song. Now all that remains is vengeance."

"Walker, I remember your song—" Gylther'yel started.

"The only song I sing is the scream of steel, the hymn of the duel," Walker said.

She was silent, bowing to his words.

"Do not fear for your lands," he said, rising. "This place is precious. It is the only home I have ever known. The only one I can remember." He turned away, looking into the sunset.

The Ghostly Lady's thin lips turned up in a bittersweet smile. "I am sorry, Walker," she said. "I did not mean to remind you—"

"It is nothing," he said, interrupting her. There was pain in his voice, pain in the suppression, but Gylther'yel said nothing.

The two were silent for a long moment. The sun dipped fully below the horizon and darkness cast its shade over Faerûn.

"Night falls," Walker said. "The third night. Time to return to my task."

❧ ❧ ❧ ❧ ❧

"Old green Drake, jolly as the day is long," rang the chorus, hollered at the top of Derst's lungs as he danced upon the table.

"Raids a town, not for food but mead!" Bars responded in his deep bellow. He tried, unsuccessfully, to push Derst off the table, but the roguish knight danced out of the way.

"Carries his booty along—" Arm-in-arm, their voices

joined in a raucous disharmony for the last lines of the chorus. "A little drink is all he needs!"

The Whistling Stag was filled with laughter. The knights sang, voices slurred with plenty of the same honey-brew of their refrain, and danced—poorly. The ditty used an old Iluskan folk melody but Amnian words pilfered from Derst's favorite bard of that southern kingdom. The crowd loved it. Bars and Derst, arms locked and feet flying, twirled awkwardly amidst a sea of smiles.

Over at the bar, Arya was careful not to allow her hood to slip and reveal her identity. As it was, she gave a small smile and raised her tankard of weak ale in tribute to the dancing fools.

The two were never more amiable than when they were deep in their cups. All their biting wit and competition vanished, to be replaced with jest and good-hearted friendship. Arya wondered if the two ever clearly remembered their sodden revels, and if they would be embarrassed that their seeming rivalry ended with only a mug or dozen of mead, ale, or elverquisst. Especially elverquisst.

Arya found herself wanting to join them, as a noble lady did not often have the chance to engage in such pursuits— Regent Alusair of Cormyr a notable exception—but she had other plans.

She had retired early, feigning weariness, and emerged without armor or sword, clad in woodsman's garb. In plain, earthen tones, Arya would not leave the sort of impression the daughter of Lord Rom Venkyr of Everlund in blue and silver would strike. Perhaps on this, the third evening, she could finally find some answers to the questions that had brought her to Quaervarr.

Finishing her ale, Arya waited until Bars and Derst were finished with their merry tune about the drunken wyrm. Then, while the crowd clapped and cheered the two staggering singers on, she set two copper coins on the bar and made her exit unobtrusively.

Arya stepped out into the night and pulled her cloak

tightly around her slim frame. Her breath crystallized before her face. While the snow that had dusted Quaervarr the previous night was gone, the air was not warmer for it. The street was deserted, and Arya felt a familiar emptiness creeping up on her, as it always did when she was alone, but she pushed it away as best she could and made her way to the other local tavern, the Red Bear.

Unlike the Whistling Stag, renowned throughout the Silver Marches for its fine brew and finer company and visited by almost every adventurer in the north once or thrice, the Red Bear catered solely to Quaervarr locals. The ale was of a lower quality and the conversations were correspondingly less lively. Still, it was an excellent meeting place for hunters, trappers, and frontiersmen of all kinds, providing a common ground where they could come after a day's work and compare tales over tankards of Keeper Brohlm's finest. The old, hardened patrons were the most likely to know about life in the Moonwood.

Thus, they were the most likely to have heard word of the missing couriers.

Arya stepped into the smoky bar, stooping to avoid knocking her head against low-hanging, mildew-stained rafters. With a tiny gasp, she managed to catch herself before she stumbled down the steps into the tavern.

" 'Ware, lass," a gray-bearded man said at her side, reaching to steady her. He forgot to set down his mug and splashed ale over them both, but he didn't seem to notice. "The Bear's not what she used to be." Arya accepted his hand with a nod and a smile and ignored the creeping wetness he had just spilled all over her wool breeches.

Taking her response as encouragement, he launched into an explanation of the rafters and the sunken floor. Local legend had it that the founder of the Red Bear had built the tavern on the finest ground available to compete with the Stag, but the curse of Silvanus on certain disloyal worshipers had caused the ground to soften and brought the tavern sinking down.

"That'll teach us to skip ceremonies for a brew, aye, lass?" he asked with a chuckle.

Arya accepted the tale with an easy manner, though it held little interest for her. It would not hurt her cause to ingratiate herself with the townsfolk. The barkeep caught her eye, and she ordered a weak ale.

"What can you tell me about travelers who pass through the Moonwood?" Arya asked the old man. "Messengers from Silverymoon, mayhap?"

"Well, the one who'd be knowing about that'd be Lord Singer Greyt." The name set his eyes to shining. "He meets all the outsiders and adventurers passing through. E'en wedded a few o' them."

Arya held up her hand. "I'm not really interested in hearing about—"

"Did I hear ye mention the Lord Singer, Elbs?" a particularly buxom serving maid asked beside their table. She was a golden-haired woman of the north with steeper curves than Arya had thought possible on a woman's body.

Arya was about to pipe up, but a huge smile painted her dining companion's face. "Annia ... Aye, lassie," he said. "Just telling Goodwoman—"

"Goldwine," Arya said. She reasoned Bars and Derst wouldn't mind if she borrowed their names. "Maid Goldwine."

"Goodmaid Goldwine about Quickwidower's wives," he said.

"Quickwidower?" Arya asked, frowning at the nickname.

"Aye, Greyt can't stay married more than a year or three," said Annia. "Just like any man, if'n ye ask me. Charmin' though—just look at the wives and babes. Though ..." A shadow crept across her face. "They was all sickly. Poor babes, only one survived to ten."

"Greyt has separated from many wives?" asked Arya.

"Aye, after a fashion. The lasses tended to meet with accidents," Elbs said somberly. "Greyt's got the rottenest luck with women. Shame, such pretty things. Died, most o' them. Or left town—just couldn't settle down. Hey, that sounds like one o' the Lord Singer's rhymes—"

The barmaid slapped him on the back of the head. "Lord Greyt certainly made that mistake," the barmaid said. "Should've ne'er settled down, but Lyetha was here."

"Lyetha?" Arya asked, wondering what the half-elf woman had to do with this.

"The woman he's always loved," Elbs said wistfully. "Lyetha, heartbroken after her husband and son disappeared. The most beautiful woman in Quaervarr." The barmaid's face turned stormy. Elbs smiled widely and patted her bottom. " 'Cept for me pretty Annia 'ere."

Apparently appeased, the voluptuous woman smiled and moved away.

Elbs turned back to Arya. "Only babe still breathing, though, be that fancy-faced Meris," he said. "Dashing, but something about him I just don't like, ye know?"

"What?" Arya asked.

"I don't be knowing," he replied. "Never talks back to his father—right respectable lad, that Meris."

"You mean respect*ful*," corrected Arya. "They are not the same thing."

"Oh aye," Elbs replied. "Even when Lord Singer goes against Speaker Stonar . . ."

As he continued, Arya nodded without speaking. She had been thinking about getting up and trying her luck elsewhere, but something about this thread of conversation was appealing. She offered to buy Elbs another ale, an offer he heartily accepted. Arya smiled, thinking that she was already on the right track to the answers she sought.

❧ ❧ ❧ ❧ ❧

Nursing his glass of heated wine, Greyt wasn't surprised to find himself alone for dinner. Claudir had set three places with the hope that he might serve his master, mistress, and Greyt's son, but, as usual, it was only Greyt who graced the table with his presence.

The dinner was elegant, Greyt decided, though too simple for his liking. Roast lamb, imported from warmer climes, was a delicacy Greyt could afford and so feasted upon regularly. Despite having lived all his life in the North, the Lord Singer had never developed a taste for the hard rothé meat from the herds that sometimes wandered the plains to the east. Trays of rich mustards and sauces provided pools of myriad colors among the winter flowers spread across the table in crystalline vases.

His preference for decadent dishes, coupled with his obsession for the various fruits and vegetables arranged in sunbursts and crescents around the table caused many to call him a "man of weak stomach." Grey preferred to call himself a "creature of delicacy and culture."

To Greyt it hardly mattered; he was, after all, Quaervarr's hero.

Greyt was disappointed a certain half-elf woman was not there to sit with him, but he was not terribly troubled. He could appreciate silence once in a while, even in his line of work.

As though in response to his thoughts, a door swung open and Claudir stepped inside. "Lyetha Elfsdaughter, the Lady Greyt," he announced.

His forehead suddenly itching, Greyt thought it might serve him best to forbid her entrance. He was about to reply to his steward's announcement when Lyetha swept into the room, almost bowling over Claudir. Greyt had to remember to suck in his breath when he saw her, or he might have berated her then, and the illusion would be spoiled.

A cascade of glowing amber hair fell around Lyetha's shoulders and her eyes blazed with sapphire light. Her face, with its distinct gold tinge, hinted clearly at her sun elf heritage. Slim and perfectly rounded, she radiated beauty in her gown of gleaming black, even as the color made Greyt wince. The frown on her full lips drew her face down, exposing soft wrinkles that hinted at her age, but she was still stunning. Lyetha had aged much more gracefully than Greyt ever would, and while they were nearly the same age, he looked at least two decades her senior.

Greyt had once thought Lyetha an incarnation of Hanali Cenali herself and pursued her with single-minded determination.

Once.

"Ah, my matchless darling," he said grandly as she swept toward him. "Do you find this evening to your liking, Morning Star?" His tone was purposefully poetic.

Lyetha ignored the compliment. She stood a short distance from the table, crossed her arms, and shifted her weight onto her back foot. "Care to explain yourself, Dharan?" she asked, the sarcasm thick on her tongue. Even so, the tone of her voice was rich, with a hint of a melody begging for release.

"I beg your pardon?" Greyt asked. He swept his hand out, gesturing for her to sit, and sipped his wine. "Pray, try some of this vintage. Amnian, I believe—or so Claudir tells me. He's always the one who keeps track. I just tell him which wines I like and which I don't."

Lyetha sat but did not follow Greyt's advice about the wine. She served herself, taking some of the vegetables on the table. After she had filled the plate, she ignored her food. Her attention remained on the Lord Singer.

"You know exactly what I mean," she said. "A bard with your long years of training and experience doesn't falter on a simple lyric, particularly one in a song you wrote yourself and have sung for almost a decade and a half."

"Don't be ridiculous," Greyt said, only half paying attention. "I would never—"

"The song about the children?" Lyetha pressed. "The missed note?"

Greyt was about to dismiss whatever she'd been about to say, but he was knocked off his guard. Of course she would ask about that. After all, it did ring with some importance to her.

"Ah yes," he said. "A minor mishap. Must be getting on in years. Watch out, I might become Elminster before you know it."

"Pausing on Ghar—on that monster's name is a minor mishap?" Lyetha countered. She stumbled over the name of Greyt's father, Gharask. "I could feel a chill, and yet. . . ."

A retort died on his lips and he looked her in the eyes for the first time that evening.

"I'm sorry, love," he said. "Coincidence, and that 'twas a cold night. No man is perfect, right?"

There was silence for a long moment. Greyt, who was purposefully not looking at Lyetha once more, could feel her eyes on him. He took a long time cutting a piece of lamb into tiny pieces and raised the pink meat to his lips. Though it was too hot, he suppressed the wince. Such an expression would not do, not in the current situation.

He noticed again her black dress. Of course Lyetha would be wearing mourning colors near the end of winter. This year made even more sense, being the fifteen-year anniversary of the murders that had claimed the last thing she had loved.

"But that name—" Lyetha started.

"Yes?" Greyt asked impatiently.

She opened her mouth to ask a question.

At that moment, the door from the inner hall flew open and Meris stormed into the room, muttering something. He wore his white tunic, but there was a black robe in his hand. No sword was belted on his hip, but the fierce expression on his face was just as dangerous as any length of sharpened steel. Lyetha started, almost leaping from her chair.

Meris stopped and scowled at her.

"Don't rise, Lyetha," the dusky scout snapped. "I won't be staying."

Greyt stretched lazily. "Meris, sit—eat with us," he offered.

"I'm not hungry." Meris didn't bother regarding either of them. "I'm going out."

"At least offer a kind word to your lady mother," Greyt said. "You've startled her."

Meris stopped in his tracks. He turned his head toward them. "I am under no obligation to show any courtesy to her," he said to the Lord Singer. "My mother was not an elf-get trollop." With that, he looked away and strode through the double doors. They slammed shut behind him.

"No, your mother was Amnian," Greyt mused as he sipped his wine.

After a moment, he became aware that Lyetha was staring at him. He looked over at her, met her cold blue gaze, and shrugged.

"Pay it no mind, dear," he said. "Young men say things without thinking. I've oft thought he needs a cool head to temper him, but I haven't found any worthy woman."

Lyetha sniffed.

They sat in silence for a few moments, then she rose and silently took her leave. She stopped at the door but did not turn.

"Dharan," Lyetha asked, without looking back. "About Gharask . . . and Rhyn. Is there any doubt that your father killed my son?"

"No, my dear. Of course, no," he replied without turning his head or missing a beat. "No more than scarlet falls the snow."

He took another sip of his wine and pretended to ignore her. It was not difficult.

Lyetha sighed and slipped out the door, seeking the refuge of her chambers.

❧ ❧ ❧ ❧ ❧

After spending plenty of silver on drinks for potential informants and learning nothing of import, Arya gave up and climbed out of the tavern. The meaty barkeep Brohlm thanked her and swept up her coins with a flick of his thick wrist.

While the customers of the Red Bear were very knowledgeable about Quaervarr's history and the surrounding lands, they knew nothing of Stonar's couriers. They had told her all about Greyt and Stonar's rivalry—the two seemed at odds over every public issue, but it was a friendly competition, by all appearances. She did not blame them—they were simple frontiersmen—but she found her search's fruitlessness irritating.

Besides, she had heard far too much about her adored step-uncle.

In the cold once more, Arya shivered and adjusted the cloak around her shoulders. The ale stain on her breeches was freezing. Not for the first time, she wished she had sent Derst on this foray instead. He was more adept at gathering information, for pressing into the right threads of a conversation, and for discerning something useful where she found only local history and superstition. Perhaps she would have him go out the following night.

Arya set out through the streets toward the Whistling Stag, where a warm bed and a pair of drunken, invariably laughing compatriots awaited her. She knew she would enjoy the former, but she wasn't especially looking forward to the latter.

Arya turned around a corner and caught sight of the Stag. She shivered and continued on, looking forward to the warmth.

A hand reached out from the alley between two buildings and caught her by the arm.

Arya tried to wrest out of the grasp, but her reflexes were too dulled by the cold. As it was, she inhaled the breath to scream, but a hand pressed itself over her mouth to stifle the sound. She tasted tanned deer hide.

"Wanderin' late at night, are ye, pretty wench?" a growling voice asked in a rough accent. "Not lookin' where ye be—Ah!" His words turned into a gasp of pain as she bit him through the leather glove. She managed to worm out of the loosened grip as he reeled, and brought her elbow back hard, catching him in the stomach. She whirled to face him, instinctively reaching for her sword—which wasn't there.

Arya turned right into a backhand slap, a blow that left her spinning and dazed. The only weapon she carried was a long dagger in her boot, but when she stooped, a knee caught her in the chin and sent her staggering back into the wall. The impact knocked whatever breath she'd been able to recover from her lungs and she sank to her knees.

Her assailant was on her in an instant, catching her by the shoulders. Before she could punch at him, he clutched her wrists with an iron grasp. "Not going to play nice?" His voice had changed, his accent shifting into something less rustic. He sounded familiar, but she couldn't recognize it through the gruffness and the pain.

"No' so intimidatin' with-outta sword, are ye, Sir Serving Wench?" The gruff, broken language was back. It might have sounded slurred, but Arya knew her attacker was not drunk. She was about to ponder the implications when another slap caught her face.

"Who said . . . I was a . . . knight. . . ?" Arya managed through swelling lips, though she was painfully aware of the Silverymoon brooch that shone brightly through her open cloak. Blood trickled from her split lip.

"Count thyself fortunate ye harlots disgust me," he said. He held a dagger to her throat but then paused. "Still, I could reconsider, seeing thy face. . . ." He ran a finger down her cheek, and a shiver ran down her spine.

Then a dark shape dropped behind the attacker, silently, with what seemed like wings billowing wide.

The man grunted as the newcomer threw him against the opposite wall. The dagger that had threatened Arya's life skittered into the shadows. The gruff attacker went for another knife, but a gleaming sword point appeared at his throat and the hand froze.

"Inadvisable," the savior rasped. The assailant cringed at his broken voice, and even Arya felt a chill when she heard it.

Arya's vision swam, but she heard the assailant chuckle.

"You not going to tell me to drop the knife?" he asked. "Just that my suit is 'inadvisable?'"

"Your choice," came the reply.

A knife clattered down. "So you're the one they call Walker," the assailant said. His voice was back to normal. It seemed familiar, somehow.

"Perhaps," her savior—Walker, she knew in her heart—replied. His manner was filled with a terrifying resolution.

"You don't seem all that impressive to me," the assailant said. "You fool us all from a distance with your cloak and your silence, but you don't impress me up close."

"Irrelevant," Walker replied. "Yours is the judgment of a coward in a mask."

Arya's vision was just clearing. She saw that Walker had not withdrawn his sword and the unnamed attacker was still standing at the end of the sharp steel. He didn't look cowed at all; rather, his stance was a challenge to Walker. The assailant wore a tattered black cloak and had his cowl pulled low. Even so, his mouth was just faintly visible stretching into a sneer.

"This isn't over, whoever ye be, Walker." He was feigning the drunken voice again and slipping away along the wall. "The People of the Black Blood will have your heart for this."

"I doubt it," Walker replied, though which assertion he doubted, he showed no sign. He kept his blade up until the hooded man ran out of the alley. Walker watched him go for a moment, sheathed the sword, and turned back toward the street.

"Wait!" Arya managed as she struggled to climb to her feet.

Startled, as though he had not noticed her, Walker turned to regard Arya. His collar was pulled up high and his face was half concealed, but Arya took careful note of his features—they were the only things she could focus upon. His pale skin and black cloak contrasted starkly in the moonlight. He was dark in dress and wild of hair, as though he were a demon come to Faerûn. Arya, however, could only see the light of his eyes. At first, his presence had been terrifying, but she found that as she looked on him, she became less and less afraid. There was something about him, something that told her he was important, a key to the entire unfolding mystery.

And there was something she could see in his eyes—a call waiting to be answered, a terrible vengeance....

Then Walker's eyes vanished into shadow as he turned away. Arya tried to follow him, but her vision swam. He was gone.

Staggering, off-balance, and with her head splitting, Arya managed to limp back to the Whistling Stag, where she could hear the sounds of raucous laughter issuing from the windows. She ignored it as she pressed through the doors and made her way up to her room.

For Arya knew two things: that her business with the dark stranger was not finished for the night, and that she would need her blade.

CHAPTER 6

26 Tarsakh

Walker strode away from the alley, his mouth set in a frown. He did not have far to go—Quaervarr had perhaps five dozen buildings and only three main streets. Few would be out of their homes after nightfall, and none would spot him as he glided between shadows.

Not that he would have cared even had he been watched. He was thinking of the woman with the auburn hair.

He had come upon the struggle in the alley by coincidence as he stalked through Quaervarr, and any other day he might have passed by without interference. Why had he saved her? He had no idea who she was. He'd never seen before, but that was not surprising. Strangers often came through Quaervarr; he himself was a stranger, in a sense.

Had he acted out of a sense of justice? Walker scowled. Justice was antiquated and meaningless—he had only to think of the murder of his father, a devotee of Tyr, for evidence. Still, the choice had not felt random; it had not been whim. Had the sight of the woman sparked feelings in him, feelings long since buried? His pulse quickened.

Walker turned to the spirit of Tarm for guidance, but his father's face was impassive. Whatever answers Walker was going to discover would come from within, where he was empty.

Using techniques perfected over long years of practice, Walker put it as far as he could out of his mind. His memory of the auburn-haired woman remained vivid, and it burned, almost indignantly, from its place in his subconscious, but he paid it no attention. He focused his attention on the task at hand—Torlic, the warrior known in Quaervarr as the "Dancing Blade."

Walker's hand went to his arm, where an old stab wound throbbed.

Torlic's was a large townhouse, built in the early days of Quaervarr and expanded later. Over the last twenty years, Torlic—a razor-thin half-elf with a penchant for the rapier—had built himself a substantial base in the Quaervarr watch, thanks to Dharan Greyt. Torlic was first lieutenant to Unddreth, though not because of his personality or any friendship with the hulking captain of the Watch. Torlic was also known for his paranoia and regularly posted his underlings to guard his own house, rather than to patrol the streets.

There were no guards that night, though, Walker observed. It seemed unlike a man such as Torlic to be unprepared, so Walker was wary. Mithral sword in its scabbard, the ghostly warrior stalked toward the house on a roundabout path, through the shadows, just in case any guards were watching from behind the darkened windows.

Leaving the front entrance behind, Walker slid along the worn logs of the outer wall and searched for a back entrance.

He could have tapped into the ethereal and walked through the barrier, but he preferred to reserve his powers for an escape, if necessary.

As Gylther'yel had done, Walker questioned the timing of his attacks. He was not worried about one of his targets overwhelming him, but fighting more than one was risky. His success depended, to an extent, on surprise, but his foes would become increasingly paranoid as they died one by one. It seemed like a tactical error, allowing them to build defenses as they grew suspicious, and as time passed....

Perhaps that was what he wanted. Perhaps he wanted to show them that all their paranoia and preparation would not save them from cold vengeance. Or perhaps he wanted them to stop him. For in the end, what could be awaiting him but the logical conclusion of his task?

He looked over at the mute spirit of his father, Tarm, who hovered three paces to the right. The man was wearing a sad, distant expression unsuited to his face. Why was he always so sad? Walker wondered. Did he hold a secret of some kind, something he could not share?

Walker doubted the spirit would aid him in his struggle, considering how deeply Tarm seemed to disapprove of his task. And, besides, for all Walker knew, Tarm might not be able to speak. Pity, since he would have appreciated scouting before he walked into potential ambushes.

Walker found a rear entrance, which was, of course, locked. Not a thief by trade, Walker had no skill in opening locks, but he had come prepared. Opening a belt pouch, he carefully extracted the contents—a small leather-wrapped bundle: a gift from Gylther'yel. Delicately, he unfolded the wrapping until an orange-red acorn stood out against the black leather of his glove.

He pondered it for a moment—a beautiful piece of nature, to be used in such an unnatural thing as murder. Gylther'yel had taught him all his skills and abilities, true, but was his course in keeping with what she held sacred? The Ethereal was as much a part of the world as the physical, but was he going too far? Was his talent, his very existence, unnatural?

For that matter, would that not make her unnatural as well?

Again, Walker looked at Tarm but, as always, the spirit gave him no answers, merely the chance for Walker to ask questions of himself.

Was Walker an abomination?

After a moment, he found that he did not know and, when he was honest with himself, he found he did not much care. In a few days, it would no longer matter at all.

Walker held the acorn against the lock and handle on the door. "Eat away the works of man," he rasped quietly in Elvish.

In response, the acorn shuddered and sank into the metal. Where it touched, ripples of red spread outward, rusting and corroding the lock and handle. The metal groaned in helpless protest, but the rust did its work.

The handle was red dust before it hit the mud.

The hinges creaked only slightly. He saw no guards or servants in the dark house. Walker calmly walked inside.

His nonchalance was, of course, an act. Walker had to assume that Torlic was ready for him; his task was too important to risk carelessly.

Walker heard a faint ringing, as of swords clashing far away, and he fell into readiness. The differences in Walker's carriage were subtle, such that only a skilled swordsman could detect them; to the rest of the world, he remained relaxed.

Walker found himself in a rear entry hall, with benches around the walls and hooks for cloaks and other garments. The place was sparse. There was little furniture to sit upon and the walls were stark. A few cloaks, mostly the black ones with the green lining of the Quaervarr guard, but that was it. The tapestries that usually adorned the homes of the wealthy were absent. Torlic's home was simple, with small, uncomfortable rooms—that of a soldier.

In the entrance room, Walker saw double doors leading deeper into the house and a pair of doors on either side. He explored the side doors first, opening them a crack to peer through. One led to a kitchen, the other to a storeroom, and neither was occupied. A pot sat over a long-cooled fire in the kitchen, and knives and small cleavers hung overhead where servants could reach them. Bundles—most likely containing bread and other slow-perishing items—sat on wooden shelves, untouched. There was a larder in the corner of the kitchen as well. The storeroom contained weapons, armor, saddles, and part of a wagon.

The door to the main room beckoned and Walker answered the call. He listened at it briefly, long enough to ascertain that the noises of the swords were coming from behind it, and put his hand on the latch. Tarm fixed him with a supplicating gaze, as though begging him to turn back, but when Walker met those eyes, the spirit turned away and walked through the wall.

Walker nodded.

His father may never speak, but his guidance was still there.

❧   ❧   ❧   ❧   ❧

Greyt was startled as Meris stormed into his study, throwing the doors wide. He tore a black cloak from his shoulders.

"Back so soon, son?" Greyt asked, looking up from the scroll upon which he was inscribing his latest ballad. Next to him rested some neglected correspondence he had meant to send to Stonar's desk when he got around to it—perhaps sometime later this year. "Claudir hadn't announced your presence, but I see time was of the essence."

"He didn't get the chance," Meris said curtly. Behind him, the gaunt steward rushed in, red-faced, apologizing over and over for the intrusion.

Greyt waved him away. "A bad day?" he asked. "Didn't find sport to your liking, eh?"

Meris stomped over to the Singer's desk and slammed down a black leather bundle. It clattered on the thick oak. "Tell me he's just a shadow now," he said angrily. Then he whirled and strode out, his feet pounding the creaking wood under the carpet.

"I need to get that fixed, it seems," Greyt said of the floor as the door slammed.

The words trailed off as he looked at the leather pouch Meris had deposited on his desk. He wasn't about to touch it, but it consumed a moment of his attention.

He went back to making notes, but the rhymes would not come. He was forcing the ballad and, like all art, it could not be demanded. Greyt threw the ink quill down on the desk.

A disgusted frown twisted his face and he seized the bundle, wincing when something within scratched him. Ignoring the blood that welled from his finger, he ripped it open, threw the contents down on the desk, and drew back in shock.

It was the snapped blade of Drex Redgill's wood axe. There was a bit of blood on it, where the jagged edge had torn through the leather and cut his finger.

❧ ❧ ❧ ❧ ❧

Torlic spun back and around, bringing his rapier singing up to parry his opponent's blade. The glittering blade snapped down and thrust under Torlic's guard, but the nimble half-elf simply twisted his rapier around and sent the thrust out harmlessly wide.

The blond watchman Narb, Torlic's opponent, slashed right to left, and the half-elf picked off the attack with a neat, almost casual parry. An attack high followed by a thrust low met similar fates, parried with quick flicks of Torlic's wrist. Narb lunged—a strike Torlic easily dodged—

and faltered. Torlic sidestepped Narb and slapped him twice on the backside with the flat of his blade, making a "tsk" sound in his throat. Torlic covered his yawning mouth with one dainty hand.

Angry, the youthful watchman lunged at Torlic, but the half-elf leaped back, spinning to land on his toes. The dancing half-elf flicked his sword back and forth, tempting his opponent.

"Try harder, Narb," Torlic said. "I haven't broken a sweat yet."

The two fought in Torlic's training room. It was a wide, open square with walls lined with weapons and practice dummies. Members of Quaervarr's Watch used this training arena for dueling and for working on their sword skills. Most of them took instruction from Torlic himself, whose sword's sharpness was surpassed only by his tongue. If fencing was his hobby, criticism was his habit.

Narb, shaking his golden mane, growled a negative. "Sorry, Captain," he said. He turned away and took a few steps. He limped from where Torlic's blade had slapped his thigh. "Me bed's callin' me louder than your sword."

Narb was handsome and young, and it was clear that Torlic had picked him for exactly those traits. The vain half-elf loved the company of men he found lovely—and enjoyed proving his superiority over them even more. Narb fingered the scar running down his otherwise flawless face, remnant of a recent rapier wound.

"Tired, are we?" Torlic asked. "Too warm? Or perhaps you're not properly motivated. Do you need another scar?" He cut his light rapier through the air, then stretched his arms.

Narb's face paled.

"It's a little too warm, I agree," said Torlic. He turned to open the window, letting in the cutting chill of the breeze.

The young watchman was walking away when Torlic cleared his throat.

"Narb, you work for me, remember?" he asked without looking back.

At the door, the watchman stopped. "Yes, but—" Narb started.

"Put up your guard," Torlic said. "I'm not done with you yet."

As he turned, Narb opened his mouth to protest then staggered away, gaping.

As though he had stepped out of the air itself, Walker stood between them, the fringes of his cloak rustling in the breeze from the window. Spikes of hair shifted around his face. His arms were hidden inside the black cloth of his cloak. His cold eyes—beautiful in the way that thunderstorms are—were fixed on Torlic.

"Your replacement seems to . . ." Torlic started, but his voice trailed off as the crushing weight of the ghostwalker's will fell upon him. His knees felt weak and the rapier in his hand grew heavy.

"Send him away," Walker rasped.

Torlic seemed to gather his senses again. "Go," he said to Narb without taking his eyes from his new opponent. "This is a duel between me and the dark gentleman."

"Should I call Unddreth?" Narb stammered, trembling with exhaustion and fear.

"Yes," Torlic said. He flicked his eyes toward the watchman. "There will be a corpse to cart away when I'm done."

Walker said nothing, but a hint of a smile might have creased his mouth—behind the high black collar.

Narb wasted no time in leaving, and the two listened to his rapid footfalls and the outer door slamming shut as he dashed off. Torlic tossed the rapier from hand to hand, cutting it through the air in practice moves.

The man in black did not move.

"So, Walker—if I may call you so, lovely boy—how long would you guess we have?" Torlic asked. His voice was almost lewd. "It's a disorganized Watch, and Unddreth is a heavy sleeper—"

"How soon do you wish for your death?" Walker asked.

"How about not at all?" Torlic asked with a whimsical smile. "How soon do you wish—"

Walker stepped aside as Torlic's blade flashed past.

Faster than the eye could follow, the half-elf had darted forward and thrust, thinking to end the battle right then. Walker swept a silvery long sword out of the folds of his cloak and knocked the rapier to the right, then parried to the left when Torlic tried to reverse his strike. Walker leaped away, his cloak swirling around him, and brought the blade left to right, low to high, throwing the rapier up wide when Torlic thrust a third time.

As the half-elf danced back, his offensive momentum spent, Walker continued his spinning attack. Eyes popping wide, Torlic barely got the sword up in time to knock the blow high enough to keep it from taking his head from his shoulders. Walker's mithral blade screeched against the rapier and Torlic pulled his weapon away as quickly as he could. He leaped back and wove his blade through the air to distract and ward off his opponent.

The warrior in black charged, ignoring the whipping blade. Torlic dived aside of the slashing long sword and turned a somersault on the floor, coming up with a main-gauche in his left hand, drawn from his belt.

Walker slashed in with the long sword, and Torlic hooked it on his rapier's basket hilt. He pulled his left arm back to jab, but Walker's fist was faster. The half-elf went tumbling backward, his face stinging, but he kept a firm hold on his weapons.

That was fortunate for him, since Walker was right there, slashing again.

❧ ❧ ❧ ❧ ❧

"My lady, what...?" asked Garion.

The voice trailed off as Arya shot the innkeeper a burning look. She would clearly brook no delay. The blows to her head had left her dizzy but intent.

She had to find the man in black, the mysterious Walker she had heard about in whispers. She felt almost desperate to see him again. He frightened her, but he intrigued her; thus, he frightened her all the more.

Arya threw open the door to her room and darted inside, ignoring the snoring bodies of Bars and Derst in the middle of the floor. Apparently, they had both tried for the bed but neither had made it.

Arya knew she didn't have time to don her plate armor, so she grabbed her shield and long sword before rushing down the stairs.

Arya heard hooves stomping by outside the door just as she reached for the handle. She threw open the door and leaped out to intercept the horsemen.

There were perhaps a dozen, dressed in the green and black of the Quaervarr guard, about twenty paces up the cobblestone street. Riding on unarmored horses, they carried spears, shields, and long swords. The horses were moving at a brisk pace, so Arya was certain something was afoot.

Arya dashed in front of the approaching horsemen, causing them to rein in. "Hold, in the name of Lady Alustriel and the Silver Marches!" she shouted, brandishing her sword high.

"Out of the way, wench!" one of the guardsmen, a young, handsome man with a scar running down his face, shouted at her. "We almost rode you down!" He drew his sword and pointed it at her. "Don't interfere—"

"Stand down, Narb," a deep, growling voice came. "Can't you recognize a Knight in Silver?" The boy seemed to shrink in his saddle, and the sword went back in its scabbard.

Arya turned. The lead watchman, a huge man on an even more tremendous stallion, addressed her. A hammer sprouted from his fist. Powerfully muscled, he might have been wider than the length of the warhammer he carried, his shoulders broader than Arya's sword was long.

"Hail," he rumbled. "Who are you who wears the colors of

Silverymoon?" He indicated her blue cloak and distinctive brooch of office.

"I am Arya Venkyr, knight-errant of Silverymoon," she said, resolute.

"Well met, Sir Venkyr, Nightingale of Everlund," the commander said, with a slight nod, sparking murmurs from the other watchmen. Arya winced to see her name recognized, but the murmurs were only about a Knight in Silver, not about Arya Venkyr.

The captain pulled his hood back. Underneath, he had a blocky face with stone-colored skin, and the gemlike eyes and distinctly chiseled features of an earth genasi. "I am Unddreth, Captain of the Watch."

"Sir Unddreth," Arya greeted him. "What business takes you at such a dark time of night?"

"Narb reports that Sir Torlic—of the watch—has been attacked by some darkly clad intruder who appeared out of the shadows," he said. "We go to his aid."

"I'm coming with you," Arya said.

"I'm sorry, my lady, but you are not mounted," Unddreth observed.

"Horses are hardly necessary, if it's in town," Arya said, fingering her sword.

"There may be a chase," Unddreth rumbled. He flicked the reins of his huge war-horse. "We need the speed."

The rest of the guardsmen kicked their steeds and trotted down the cobbled streets. "I appreciate the offer of aid, but we cannot delay longer."

"My horse!" Arya shouted to the stable boy, who was peeking out the stable door at the commotion. Unddreth bowed his head slightly, turned his steed, and made to trot away.

"Don't bother," a voice came from the side. Arya whirled, and Meris was there astride his stallion, dressed in his distinctive white leathers. "I'll take you."

When Meris appeared, Unddreth stopped and looked at him warily. "We don't need your help, Wayfarer." The surname was a condemnation, akin to calling Meris a bastard directly.

Though the edge of his mouth twitched slightly, Meris ignored the genasi as though Unddreth's voice, the crashing of boulders, were but the breeze. He extended his hand. "Come."

Arya took a step back. "My thanks, but I'd rather ride with Unddreth," she said, narrowing her eyes.

"That brute's horse can barely carry him," Meris said. He smiled, an expression that might have been pleasant had Arya not known him better. "Let me make amends for my rude behavior earlier."

Arya hesitated, looking at his outstretched hand. She didn't want to take it, but it was a seemingly good-hearted offer. The code of knighthood, to which she had sworn, would not permit a personal bad sentiment to interfere with duty. Unddreth was watching and weighing her; Arya knew the significance of her decision.

The stable boy appeared then, leading Arya's horse, Swiftfall, fully saddled. The crimson mare neighed in friendly recognition, but quieted when it saw Meris's black stallion.

"Oh look," Arya said pointedly. "My horse."

Meris sneered. "Suit yourself," he spat. He turned abruptly, dug his heels into his stallion's flanks, and burst away.

Unddreth nodded to her, a slight smile on his blocky features, and rode off.

Arya, not weighed down by armor, easily vaulted into her saddle and followed them. The stable boy ducked out of the way just in time, and the knight-errant was away, racing down the street to the house of Torlic.

❖ ❖ ❖ ❖ ❖

The long sword came down over his head, and Torlic barely deflected it with both weapons. The black-clad warrior was deceptively slender—his frail build belied strength equal to even Unddreth's might! Torlic was on the defensive, constantly retreating, keeping his weaving blades moving to ward off Walker's blade.

"Is this it?" Torlic sneered. "You call this skill?"

Walker slashed diagonally, and Torlic parried, but the warrior in black slid the sword down the rapier and main gauche, locking the hilts on his own. He gazed into Torlic's eyes with something akin to fury. Torlic took that as a good sign.

"Having some trouble?"

No reply.

"What are you, mute?"

"Silent as the grave," Walker said calmly.

"That's not polite, my lovely boy," Torlic mocked.

Walker did not reply but gritted his teeth.

Torlic peered harder at his opponent. Walker was younger than he had seemed at first. "Impressive entrance, frightening dress, but no skill," Torlic said. "You have no business fighting a real man."

Walker smiled. Then he threw Torlic tumbling back with a heave of his shoulders. The half-elf rolled, blades held wide, and went into a crouch. He came up slashing, but Walker had not followed.

Rather, the dark warrior stood, eyes burning, in the center of the room once more. The only difference between now and when he had first appeared was that he held his mithral sword outside of his cloak, pointed down at the floor. The blade was touched with translucence, making it appear almost ghostly. Torlic felt the weight of Walker's presence once more, only now it seemed sharper, more focused.

"That's a shatterspike blade, is it not?" the half-elf asked. He looked at the nicks it had left on his rapier. "Interesting," he continued when no reply was forthcoming. "Come dance with me, boy, whoever you are," Torlic said, weaving his blade before him. "I wasn't careful before, and you caught me. It won't happen again. I'm through toying with you." He pointed his blade at Walker's eyes. "Dance with me, boy: I'll be the last thing you ever see."

Even as Torlic spoke the words, he could feel the heat bleed out of the room and Walker's stance become even firmer. It was almost as though the half-elf had just thrown down his blade and admitted defeat. Above it all, though, Walker seemed to pulse with an icy resolution that set the ever-confident Torlic back on his heels.

"I'm sorry, have we met?" Torlic asked, noticeably flustered. "Some fool I chased out of town? Some angry merchant I swindled? Some jealous, cuckolded husband? Lover? Some pretty thing I scarred?"

Walker was silent.

"You know, it doesn't matter." Torlic shifted his grip, turning his knuckles skyward. His blade flashed in the dim light. "Or, at least, it won't matter in a moment."

Torlic thrust forward, rapier flashing out like lightning and dagger whipping, ready to block a counter attack. Walker leaped at the last moment, seeming to fly back and under the blade. His trailing foot caught Torlic's wrist and knocked the blade harmlessly high, and his other foot struck the half-elf in the chest, knocking him back. As though not exerting himself in the least, Walker rolled backward in the air and fell to his feet. His cloak flowed behind him.

Torlic staggered back, righting himself with effort, only to find Walker standing before him, that same stoic expression on his face.

Impressed, Torlic slashed right, and left, then right again, but Walker dodged each blow. Whirling, Walker knocked the rapier away, but Torlic allowed the parry to spin him the same way, and his dagger shot out. The half-elf sneered, thinking this to be a deadly strike.

Walker continued spinning as well, and, to Torlic's astonishment, he floated into the air. With matchless grace, Walker leaped over the chest-level thrust. The shatterspike slammed down, and Torlic barely managed to block it. The blades sparked and the half-elf staggered back.

When he looked up, blades held low, Walker landed and faced him, nonchalant, his sword held down.

Torlic was shaking with anger. "Enough," he snapped.

With a furious snarl on his lips, the half-elf came forward in a rush, low to the ground, balancing on the balls of his feet. As he ran, Torlic waved his weapons around him in a whirlwind flurry, faster than any but the greatest duelist could follow. As he came on, he jumped, rolled, cartwheeled, and twirled through the air, in a confusing and dizzying charge.

This devastating acrobatic rush, seemingly reckless but actually tight and controlled, was an elf technique Torlic had used to slay his greatest enemies in his adventuring days. No orc chieftain, no fencer, no knight, no swordsmaster had ever been able to stand against it.

Leaping headfirst, Torlic lunged at Walker, both weapons before him. The ghostly man took a single step back and swept his sword as though to parry. As he flew through the air, Torlic snapped back then forward with his right arm, bringing his rapier just out of line with Walker's parry and punching it forward again. Walker's sword swept through the seemingly vanishing rapier, making no contact, and Torlic threw the main-gauche wide, as though deflected, to disguise his feint.

The rapier, pulled and thrust just in time to avoid the parry, darted for Walker's chest.

Torlic gave a triumphant cry as the blade drove through Walker, lancing his heart and punching out his back.

❧   ❧   ❧   ❧   ❧

Arya spurred her horse ahead, but the guard's horses crowded the road and so she arrived at Torlic's townhouse with the last of the guards. When she arrived, several of the soldiers were already milling around the door and two were slamming their shoulders against it. Meris had dismounted and was standing among them, snapping at the watchmen pounding on the locked door.

"Swords inside," a watchman shouted as Arya pulled up next to them. "I hear steel!"

"Mielikki's scowl. We need a battering ram!" another cursed.

"Stand aside!" Arya shouted.

Protests on their lips, the watchmen turned toward her, but then their eyes went wide in shock and they leaped aside. With a pump of her legs, Arya's reddish mare slammed both hooves into the shut portal. The door caved in with a crash and its hinges snapped.

"Battering horse," Arya explained to the staring watchmen. "Just as good."

"Inside!" Unddreth ordered, leaping out of his saddle.

With a short cheer to the Nightingale of Everlund, the watchmen rushed inside. Arya slid off her steed, right in front of a startled Meris. She flashed him a quick, wry smile, drew her sword, and ran after them.

Meris's eyes smoldered.

❂   ❂   ❂   ❂   ❂

They stood, Walker transfixed on the half-elf's sword, for a long moment, Torlic smiling with his offhand held artfully back and Walker with his eyes shut. The ghostwalker seemed almost translucent, as though the blade had stolen his very essence.

Then Walker's eyes opened. Torlic looked at him, confused.

The ghostwalker stepped to the right and became clearer, as though he had been but an illusion and was only now taking on solid matter.

The mithral long sword swept between them, cutting Torlic's sword neatly in two. Walker continued the spin, his left hand going out.

Too late, Torlic saw steel glinting in the ghostly man's hand. The dagger jabbed into his ribs. All the strength went from Torlic's legs and he collapsed.

The broken sword hilt tumbling from his shaking fingers, Torlic looked up at his opponent in astonishment. Walker shook his cloak, and the rapier blade swayed with it. The blade had gone right through his ghostly body and done no damage. Walker's body had only become material once the blade was outside his flesh. Now, it was stuck through fabric. Walker pulled it free and the blade came out sparkling clean.

Torlic saw, even as his vision swam in a sea of red, half a dozen guards rush into the room behind his attacker. He also could have sworn he saw a sad face flickering at the edge of his vision—the face of an old man mourning a loss.

Torlic had nothing at all to say as Walker slashed down with the shimmering mithral sword, angling for his head.

❧ ❧ ❧ ❧ ❧

"You! Halt in the name of the Silver Marches!" Arya heard Unddreth shout from within as she ran into the house. The clashing of swords and more panicked cries followed the shout.

She rushed through the open door into the training room but pulled up short, along with three other guards in Quaervarr watch uniforms. They watched the spectacle before them, stupefied expressions on their faces.

Walker whirled among the guards as a dervish, his sword darting right and left to parry blows, whipping back and forth like a leaf in a hurricane. Three watchmen, including Narb and the hammer-wielding Unddreth, were hacking at the black-clad warrior, who stood over a corpse Arya could only assume had once been Torlic.

Rapier in hand, Narb lunged from the right. Walker leaped to the side, his cloak trailing in a circle as he spun away. Narb's rapier sparked off Unddreth's shield, causing the genasi to shout and falter in his low attack. Leaping over the swinging hammer, Walker whirled in the air, batting the third guard's sword out of the way and snapping up an elbow to strike the back of Unddreth's blocky head. With a confused grunt, the genasi staggered forward and fell bodily against Narb. They went down together in a heap.

Without hesitation—without even losing a beat—Walker

stepped forward to engage the third guard, a ruddy-cheeked man whose movements had suddenly become much more frantic.

"What are you waiting for?" the cruel voice of Meris shouted almost in her ear. Turning, Arya saw the wild scout with a sword in one hand and a hand axe in the other. "After him!"

"Begging your pardon, Sir," one of the guards said. They had entered the room but hung back warily. "What good can we do against—"

Meris swung his axe around and lodged it in the door-frame with a thunk. He reached over and ripped the light crossbow from the watchman's belt. "Must I do everything?" he asked as he took aim.

"But ye'll hit Delem!" the soldier protested. He reached out to knock the weapon away, but not before Meris fired.

As though he sensed the projectile coming, Walker spun, but not out of its path. Rather, as it streaked for the hapless Delem's head, Walker shot out his arm to intercept the bolt. The ghostwalker scowled as it clanged off his left bracer, and the impact sent him stumbling away from Delem, shattering his momentum. The young guard, oblivious to the attack, seized the advantage and pressed after Walker.

"You see?" Meris said. He reclaimed his axe—and a chunk of the wall in the process. "Break his focus, and you win the battle. He's ours now." Then he charged into the fray, leaving the hesitating guards scrambling to catch up.

Arya took a step forward, but no more than a step, for she was immediately on her guard.

Walker, who had been retreating before Delem's press all the way to the rear wall, suddenly leaped over Delem's low slash, kicked off the wall, and flew over his head. Delem's sword slashed in, but instead of finding Walker's flesh, it cut into a thick oak beam supporting the wall and ceiling. Ignoring the stuck watchman behind him, Walker rolled and came up in a rush toward the exit—right into the thick of the oncoming guards.

Meris, charging at their head, hurled his axe with a flick of his wrist and pulled his sword back to slash. Walker's mithral blade snapped around, as though of its own accord, and batted the axe aside. It sailed, end over end, to lodge itself in the wall near Delem. Meris slashed, but Walker dived over the sword, rolled, and came up running, leaving a startled wild scout behind.

The other guards came against Walker, but hesitated under the intensity of his gaze. He knocked aside one half-hearted attack, spinning to his right, and knocked the second guard's blade away with the same swing. This guard staggered back, stunned at the speed of the parry, and Walker kept spinning. As he came up again, he punched the third guard in the face, knocking him down, and continued his spin, his shatterspike coming around ...

To spark and lock against Arya's drawn blade, low to the ground.

His momentum spent, Walker settled to his feet and stood against her. He had expected she would give way as easily as the guards, but she did not. Instead, she remained in place, determined, the last obstacle standing between Walker and freedom.

Their eyes met, her steely orbs standing firm against his fierce, dark gaze. There was danger, there was threat, there was resolution, but Arya did not flinch. Exerting her full strength, she held his blade in place, a hand's breadth from her face. They battled, a contest of wills that both knew was of deathly importance.

Of a sudden, Arya realized Walker's eyes were blue. The blue was obscured, hidden beneath the darkness, but definitely there. Her heart leaped and her breath caught.

Then, just like that, Walker pulled away, whirling back in exactly the opposite direction. Meris had reversed his charge and was coming back, but Walker made no move to meet him. Instead, he bounded toward a dark corner and melted away, as though into the very shadows.

No sooner had Walker vanished than Meris's throwing dagger imbedded itself into the wall where he had gone. The wild scout, deprived of his opponent, whirled and searched, but there was no one to be found, except for groaning and disoriented guardsmen.

"Beastlord's bloody—" cursed Meris. Then he stopped, seeing Arya looking at him in shock.

Meris sheathed his sword slowly and deliberately, and retrieved his thrown axe and knife. Without a word to Arya, he shot her a vicious glare and stamped out into the night.

Finally, the knight remembered to exhale.

CHAPTER 7

27 Tarsakh

Parry, parry, thrust, parry, thrust," Greyt intoned silently as he worked through the familiar movements. His opponent fell back with each of his attacks, but pressed when Greyt took the defensive. The Lord Singer's hand lacked the speed and strength of youth, but it was all the more deadly for experience.

His opponent thrust high suddenly, his sword a silver blur.

Greyt ducked, his knees bending apart. The weapon passed harmlessly over his head. Even as the younger fencer tried to reverse his blow, Greyt's rapier slashed open the dark leather covering the man's side. A line of bright red appeared on his pale flesh.

As his opponent staggered back, Greyt took the opportunity to cuff him on the side of the head. "Keep your guard up, fool!" he shouted. "I should run you through for your stupidity!"

"I'm sorry, Lord Singer—" Tamnus said, dropping immediately to one knee.

Greyt promptly kicked him in the face, launching him backward. Blood streamed from his nose. When Tamnus looked at him in shock, the Lord Singer's mouth was hard.

"Did I say the duel was over?" he snapped. The aide shook his head. Then he cringed when Greyt raised his rapier once more, as though to thrust it through Tamnus's head.

A banging at the door startled Greyt, and he almost thrust. A tingle ran down his spine, and he whirled on the portal.

"Who is it?" he shouted.

"Captain Unddreth, Lord Singer," a rumble came. "I wish an audience with you."

The bard ran a hand through his graying hair. Then he turned on his training aide with a vicious glare. "Out of my sight," he ordered with a hiss. Tamnus wasted no breath in hesitation. He ran away, clutching at his side in obvious pain.

Greyt cared not. When Tamnus was gone, Greyt flicked the blood off his rapier and sheathed it. As he wiped the sweat from his brow, he assumed a more comfortable stance.

"Come," he called.

The doors swung open and the massive Unddreth entered Greyt's ballroom. The floorboards, hard, good wood, did not creak, even under his heavy boots. Situated in the center of the mansion, the ballroom was the largest—if not the finest—room in Quaervarr. Tapestries of scarlet, bold white, and vibrant purples adorned the walls, laced with ivory and gold thread. In the center of the ballroom, marble statues of dancing nymphs poured water from basins down into a great copper fountain. If it had not been so dismal outside, sunlight would have cascaded through high, stained glass windows depicting dancing fey, dueling heroes, and wheeling dragons.

If Unddreth was impressed as he entered the grand ballroom—useless in such a small town—he showed no sign of it. His blocky face was stoic, as always.

"What is it, Captain?" Greyt asked.

"I bear grave news," the earth genasi growled.

"Of course you do," the Lord Singer said. He started away, toward a tapestry depicting a dragon in flight. Unddreth did not follow. Greyt thanked the gods for that.

"I have come to inform you of a murder that transpired last night," Unddreth said. "Sir Torlic, a lieutenant in the Quaervarr guard, was killed in his house last night."

"What do I—" Greyt started angrily, but stopped himself. "Why bring this to me?"

The genasi's lip twitched. "He was once of the Raven Claws," Unddreth said. "I thought perhaps you might help me find the one who killed him."

"Ah." Greyt wanted to claim that he knew nothing, but that would make Unddreth suspicious. "I well remember our days on the road, but I know of no enemy who would kill him, nor even seek to attack him in his humble abode."

He had thrown out his hand in imitation of a performance and now became aware of a small spot of Tamnus's blood on his palm. He clenched his fist and looked back at Unddreth.

"Perhaps Jarthon and his People of the Black Blood. They have been quiet for long enough. Could your soldiers have relaxed their guard, I wonder, Captain?"

Unddreth's already dark complexion became black. "I personally fought the man responsible," he said. "And he was no werebeast. We are dealing with another attacker, one very skilled with a blade, and possessing powers I have never seen before."

"Powers?" Greyt asked idly. He peered intently at a tapestry of a military victory, with a knight of Cormyr leading a host of soldiers. One of the Azouns, perhaps? He could not recall.

"The villagers are whispering about a shadowy man named Walker," Unddreth said. "That may have been him."

That produced a stir in Greyt. The name sounded like a discordant note on his yarting. He rubbed his gold ring, as was his habit.

"And what do you want me to do, kill this shadow for you?" Greyt said, suppressing his reaction. "You and your soldiers find this attacker and deal with him as is proper.

Or . . ." He drew his rapier with a flourish. "Could it be you have come to ask for the aid I can offer?"

"We need none of your thug rangers, Greyt," Unddreth spat. His animosity toward the Lord Singer was matched only by his contempt for Greyt's servants—as Greyt well knew. "Undisciplined scum, all of them. Especially Meris the bastard."

"I can't argue," the Lord Singer laughed, unsurprised. "It's very true."

Nor was he surprised that Unddreth had spoken so crassly. Unddreth had always been free with his tongue—it came from being raised a commoner. Greyt waved the captain away and sheathed his sword.

Blaming the Black Blood was a ruse—for all Greyt knew, the bastard werebadger and his kin were all prowling Malar's infernal forests in the Abyss, or wherever Malar's forests were. He cared little for theology.

After a moment, Greyt looked back and saw that Unddreth had not moved.

"You're still here," he said.

"I am." Unddreth, not prone to fidgeting, gazed at him stonily.

"There is more?" Greyt asked.

"Speaker Stonar left the city in your hands," Unddreth said. "Thus, when an event transpires that threatens the welfare of the city, it is your responsibility to deal with it, is it not?"

"And I have," Greyt said, a hint of anger creeping into his voice. "I want you and your soldiers to find this attacker and kill him. Or her. Or it. Just do what you are paid to do."

Dim-witted Unddreth. Greyt scowled. *Are you as stupid as you look?*

"We must inform Speaker Stonar of the event," Unddreth said.

Not stupid then, Greyt decided. He should have foreseen the suggestion.

He didn't miss a beat, though. "So send to the druids to communicate with their magic," he said dismissively. "They may not be under our control, but they will aid us."

"I already have," Unddreth said. "Something blocks their magic, some barrier they cannot pierce."

"Probably another of their foolish excuses—a damned equinox or something," Greyt said quickly. It was plausible, after all. Quaervarr was a frontier town in every sense: unless matters were really out of hand, the people preferred to settle their own problems, without help from the High Lady or her armies of mages. The druids would expect no less from the Watch. "Or it's a sacred time for their gods, or perhaps the guild of Silverymoon has better things to do than listen to our minor complaints—"

"So we must send a courier," Unddreth said.

"I'm sure that's not necessary," Greyt said with a shrug as if he meant to forget the whole thing. "As you said, it is only one man. Some independent town we would be if we ran to Silverymoon with our troubles every time a lunatic crops up. How much trouble can one man be? Take a few of your best soldiers and scour the Moonwood for him."

Unddreth hesitated, but finally nodded. "As you command, Lord Singer," he said curtly. Turning on his heel, the genasi strode out of the ballroom.

Greyt watched his retreating form for a long moment, tracing with his eyes the image of the white stag emblazoned upon the huge shield Unddreth wore on his back.

"As I command," he repeated to himself with a grin. He liked the sound of that.

❧ ❧ ❧ ❧ ❧

Wrapped in steel, Arya was approaching the front doors of her uncle's manor when they flew open and the hulking Unddreth stamped out. His face was even harder than usual. She dropped into a light bow.

"Well met, Captain Unddreth," she said.

The genasi's frown turned to a soft smile when he saw her, and Arya was acutely aware of her appearance. Her silver armor gleamed and her auburn hair burned in the soft light. Shining on her breast, the badge of the Knights in Silver—a clasp with the sigil of Silverymoon—secured a deep blue cloak around her shoulders. Arya knew Unddreth admired her simple elegance, and embarrassed warmth blossomed in her cheeks.

"Good morning to you, Lady Venkyr," Unddreth said. He gestured to the sword belted at her hip. "Going about armed, are you?"

She smiled shakily. "One can never be too careful," she said in reply.

"True." He patted the warhammer at his own belt. "Very true."

His face was still stony. Something about his voice, though, told Arya that he was thinking about the audience with Greyt he had just left. He perked up, though, when he caught her staring.

"Thank you for your assistance last night," he said. "I hope it is clear that any momentary hesitation or doubts about your abilities—or loyalties—have been put to rest."

"It is, Captain," Arya said. "I serve the Silver Marches, so I serve Quaervarr as well."

Unddreth bowed his head then plodded on his way.

Arya nodded, smiling as he went. She had read the characters of many people in her time with the Knights in Silver, and she knew that there went a just and noble soldier.

As Unddreth walked farther away, though, Arya looked back to Greyt's doors and her smile vanished. She turned smartly on her heel and headed to the portal, where she rapped the gold wolf knocker. She pulled the cloak tighter around her armored body, trying vainly to warm the cold steel strapped around her limbs. Armor was impractical in this cold, but she wanted to be in full uniform when she confronted her uncle once more.

Claudir arrived in a moment to take her inside. The steward looked at her with the same uninterested, detached look he always had. He led her through Greyt's spacious manor without paying attention to her. Once Claudir had ushered Arya into Greyt's study, he sniffed, as though to assure her that Greyt would arrive shortly, and left without a word.

"Took you long enough," came an angry, nigh-angelic voice, startling her.

In the center of the room, a beautiful woman in a dark gown was standing, facing away from her. When she turned and saw Arya, she started and assumed a confused expression.

"I . . . I'm sorry, I thought you were someone else," the lady said. Golden curls fell around a beautiful, oval face. Her ears were slightly pointed. "I am tired." She moved to leave.

"Lady Lyetha," Arya said finally. She dropped into a bow. "I'm sorry; I did not recognize you for a moment. I am Arya Venkyr, stepdaughter of your Lord Husband's sister."

Lyetha paused, looking at Arya again with fresh eyes. Her orbs were sparkling sapphires, and something about their intensity made Arya's breath catch. Her serenity brooked absolutely no display of emotion. This was a noblewoman if Arya had ever seen one, and the knight was a personal friend of Alustriel herself.

"No need for me to worry, then," she said dismissively. Lyetha swept out of the room, leaving a confused Arya in her wake, and that was that. Lyetha was gone.

Arya would never speak with her again.

❂ ❂ ❂ ❂ ❂

Time passed.

Eventually, the lady knight, bored, looked around for something to distract herself. While she waited, Arya scanned the titles of different tomes with disinterest. Lord Greyt kept epics, poems, treatises, and battle records. Arya recognized names, but that's where the interest ended. Though she could read and write Chondathan, Iluskan, and even some Damaran, thanks to schooling at her father's house, Arya had never fancied herself a scholar. Books were for sages, the nobility, and wizards, not knights. Still, there was nothing else to do in the small study, so she browsed the shelves and desk.

After some time, Arya noticed a small amulet on the desk. It was gold, in the shape of a five-pointed leaf cunningly cut and delicately formed. Tiny Elvish runes were etched on the back.

Arya wished she had paid more attention during Elvish lessons, but she could make it out. "It is easier to destroy than to create," she read out loud. She pursed her lips in thought.

The door clicked and she looked up with a start, hoping it was Lyetha returned to collect the pendant so she could ask her about it, but her hopes were in vain. Instead, Greyt came in, dressed in soft leathers embroidered with gold thread that set off his similarly colored hair. Without thinking, Arya slipped the pendant into her pocket.

By his mussed mane and smoldering eyes, Arya could tell Greyt was not pleased. Whether this was because of her interruption or not, Arya did not know, but she found she did not truly care. Somehow, she felt less uneasy when he was less than comfortable. His arrogance and supercilious manners were gone.

"Ah, Niece," Greyt greeted her. "To what do I owe this dubious honor?"

Arya winced. She retracted her earlier observation about his manners.

"Not the best of mornings, eh, Uncle?" asked Arya. At least he was overt. She preferred when people did not hide how they really felt. Arya, honest herself, valued honesty in others. It was part of why she found court life stifling.

A wry smile creased his face. "Mayhap," he said. "I am quite busy this morn with affairs of state—er, Quaervarr, that is. I am in charge in Speaker Stonar's absence."

"Precisely the reason I desire an audience," replied Arya. "I have come to tell you something, something you should know."

"And that is?" asked Greyt without any real interest. He crossed to the sideboard and poured himself a glass of Cormyrean red. With a halfhearted lift of the bottle, he extended an offer to Arya, but she declined with a wave. He flopped into his chair.

Arya took a deep breath before she next spoke, for against her better judgment, she was about to reveal an important secret.

"Lady Alustriel is concerned about the disappearance of several of her couriers, who have set out for Quaervarr but never returned," said Arya.

Greyt looked at her blankly. "And what does that have to do with either of us?"

"My mission to Quaervarr," explained Arya, "is to investigate those disappearances."

He did not seem surprised in the least, a fact that made her wince.

"The North is a dangerous place," Greyt replied with a shrug. "The People of the Black Blood were a danger in the Moonwood, and who knows what might have replaced them in the last months? I can't guarantee safety, and neither can you."

"It's not that simple," Arya said.

"No?" Greyt asked as he sipped his wine.

"No," asserted Arya. "All the messengers had two things in common—all were young women, and all were alone."

There was a moment of silence in the study.

Then Greyt laughed, long and loud. When his mirth finally subsided, he managed to speak between deep chuckles.

"I'm sorry, Niece, but I can't say I'm surprised," he said. "I've said it before, and it holds true now. 'The road for a man, home for a woman.' I believe a bard from Westgate said that . . . Now, what was his name? Mayhap not."

Shocked, Arya felt irritation rise in her throat and had to clench her fist to avoid striking him. Her reputation for stubbornness and temper was not undeserved. She had cast off her responsibilities in Everlund, despite her father's wishes, because of just such a discussion. But losing her composure as a Knight in Silver simply would not do.

In the meantime, Greyt continued his mocking laughter. She could not help but feel it was partly at her expense. Soon enough, she could take it no longer. She wanted to say something to stop that laughter, and she spoke before her mind worked.

"Are the streets of Quaervarr even safe? Can you not protect your own people?"

"Niece, know that your safety is of top concern," Greyt added, seemingly at ease. "The attack upon your person last night will be investigated. To tell you the truth, I wouldn't put it past this—what did you say people called him? Walker?"

Arya suddenly felt cold. "The attack upon my person?" she said softly. "I never said I was attacked last night."

Greyt's eyebrow twitched but his smile was firm. "Unddreth must have reported it," he said dismissively. "I say, a Knight in Silver attacked in my own streets—"

"I haven't told anyone about last night," said Arya. "And I never mentioned Walker."

Greyt's smile slipped. The two were silent for a moment, Greyt staring at her with something that was not quite confusion. Then he stood, walked up, and loomed over her. Her anger gone, Arya trembled for a different reason entirely. Through discipline, she held her body firm, but she could do nothing about the emotion written in her eyes: fear.

She looked at Greyt for a long moment, and she saw nothing but cold, calculating anger in his face.

Then he moved, and Arya almost drew her sword. As though he did not see, Greyt continued his step to the sideboard and poured himself more wine.

"Are you sure I can't tempt you?" he asked, raising the glass. " 'Tis quite good."

"No," Arya said firmly.

"Pity." Greyt smiled a half grin but his eyes were smoldering. Then he shrugged. "Well, suit yourself." He went back to the chair and collapsed into the cushions. "I'm very tired, Niece, and feeling my age. You'll excuse me if I don't walk you out."

It was not a question.

Arya nodded, turned on her heel, and left the room as quickly as walking allowed. She could feel Greyt's eyes boring into her back the entire time.

As she left Greyt's study, Arya was not surprised to see Greyt's cruel-faced son leaning against the wall, bedecked in his white leather armor. She was not surprised that he had been listening.

Arya nodded to him, not about to say anything, but he held up a hand to stop her.

"You know him, this murderer," Meris said. "This . . . Walker."

"We have met," replied Arya. "Briefly. He saved me from a masked attacker."

"A great Knight in Silver needed saving?" asked Meris incredulously, snidely. "This attacker must have been quite skilled to defeat you."

He sounded just a bit too proud, and Arya couldn't resist the bait. "A coward," she corrected him. "A knave who attacked from the shadows, like a filthy rat."

The corner of Meris's mouth twitched but the wild scout said nothing.

Arya felt that twitch stoke her anger, which had already been smoldering, into a hot blaze. She stepped toward Meris, hand on her sword hilt. " 'Twas fortunate Walker appeared in time," she pressed. "He saved the coward from me."

Meris eyes narrowed, and he stared at her coldly. "I doubt it," he said, his tone betraying a seething outrage.

"Meris, come!" Greyt shouted from inside the study.

"Better not disobey," Arya said to him, refusing to blink.

"I'm not the one who should be obeying, lass," Meris almost spat.

Arya did not back down. "I do not fear you, cousin," she said. Then, leaving him with the implicit challenge, she turned and walked away.

Meris allowed the tiniest of smiles to creep onto his face. "I doubt that also," Arya heard him whisper. "I doubt that very much."

"Now!" came Greyt's shout.

Meris turned and entered the study, allowing the door to swing closed behind him.

❖ ❖ ❖ ❖ ❖

Greyt was standing in front of the desk, awaiting him. Books on high shelves surrounded the Lord Singer, and he was holding one in his hand, idly scanning through the lines of text.

"Father," greeted Meris as he walked up to the Lord Singer.

Greyt greeted the dusky-skinned youth with a vicious slap to the cheek. Meris reeled, stunned, and looked back up at his father in shock.

"You lazy, incompetent fool!" Greyt shouted. "Your lax patrolling of the Moonwood has jeopardized our plans!" He slapped the book against the wall, and the pages fluttered all around.

"Really, Father . . ." Meris started.

"And now, right when opportunity knocks, when Stonar—" The words dissolved into a snarl, and he glared at Meris. "How can you be such an idiot, to attack her in the very street? Have I not done enough for you? I've turned a blind eye to your indiscretions for years, even ignored the untimely deaths of your siblings. Of all my blood, you were the only one worthy of my legacy, and this is how you repay me? With betrayal?"

"Father!" Meris growled.

Greyt slapped him again. "How like an ignorant child you are! Incapable of controlling your own base desires. You sicken me."

Meris stared at his father in shock, then anger, and assumed a sullen expression. Though he was outwardly chastened, his rage burned. Meris's fingers itched to clasp his sword. He admired his father, true, but Greyt could not escape a measure of his contempt—probably as much contempt as Greyt felt for Meris in return.

Still, the wild scout stayed his hand, once again aware of that same nervous suspicion that had protected Greyt from his rage thus far. Meris never ignored this feeling, a sense that he was walking into a trap. There was something Greyt was hiding, some protection the Lord Singer kept hidden, and that dissuaded Meris from attacking him.

"Whatever I can do to make amends, Father," Meris said.

"Merely speak the word, and it shall be done."

"Watch over the house of Bilgren tonight," Greyt said. "I fear he will be next to suffer Walker's ire. He is the last of the Raven Claw band, and that may be—"

"Except yourself," clarified Meris. When Greyt frowned, Meris reiterated it. "The last except yourself."

Greyt looked at him none-too-pleasantly. "Go to Bilgren and make him wary," he said. "I doubt even the barbarian's fanciful weapon—that gyrspike, or whatever it is—will be enough to save him. Protect him the night through, and prove yourself true."

Meris accepted the rhyme with a grimace.

"And continue the search for Stonar's supporters," said Greyt. "The druids are our enemies as is, I fear, that fool captain. As for the owners of local businesses, I want them persuaded to see my side of things or taken care of, understand?"

Meris nodded and frowned.

"What is it?" Greyt demanded. He drew himself up taller. "You have something to say?"

Meris stared at him angrily for a moment then looked away.

"I will not fail, Father." He turned on his heel and stalked out the doors of the study.

"See that you don't," Greyt growled.

❧ ❧ ❧ ❧ ❧

The door slammed shut, and Greyt smiled authentically for the first time that day. It always pleased him when things turned out exactly as he wanted.

Business needed to be tended to, though. He allowed the elation of the last few moments to settle, then he set the glass on the sideboard and poured himself another. He slipped an amulet out of his tunic—a piece of amber in a rough ovoid shape—and rolled it between his fingers. The amulet was warm.

"You heard all that, I suppose?" he asked aloud.

"Of course, Lord Greyt," a disembodied voice said

immediately. A gaunt form clad in a gray robe shimmered into being, shedding invisibility the way one slips out of a blanket. "All three interviews."

"And?" He did not look up but kept his eyes fixed on the amber gemstone.

"You acted more or less correctly," the cloaked man said. His voice was calm and level. Though magical power seemed to surround him like a corona, Greyt was not disturbed. "The Beast must be wary of the Spirit of Vengeance."

Greyt knew the cryptic names were references to Bilgren and Walker respectively. "And Arya?" Greyt asked.

"The Nightingale is suspicious," the wizard said. "She searches for the killer of the couriers, and she suspects that the Spirit of Vengeance might be that killer. She also suspects, however, that you might be that killer."

Greyt dismissed that with a snort. "But who is he?" asked the Lord Singer. "Don't play the mysterious cloaked figure with me—take off that cowl and tell me who he is!"

"Who?" the man asked as he pulled back his cowl. Beneath, the pale skin of a moon elf sparkled in the candlelight, and emerald eyes glittered.

Greyt rounded on the wizard. "You know very well 'who' I mean!" he shouted. "Who is Walker?"

The wizard spread his slim hands. "You have made many enemies in your travels, my lord," he said. "I know not who he is. Only that his vengeance is old."

Greyt was about to shout again, but he bit his tongue. "Talthaliel," he asked sweetly, running his finger along the amulet. "Why do I keep you around?"

"Because I am useful," the wizard replied matter-of-factly.

"You are," Greyt said. "And why are you useful?"

"I see many things," Talthaliel said.

"And how do I have power over you?"

"You have that," the diviner replied, nodding at the amber crystal on his necklace.

"Exactly," Greyt said. He clenched his fist around the gemstone.

"You may stop," Talthaliel said. "I shall do as you ask."

"That's better," Greyt said. "Now tell me who Walker is."

"I cannot," replied the diviner. "Powerful magic shields him, magic I cannot pierce. Not his own magic, but that of a protector. I can feel the other shielding him—a powerful, ghostly presence, but certainly alive."

"Then he is not a ghost," Greyt said.

Talthaliel shook his head. "A mortal man with magic on his side."

"You can tell me nothing else?" Greyt asked.

"Only that he can be killed, and the Wayfarer is eager to do so," Talthaliel said.

"You are maintaining the communication barrier around Quaervarr?"

"As you command," Talthaliel said, nodding. "Several attempts have been made to pierce my magic, but the druids do not approach my skill. Nor do they come to town often—there is little suspicion. None will hear of your activities to undermine the Lord Speaker."

"Still," Greyt said. "With some murderer killing people, questions will be asked. Someone could go to that trollop Clearwater and ask for a sending to Silverymoon or even Everlund—Unddreth already has, and I could only deflect him this once. If they realize that someone is keeping a barrier up, our plan would be ruined. You and I cannot battle the Argent Legions or a handful of the Spellguard from Silverymoon. The last thing we need right now, while Stonar is gone, is someone running for help."

Talthaliel said nothing.

"And my son," Greyt mused. "What of him? Will he fulfill the vision any time soon?"

"There is malice in his heart, but not in his mind . . . yet, at least," replied the seer. Greyt's expression became dubious. "My two-fold vision will hold true: Your son will come to kill you, and your son will not defeat me."

Greyt smiled. He so enjoyed knowing the future before his opponents did.

CHAPTER 8

28 Tarsakh

Spirits of the dead ebbed and flowed around him, whispering of hunts long past and unfulfilled dreams, but Walker, as always, hardly listened. He sat legs crossed, staring into the blurry, bleak world of the spirits, and thought.

Two of his foes lay dead and two were alive. Indeed, the spirits of Drex and Torlic hovered around him, silently awaiting the completion of some unfinished business.

Walker's death had come at the ends of four weapons, and four hands had held those weapons.

At least, he thought so.

Dying had shattered his memories; he could remember hazy fragments about the murder and only flashes from before that. As far as Walker was concerned, his life began that night fifteen years ago. He fully remembered his attackers only when they spoke the words he could not forget, the words they had spoken that night long ago. . . .

Instead of focusing fruitlessly on the past or on the future that inspired no interest, Walker thought about the present. Two men were dead and two were going to die. He knew Greyt was one of them, and he would soon know the other for certain. Drex had said Torlic's name, but the half-elf had not pointed him toward a third. Walker had to know, and he simply could not remember.

As though drawn to Walker's violent thoughts, Tarm appeared. His father had vanished before the fight with Torlic and had not reappeared since. Was he reproaching his son for his task of vengeance?

"I avenge us, father," said Walker, though he knew the spirit would not reply. "Why does this displease you? Is this not the justice you worshiped? What regret do you wish to express?"

Tarm was silent, as always. Not once in fifteen years had he answered his son's queries.

"Will you not speak to me?" Walker demanded. "Am I not your son?"

Silence.

A stray thought passed through his mind and became the focus of his attention. It was the face of a woman—the woman with auburn hair. Who was she? Why did she stick in his mind? What did she have to do with his task?

He turned to ask his father—in the hope that he might be able to decide for himself by hearing his own words—but Tarm vanished.

It could mean only one thing.

A sparrow that flickered in and out of the Ethereal world flapped down out of the sky. The blurry remnants of spirits flinched away, terrified. The tiny bird, as it landed on a fallen twig, did not seem to notice.

You did it again. It accused in its ghostly voice, which no mortal would have heard. Or, at least, no purely material listener.

Walker did not dispute the point. He had been waiting

in the grove for Gylther'yel to return, and he had known what she would say.

Indeed, two nights past, he replied in the same ghostly tongue. The pale bird grew larger, its wings became arms, and its beaked face grew into smooth elf features. *The dancer Torlic has joined the woodsman Drex in death. Lord Greyt knows they were not isolated attacks. He will quaver in terror.*

He breathed out and allowed his body to return to the Material world. Vibrancy returned to his surroundings. The grass became green in place of dead gray, and the trees waved soft needles, not skeletal limbs. All around him, he saw soft life where before had lurked only death.

A dubious elf face awaited him. The ghost druid stood, a deep gray cloak wrapped around her bare golden flesh—Gylther'yel disdained excessive clothing when she ran or flew through the woods in wildshape. "Terror?" Gylther'yel said without mirth. "I hardly think two murders in the night will inspire terror."

Walker shrugged, as if to demonstrate that it did not truly matter.

Gylther'yel's face was impassive, but her eyes burned.

"You have not come here to upbraid me," he said. "There is something else."

A hint of a smile played on her golden face.

Walker narrowed his eyes. He knew enough to be wary when Gylther'yel was angered. "Where have you been these last days?" he asked carefully.

"Where you should have been," the druid said. "Watching over my woods."

Walker's brows furrowed. He knew of her spies—almost every bird and forest animal within miles. They watched for her, and she did little. Unless. . . .

"What does that mean?" he asked.

"I have decided my student needs a lesson in inspiring terror," she said coldly. "Three miles east of here, hunters come for you." She held up a ragged piece of leather that bore the Whistling Stag sigil of Quaervarr. "I will teach them the penalty for trespassing into my woods."

"Who are they?" Walker asked, reaching for the cloth.

The sun elf shook her head. She dropped the torn bit to the ground. "I have spent the last fifteen years teaching you to avoid such irrelevant questions," Gylther'yel said.

The sun elf grew and her face extended. She fell to all fours as her limbs shortened and she grew the sleek fur of a ghostly, golden fox. As her body shifted into that of the animal, Gylther'yel faded out of his physical sight and into the Ethereal.

The ghostly fox flashed him a fanged grin and bounded off into the trees, heading east. Walker turned to run after her, but then he remembered the discarded leather scrap.

Tentatively, for he knew the pain that this could bring, he stooped low and picked it up between gloved fingers. It was a ragged piece, torn from the hauberk of a suit of hunting leathers. Slowly, gently, Walker drew his black leather glove off, revealing a pale, long-fingered hand.

Hesitantly, he rested his fingers on the leather in his other hand and closed his eyes. Images flowed into him then, along with an emotional swell that blew the breath from his body. The psychic resonance of the piece carried whisperings of memories and visions, hopes and fears. He hated this power, which would manifest whenever his bare fingers touched something not his own, but it was necessary at times.

A round-faced woman, cheeks rosy from the morning chill ... two little boys, playing at rangers and orcs with wooden swords ...

Sweat dripped down Walker's forehead and his body burned with phantom pain, but he gritted his teeth and held on. The resonance was not strong, but it could overwhelm him if he lost control.

A soldier, not heroic but strong of heart....

The visions faded as Walker dropped the leather to the ground.

He dived into shadows, racing his mistress. Leaping along in the Shadow Fringe, Walker ran faster than any mere mortal could. Ghosts flitted past his peripheral vision and reached out imploring arms to slow him, but Walker was firm in his cause. He gripped the hilt of his shatterspike and prayed he would not need it.

❖ ❖ ❖ ❖ ❖

The distance was not great, covered in almost no time through the shadows, but it was only by luck that he found the hunters. Under a darkening sky, with clouds rolling across the sun, the shadows were dissipating, but he could make it. Walker leaped to a shadow near a giant of a man he had fought before. Then he dispelled his shadowwalk and stepped out within a sword's length of the captain.

"Leave these woods now," Walker warned.

"'Ware!" Unddreth shouted. A mighty warhammer came around at Walker. "He's here!"

The ghostwalker ducked the swing and stepped inside Unddreth's reach. He grasped the hammer arm in both hands and stared into the genasi's eyes with the full weight of his gaze. "Fools," he said. "You must leave now."

Unddreth strained against the grip but could not break it. He puffed himself up as large as he could, refusing to be intimidated. Walker swore inwardly.

"Let the captain go!" came a shout from behind him.

A dozen guards were all around Walker, swords drawn and crossbows trained on his face.

Walker ignored the threat. "Leave now," he reiterated. "You do not understand."

Unddreth grimaced, his arms straining. "You are under arrest, by order of Lord Singer Dharan Greyt, by the power vested in me by the Silver Marches Confederation—" he rumbled.

"You must leave, or you will surely die," Walker replied. Clouds were gathering overhead and thunder rolled. "The Ghostly Lady is coming."

"A legend," Unddreth said. "In the name of High Lady Alustriel and the Silver Marches, I place you under arrest—"

Walker interrupted him again. "I see you are a good and honorable man. If you are concerned for the lives of your men, you will leave." Suddenly, the ground beneath Walker's feet became porous and soft, losing its consistency until it was as thin as quicksand.

"No," he rasped as he sank down. "Gylther'yel! No!"

One of the crossbowmen started and shot a bolt at him, which Walker instinctively batted aside with his steel bracer. "Men of Quaervarr, run—"

Before he could croak out more of the warning, the earth swallowed up his face and he could see and speak no more.

Then the heavens rained fire.

❧ ❧ ❧ ❧ ❧

Trapped in a womb of dirt, Walker could barely move his limbs. He could only imagine what was transpiring above him. More than that, he could feel, rather than see, death. He would have taken on ghostly form and leaped up through the earth, but Gylther'yel had woven an ethereal net over him. She knew his powers only too well.

Thus, his options exhausted, Walker took a gulp of trapped air and began wriggling, then digging upward, hoping against hope he would arrive in time.

Finally, his reaching fingers struck air and he hauled himself out of the hole in the ground.

The scene that greeted him was one of fury and devastation. Mist mingled with smoke in the glade, blurring his vision. The grasses and trees were singed as by an inferno, and the few standing guards were limping and pulling at icy shards embedded in their flesh. Several of the men were struggling against the limbs of trees, which had reached out to ensnare them. Ghosts of the dead and groans of the dying surrounded him.

Walker counted six living guardsmen, and the captain. Unddreth swiped his hammer at a pack of ghostly wolves that had encircled him, their eyes gleaming with malevolence. The rest of the men had been reduced to cinders or frozen into blackened statues. All killed ... destroyed by nature's wrath.

As Walker watched, a bolt of lightning streaked out of the clouds and struck Unddreth directly, throwing him down. The genasi, dazed, struggled to beat off the wolves as they swarmed him. Even as he punched one aside, another wolf leaped atop him and grabbed his arm in its jaws.

Walker leaped to his defense, his sword slashing back and forth, cutting through ghost wolf after ghost wolf. Because of its enchantments, Walker's shatterspike existed in both the Material and Ethereal worlds, so its ghostly touch slew the shadowy creatures as though they were flesh. The wolves fell back, snarling. Shimmering shatterspike in hand, Walker stood over the fallen captain and threatened any wolf that came too close.

Gylther'yel appeared out of the mist, her gray robe making her golden skin appear luminous in the half-light. "This is foolish, Walker," she said with a mirthless smile. "Step aside and let my children do their work."

"Impossible," the ghostwalker said. Just then, the remaining soldiers stopped moaning, as though the pain of their wounds had vanished under the icy press of his will.

"Do not presume to test your powers on me," Gylther'yel warned. Her voice was soft but there was righteous fury in her eyes.

If Walker's resolute aura made him intimidating, Gylther'yel's presence could have slain ordinary men with its terror and majesty. Even Walker felt weak, but relief and encouragement flooded through him, assuring him that his was the right course. Not even pondering the source of such feelings, he stood firm against the ghost druid, his teacher.

"This is what I must do," Walker said. He slid his sword back into its scabbard. "These men have done nothing against you, or against your woods."

"They are humans. That is enough," Gylther'yel said. Her words were calm and her face was composed, but her eyes were seething. "They come into the forest that I love, they murder the animals that are my brothers and they rape the trees that are my sisters. They bring axes. They bring lances. They bring fire." The bright flame burning in her palm diminished, as though she had just realized she'd held it. Gylther'yel turned back to Walker. "They carry death with them, child. Never will I accept them. They are a disease, a blight, a hungry flame."

"Not all—" Walker started.

"All!" Gylther'yel hissed, and her soft voice held the fury of thunder. "I am pleased when you kill them, for you purify them. Death is the only purity they can hope for, the only purity any of them can know—it is far more than they deserve."

Walker was about to protest, but then a soldier rose up behind the druid, sword raised high as he advanced on the petite elf. Walker held up his hands to ward off the man, hoping the gesture came off as peaceful to Gylther'yel.

The sun elf held up a delicate hand of her own, as though in reply, and Walker felt a sinking feeling in the pit of his stomach.

Sure enough, vines snaked out of the ground and wrapped themselves around the soldier's legs and body. The man gawked as the vines completely entangled him and twisted the sword out of his hand. The small sun elf turned toward him with a smile on her face.

"An example," she said. Then, addressing the soldier directly, "Take freedom in death."

"Gylther'yel, no!" Walker rasped. He stepped forward, but the wolves nipped at him.

The druid spoke words of power and pointed one finger at the guardsman. The shadowy radiance surrounding her hand shot toward the man with an unholy scream, one that might have been nature herself. The man's eyes glazed over and he did just as she had commanded. The vines held up the corpse in a mocking parody of an erect stance.

The sun elf turned back toward Walker, but now there was the business end of a long sword in her face. Holding the hilt, a pace distant, was the ghostwalker himself.

"Let them go," he commanded. "Do not argue."

Gylther'yel looked up the blade at Walker's face as though the weapon were not there.

"You care for these defilers?" she asked. "Have I not taught you better than this, these fifteen years?"

"I learn slowly, perhaps," replied Walker. He did not lower the shatterspike. "Let these men go free, or I shall leave instead."

Gylther'yel had no reply, except to widen her eyes, just for an instant.

Silence reigned as the two, mentor and student, standing apart, engaged in a contest of wills. The ghostwalker, with his determination and resolve, faced down his teacher, who had taught him everything he knew. The silent battle raged for some time. The only sound was the dazed captain's panting.

Then the sun elf closed her eyes and looked away, down ever so slightly. Walker nodded and lowered the sword.

"Go," Walker said to Unddreth and the remaining guards. "And never return."

They all looked at one another. Though neither the elf nor the ghostwalker had made anything more than the slightest of movements, all present in the grove knew they had witnessed a tremendous struggle, surpassing even the devastating druidic magic that had been arrayed against them. The soldiers stood, gathered up their arms and equipment, and moved to the bodies of their companions. They hesitated when Gylther'yel cast them a baleful look.

"Tell them to leave the dead for the earth," Gylther'yel ordered Walker.

The ghostwalker's cloak swirled in the wind, but Walker made no other move. The sun elf's lip twitched but she said no more.

They waited as the soldiers gathered their dead and wounded, slinging the former over their shoulders and helping the latter stagger back to Quaervarr. Unddreth gave Walker a deep, measuring gaze as the Quaervarr soldiers left the clearing—a gaze filled with respect—but the ghostwalker's eyes were fixed on the petite yet imposing sun elf before him. They waited until the soldiers were far away.

Gylther'yel assumed her ghostly wildshape once more, this time taking the shape of a nimble, golden doe. Then she stared at the ghostwalker levelly with a gaze that told Walker, in no uncertain terms, that he would regret his decision.

Soon he was left alone with his thoughts, his doubts, and the spirits. Ghosts flitted about, most of them of creatures long passed and a few the mournful souls of the soldiers who had died that day. Walker could not see them—he had not tapped into his ghostsight, wanting to do this battle as a mortal man—but he could feel them. They begged for his reassurance, his guidance. It was something he could never give.

As always, the sadness came to him, intensified now that it seemed he had rejected the one being, his teacher, who could understand his power and his curse. This was the first time he had threatened Gylther'yel and it was the first time he had opposed her wishes directly.

He knew things could never be the same with her again.

Pulling his cloak tightly around himself, Walker began the long trek back to Gylther'yel's grove and imagined the reception he would find there.

❂   ❂   ❂   ❂   ❂

The thing that displeased Greyt the most—and it was possibly the only thing that truly displeased him at the moment—was that he could not compose while inebriated, and he was definitely in his cups that evening. The three empty bottles of Tethyrian and Amnian wine surrounding him attested to that.

The loss of musical talent could be justified, though, for this was a time of celebration.

He had just received word that Unddreth had met with great unpleasantness in the Moonwood, and while the thick-headed captain continued to deny it, rumors were spreading through the town like wildfire that the mysterious Walker had killed half a dozen soldiers and wounded as many. Greyt suspected something more sinister was at work, for he knew what guarded the west Moonwood.

The common citizen, though, knew nothing of the Ghostly Lady; she was but a child's story. Walker, on the other hand, seemed real enough. With every retelling, his story became more extravagant, and now the man in black seemed to be guilty of at least two score murders and was thought by many wise citizens to have destroyed the Black Blood and perhaps Silverymoon single-handedly.

Greyt's mind was cloudy with drink, but he felt in his gut that this was exactly what he needed—an outside threat to distract the people and make them examine their security—one that was not the Black Blood, despite how useful the cult had been. After all, Jarthon and his beasts, before those damned adventurers had driven them out, could be dismissed easily as frenzied savages who picked victims at random.

But a murderer on the loose—a cold-blooded, methodical, unstoppable killer—during Stonar's absence would upset the balance, and Greyt could make it swing in his direction.

Who would the frightened townsfolk run to but the Lord Singer, an adventurer himself, with contacts to be called in and experience in dealing with monsters and killers? Talthaliel's warnings that Walker was a wildcard to be watched seemed irrelevant.

There was still the matter of the Venkyr girl, however, and that was what plagued Greyt's mind now. Talthaliel's warning that the girl was clever and insightful set off bells in Greyt's head. He had to keep Arya away from this Walker. Their meeting—as Talthaliel had warned—would bring only bad consequences.

Just as he was pondering this, there was a knock at his ballroom door and Claudir stepped inside to announce that "Lady Arya Venkyr and her companions" waited without.

Intrigued, fighting the muddiness in his head, he waved for the steward to show her in.

"Uncle, I must protest," said the knight as she stormed in. Her appearance was stunning in her silvery armor, aided in no small part by the flush of anger. The other Knights in Silver who were her companions walked in as well, clad in their armor and bearing their weapons. So she had decided she could not come alone, eh? Greyt frowned.

"I went to speak to Captain Unddreth about his encounter in the Moonwood," Arya said, "and I was turned away—not by the Watch, but by your guards."

Greyt waved his hand through the air. "So?" he asked, his head rocking woozily.

"He's fairly tipsy," Derst observed quietly to Bars.

"Done in by Moradin's hammer," the paladin agreed.

Arya seemed not to notice. "I really must be able to continue my investigation into the disappearances of the couriers, and anything related to Walker could help to—"

"Didn't I tell you to leave that alone?" interrupted Greyt. He rose from his chair and pulled himself up to face her.

"He smells terrible," Bars murmured to the roguish knight.

"Like you did last night, after spilling that venison stew all over your tunic," replied Derst under his breath.

Brows arching, Bars gave an almost imperceptible nod.

Arya screwed up her face in distaste at Greyt's foul breath. "Excuse me, Uncle, but I am on an assignment from Silverymoon to investigate the disappearances—"

"What's this preoccupation with Walker all of a sudden?" asked Greyt, cutting her off. Arya's companions looked at each other. "It almost sounds like you're infatuated with him." Her mouth dropped open. "Ah yes, dark and mysterious . . . is he handsome? A thrilling lover?"

"Well, that was uncalled for," Derst said with a frown. "Aye, Bars . . . Bars?"

Though he did not speak, it was clear that Bars agreed, for he flushed, stepped forward, and dropped his hands to the maces at his belt.

Greyt saw this and his face skewed up in a crooked smile.

"Oh, a hero, eh?" He pushed his slim chest out and stepped right up to the hulking paladin, a man nearly twice his size. The Lord Singer stood a step higher, so their eyes were almost level.

Bars refused to back down before him, and Greyt laughed in his face. "The gallant knight stands to defend his beleaguered lady, the way all the stories and ballads tell; all flowery, all heroic . . . all lies."

"Take back what you said," Bars said. Greyt flashed a mocking smile in the paladin's face but did nothing of the sort. "I won't ask again."

"Very well," Greyt said with a shrug. "I take it back, then."

Bars gave him a long, measured look—one that the Lord Singer answered with a gaze of haughty disdain—and backed away. The Lord Singer grinned, put a finger to his forehead, and broke down in a laughing fit.

"Heroism," he cackled.

"Please, uncle," Arya said. "You are drunk."

"Yes, yes I am," the Lord Singer replied with a dazed smile.

Then he lunged forward and seized Arya before either of the other knights could react. He pulled her face to his and went for her lips.

He ended up on the ground clutching at his groin where Arya had kneed him.

"G-get away from me!" stammered Arya.

The Lord Singer, nearly unconscious from drink and pain, was in no position to argue. The three knights hurried out the door, Bars trying to convince Derst that it was all right because the knave was drunk, Arya casting her step-uncle warning glances, and Derst exclaiming at the top of his lungs that they had both taken leave of their senses. Meanwhile, Greyt, face flushed and brows knitted with fury, struggled to growl at them.

Arya Venkyr would regret this, step-niece or no.

CHAPTER 9

28 Tarsakh

As storm clouds rolled overhead and the residual light from the setting sun faded, Walker made his way back to Quaervarr with a heavy heart and a head full of worries. His sword felt leaden in its scabbard and his clothes similarly weighty because of the light rain. As he had expected, the ghost druid had been nowhere to be found in the grove, but he had still felt her presence, watching him. And, as always when he felt her eyes upon his back, the ghost of Tarm Thardeyn was nowhere to be found.

Any other man may have feared Gylther'yel's retribution, but Walker thought little of this course of events. This was simply the way of things with his teacher, the only mother he had ever known: a mother who neither loved nor forgave.

Elves' memories were long and their scorn hot, she often said to him, and after fifteen years he knew it was the truth. But there was nothing he could do about it, so Walker focused on the task at hand—slaying the third and last of Greyt's henchmen.

At least Walker thought that the giant of a man they called Bilgren was the third attacker—he would not know until he faced the barbarian, until he could feel that same soul of hatred he had sensed that night fifteen years before.

In keeping with his thoughts, the rain strengthened from a dreary drizzle to a gloomy downpour.

Eluding the grim-faced guards at the sole gate of Quaervarr was not a problem. Though they were sharp-eyed and suspicious, clutching their silver-headed spears tightly, visibility was reduced to almost nothing in the rain. Walker slipped through the shadows, hidden in his heavy cloak, within a sword's length of the guards.

A shadow in the rain, he made his way up the empty main street. Few townsfolk came out on a good night, fewer when it rained so heavily. Walker did not need his eyes to navigate the town, for he had walked its streets many times before, unseen and unknown by the townsfolk.

As the street opened up into the main plaza, the rain let up for a moment, and Walker lifted his head. He could see the lamplights bright in the windows of Greyt's manor. He could see faces inside those windows and the shadowy silhouettes of moving figures, but he did not think much on them. He knew that he would be inside that place soon enough.

He turned north and started down the road toward the oldest part of town, through the original shadowtop gates, where the first settlers had set up camp in what would become Quaervarr. Townsfolk claimed that the additional settlers carried a shade of cowardice because they had stayed south, close to the Silverymoon road, where help could come the fastest. It made for a tiny difference, but the northern Old District carried more of a frontier feel.

Bilgren's house, a stout former tavern the barbarian had bought for its ale store and wine cellar, squatted dankly a few buildings down the road next to an unmanned merchant wagon filled with goods in bundles. The entire place seemed worn and abused, even at this distance. The second floor balcony had half-collapsed from mildew and rot and most of the windows were boarded up. The building might have seemed condemned but for the thick iron door set in the front. Carved with roaring tigers, the door represented Bilgren's measure of his own strength—local legend said the barbarian had carried the several hundred pound door single-handedly from the smiths of his homeland, hundreds of miles distant.

Lost in his thoughts, Walker was completely surprised when a hand reached out of an alley, seized him by the shoulder, and yanked him from the hazy night into pitch darkness.

Walker recovered enough from the surprise to draw his shatterspike in the blink of an eye and slash up and across at his unseen attacker. The hand released his shoulder and the dark figure leaped back, but Walker did not let up. He followed, his blade thrusting up and down, then slashing right to left. The first thrust the attacker managed to dodge and the second scraped off hard steel, as of armor. The high slash slammed against a hastily raised shield, a parry that barely managed to block it. The shield did not resist the sword's cut directly, but instead let the slash continue, straight into the wall of a nearby building, where the shield held it.

Releasing the sword, Walker lunged forward and shouldered his opponent, who was already off balance, against the wall of the nearby building. A long sword came up, held in the attacker's other hand, and Walker immediately stepped inside its reach, putting his shoulder against the upper right arm, and held his opponent against the cracked timber wall with his body. The overhang stopped the rain from falling on Walker's head, but the darkness obscured his attacker's face.

"Stop—" he started to say, but a flash of lightning overhead lit the alley for the barest of instants and bathed his opponent's face in light.

It was the auburn-haired woman, the one he had happened across in the alley, saved from an unknown assailant, then confronted in Torlic's house, all within a short amount of time.

"You—" began his next question, but it cut off in a grunt as pain exploded up his leg from where she had stomped hard on his foot. He staggered back and a knee met his midsection. Walker doubled over, the air stolen from his lungs, but managed to reach up for his sword, still stuck in the wall.

The woman made no move to attack, but she kept her sword up as she stepped away from the wall. "A less honorable woman would have put that knee between your legs," she observed casually as she wiped a lock of auburn hair out of her face with her sword arm.

Walker managed to right himself, holding himself up against the opposite wall until his stomach cramp disappeared, and his eyes adjusted to the darkness.

The knight saw that he was vertical again and smiled. "Now—"

Whatever the knight had been about to say became a startled gasp as she leaped back, barely avoiding a silvery blade through the ribs as Walker lunged. She slapped the sword away and fell back into a defensive stance, shield up and ready.

That was fortunate—for her—because Walker's second slash came not a breath later, slamming into her shield with bone-numbing force. The fine steel held, though the keen shatterspike left a wide notch in its surface.

The knight attempted to swing back, but Walker parried the sword out to his left, spun toward her, dropped the shatterspike, grabbed her wrist, and rolled along her arm, coiling up to her sword hand all in one smooth movement, holding her blade away from him. Then he punched her stomach hard with his off hand and slammed his palm against her sword hand, knocking the sword from numbed fingers. Uncoiling once more, he slammed her back against the wall, and held the point of a knife to her throat—a knife that he had slipped from his left sleeve.

In the space of a breath, he stood, back to her front, her right hand in his, holding her against the wood.

Walker hissed in her ear. "Now—"

She twisted her hand and pulled a dagger from his right wrist sheath. Walker's eyes widened, but the surprise did not stop his reflex. With his free hand, he slapped the blade away.

"Well, that's out of the way," she said, half jokingly, as the knife fell to the ground.

"What?"

"You don't understand," the woman said. "I'm not here to fight you—"

"Then why are you here?" Walker demanded, so harshly that the knight flinched.

Then, as though she had steeled herself with the same icy resolve that ran through Walker's veins, the knight's face went calm.

"Are we through interrupting each other?" she asked slowly and levelly.

"Are we?" Walker kept his voice calm.

"What kind of answer is that?" asked the knight. "Obviously, I'm in no position to surprise you with an attack, so it's really a matter of whether you—" Walker was impassive as he held the knife to her throat. The knight swallowed. "Right, well, let's assume that's a 'yes.' In that case, I'll tell you why I'm here."

"Indeed."

Though his rasp was chilling, the knight, unafraid, was staring into his sapphire eyes, a gaze that made him uncharacteristically uncomfortable. It was not a sensation he was used to. Fortunately, her eyes were drawn to a silver gleam on his finger—the wolf's head ring. Walker shifted his stance, pulling her attention from the ring.

"Will you do something for me?" she asked after a moment.

"Perhaps," replied Walker.

The knight lifted her chin, heedless of the blade poised

there. "Allow me to speak without attacking?"

Walker's face was impassive.

"My name is Arya Venkyr of Everlund, Knight of Silverymoon," she said.

"Men call me Walker," said the man in black.

"I know," said Arya. "I have seen you before—"

"And?" Walker hissed, forcing her back to the former subject.

"I'm here on assignment to investigate the disappearances of half a dozen couriers—"

"Couriers?" asked Walker, unfamiliar with the term. He spoke Elvish more often than Common.

"Messengers," said Arya. "They have vanished over the last few tendays—"

"Then why are you here?" came the interruption.

Arya's brow wrinkled. "The couriers, they—"

"No, why here—why follow me?" corrected Walker. "I know nothing of your couriers."

"You do know something," she said. "Something that will help in my invest—"

"I know nothing of your couriers," repeated Walker.

"How do I know you're telling the truth?" asked Arya. Walker turned the knife he held to her throat. "Well, I suppose I'll have to take your word—"

"Indeed," said Walker.

Then he took the blade away from her throat, though he made no move to release her. He did not even realize he was still holding her until she tilted her head, examining his face.

"It *was* you, wasn't it?" she said excitedly, as though making a discovery. "You saved me. You're not as old as I thought—you can't have seen many more winters than me. Why do you wear your collar so high? What are you hiding?"

Not answering any of her questions, Walker released her and stepped away, toward his fallen sword. She stood there for a heartbeat, massaging her stung wrist. Then, as though remembering something, she clutched the trailing edge of his cloak and stayed him.

"You're going after one of Greyt's friends, Bilgren," Arya said, holding him back.

Walker shrugged, as if to concede the possibility.

Arya continued. "Turn back. Knowing my . . . knowing him, it's probably a trap."

Walker smiled. "It matters not," he said. He turned. "If you knew how I am committed, you would not stop me." He pulled his cloak out of her grasp and stalked away.

✦ ✦ ✦ ✦ ✦

"Wait!" Arya shouted, not knowing why. She had almost let him fade away into the shadows, but something within wouldn't let her.

He turned, showing no emotion at all in his face, but she could tell he was confused.

The rush of words burst out of her faster than her mind could hold it back. "I wanted to thank you for saving me the other night."

Walker's expression did not change, but Arya could feel something shift. That had startled him. He stood still for a moment, gazing at her, and she felt none of his bitter, icy resolve burning at her. Instead, he seemed almost a simple man gazing at her through the darkness.

"You are welcome," Walker said quietly. He turned, bent low to retrieve the weapon, then headed back toward the street. Then he paused and looked back.

"What is it?" Arya asked, knitting her brows in confusion.

"I apologize for frightening you," said Walker. "You were in no danger." His voice was soft, almost gentle.

It is the curse of quick words—when one shouldn't respond, they come, and when one needs to speak, they are mysteriously absent. When Arya could not form a reply, Walker bowed his head and turned to go.

Arya blinked. What a quandary this man seemed: a creature of darkness, with vengeance burning in his eyes, and yet he had saved her. Arya felt the same conflicting duality as she looked upon him. On the one hand, his cold stare frightened her, and the rage she had seen in his eyes sent chills down her spine. But on the other, he intrigued her, taking her beyond her initial curiosity. And something told her that he hid much behind those blue eyes, beneath that black cloak....

That thought made her blush, but she hadn't meant it that way. Too much time around Derst, perhaps.

Now, Arya realized with a start, Walker was going back into the shadows, but slowly. There was more he wanted to say, she could sense, but he did not have the words. Something about the way he carried himself and the way he moved set her heart to racing.

"Stop!" said Arya without meaning to. She realized she'd stopped him a third time.

Walker turned back, and his eyes appraised her. "You possess courage," he said.

It sounded almost mocking, and Arya puffed out her chest. "Why do you say that?"

Walker may have smiled behind his high collar. "You do not fear me."

"Should I?"

Walker's gaze was her only answer.

Arya felt her defiant spirit flaring, and a retort came to mind. Her mouth was moving first, though, before she even considered what was to come out.

"Evil holds no terror for me," said Arya, baiting him.

"Then you should feel terror indeed, for I hold no evil for you," said Walker. "Only vengeance for my foes."

"Vengeance is evil," she argued.

"Vengeance is beyond good and evil," replied Walker.

They were silent for a long moment. Then, leaving it on that cryptic note, Walker turned and walked away.

Arya made to follow him but stopped, a thought having occurred to her. She reached in her pocket and fingered the gold amulet she had accidentally taken from Greyt's manor. She ran the other way down the alley.

❧ ❧ ❧ ❧ ❧

Wiping rainwater from his nose, Walker pushed Arya's warning out of his mind as he approached Bilgren's house, though he kept his hand on his sword.

Arya. So that was her name. A beautiful name, for a beautiful. . . .

Growling inwardly, Walker shoved the thoughts aside.

The caravan in front of the decrepit former tavern bulged with crates and bundles of silks from Kara-Tur. He found it odd that merchants would stop in this part of Quaervarr, and even odder that the merchants would leave their wagon, fully loaded and unguarded.

An odd sensation of paranoia crept through him.

Strange. Why should he feel unnerved? Was this merely Arya's warning coming back to haunt him?

He was pondering this when the lids of the crates burst open and soldiers, glittering steel in their hands, poured out into the rainy night around him. These men were dressed in dark leather and carried swords, daggers, and axes, most with a weapon in both hands.

Caught momentarily off guard, Walker barely drew his sword in time to deflect the first slash of a ranger's blade. He twisted aside and winced as the man's dagger scraped past his side. Fortunately, the blow was cushioned by the magic of his bracers and drew little blood. He countered with a vicious punch to the jaw, laying the man low, but two were waiting to take the fallen ranger's place, swords darting for his life.

Walker spun, throwing his cloak up high to distract them, and the blades stabbed right through the thick cloth, one narrowly missing and the other sparking off his left bracer.

Continuing the spin, Walker yanked his cloak hard to the left, and the cloth pulled the swords along with it, dragging the rangers off their guard. He reversed the shatterspike in his left hand, followed the spin, and cut one of the rangers down with an underhand slash. Even as the man fell, Walker leaped backward into the middle of the street, warding off the dozen attackers with his blade.

One came forward, and Walker batted the sword aside, but his counter went to parry the sword of a second, coming from his unarmed side. A dagger snaked in and Walker slapped the man's hand, disarming him, caught the falling weapon, and jabbed it into the first attacker's belly, all in a blur of motion. The man cursed and kicked out, but Walker twisted aside to dodge.

Then white-hot pain slashed across his back, and Walker lost his focus. He ducked under the next slash and thrust his blade behind him. The flanking ranger leaped back with an oath.

Walker rose. The angry-faced rangers, many sporting scars and eye patches, sneered at him. More men came out of the surrounding buildings, until Walker found himself facing thirty men, all armed to face a small army. They did not advance—Walker's aura of deadly resolve kept them at bay for now—but they kept Walker carefully surrounded.

The huge iron doors of Bilgren's tavern home creaked open and two figures came out, one with dark curls, clad in white leather armor, and the other a hulking giant of a man, wrapped in furs and carrying a long weapon with a sword blade extending from one end and a single chain flail from the other. The latter man's thick red moustache quivered as he guffawed loudly.

"Ah, ha ha!" the huge man bellowed. "Look at the rat me trap has caught!"

"My trap, Bilgren," said the smaller man. "My trap. You'd have just fought him alone."

Bilgren roared with laughter. "Ye be right, little Meris, ye be right." He spun his gyrspike before him, blade over chain. "An' now I'll do the like anyway."

Meris raised a finger and opened his mouth to speak but then shrugged. "Whatever you say," said the dusky scout.

Walker, bleeding from half a dozen small wounds, kept

warding the rangers away with his threatening blade and gaze. Then the rangers drew back and lowered their swords, allowing Walker his circle. The ghostwalker stood up as straight as he could, held his blade low, and stared at the huge barbarian coming toward him. Bilgren shouldered his way through the rangers and stepped into the circle with the bleeding ghostwalker.

"Thy race be run, dark man," Bilgren rumbled, holding his weapon ready. He twirled it in front of him and across to both his sides, then over his head, with astonishing grace given the weapon's size and Bilgren's bulk. He finally snapped it down and held the flail and sword handle in his two huge hands. "I only regret that a sickly goblin like ye could kill me friend Drex." He lifted his gyrspike over his head in challenge.

Walker's grim scowl did not waver. He lifted his shatterspike, accepting the barbarian's challenge.

Bilgren roared and leaped in, attacking with reckless abandon. It was a berserk fury, a terrible blood frenzy Walker had observed many times in animals backed into corners. The rage would heighten Bilgren's strength, speed, and endurance. Against Walker, already injured, the advantage was clear.

The fight would be a quick one, unless Tymora intervened.

Spinning his gyrspike, Bilgren slashed down at Walker's head. The smaller man made to parry, then leaped aside, dodging the blow and the spiked ball that smashed down after it. Working with both hands, Bilgren continued the swing, allowing the sword and flail to slash past the side of his body. For such a huge man, he possessed remarkable speed. Bilgren turned and brought the weapon horizontally right to left, turning the swipe past his side and allowing the flail to swing. Walker managed to whirl away in time, the flail passing within a hand's breadth of his chest.

Meanwhile, a dagger slid into Walker's hand, and he let fly.

Walker landed and went to one knee, one hand low, and his cloak spread out around him. Bilgren gave a gasp from behind, and the ghostwalker closed his eyes as though mourning. The street was silent.

Then a sound broke that silence—a loud, booming laugh.

Walker turned to see Bilgren looming over him, a dagger stuck to the hilt in his right arm. The barbarian looked at the wound idly, then ripped the knife from his flesh with the slightest of winces. He tossed it aside and swung the gyrspike, keeping the sword blade against his arm.

Eyes wide, Walker managed to duck the flail by throwing himself on his back.

Bilgren followed through and took the weapon behind his back, turning it like a staff, and the blade came back around his right side. Walker leaped to the opposite side of Bilgren's body, but the barbarian kept the weapon slashing after him. The ghostwalker managed to parry aside the sword blade but the spiked ball clipped his shoulder and sent him spinning to the ground.

Intense pain lashed through Walker and blood flew from his lips. He pushed on the earth, trying to force himself up from where he lay on his belly, but he could not muster the strength. He tried to summon up the ghostly powers that would allow him to escape by walking through the very earth, but the necessary focus eluded him. For the first time in the life he remembered, Walker felt his resolve and his calm slipping away.

The rangers laughed and jeered all around him. A flat, emotionless expression was painted across Meris's dusky face, but something burned in his eyes.

In those eyes, something . . . Anger, yes. Rage, yes. But something else. . . .

Looming over him, the bearlike Bilgren spun the gyrspike over his head. "Not used to facing death, are ye, dark man?" the raging barbarian roared like a lion. "How does it feel? To know I be about to crush ye—"

"Sir Bilgren!" a voice shouted from somewhere.

Startled, the barbarian watched, stupefied, as a lance stabbed into his shoulder, lifting him up and out of the circle.

Holding the other end of that lance, Arya burst into the circle on the back of a charging steed. The confused Bilgren, borne aloft on her lance, flew back and crashed bodily into the full trader's wagon. Nightingale-and-Moon shield in one hand and lance in the other, Arya scattered the surrounding rangers like children with her furious gaze and, more tangibly, with the hooves of her war-horse. Her lance now freed, Arya swung it around in a wide semi-circle, knocking half a dozen rangers to the ground.

"Up!" Arya shouted to Walker. She dropped the lance and reached down.

Somehow, the ghostwalker managed to muster his strength and rise to one knee. He reached up, caught hold of her hand, and pushed himself up as she pulled. Together, they hauled him onto the horse. Arya gave a shout and the steed leaped through two rangers, throwing them to the ground, and sprinted away from the battle, south toward the center of Quaervarr.

"Strumpet!" came Meris's shout, and a light axe whirled end over end toward them. Arya got her shield up in its way and the weapon skittered off Everlundian steel.

"Wh-what are you doing?" Walker choked out, blood trickling down his chin.

"My turn to save your life!" the knight replied with cheery ardor. She flicked the reins again and the horse leaped into a full gallop.

"Head west . . ." Walker murmured. "My grove. . . ."

Arya nodded and spurred the horse toward the outer gate of Quaervarr.

Meris's rangers were in hot pursuit, running full out as fast as their legs could carry them. Thus, when a rope suddenly came up between the two old gates, fully half a dozen were caught off guard, took it in the chest, and stumbled to the ground. The rope fell as two men dressed in tabards of the Knights in Silver stepped out from the sides of the gate.

"I don't know how you talked me into this one, Derst," the larger man rumbled. "Covering their escape—"

"The old duty and honor trick," his weasel-faced companion said. "Gets you every time."

Spinning the two light maces he held, Bars laughed grimly, conceding the point.

❧ ❧ ❧ ❧ ❧

"Stay with me, Walker," whispered Arya, surprised at how worried her voice sounded.

They had burst out Quaervarr's main gate, not slowing as the stunned guards threw themselves into the mud. Bearing her two riders, Swiftfall leaped with a whinny into forbidding cold.

More than any pursuit, Arya feared for the wounded man who clutched her waist so fiercely.

That grip was inexplicably distracting, but as they rode, the arms slipped and the hug loosened bit by bit as Walker lost more and more blood. Thus, even as his touch filled her with an unexpected tingling, it also wracked her with a sense of dire urgency. She spurred Swiftfall on all the faster, heading south.

"Drink this," said Arya, handing him a potion from her belt. The vial was marked with the Dethek rune for healing. Walker choked down the milky liquid and nearly gagged, but the potion spread its healing warmth through his body. "It's not much, but Swiftfall can get us to Silverymoon this night—"

"No!" Walker hissed so sharply that Arya started. "No . . . I cannot . . . leave. . . ."

Arya opened her mouth to protest, but shut it once more. "All right, all right," she said. "Where do we go then?"

"West," said Walker. "West to my grove. . . ." He trailed off into silence.

Frightened, Arya started to ask if he were awake—or even alive—but at that moment, the ghostwalker leaned his head against her strong back, repeating his directions in a whisper.

Arya turned Swiftfall to the right, toward the Dark Woods. "We'll be safe, old lass," she said to the horse, stroking her mane. "No one will think we ran where you can't run."

They broke into the woods and left the road to Silverymoon—and safety—behind.

❀ ❀ ❀ ❀ ❀

Greyt's rangers were up long into the night, pounding on doors and interrogating townsfolk, looking always for the two knights—one huge, and one tiny. After a short skirmish, the knights had disappeared, and try as the rangers might, the knights were nowhere to be found. Oaths, growls, threats, and even the clashing of weapons filled the air, and little of Quaervarr got any sleep.

Meanwhile, on the edge of town, beneath the eaves of a certain Bullot Feyfoot's stables, a loud oath was heard, seeming to come from the air. A stray dog, hearing the curse, yipped and backed off from the invisible barrier its nose had struck just an instant earlier.

"Derst, where the Hells are you?" Bars asked aloud. The invisible paladin shifted and almost lost his balance, nearly falling to the cobblestones. He could not, after all, see his feet.

"Right here, actually," came a voice from beside him. The suddenness made Bars jump, then fall.

"Beshaba's horns!" Bars covered his mouth as though to pull back the foul words. Since he couldn't see his hand, he poked himself in one invisible eye.

"Watch yourself there, you big oaf," said Derst. "You almost crushed me!"

"I can't 'watch myself,' orc-brain!" shouted Bars. "Your Tyr-cursed potions made us invisible, remember?"

"Well, obviously. . . ." he trailed off. "I always find invisibility comfortable, don't you?"

"How do you turn the damned things off?" growled Bars. "I feel . . . disconnected, as though I'm outside my body. A ghost." Like Walker, was his next thought, with a chill.

"Oh, you're all right," replied Derst in a tone that indicated he had rolled his eyes. "Well, I suppose I'm used to it, and my senses are a little sharper than yours. I'm tempted to just leave the invisibility on and let your small brain figure it out." Bars felt a heavy tap on his shoulder, a light push, and Derst shimmered back into visibility.

"See, it's that simple," said the wiry knight. "You remember how I told you not to hit anyone until—" Then a heavy force struck his stomach, and the smaller man doubled over with a gasp.

The paladin faded into view. "You're right, that was simple," said Bars, cracking his knuckles.

Derst just moaned.

"Funny, didn't mean to hit you so hard. Right then, Sir-Plans-A-Lot, what now?"

Slowly, Derst recovered himself and stood up straight. "To the stable," he muttered. "There's a trap door, used by those who Har—er, do business with me, in certain unpleasant circumstances a little like these. Tight quarters, though."

"Joyous," Bars said glumly.

CHAPTER 10

28 Tarsakh

Arya did not know how long they had been traveling through the forest, Swiftfall picking her way between fallen limbs and avoiding holes in the ground. The deeper they went, the darker it became and the less at ease she felt. The silence of their ride did not help. Walker was far from talkative. Nightmares had gripped him earlier, and he had called out strange words she had not recognized, but they seemed to have passed, leaving him silent.

At first, she had filled the quiet with the tale of how she came to be in Quaervarr, of the vanished couriers, and of her suspicions about Greyt. Now, the knight divided her focus between ducking under tree branches and thinking about the mysterious man slumped against her back. He had long since stopped murmuring, and now she didn't know if he were even still breathing.

"Walker?" she asked. "Still with me back there?"

When there was no response, Arya turned her head back to look at Walker. He sat slumped, eyes closed, on the back of the horse. "Walker?" she asked in a frightened whisper. "Are you—still alive?"

His eyes flickered open and his intense blue gaze found her worried face.

"Of course," said Walker. "I shall speak up if I feel about to expire."

Arya looked away, hiding her relief. At first, she was upset he had frightened her, and that his voice had been almost mocking, but she laughed. It was appropriate, since she had sounded like a frightened little girl.

"Was that a jest?" she asked with a half smile.

Walker did not reply except to release her waist.

"What's the matter?" asked Arya, worried again, clutching at his hand. He felt so cold, even through the glove.

"I can sit on my own," Walker said. She heard a tiny elf touch to his voice.

"You've lost that much blood and now you can sit on your own?" Arya asked, doubtful.

"Healing." His rasping voice was soft.

"No one heals that fast," Arya said. "You were on Kelemvor's doorstep when I pulled you onto Swiftfall's back. How—"

Walker's right hand came up from her side. In the moonlight, a tiny sapphire glistened from within a silver wolf's head ring wrapped around the fourth finger.

"You have many secrets, it seems," said the knight with a nod of approval. "Lone wolf."

Walker nodded. Looking away, Arya bit her lip in thought. She was familiar with rings that healed their wearers—a warrior in the field did not always have a priest's healing at hand—and how powerful such rings could be. Still, she did not know how healed he was.

"Put your arms back around me," Arya said finally. "I don't want you falling off—I'm too tired to pick you up again."

Walker hesitated, but he did as he was told. She supposed

the order was half for his benefit and half for hers. It was bitterly cold and though his arms were not overly warm, Arya welcomed them. His proximity reassured her against the dark of the forest.

That was what she told herself, at least.

"Talk to me," said Arya after a moment. "I've told you all about myself; what about you?"

"What shall I tell?" asked Walker. His voice still rasped, but he did not sound so deathly now. "I walk with ghosts. I have my task. That is all."

"Your task … you mean killing people?" She felt him wince at her harsh tone, and she quickly amended. "People who wronged you? Hurt someone you loved? Greyt? The others?"

Walker said nothing and silence fell again.

"I'm still not convinced you're not the one attacking those couriers, you know," Arya observed after a moment. "It's quite a coincidence, that I run into you exactly when I'm investigating those attacks—"

"Yet you aid me now," Walker replied. "Why?"

Arya paused. "My … Lord Greyt wants you dead, and that's enough for me." She was not sure why, but she stopped herself from drawing a connection with her step-uncle. "The same man is trying to kill us both, whatever his plans might be. Then the man's son, gods above, he's just as dangerous—"

Walker perked up. "Meris?" he asked, interrupting.

Then he stopped and looked around. "Wait." His arms were gone from around her waist.

Arya had been about to respond, but the urgency in his voice cut her off. "What is it?" she asked. Swiftfall whinnied and paced nervously.

"Something draws near," said Walker. "Something powerful."

He swung down from Swiftfall's back, landing on his feet and appearing not the least bit weakened.

"What is it?" she asked again.

"Stay there," Walker said. "I shall look."

Then he vanished into the air, as though he had never existed.

"Walker?" asked Arya, surprise in her voice. She could no longer even feel his living presence. She and Swiftfall seemed alone in the dark forest. "Walker!"

❖ ❖ ❖ ❖ ❖

"Walker!" came her panicked cry.

The ghostwalker did not answer, but it was not out of rudeness. Rather, he understood that she would not have heard his voice had he spoken. Ethereal himself, he would be just as hidden from whatever approached.

In the Ethereal, the night was not as dark, or perhaps it did not seem so because everything was gray and blurry. Arya and Swiftfall were luminous beings seen from that realm—so vibrant that their flesh and bones seemed made of blazing sunlight. The knight looked around frantically, trying to find him, and Walker felt an odd twinge of regret that he had not given her more warning before he had shifted into the Ethereal plane.

It was difficult to see beside the shining horse and rider, but Walker was immediately aware that the three of them were alone. The spirits that always seemed drawn to him had vanished as though driven away by some greater force.

Walker bit his lower lip in thought. What could frighten spirits of the dead?

It did not take more than a moment for his question to be answered, for in that moment a huge, roiling creature of flame emerged from the trees ahead of them.

Walker's eyes widened as he looked up at the creature. Vaguely human-shaped, it towered over him like a giant composed entirely of shadowy fire.

The most significant thing he noticed, though, was that the creature existed on this—the Ethereal—plane.

He had heard of elementals, but never a beast of this ghostly sort—nor did he have any idea how to battle one. He did know two things, however: being ethereal would not hide him, as had been his intention, and the beast was coming fast.

Drawing his shatterspike, Walker stepped back into the Material and put his hand on Swiftfall, as though he could command the horse to carry Arya away with but a touch.

Indeed, his sudden appearance startled the animal, even as his ghostly aura had unnerved it. Carried past the realm of comfort, the horse panicked and snorted.

"Run!" he shouted to Swiftfall. "Flee!"

Then he rushed toward the elemental. Though it was invisible on the Material plane, the creature, in all its fiery fury, was fully visible to his ethereally sensitive eyes.

Arya, however, did not share his ghostsight. To her, the ghostwalker charged toward empty air.

"What? What are you—"

Her voice trailed off as the creature manifested, shimmering out of the Ethereal directly in front of her.

The forest erupted into an inferno of gray-silver fire, translucent flames shifting like ribbons of burning silk. It made no sound—even the raging flames, which should have roared, burned silently. The ghostfire elemental loomed over her and pulled back one of its massive tendrils. Arya, shocked at its sudden, majestic appearance, stared into death itself.

"Arya!" shouted Walker.

He slashed down into the mass of flame and the weapon pulsed with cold, ghostly power. It bit into the elemental, disrupting its essence and causing the creature pain. It bucked and turned toward the ghostwalker, growing a new fiery arm to lash at him. Walker stabbed his sword at the creature, warding it off, and ducked its swipe. He retreated and the elemental followed.

The knight, broken from her spell, swung down from Swiftfall and slapped the horse's rump. With a whinny, Swiftfall ran and Arya stalked back toward the ghostfire elemental, drawing her sword.

"What are you doing?" hissed Walker as he thrust at the

elemental again and ducked its countering swing. "I told you to run!"

"You told Swiftfall to run," corrected Arya. "I have no intention of leaving you behind!"

She slashed her sword into the elemental with all her strength, but the blade passed through the ghostfire with no effect. "What, by Torm's blade?"

"I told you to flee for a reason!" shouted Walker. "Your blade is useless! Look—"

His warning cut off, incomplete, as a fist of ghostfire slammed into him. The elemental was certainly material enough to knock the man tumbling back through the air. Walker's body cracked against the thick trunk of a fir and he slumped to the forest turf, momentarily dazed.

The opponent with the stinging sword defeated for the moment, the creature turned its attention to the opponent whose hair resembled its material body in the moonlight.

The knight ducked as fiery tendrils struck out at her and scrambled back, leading the creature from the inert Walker. As she went, she uncorked a potion from her belt and splashed a silvery substance onto the sword. It suddenly glowed in the firelight with a cold blue radiance. "Come!" she shouted. "Come, demon-spawn!"

The elemental was only too happy to oblige, and flames roiled as it flowed toward her. Before Arya could escape, the creature raged around her. Arya swiped, slashing at the beast with her fine steel, but the blade swished through the ghostly flame with no effect. The elemental flickered between the planes, such that it was only really there half the time—the other half of the time, it was hopelessly ethereal.

She ducked an attack and slashed again, and this time the sword did not pass through harmlessly. Instead, the blade bit into its essence, causing it pain.

The creature swung a huge, fiery tendril at her, and Arya drew up her shield desperately. The ghostfire arm, however, passed right through the stout steel shield and struck Arya's arm full force. The knight screamed as the ghostfire tore at her flesh, her strength, and her spirit. Arya fell to her knees.

The scream jolted Walker from his stunned daze and the ghostwalker climbed to his feet. He ran toward the elemental, retrieving his blade from the ground. The elemental raised a fist in the air, preparing to bring it down on the staggering knight, but Walker lunged in and stabbed his shatterspike into its fiery depths. The creature whipped away from Arya.

Walker snapped his blade up to block the elemental's swipe. Its punch did not pass through the weapon, enchanted as the shatterspike was, but the force threw Walker to the ground. The ghostwalker struggled to rise, but the elemental slammed its arm down on his sword again, crushing him to his knees. The elemental flowed over him and held him down, manifesting entirely into the Material world, preventing him from rising.

The forest was suddenly lit with red, raging, material flame, and those flames licked at Walker around the sword. He gritted his teeth against the heat. Walker delved into his ghostly focus and distanced himself from his body so that he could ignore the pain.

Arya, seizing her opportunity, slashed at the elemental with two hands on her sword hilt. The temporarily enhanced blade cut into its fiery body but had little effect. The elemental countered and the knight managed to block the incoming punch with her shield. Though the fire did not strike her flesh, the force of the blow sent her reeling back. A second strike sent her flying into a fir tree on the other side of the clearing, where she crumpled to the ground, thrashing and moaning.

Amidst the pain of the flames, Walker blinked through the blood in his eyes and looked at the elemental standing over him. He stopped moving, allowing his body to go limp as though he had died from the flames. It was not a difficult task, for Walker could feel his flesh blistering and blackening and see that his bracers were white hot. He could endure, though, if only he could convince the elemental to leave. . . .

Sure enough, the weight on Walker's chest vanished as the ghostfire elemental faded from the Material. His tearing eyes could see that it was not gone. Rather, the creature had turned from Walker's inert form and now flowed toward Arya.

With the elemental no longer standing on him, Walker struggled to push himself to his feet. It was, however, to no avail. Scorched and blackened, his body would not obey his commands.

"Ar-Arya . . ." he called, but the knight was unconscious.

Walker felt his concentration wavering and his burned body crying out in pain. The burning specter loomed over Arya and raised its two fiery appendages to crush her. He tried again to move, but he could not even lift his scalding sword from the ground.

Arya was about to die, and there was nothing Walker could do.

Nothing, except for the last action he would ever consider.

"Gylther'yel!" Walker shouted, blood spurting from his lips. "Aid us! Gylther'yel!"

He called for his mentor with all the breath he could muster. He knew that she was watching and he knew how much she hated humans such as Arya, but he knew that she could not leave him to die, not after she had spent fifteen years to mold him as her guardian.

Nothing happened.

The elemental paused in its attack as though to laugh at him, though it made no sound.

In that moment, Walker felt hope die. Gylther'yel was too far away. This creature would slay them both. He felt like a fool.

The beast turned and raised its fiery tendrils to batter the knight to a scorched pulp.

Then the forest became utterly black as a dark cloud moved over the moon. The ghostfire provided the only light.

The air around the elemental chilled and hail began to fall. The creature paused, as though it heard something Walker and Arya could not, and shifted again, shedding its body. Hail battered at its suddenly diminished flames. The magic struck it even though it was incorporeal—the spells were halfway between the planes.

"Gyl ... Gylther'yel ..." rasped Walker.

Then a bolt of lightning shot from the sky and slammed the elemental to the earth. The elemental burned low, stunned, and another bolt struck it. The elemental struggled to rise and lash out at the knight, but a third bolt struck it, then a fourth, and a fifth. Lightning bolts flew from the clouds and battered the beast to the ground.

The elemental, reeling from the blows, managed to rise, but then the hail increased and a veritable ice storm descended upon the creature, icy shards tearing apart the flames.

When the dust and fog cleared, the elemental was no more. The last flickers of ghostly flames licked up into the sky and vanished. Arya slumped against the tree, knocked out cold but unscathed save for several burns and a thin stream of blood that trickled slowly from her split lip.

Gray-green cloak billowing and whipping around her slender figure, the gold-skinned Ghostly Lady stood in the elemental's place, hugging her arms around her stomach. Her waist-length golden hair wafted around her cold face like fire. She looked down upon Arya exactly as the elemental had.

Walker, as he watched, was not sure he was any less afraid for the unconscious knight.

"I am your teacher and your friend," Gylther'yel said to him. The slow, beautiful Elvish sounded out of place on the battlefield. "I brought you back from death and raised you as my child, taught you all your skills and powers, and this is how you repay me? With betrayal?" With the last word, Gylther'yel's voice rose in volume above an undertone—it was the loudest Walker had ever heard her speak.

She stared down at Arya, and her hand pulsed with black

energy, the killing magic that she had wielded against the Quaervarr soldiers.

"Gylther'yel, please," croaked Walker. His voice was broken and wretched. "Spare her ... She saved me ... If you must be angry ... be angry at me...."

"I am not angered that you disobey," replied the Ghost Druid. Her fingers, blazing with destructive power, twitched idly. "I am merely ... disappointed that you do not heed."

Then she waved, like brushing aside a flea, and the power crackled out of her hand. She walked over to Walker and placed her hand upon his forehead. He might have flinched, having seen the terrible magic she had just held, but he trusted the ruthless sun elf. The same hand that dispensed death so easily could also caress life into mortified flesh.

Gylther'yel's druidic magic soothed his mortal burns and he sensed—rather than felt, for his focus separated mind and body—his flesh re-knitting.

"I will allow you this diversion, while it lasts," said Gylther'yel. She stood, watching his wounds heal. "But know that you have brought this, my disappointment, upon yourself, and remember that the next time you cry to me for help, I will not be so quick to answer."

With that, the Ghostly Lady was gone. She vanished into the air as quickly as she had come, blown away with the passing mist and clouds.

Walker, his body healed such that he could move, pushed himself to his feet. He crossed to where Arya had fallen and, slinging the unconscious knight over his shoulder, began the trek west through the dark woods, on foot, seeking the sanctuary of his grove.

He prayed that he would have the strength to make it that far before he collapsed.

CHAPTER 11

29 Tarsakh

A heavy rap at the door awakened him. Stirring from troubled dreams, at first Greyt thought the knock was the sound of ribs crunching under a blow and he gave a startled gasp. He awoke but could see nothing in the darkness, as though he were blind. He soon realized, however, that he was alone in his bed and, exploring with his hands, that his body was whole. After a few tense breaths, the rap sounded again.

"What is it?" shouted Greyt.

The sickly-thin Claudir entered, robes carefully pressed and neat as always. He gazed imperiously down his thin nose at the Lord Singer buried under a small mountain of furs. "Important business, sir," he said.

"What could be so important?" Greyt threw back the covers and slid out of bed. He crossed to the window and yanked the latch open. The sun had not yet risen. The cold air surrounding his bare body sent shivers down his spine. "Especially before dawn?"

If Claudir minded or even noticed the Lord Singer's nakedness, he gave no sign. "There is a large group of townsfolk at the door," he said. "They have gathered in the square outside and wait upon your pleasure."

Greyt cursed under his breath, translating Claudir's words into tactical terms. "What is the general mood of the crowd?" he asked.

"They seem somewhat . . . ill at ease."

Greyt cursed again. "Angry mobs never 'wait upon your pleasure.' " He wrapped a blanket around his body. "Fetch my robe, yarting, and sword. I'm going out."

"Of course, my lord." Claudir bowed slightly. "Shall I send for several guards, two to escort you and half a dozen to filter through the crowd?"

"Naturally."

Claudir moved to leave, but Greyt stopped him with a call.

"And bring me a bottle of elverquisst after," he said. "I'm either going to toast a great success or the bodies of a dozen ignorant villagers. Or more."

"Of course, my lord," said Claudir with a bow.

❧ ❧ ❧ ❧ ❧

The crowd gathered in the courtyard of Greyt's manor, spilling into the main plaza of Quaervarr, was just as "ill at ease" as Claudir had described. Almost three hundred villagers stood in the plaza; nearly a third of the town's population. Most bore weapons, whether new purchases or dusty heirlooms, and others carried the saws and axes they used in woodworking. Those who did not carry weapons carried torches. Frowns were smeared across most of the faces and angry shouts rang out from the crowd.

"Well, sounds like the Lord Singer's going to get it," a thin voice observed, as though to no one in particular. "This reminds me of that time in Newfort, when we—"

"Derst, must you bring that up again?" the hulking man by his side whispered. Facing away from one another, the two warriors seemed totally unconnected, and their soft words were lost in the crowd. "That was not the best of experiences, and I'd rather not—"

"As I recall, we had gathered before the Hero's Reward and called out Mayor Uhl—"

"The situation quickly turned on us, and we had to flee the town," said Bars.

"Well," argued Derst. "That was hardly my fault."

"Your plan."

"Well, if you'd remembered the horses—"

"You distinctly said: 'leave the horses behind. We'll be back for them later.' "

"No fair pointing fingers," argued Derst. "But since we're on the subject, if you hadn't exposed our identities—"

"If you hadn't slept with Uhl's maid Emmi, we wouldn't have had to hide our identities."

A smile crossed Derst's face. "Ah, Emmi," the roguish knight said silkily. "Bars, you know I can't resist a pretty smile and a well-rounded ankle—"

"I suppose you didn't notice her chest," murmured Bars.

"Well, a little," he admitted. "It was hard not to, with a bodice like—"

At precisely that moment the Lord Singer swept out from the double doors that marked the entrance to his manor. He stood upon the raised entryway overlooking the crowd in his golden robe of office, carrying his fine yarting under his arm. To all appearances, Greyt looked as though he had been up all night and might be heading out to a dinner party. Bars and Derst knew better, though. Greyt's eyes gave him away: red-rimmed and containing a hint of savage anger. The eyes of a tired man on edge.

"My neighbors and friends," Greyt said in his smooth baritone. "To what do I owe the honor and pleasure of this visit?"

At his tone, the crowd quieted, except for a few discordant

shouts. Derst swore. Greyt's disarming manner had just that effect: disarming.

One man, however, was not so affected. Black cloaked, he stood tall in the middle of the crowd and spoke in a rumble.

"Lord Singer," he called. "We demand justice."

"Sounds like you, Bars," said Derst. "Always straight to the point."

The paladin did not reply.

"By all means," Greyt called back with a smile. "I didn't think you'd all risen early to bid me a good morning."

There were a few scattered laughs.

"Really? That's exactly the reason I'm here," murmured Derst.

"Derst, that wasn't funny," Bars muttered in reply.

"In Speaker Stonar's absence," the cloaked man continued. "You are our defender and our lord. We demand protection. The fighting on the streets must cease, and your soldiers—"

"I find that demand ironic," Greyt shouted back. The crowd was stunned to silence. "Especially coming from you, who are supposed to keep the peace, Captain Unddreth."

A collective gasp ran through the crowd as the earth genasi pulled back his hood. The scars and bruises of battle still decorated his face and, if anything, added intensity to his words.

"Your men spent all night searching for some stranger, swords drawn, injuring or frightening the townsfolk," Unddreth accused. "This cannot stand!"

"A 'stranger?' Walker is a murderer who has been attacking our people for days!" Greyt corrected. "Many men are already dead and you insist I call my rangers back—you demand I leave our lands unprotected? I do what I must to stop this killer—for the watch has found nothing but failure." Unddreth shivered at the barb. "You protest my methods?"

"Speaker Stonar would have—" Unddreth began.

"Speaker Stonar left us in our time of need!" Greyt

interrupted. "He refused to protect us, either because he would not or could not. He fled to our noble High Lady Alustriel when his countrymen cried out for aid! I can only hope she sees his cowardice or discovers his culpability."

Confused frowns answered from the crowd and Greyt chuckled.

"Guilt," he clarified, and the people cheered.

"A bid to rule Quaervarr?" Derst asked skeptically. "That's not like—"

"I know," returned Bars. Anger coursed through him. He hated politics and its machinations, but he understood the game. Greyt played the crowd like a yarting. "Not like the Greyt we know. He hates this city."

Greyt waited until the cheering died down. "I cannot believe, however, that Stonar is behind this," he shouted. "He is a good and just man, with nothing but noble intentions. I refuse to believe he is anything but ignorant—an unwitting piece of the puzzle."

Derst and Bars shook their heads. Not a power struggle, then.

"I believe the killer is acting on his own," Greyt said, "A lone villain murdering our people!"

"He is no villain!" Unddreth shouted, but his words were lost in the hubbub of frenzied shouting.

"Stonar must be told!" came a shout from the crowd. "Cast a sending to Silverymoon right away and bring him, along with a unit of the Argent Legion—"

"Impossible," came a voice that should have been too soft to penetrate the noise of the crowd but projected loudly all the same. At the sound of that voice, the crowd parted around a cloaked figure. Bars and Derst looked and saw a shapely half-elf woman in a leather cloak, flowers laced through her shockingly light hair and feathers adorning the end of a gnarled staff she carried. Though the morning was chill, she wore only a light leather tunic and leggings. Her face, flushed in the cold, was young and smooth, but her eyes were both knowing and wise.

Bars was at a loss for words. "Who is yon lady?" he asked Derst.

"Now that's a woman," the knight replied. "The Lady Druid Amra Clearwater, of the Oak House. Powerful, skilled, and an excellent tumble between the sheets." The paladin gave him a sidelong, warning look. Derst cleared his throat. "I mean, so I've heard."

The beautiful half-elf continued in a light voice. "Some barrier thwarts our spells, as though a dark moon rises over Quaervarr and shrouds our sight," she said.

"A magical barrier?" asked Greyt. "Then our enemy is more powerful than I thought!"

Cheers mingled with gasps of horror. The crowd fixed its eyes on the Lord Singer. The roguish knight and the paladin looked at one another, utterly confused. What could Greyt be thinking? Did he want to start a panic?

Silence, tense and fearful, gripped the square.

Greyt grinned. "Fear not, though, for the danger has passed," he said. "Thanks to my efforts, the killer is in our hands and we shall question him to find—"

"He escaped!" Bars shouted, cupping his hands around his mouth. "The killer escaped!"

"Dolt," Derst cursed under his breath, turning his head so as not to be recognized.

❧   ❧   ❧   ❧   ❧

Greyt swore inwardly, angry at this news. He had no doubt it was true. He had ordered his men to take Walker alive or dead but at all costs to take him. Incompetence and failure vied for his greatest frustration.

He moved to rub his gold ring, but found he had taken it off. Around his finger was a shallow indentation, reminding him of the first ring he had worn there, the ring that had inspired his seal.

His mind snapped back to the situation at hand. Walker's escape snarled Greyt's carefully laid plans. He was momentarily unsure how to proceed. His criticism of the watch would not carry the same weight if his own men could not capture Walker. And, loose, the murderer could talk to Unddreth, Amra, or even Stonar himself, and all would be lost.

Then the solution presented itself. The Lord Singer's quick mind found a way to approach this news that simply delayed his plans and, perhaps, even strengthened them.

"A testament to the power arrayed against us. Surrounded by attackers, cut off from the Marches . . . For all we know, there could be a war brewing just outside our borders!"

The crowd gaped.

"Save us, Lord Singer!" came a shout, a call that was quickly picked up throughout the crowd. Shouts of his nickname, "Quickfinger," and praises of his heroism reverberated around the square. "Save us!"

Greyt smiled and bowed. "The killer was in my hands, but he escaped. He will not escape again." He drew his rapier in a flourish and held it above his head. "Thirty years ago, I took up this sword against the giants of Fierce Eye, when the Raven Claw band was first formed. Know this now and know it true: mine every breath shall shield you!"

As he sang the last few words, rhyming poorly, but it did not matter with such simpletons, Greyt seemed to grow: a trick he managed by standing up straight, where he had formerly bent his knees. A bit of bardic magic set his sword blazing with fire and illumined his face. The crowd was in awe.

Time for the final touch.

"I promise you, people of Quaervarr: as I was your hero then, so am I your hero now!"

With that, he released the illusory fire and the blade seemed to explode in flames, sending sparks flying over the crowd. These vanished before they struck flesh or clothing, and the people gaped in astonishment. They burst into cheers and shouts, calling for Lord Dharan "Quickfinger" Greyt, the hero of Quaervarr. The Lord Singer basked in the adulation and praise, his heart rushing despite himself.

Ah, the thrill of heroism ... how he had missed it!

"Send out riders!" came a call above the crowd, and the thrill died like a snuffed candle flame.

"What?" Greyt mouthed, looking over the suddenly silent crowd.

"Send out riders," Amra Clearwater called again. "Speaker Stonar must be informed."

"My lady, really," Greyt said as all eyes turned to him. He halted himself, thinking quickly, for the half-elf druid was widely respected and even feared for the powers of Silvanus she commanded. "We cannot simply go running for help every time—"

"But Geth does not know," argued Amra. "Let us assuage his ignorance—give him the chance to do his duty. Let him help!"

Greyt swore inwardly, trapped by his own words, but he saw a way out, one that could turn this to his advantage.

"A rider then." Greyt said. "But the Moonwood is dangerous—it is too easy for one of our own to be lost and slain!"

That elicited a gasp of horror from the crowd, but he waved them to silence.

Greyt smiled. "One who knows the land and its powers. One of your druids perhaps, Lady?"

All eyes turned to Amra, and the half-elf frowned. Greyt knew she could not refuse, not after she had challenged Quaervarr's hero so openly.

"Fine," said Amra with clear hesitation. "I shall send one of my own."

"Excellent," Greyt shouted with a flourish of his hands. The threat past, he grinned. "Now, for the rest of you: go back to your homes and rest your heads, safe in your beds. Your hero protects you all, great and small."

If the cheers had been loud before, they erupted like a volcano now. Hundreds of eyes stared at Greyt in sheer adoration and absolute faith. He was their hero, their master, their shining knight, and he was fully in control of this situation.

Secure in his role, Greyt gave them one more smile, waved, and went back inside his manor to the cheers and shouts of devoted friends.

❧ ❧ ❧ ❧ ❧

Meris was waiting for him inside the entry hall. "Overdone," said the wild scout.

"Perhaps," allowed the Lord Singer. "It matters little when dealing with the sort of fools who make up frontier towns such as Quaervarr." He beckoned Meris with a wave and began walking toward his bedroom. "Walker escaped?"

"Yes."

"This upsets my plans," said Greyt. "But not irreparably. The trap failed?"

"Walker is formidable, but we had him. He only escaped with help."

"Who?" Greyt asked, though he had already guessed the answer.

"My cousin and her paramours," Meris spat. "She burst in and rescued him. Then her wretched lads covered their escape."

Greyt sighed. "Ah, Niece, Niece, you disappoint me. So obvious, so unsubtle, so . . . like a knight." He paused at the door to his bedroom. "I have a task for you, boy."

"I can hunt them both down tonight," offered Meris in a harsh whisper. "I need only half a dozen men—"

"No. Another task." Meris furrowed his brows in confusion and Greyt suppressed a smile. "That whore Clearwater is sending one of her lapdogs to warn Stonar of all this. The last thing we need now is our beloved Speaker returning at the head of an Argent Legion. Everything would come undone. Send your rangers into the woods—"

"Consider it done," said Meris. "I'll take care of it personally."

As soon as he realized it was still open, Greyt closed his mouth and regarded his son. That had been too easy, Meris's agreement too fast. Greyt searched the young wild scout's features, but the dusky face was unreadable. Neither could the Lord Singer read Meris's body language—except for the single hand on the sword hilt that spoke volumes.

"Yes," Greyt said, very softly. "And I promise, when you return, Walker and Arya will be yours. Just ... do not delay. Silverymoon isn't a day away." The rhyme held none of its luster, and was a death sentence coming from the Lord Singer's lips.

Meris smiled but did not speak. With a curt nod, he turned and padded away.

Greyt watched him go. So Arya's tale had been true: Silverymoon was searching for lost couriers, and Meris was involved somehow. The Lord Singer wondered how this could have escaped his notice. This was a surprise, and nothing pleased Dharan Greyt less than surprises when he was not the one behind the mystery.

Greyt might have asked aloud, but he knew Talthaliel was already weighing this, having read Greyt's thoughts faster than the Lord Singer could have articulated them.

With a derisive whistle, Greyt decided to let the diviner puzzle over this dilemma. He had more important things to do, the first of which was keeping an appointment with his bed.

Greyt opened the door and stopped short in surprise. The woman sitting on his bed was facing away from him, her features shrouded in darkness, but he would recognize that silhouette anywhere.

"I did not expect to see you here," he said coolly.

"I did not think you would," said Lyetha. "I have not been in this room for many winters."

She shifted. She wore nothing beneath the white silk robe wrapped around her delicate curves. She looked so beautiful in the moonlight that Greyt's breath caught. Though he had known her over thirty years, the half-elf did not seem to have aged more than a decade. She still possessed the same youthful vibrancy that had first attracted him.

"It was not always that way," said Greyt. He slid down onto the bed next to her. "There was a time when you called this room your own." He extended his arm around her, and Lyetha did not recoil from his touch. Rather, she leaned her head against his shoulder. "I remember when first we—"

"So you will be a hero again," whispered Lyetha in a soft, hopeless voice.

Greyt blinked. The sweet honey of her voice was filled with bitterness. Lyetha spoke of great things for her husband, but the way she said it turned all the praise to worthless, crumbling ash.

"I have always been a hero," Greyt said with a little smile, an attempt at cheer. "You should know that, beloved." He had not even meant to say the last word, but he found, deep inside, that it was not a lie.

For the first time, Lyetha looked at him, and he saw her azure eyes gleaming into his own. She was as beautiful as he had ever seen her. Her ruby lips parted slightly and she smiled at him. She ran a silky hand down his cheek.

"It is not long until dawn," the half-elf woman said. "The moonshadows grow longest in this dark time."

"Yes." Greyt smiled. He remembered those words, the words she had spoken to him that first time they had awakened together.

He bent in and kissed her. After a long moment, she returned the kiss, releasing her robe and holding his face with both hands.

❧ ❧ ❧ ❧ ❧

Later they lay in each other's arms in silence and watched the sunrise out Greyt's window, rising somewhere past the Moonwood.

"Love," whispered Greyt.

Lyetha did not respond, but he could tell by her breathing she was listening.

"I know I am a hero in their eyes, the people of Quaer-varr, but I care nothing for what they think." His voice wavered, but he ignored his own misgivings. "I only care what you think."

Lyetha met his eyes. "You have been very good to me, my love," she said, touching his cheek.

For a moment, Greyt could see the old fire in her sapphire eyes, and his heart felt so light.

Then she sat up and pulled her robe around her shoulders. "But you have never been a hero, and I fear you never will be," she finished.

His eyes widened and softened. She could not have stung him more with a knife.

Then she stood and walked silently away, leaving the Lord Singer to greet the morning with damp eyes.

CHAPTER 12

29 Tarsakh

She woke from a dream where a hauntingly beautiful melody surrounded her, bathing her in its dark warmth, like a lover draped in a black cloak....

Awareness returned to Arya gently as she relaxed in the grove, bathing in the warm dawn sunlight that pierced the clouds overhead. The grass was softer than any bed she had ever known. The breeze was cool and soothing and, despite the winter, the air felt almost warm. She was dimly aware that her armor sat stacked a couple paces to her right. Clad in the light garments she wore beneath, she stretched languidly.

It was only when she rolled over onto her side that Arya remembered where she was and how she had come there. She saw that Walker lay limply on his back a short distance away. His cloak pooled around him like blood and the black of his heavy collar made the exposed half of his face seem a skull.

"Torm's shield," Arya breathed. She pushed herself to her knees and crawled over to Walker. Her limbs were surprisingly sore, and she took quite some time to make it those few steps.

"Walker?" she asked. She unlaced his collar so that he could breathe and saw his face for the first time. His handsome elf-touched features were pale and clammy, and his limbs were stiff. She slapped his cheeks and listened at his lips, but there was no breath. Neither could she feel his heart beating within his chest. "Walker!"

Arya tore open the leaf-shaped clasp of his cloak and pulled the dark leather apart. He wore a much-patched cuirass of boiled leather under the cloak and she immediately unlaced the clasp at his shoulder. Her dexterous fingers, used to working with armor ties, had it free in moments, and she ripped it off to give him space to breathe. She was almost surprised to find that his face was not scarred.

Walker's chest, muscular and pale, was another matter. Upon his skin lay a network of crisscrossing scars from countless wounds, some minor, some serious. Standing out against his bone-white skin, four wounds in particular caught her eye. Two seemed half-healed: a shallow cut on his chest where his ribs had been crushed and a devastating scar on his upper chest, near his throat. There were two others—a gash on his shoulder and a puncture in his left arm—that were closed and seemed to be healing. The scar below his throat was the worst, a sort of wound Arya had never seen a man live through.

At first she thought the wounds had been inflicted the night before, but she did not recall seeing Walker stabbed. No, they must be old injuries. Why they still looked fresh, refusing to scar, she did not know.

Then she snapped back to reality. Arya had been around dead bodies in her time, and nothing distinguished Walker's body from a corpse.

Had Walker made it to the grove alive only to die in the night? Arya remembered nothing beyond the ghostfire elemental's attack. Had she fought so hard to save Walker only to fail now? Had she lost him before she could figure out the key to this whole mystery?

Tears leaking down her cheeks, Arya knelt beside Walker and pleaded with him to wake, open his eyes, and rise up.

Then, to her surprise, he did.

Walker's eyes flickered open and he looked up at her in confusion.

"What is the matter?" he asked matter-of-factly, though worry flashed through his eyes.

Blinking with wonder, Arya thought her senses had deceived her. "Walker?"

"Of course," said the ghostwalker. "What is wrong?" He sat up with startling smoothness of movement, looking around for attackers, and Arya stumbled back, stunned.

"N-no," she stammered. "I-I just thought you were . . . you were. . . ."

"Dead," finished Walker, his voice a dry rasp. He made no move to replace his leathers. She noticed he rubbed at his silver ring, as though reassuring himself.

"Yes," whispered Arya. Remembering the tears on her cheeks, she wiped them away with an embarrassed jerk.

If Walker had noticed the tears, he made no sign.

Rising, Walker drew his sword and stalked around the clearing, peering into the shadows cast by tree branches. It was a wide grove, surrounded on all sides by towering shadowtops and firs taller than any Arya had seen before. A stream ran through it, and a few boulders were scattered around in piles. A doe and her two young stood on the other side of the grove, drinking at a small pool, paying no attention as Walker made his way within an arm's length of them, though he paid them scrupulous attention.

Alone for the moment, and without worry gripping her, Arya felt surrounded by the deepest feeling of peace she had ever known, as though this grove were a font of the primeval nature that had given birth to humankind and all races of Faerûn. She had heard rangers and druids speak of the tranquility of the natural world, but she had never felt it herself. Everything seemed right, in balance ... all except for the shadowy man walking toward her.

"What is it?" asked Arya, surprised at how calm her voice sounded. "What were you looking for?"

"No one," answered Walker, sitting down cross-legged before her.

It was not until he fixed her with his sapphire gaze that she realized he had not answered her question as she had asked it, but by then it did not matter.

The two sat and stared at one another, neither speaking.

Arya was not sure why, but she felt more comfortable around this man who looked so forbidding than she felt around her friends. She was peripherally aware of his cold aura, but she saw through it. In the light, his eyes shone blue and his hair was a dirty blond. His ears were slightly pointed, though not as pointed as a half-elf's. This man definitely had elf blood in his family line—perhaps even a parent who was a half-elf.

"Why have you brought me here?" she asked, without really meaning to speak.

"I do not know," said Walker.

"You don't know or you can't tell me?"

"Either," came the soft response. Walker reached for the cloak discarded at his side.

Arya caught his hand and his eyes shot to hers. She shook her head. "It's all right." She motioned to his scars. "They don't frighten me."

Walker seemed assuaged by this, but he still hesitated before he sat back, no cloak in hand. Arya had watched an inner conflict take place, she knew, but whether it was over his cloak or her hand on his wrist, she did not know.

She smiled. "You haven't been around many women before, have you?"

For just an instant, the thick aura of resolve slipped from around Walker and she caught the hint of an ironic smile.

It might have been the first real show of emotion she had perceived in him.

"No," he said. "I apologize if I seem ... distant."

"No," said Arya. "No need." She put out her hand to take his again, but he pulled it out of reach. At first she felt hurt, but then she saw the pain in his eyes.

"What's wrong?"

"Until I met you," whispered Walker. "No one had ever touched me without violence."

A wave of sadness washed over her. "No one?" she asked. "Not even your mother?"

Walker's face became stony. "I have no mother," he said. "No father." His eyes closed. "My life began fifteen years ago. The day I was murdered by Dharan Greyt." His face twisted in awful hatred for a breath, then smoothed again.

Arya sat in stunned silence.

"I wield powers beyond your world. You cannot under-stand." He opened his eyes and looked at her. "Having never died, that is."

"How do you know a priest has never raised me from the grave?" asked Arya with a raised eyebrow and a tiny smile.

"The same way you know I have not known many women," said Walker. "I can tell by looking at you."

Arya conceded the point. "If not parents, then who taught you these powers?"

"My teacher is not as important as her teachings. I feel the pulse of the earth, the power in every leaf, rock, and tree. It is not the vibrant life, but the opposite, the spiritual energy of the dead. You cannot see the spirits around you, but they are there. I see them at all times—even now, in this very grove, all around us. Dozens."

"The souls of the dead? Ghosts?" Arya's face went pale as she looked around the grove in vain. She could see nothing but the forest—even the doe and her fawns had bounded away.

"Not ghosts," explained Walker. His voice sounded almost

clear. "The departed are not fully departed. They wait for something to be resolved—unfinished business. Just as I have unfinished business with Dharan Greyt."

The comparison sent a chill through Arya.

The noon sky darkened as the clouds that had merely been lurking before asserted their presence over the sun.

"Rarely, I find wraiths, specters, haunts—all things men call the undead," Walker continued. "These are not the same spirits that surround us, but dead people, fully formed in spirit. They grow jealous of the living and malevolent. These spirits avoid such as I, for they have no new secrets to tell, no new horrors to show us that we do not know. But the other spirits—they are always there."

Arya shivered. "And these monsters . . . surround us all the time?"

Walker's eyes flicked back to her and he shook his head. "They are not monsters. The spirits that surround us—spirits most cannot see, even with magic—are mere figments of departed souls. They are tiny echoes of those who have lived, loved, hated, and died. They exist so long as someone lives to remember them, so long as someone listens to their whispers, and so long as someone looks for them." He smiled wistfully. "As I do."

Arya's heart fluttered at that smile. Describing the mysterious spirits as though they were his children, Walker seemed almost happy. She felt her body grow warm all over.

Hardly aware that she was doing it until she had done it, she reached out and placed her hands over Walker's ears, pulled his face to hers, and pressed their lips together.

At first, Walker sat in stunned shock, then the kiss took on a mind of its own.

Then he seemed to remember himself and pushed her away. Arya fell back onto the ground and gasped, finally aware of what she had done. Her cheeks flooding with heat, she grinned sheepishly and stammered an apology.

"I'm-I'm sorry, I didn't—"

He wrapped strong arms around her and pressed his

lips against hers, and she lost herself in that embrace. For a sweet moment, as he held her, she felt safe and secure for possibly the first time in her life.

And for just one thrilling moment, she felt exactly where she was meant to be.

As though realizing what he was doing, he broke the kiss and scrambled away. She sat there for a breath, held in the lingering sensation of his lips, before her senses returned.

"What's the matter?" she asked.

"No," said Walker. "I cannot."

Arya sat back, weighing him with her eyes. Walker made no move, except to look away into the darkening sky. His words had been simple, short, and seemingly empty, but expressed a pain that tore at her heart.

"Will you do something for me?"

"Perhaps," replied Walker.

"Sing."

❧ ❧ ❧ ❧ ❧

The druid courier paused on her mare, furrowing her brow.

There was nothing unusual about the road, at least nothing she could see. The sun was shining and a stream trickled water down a side path. The wind was not overly cold today—it was, perhaps, the first warm spell Quaervarr had known in a long time.

"No worries, girl," Peletara said to her mount in the druidic tongue. "Just thought I heard something, that's all."

The chestnut mare snorted.

A crossbow bolt flew out of the boughs of a tree farther up the road, driving into one of the horse's eyes. The mare, killed instantly, fell, trapping the startled druid beneath her. The huge weight fell on her leg, snapping it, and Peletara gasped in pain. She looked all around for her attacker, struggling to draw her sickle.

A black boot stepped on her hand.

She looked up, following the length of black breeches to

a mottled green and gray cloak that had, until just then, blended in perfectly with the trees.

Peletara recognized him.

"Lord..." she said. "Lord Meris?"

He smiled. Even as his sword scraped out of its scabbard, the attacker bent down and traced a finger down her cheek.

The touch of death.

❧ ❧ ❧ ❧ ❧

Walker stiffened, as though something had gouged him. Arya reached out, but he shook his head.

With a troubled look, Walker turned to her.

"What?"

"Sing for me," she repeated.

Walker hesitated. Then he shook his head. "My song was ended," he said. "Fifteen years ago."

When he was distracted, Arya kissed him. She pressed her lips against his cold mouth, kissing him gently at first, then in passion and hunger. She could feel the heat that lurked beneath his icy lips, felt it begging for release.

She pulled back, staring into his eyes, and placed her hand on his cheek. "I want to hear the song they tried to end."

Then she was away from him again. He had pushed her back. "I cannot," he said. His voice was sad. "Not now. Not ever."

"But Walker..." Arya said.

Then, as though helpless to reply, he began to sing. Voice broken, song discordant and ragged, still there flowed a certain beauty through its shape, in the rise and swell of his music. Arya heard, rather than saw, the man he might have been, a golden god who had once sung in these woods but now walked in darkness.

After a moment, she became aware there were words to his song, words that flowed and ebbed with a melodious disharmony that was inexplicably balanced. They were in Elvish, and she did not understand them on a conscious level; the words cut to her soul.

There was pain, hatred, and vengeance. Walker sang of his death, sending images into Arya's heart that sent chills through her body. Without realizing it, she reached out to take his hand, as though to comfort him.

He ripped his hand out of her grasp so quickly the silver ring came off in her hand, but he did not notice in the singing, and she did not notice in the listening.

She found herself wrapped in the melody of his voice. Torn and shattered, leaping between notes no bard would play together, and perfect. The haunting melody enfolded her like a cool, dark blanket, and she felt her senses floating free of her body.

Walker's voice trailed off, but Arya, lost in his art, hardly realized it. Her heart was throbbing and breaking all at once. It was simultaneously the most blissful romance she had ever heard and the saddest tragedy she could have imagined.

When she finally looked up, she perceived, through tear-blurred eyes, that he was staring at her.

"Is that not ugly?" he asked. He had misinterpreted her.

"Walker—" she started.

"I am lost to you, Arya," Walker said, interrupting her. "All that remains is my task, and when it is done. . . ." He trailed off, and the silence was palpable.

Bitter emptiness welled within her. "Walker," she said. "That's not your name, is it? What is it, your name, so that I can—"

With a frustrated growl, Walker slammed his fist into the ground, and though she could hear bones crack, he did not seem to care. Then he coughed so violently Arya wanted to cover her ears. Blood came up—the legacy of ancient wounds. Arya touched his hand in concern, closing her fingers around his. If Walker noticed, he made no sign.

When he spoke, his voice was calm but sad. "I do not know," he said. "Where do these songs come from? I do not know. How do I remember them? I do not know. If I remembered my own name, would it still hold true? Would I still be . . . I . . . ." The last words were quiet, helpless.

He seemed on the verge of opening to her, as though....

Then nothing. He fell silent again.

Arya felt frustration well within her, along with deep sympathy. How long had this tortured man existed in this state? He could not open himself, could not confront the demons of his past, the feelings of his present, or his fears of the future. Whenever he tried, whenever he came close, he would cough violently as though to tear himself in two. Sometime in his past, Walker had forgotten how to feel. He was a man without fear, hope, or love.

But no, that was not it.

Her heart denied that. It told her he couldn't open up, not because he had forgotten, but because he could not face what would come.

Trusting her feelings, Arya reached out and took his hand.

Walker pulled away.

"Walker," Arya said. She leaned in again, but he pushed her back, gentle but firm. He pulled his gloved hand from her grasp.

"Do not do that again," he rasped, menace—and pain—dripping from his broken voice.

❧ ❧ ❧ ❧ ❧

Somewhere in the trees above them, a pair of phantom lips smiled.

"Yes," said the feminine voice.

Having said that satisfied word, the face became that of thrush. The bird beat its wings once and was gone.

❧ ❧ ❧ ❧ ❧

Arya turned away, and he could see her shoulders shaking, whether because of fear or relief he did not know.

There. He had done it.

Walker had just reinforced everything his training had

taught him. Everything Gylther'yel had hammered into him about being alone, everything he had learned about the dangers of bringing others into his violent life, everything he had thought in these last fifteen years was coming true once again.

He would not, could not share his bleak, bloody, and short existence with anyone. No friends. No lovers. No family.

He was the spirit of vengeance, meant to walk alone.

He thought he caught a glimpse of Tarm Thardeyn out of the corner of his eye, but the spirit was not there when he looked. A wave of sadness came over Walker, but he let it pass through him, leaving him empty.

Now that he had done it, how did he feel?

He should have felt nothing. All his experience told him he should feel nothing but ice inside, project nothing but cold outside, and take comfort in his retreat from the world of the living. The dead understood and never judged. The spirits that surrounded Walker would never turn away in fear.

But that was not the way he felt. Instead, he felt ... he ...

He did not know, and that was what frustrated him.

"You should go," he said, as much to stop his thoughts as to break the silence. "I am ..." Then nothing, not even the word he had meant to say, which was "sorry." He wanted to say more—about his fears, his quest, anything more—but the words would not come. He had forgotten how to speak them, he thought.

But all the while, he knew he had not.

Some tiny voice deep in his frozen heart, a voice he had kept hushed for so many years, was trying to tell him how. And he knew. He understood. He was just ...

"Afraid," he breathed.

Arya had risen as though to leave, but she turned back. "What?" she asked, her voice a shade above a whisper.

Instantly, Walker was silent, but he had already said the word, and it had been enough.

Arya saw then, as through a tiny crack in his stone will. She saw Walker with his defenses down, terrified, empty, hollow . . .

And alone.

"It is nothing," he said.

Arya heard the pain in his voice—not so much in his words, for they were few, but in how he spoke them. He was struggling with himself. Walker had been forced to face death, the hellish cry of vengeance, and fear of himself, and he had done it all alone.

Arya made a decision then, a decision that would steer the course of her life until her last breath. She gathered the courage to look into his blue eyes. She suddenly became aware of a small object in her hand—a silver ring. His one-eyed wolf ring. Arya gently took his left hand and began drawing off his glove.

❖ ❖ ❖ ❖ ❖

"What are you. . .?" asked Walker.

As she bared his flesh, though, his thoughts leaped to his abhorred power to sense spiritual resonance, insights that would steal images from her thoughts and cloud his vision. He did not want that emotional turmoil—he did not want to lose himself when Arya was there, her beautiful face before his.

But she was touching his skin, and there was nothing. No resonance, no visions, no knowledge—only the warmth of her skin.

She pulled the glove entirely off, and with it went Walker's last line of defense, the barrier between him and the sword. Like the walls he had built around his heart, his gloves hid him behind a layer of black. And now she had stripped that defense away. She laced her fingers through his. So soft, so warm. . . .

"Arya—"

She held up his left hand—the wrong hand, but he hardly

noticed—and slipped the ring on to his fourth finger. She reached delicate fingers up to brush his cheek.

"Your song," she said, "was beautiful."

Some part of Walker—the fearful part—wanted to argue, scream, or turn away, but he could not. He merely sat, dumbfounded, as she caressed his cheek, then leaned her head against his bare chest.

Then it occurred to him. Though he had touched Arya's hands, kissed her lips, and hugged his arms around her waist, he had not felt any psychic resonance from her. No visions. No feelings. He simply felt what she felt. This unknown sensation would have had him collapse into tears just as soon as he'd have clasped the woman in his arms. It might have frightened him, this lack of resonance, as he had not imagined it possible, but he understood intuitively what it meant.

And that frightened him even as it set his body tingling.

"You cannot," he said. "Arya...I...I live for vengeance. It is my unfinished task. When this is over, I will have nothing else. I will die—whether in battle or in silence. There is nothing for you here; only darkness and a grave."

Arya gazed into his eyes, and he could see tears sliding down her cheeks. "I do not care," she said without trembling.

Walker was overcome with a new wave of feeling, which frightened even as it excited him. At first, he thought he had never felt the sensation before, but then he discovered that it was there, buried deep, beneath the ice and shrouded in the mists of his heart. It was warmth in his chest, a feeling of loving and being loved.

His eyes slid closed—eyes that were bleary from the moisture gathering there.

This time, when she leaned in to kiss him, pressing him down, he did not stop her.

CHAPTER 13

29 Tarsakh

W *andering child...*

Miles south of Quaervarr, Meris froze where he walked, sliding the kerchief along his blade. He extended his senses into the surrounding forest. The words might have been a figment of his imagination. He could hear nothing but the chirping of birds, the swaying branches, and...

Where have you wandered, Wayfarer?

Meris started in terror. He heard nothing, but there were the words, spoken in a mocking female voice in his mind!

Feeling his flesh tingle, Meris let the kerchief flutter to the ground and drew his hand axe. He whirled around, searching every shadow and treetop for the speaker.

"Who's there?" he shouted, brandishing his weapons. "Show yourself!"

Haunting laughter sounded in his head, so soft as to be barely present.

He sensed a presence behind him and whirled, letting fly his hand axe. The weapon cut into a fallen tree trunk.

A terrified squirrel, which had barely dodged the deadly missile, scampered out of sight.

Who do you fear, Meris Wayfarer, son of Greyt?

"What do you want from me?" Meris waved his sword in the air.

What do you want from me? came a reversal.

He could see no speaker, only the forbidding trees of the Dark Wood. The canopy seemed to have grown tighter, swallowing the sunlight overhead.

"Who are you?" Meris's voice was a shriek. "Who speaks?"

More soft laughter. *You know me, Wayfarer. You have always known me.*

Meris ran to the fallen trunk and recovered his axe. Without pausing to search the clearing again, he pumped his legs as fast as he could, running toward Quaervarr.

He hoped the whispers would not follow.

❧ ❧ ❧ ❧ ❧

The watchmen at the gates of Quaervarr were glad to see a spot of sunshine, particularly after the events of the last few days. So many folk were disappearing, victims of the Ghost Murderer, it seemed. Mostly heads of businesses, prominent leaders, and rich folk. It threw the town into chaos. This weather, however, seemed to carry hope. The watchmen relaxed and enjoyed the light and warmth of the coming spring.

Meris neglected his usual subtlety when he ran up to the gates. Though he had sheathed his weapons, the darkly clad figure running toward them jarred the guards, who crossed their spears to bar his path until they recognized the scout's face.

"My lord?" they asked as he shoved their weapons away and rushed into town.

Once he was inside, Meris calmed his breathing, but his heart still raced. He left the main street for an alley and shed his black clothes in favor of the white leathers he had placed in the alley beforehand. No one must see him in black—no one ever had. The watchmen were an exception he would have to take care of.

Clad in the fresh armor, he strode down the street to his father's manor.

Claudir tried to stop him at the door, but Meris shoved the thin servant away and stormed in. Without waiting for his name to be announced, he threw the doors to the ballroom open and approached the Lord Singer.

Greyt was dressed resplendently, as always, but his face was haggard and worn, as though he had slept little that night. The ballroom was as opulent as ever, but the statues and tapestries reflected Greyt—old and shabby. The Lord Singer had been musing about something when Meris came in, but he looked up immediately. His look was glowering, his eyes shot through with blood.

Never, in Meris's memory, had the old man looked so weak. A part of him wanted to ask what was wrong, perhaps in a show of familial friendship, but Meris despised his father in that moment, more than he ever had before. He held his tongue.

"To what do I owe the honor of this impertinence?" asked Greyt. His voice did not sound melodic at all. At his wave, Claudir, following Meris, left and shut the doors.

Meris trembled, but he pushed the memory of the ghostly whispers from his mind. "I come to report," he said. "The courier is dead, slain by a man in black—as is her horse, so even those cursed druids can't find out what happened. The woman was killed with a sword, as Walker uses."

"And if a priest thinks to conjure the dead?"

"The girl recognized me before she died, but I buried her head separately," replied Meris in distaste. "Let the corpse try speaking without a mouth."

"How about the others?" pressed Greyt.

Meris bristled. So his father had puzzled out his habit

of waylaying the couriers. No matter. "A man in black," he said. "Unidentified. I—you are quite safe."

The Lord Singer sat back in his chair, weighing Meris. "Good," he said shortly.

Meris might have thanked Greyt. Then he realized it had not been a compliment—or even directed at him—and sneered instead.

"Now, I want you to find and kill Walker," said Greyt. "Bring me back his head, and I will be the hero of Quaervarr—their savior."

Meris had to work hard to keep from laughing. Some "hero." He could not even take care of his own murders.

How pathetic Greyt seemed to him then, how frail. If Meris had wanted to, he could have walked up to Greyt and run him through, or crushed the Lord Singer's skull in his hands. What wards could he possibly have? He was not even wearing his rapier, flimsy weapon that it was.

Greyt narrowed his eyes. "Try it," he said.

"Try what?" asked Meris. Had the Lord Singer heard his thoughts?

"You want to kill me, then do it," said Greyt, rising. When Meris's eyes widened, the Lord Singer laughed. "Oh, don't be so surprised. The hatred is written on your face. You are as easy to read as the simpletons who live in this town."

Bristling at the insult, Meris reached down and grasped the hilt of his long sword. He did not draw, though, for the tiny fear had returned; the fear that Greyt was hiding something, some defense that Meris could not perceive.

"Come on, draw," Greyt egged his son on. "You think me old, weak, frail ... what was it? Pathetic. And that's what I am, a pathetic old man, unarmed." He spread his arms wide. "Draw, and run me through."

"What trickery is this?" Meris hissed.

Greyt ignored him. "Draw your sword, boy," he commanded. "Run me through. I have no defense." He stepped within Meris's sword reach. "Kill me. Or are you afraid?"

"Afraid?" asked Meris. "Afraid of a pathetic old man?"

"Afraid of a hero!" asked Greyt, his eyes shining. "Afraid of killing a hero, afraid of facing a town of vengeful woodsmen, women, and children?"

"I fear no ..." Meris trailed off. The words would make no difference, for his father was mad. He knew it then, knew it beyond doubt. Instead, Meris set his jaw and said nothing, though he kept his hand on his sword.

"Then draw," Greyt said, his voice low and biting. "Attack."

Meris did nothing but fight to control his trembling hand.

"Attack, coward!" ordered Greyt. "You are my dog! I order you to attack!"

Meris stared at him. Greyt had never been this abusive, had never badgered him like this. He knew that Greyt was his father, his own flesh and blood, but ... He did not know what to do.

"Attack!" shouted Greyt.

When Meris said nothing, the Lord Singer slapped him hard across the face. The scout looked back, his eyes furious, and Greyt laughed.

Meris felt his mouth drawing up into a sneer. The screaming creature before him was no longer a man to be respected, admired, or even feared—instead, he was merely a weak fool like the other villagers of Quaervarr. Only a tiny voice in the depths of Meris's heart protested that this man was his father.

"Attack, bastard!" Greyt screamed, spitting in Meris's face.

That one word—a title Meris had always worn without any show of emotion, a name that spoke of obdurate bitterness and a gulf between them that could not be crossed—cut him deeply, down to whatever he had left of a soul, and forever silenced that tiny voice. Here was the one man—the one being—he had ever felt any connection to, and to hear that damning word. ...

"Attack!"

Meris almost did. But even as he sent the command to his arm to draw the sword, he felt that haunting fear in the back of his mind and all his anger become terror. He flinched away, averting his eyes, unwilling to let the Lord Singer see him afraid.

Greyt chuckled. "As I thought," he said, turning. "You disgust me, coward." He walked back to his throne and sat, draping his gold-laced cape across the arm.

Meris paused at the door and looked back. His gaze held nothing but hatred. Then Meris turned on his heel and walked out without a backward glance.

❧ ❧ ❧ ❧ ❧

The Lord Singer waited a moment after the doors shut behind Meris then he raised his hand in a particular signal. Talthaliel stepped out of the air at Greyt's shoulder.

"That was unwise," observed the elf seer. "What if he had done it?"

"You were there, weren't you?" the Lord Singer asked irritably. "I was never in any danger. Besides, your vision said he won't defeat you."

"What if I err?"

"Have you ever erred?"

Talthaliel nodded, conceding the point. Greyt's face was calm but his eyes were furious.

"Still, I advise caution," the elf continued. "Words spoken in haste and without calculation lead to mistakes. The Spirit and the Nightingale are no threat. But send the Wayfarer after them and—"

"Silence," snapped the Lord Singer without looking at Talthaliel.

"But—"

The man swung around and slammed a fist into the diviner's jaw. Talthaliel, startled, toppled to the floor. The Lord Singer stood over him, took the amber amulet out of his tunic, and dangled it in the air.

Talthaliel did not move.

His anger spent, Greyt returned the amulet to the inside of his tunic and stepped off Talthaliel. The elf seer didn't make a sound as he climbed to his feet.

"Now, are you maintaining the barrier to magical

communication?" asked Greyt.

"Yes ... *Lord*." The word came hesitantly.

"Have you learned anything new of Walker or his protector?"

"Nothing, lord."

"Why do I keep you? A seer who never sees anything I need!" Greyt fumed.

"My sight is keen at times," the diviner said. He did not mean to continue, but the words came out before he could stop them. Emotion was so rare that it startled him. "Even if your son did not see it, I saw what truly passed between you in those moments."

Greyt's eyebrows rose, though whether in surprise or fury was unclear.

The elf hesitated, but the Lord Singer glowered at him. Anger, then.

"Speak, seer," he muttered, pulling at the chain around his neck.

"The balance of power is upset, Lord," Talthaliel said. Greyt pulled the amber amulet out again, but the diviner could not stop himself. "A time is coming when that balance will shift, and it will not be in your favor."

Greyt held the amber amulet in his open hand, but his hand twitched to crush it. He was trembling with barely restrained hate. "And?"

"I read the Wayfarer's heart," said Talthaliel. "His decision is made. As of now, he is your enemy. He could have loved you before, but he will never love you now."

Greyt's fist snapped around the amulet and Talthaliel's jaw closed with an audible clack. The two stared at one another for a long moment, their wills struggling across the short distance that separated them.

It was the Lord Singer who broke the silence first. His challenge was low and cold. "By all means, slave, keep speaking." His fist was closed tight around the amber gemstone, and Talthaliel could almost feel the hungry pressure of his fingers.

The diviner bowed, indicating that he had nothing to say.

"Well, if you're finished," said Greyt. He held the amber amulet up between them. "I suggest that if you want this gem to remain intact you still your impudent tongue and get out of my sight." He turned away.

"I only give counsel based upon what I see," Talthaliel reminded him. "You should listen. After all, you are the one, Lord Hero, who said I never err."

The Lord Singer whirled, gem in hand, ready to curse the diviner for his impertinence, but Talthaliel was nowhere to be seen.

The Lord Singer sighed, loud and long, and shuffled to his throne. He slumped down, threw his cape wide, and rested his chin on his left hand. The Greyt family wolf sparkled on his hand in the afternoon sunlight from the high windows. Sitting there brooding, Greyt seemed to have aged years in just the past day.

❧ ❧ ❧ ❧ ❧

A knock sounded at the door.

"Come," Greyt called absently.

The door opened, and a woman's face peered through. "Husband?" asked Lyetha in a tentative voice. "May I speak with you?"

Greyt did not look up, but he did wave slightly—it was an almost imperceptible movement. He was thinking, and she didn't even distract him.

Lyetha, dressed in a shimmering red gown, swept in. Her dark, mourning colors were gone and her hair, which had been simply pulled back and seemed dull brown before, was a gleaming, golden cascade down her back. Even her words had lost the cold formality they once had. She approached the throne with a spring her step had not known for over a decade. The change that had come over her the last few days was startling—it was as though she had gone back in time fifteen years.

Greyt hardly noticed. "What is it?" he asked, disinterested.

The half-elf stopped at the foot of the dais and paused, looking up at him. She had weighed matters in her head and in her heart, and now she hesitated to do what she had intended.

"I . . . I wanted to tell you something," she said.

"Yes?" He did not look at her.

Lyetha opened her mouth to speak, but closed it. Instead, she looked at Greyt's averted face, seeing the lines of fear, discomfort, and hate there. His gaze was far away. For a time, she thought perhaps he had changed, but she saw once again the bitter, cynical, cruel, and very old creature he had become.

"What is it?" he repeated, still not meeting her eyes.

Lyetha shifted her gaze away. " 'Tis . . . 'tis nothing," she said.

Greyt did not argue. He merely shrugged and blinked once.

Picking up her skirts, Lyetha went away, slowly at first, but her steps picked up speed until she was running. She could not let Greyt see the tears leaking down her cheeks.

She need not have bothered, for the Lord Singer did not even look up.

❧ ❧ ❧ ❧ ❧

Somewhere in the shadows, another pair of eyes watched.

"You could have saved him, Elf's Daughter," mused a spectral voice. The words were too quiet for Greyt to hear. "Just then, you could have saved him."

The Lord Singer shivered once, but he did not wonder why.

Sighing, Talthaliel closed his invisible eyes.

"And so it begins."

CHAPTER 14

29 Tarsakh

Still no sign of 'em, sir," Darthan reported. "Even the horse's trail has disappeared, as though ..."

He trailed off and bit his lip.

"As though what?" asked Meris, though he knew the answer.

"As-as though the f-forest swallowed it up!" the man stammered.

Meris swore despite himself. This damned "cursed forest" nonsense was giving him nothing but trouble. He resisted the urge to slap sense into the jittery Darthan.

"Keep pressing west," Meris said. "Deeper into the Dark Woods."

"D-Deeper?" Darthan swallowed.

"Forget this fanciful 'Ghostly Lady,' " he ordered. "The woods are probably 'haunted' because Walker makes them that way. Well, tonight we're going to undo his efforts."

"If we ever find him," a ranger said from the side. The comment was greeted with snickers and other less optimistic grumbles.

Meris was tempted to lash out at the speaker, but he had to agree.

He and his eight rangers had been searching the godsforsaken forest for most of the day, and it was near midnight. The stolen Quaervarr watchman's uniforms they wore were not as comfortable as woodland garb. The cloudy afternoon had become a dark night, albeit one with a bright moon. Unfortunately, because the canopy was packed so densely, little light shone down, and they were forced to carry lanterns to illuminate their path.

In the weak radiance of the lanternlight, every tree seemed to loom over them, stretching skeletal limbs to grasp at loose clothing and stragglers. The wood was black—in the case of the shadowtops, duskwood, and firs—or luminous white—in the case of some trees of a kind even Meris had not seen before. The men shied away from these mysterious white trees and Meris could not fault them. Low-growing helmthorn bushes sprouted everywhere, jabbing long spines into a ranger's flesh at every turn, prompting more than a few curses. Deep in that black and ghostly forest, the irritating shrub took on an even more sharp and sinister appearance in the mist that covered the ground. The forest brooded silently but for the occasional bird cry from trees directly overhead, causing rangers to jump and draw steel or point arrows at nothing.

If there were ever a haunted forest, Meris imagined it would feel like this.

Keeping his weapons ready, he took lead in the group, searching in vain for signs of tracks or, failing that, signs that they were not turning in circles.

Even now, they crept through another stand of shadowtops and cut at some especially thick patches of helmthorn. Meris watched the work grimly. All the while, his mind wandered elsewhere.

He was thinking about the dark-clad Walker—the man he had confronted three times but never really fought. Meris did not understand why his father feared Walker so much—the dark man did not seem so powerful or commanding in person, just crafty and treacherous. He was a coward, Meris decided, so afraid of the world around him that he hid behind a high collar and an assumed name, a dark face he thought would protect him.

Meris smiled. He wanted to be the one to cut that face off.

Distracted as he was, Meris failed to notice anything unusual about his two newest recruits—a thin weasel of a man and a hulking brute almost as large as Bilgren. They slouched in their cloaks, searching the misty ground for tracks. In fact, if Meris had paid any attention, he would have recognized the voices that traded soft repartee in the background.

"Did I ever tell you how I once walked to Mirabar from Everlund?" the small one asked. "It took three tendays of constant travel: no sleep, no water—"

"Shut up, mutton head, or my fist'll send you on another journey," the big one replied.

"Will you be there to keep me company on this new journey?"

"Of course not!" came the growling reply.

"Well, thank Tym—I mean, Beshaba." The short man sighed in relief. "I was worried I was cursed to spend eternity with the likes of you, Winebelly."

"And I with you, Leadthief."

Meris's lieutenant pushed back through the brush. "Silence, you two," Darthan snapped. "Haven't you heard of the word 'stealth?'"

"I've heard of it," the man called Winebelly replied.

"Then try it," Darthan growled. "And if it doesn't work, I'll be back, and it won't be a warning next time."

Winebelly glowered at Darthan's back as he went. Leadthief, on the other hand, laughed aloud and called after the ranger. "If Wine 'ere can sneak out of a maiden's bedroom afore her pa wakes up and gets the axe, he calls that 'stealth,' " the weasel man said.

"Leadthief, you ever heard of being knocked cold to the ground?"

"I've heard of it—"

Then a whisper cut them off. Forbidding light burst through the trees, dazzling the men. Blades fell from limp hands and the rangers threw themselves to the ground, shaking in terror. "What, by the Hells?" they asked.

Meris was the only one not bowing or cowering in terror. Meris stood tall and strong with his long sword and hand axe drawn. He spread his arms wide and bowed.

"Hail, Ghostly Lady."

❀ ❀ ❀ ❀ ❀

It was not until her eyes opened that Arya realized she had nodded into a warm, dreamless sleep. The sun had just set. Though she wore only a light undertunic and breeches, she was not cold. She sat up and looked around expecting to see Walker sitting some distance away in his usual cross-legged, meditative pose, but the clearing was empty save for a small cookfire over which two small animals roasted. Her auburn brows furrowed, but then she felt a soft hand brush her cheek. Strong arms wrapped around her.

A smile spread across her face. "How long have I slept?" she asked.

"Through the sunset," came Walker's reply. His voice was low and melodic, even as it was fragmented. She shifted in his arms, and he held her tighter.

"Have you been watching over me this whole time?"

"No," said Walker. Startled at his answer, Arya turned her eyes to his partially hidden face. He had buttoned his collar halfway up but not donned his cloak again. He gestured toward the cookfire. "Hunting as well."

The knight smiled and laughed. Heedless of how her garments clung to her slim frame, she sprang up and crossed to the cookfire. There roasted two wild rabbits. They were slightly blackened, but when she prodded one with her knife, rich juices flowed out and sizzled in the fire.

Arya realized she was famished. She removed the spit and carried it back to Walker, but the ghostwalker waved the meat away. Obliging him, she sat and bit into one of the rabbits. It was plain, not flavored, but it was the most succulent thing she had tasted in a long time, due in no small part to her growling stomach.

"I am not hungry," said Walker when Arya pressed.

"But you need food, do you not?"

Walker did not reply, but held up the hand with the silver wolf ring.

Arya shook her head. "I might have guessed," she said with a smile.

Neither rabbit was small, but she wolfed down both in short order. She was too hungry to stand on ceremony, but when she felt Walker's eyes watching her, she became self-conscious. With an embarrassed laugh, she finished the second rabbit and wiped her fingers in the soft grass.

Walker said nothing and Arya felt profoundly comfortable in the silence. His sapphire eyes burned, but he did not match words to his gaze. Could not.

At least, though, they had made progress.

She scooted closer to him, leaned in, and rested her head on his shoulder. Walker sat frozen for a moment, seemingly unsure how to approach the situation.

Then he put his arms around her, and the knight melted.

"Walker, can I tell you something?"

To her astonishment, his answer was not "perhaps." Instead, Walker said, "Yes."

She leaned back into his chest and encircled his arms with her own. She gulped, steadying herself.

"You've never felt this way before," she said. "I can see it in your eyes. You've never had someone to love."

Walker looked at her in confusion, but Arya knew it was not because she was wrong—it was because he was unfamiliar with the term. She felt a twinge of sadness, but tilted her head back and to the side, so that she could kiss his cool lips.

They needed no words.

❧ ❧ ❧ ❧ ❧

The semi-transparent image of a beautiful elf lady stood before him, dressed in a long gray gown that trailed away to nothing. She seemed to melt out of the mists, and indeed he saw little of her features distinctly except for her burning red-gold eyes. The ghostly face raised its eyebrows, but Meris saw that any surprise was feigned.

Meris made no move to sheathe his weapons, even though he knew they would be useless against this spectral apparition.

You are not afraid, the feminine voice said in his mind. It was obvious that the other rangers heard it as well, for they cringed and gasped.

"No."

Why? It seemed she was more amused than angered.

"How do you know me?" asked Meris.

That is not an answer, she replied.

"But it will suffice. Tell me how you know me, and I will tell you why I do not fear you."

The Ghostly Lady smiled, and it was a beautiful if unnerving expression. She drew mistlike fingers along Meris's cheek and he was surprised to feel a cold, physical touch. Stunning in the moonlight, her face had a smooth, hungry look to it that excited Meris's body in ways he had not imagined—even in the arms of the barmaids and hunters' daughters of his youth, even when he looked upon Arya's lovely form.

Then she laughed. "I do not need to answer your question, Meris Wayfarer," she said aloud, and he was surprised to hear her voice in his ears. "For the answer is written upon your heart: you do not fear me, because you fear nothing. You have overcome your last love and, with it, your last fear ..." She fixed his eyes with her own. "Your father."

In a flash of movement, Meris drove his long sword through the Ghostly Lady's heart.

A long breath passed between them. Then she looked down at where the weapon protruded. No blood oozed from her breast. It had passed through her like so much mist. In contact with her ghostly body, the blade became chill as ice, but Meris held it even as the cold burned his hand.

"Impressive," she said.

He held it as long as he could, gritting his teeth, but it was too much. With a gasp, Meris let go, and the sword stayed, borne aloft in her body. The elf smiled.

"You have great spirit, Meris Wayfarer." She slid away, and his sword fell to the ground, chilled. She seemed unhurt. "I am Gylther'yel, and I need your aid."

Meris's eyes narrowed. "My aid?" he asked as he rubbed his hand.

She nodded.

He looked down at his long sword, white with cold. "My sword?"

"Let it lie," replied Gylther'yel. "I will find you a greater, when you have accomplished your task for me."

"And that is?" A little smile tugged at the corners of Meris's mouth.

"Rats infest my woods. I want you to remove them."

❧ ❧ ❧ ❧ ❧

Arya and Walker sat together in the grove, bathed in moonlight, their eyes only for one another. The sun had set and moon had risen, but they hardly noticed, holding one another through the night, relaxing in blissful eternity. The grove lay peaceful around them and Selûne smiled down from high overhead.

· Arya hardly believed it. It had all happened so fast. She felt as though her entire world was to be found in Walker's arms. All seemed right.

All except. . . .

With a start, Arya remembered what had brought her to Quaervarr and the strict orders that demanded she return to Silverymoon with her news.

Without thinking, she broke free of Walker's arms and stood. She scanned around for her equipment, and finally found it beneath a tree on the edge of the clearing.

"What are you doing?" Walker asked, rising from where he had sat beside her.

"I have to go," Arya said. "I'm sorry, but I have to."

"No, you do not." Walker stepped to her side.

"I have to report Greyt's activities," argued the knight. "My findings, my suspicions . . . Grand Commander Alathar needs to send more knights to—"

"No more knights!" snapped Walker, so fiercely Arya whirled to look at him. She made to speak, but he collapsed to his knees, awful coughs racking his body. Arya reached out to comfort him, but he flinched away.

Finally, Walker looked up. "No more knights," he repeated.

"But—" Arya began.

"Fill the town with swords and Greyt will be untouchable. He will twist free of any hold your order puts on him, I promise you that." Walker's eyes burned. "Leave Greyt to me."

Arya noticed he had not said anything about Meris but she dismissed it. "Walker, I cannot allow you to—"

"Leave them to me," he repeated coldly. His eyes sent a chill down her spine. "Justice will be done."

"And 'twill be, when I return from Silverymoon at the head of twenty Knights in Silver, a hundred from the Argent Legion, and half a dozen from the Spellguard," she argued hotly. Arya felt her natural defiance flaring.

"Greyt and his henchmen will be dead long before you get here," Walker said.

"Walker, my honor does not allow for vigilante—"

"Damn your honor!" he shouted. "Damn all honor. How many lives has honor destroyed? How many innocents has it slain? It is nothing. It is worse than nothing."

The color drained from Arya's face. This man she had

shared herself with, this intoxicating, mysterious warrior she had known only a brief time but with whom she felt she had spent a lifetime, was spitting upon the knighthood she loved so deeply and the honor that gave her life purpose. That honor bound her more tightly than chains of steel, but she remembered the soft, tender grasp of Walker's arms. Which held her heart tighter—honor and its obligations, or love and its freedoms?

These things warred in Arya's heart in that moment, and the scrape of steel as her blade left its scabbard told them both which had won.

"My duty lies to the south," said Arya, pointing her sword toward Silverymoon. "Stonar and Lady Alustriel must be warned. I'm sorry. I have to go. But I'll come back. I promise. Just do not try to stop me."

Walker's eyes, burning upon her face, fell. He looked away, focusing on some object unseen a little ways away.

Arya nodded, sheathed her sword, stooped, and slid on the greaves of her armor. She looked back, her eyes firm, but Walker's gaze remained averted. Seeing that the ghostwalker did not protest, she picked up her breastplate.

Then his voice came, soft and calm. "You do not have to go."

Arya hesitated as she adjusted the breastplate into place, but only for a moment. She fit it snugly around her breasts and smooth stomach. The armor was perfectly fitted—her father had paid the finest armorers in Everlund for no less.

"Yes, yes I do," said Arya. She fell to the clasps.

Walker's deep blue eyes were tangible on her back, and she tried not to feel them.

"I do not want you to go," he said.

Arya looked sidelong at him. "You have your task, I have mine," she said with determination and not a little bitterness. "You can come with me if you want, but I cannot stay here. I don't have that choice. My duty compels me to go."

Walker had no reply to that. The last breastplate clasp snapped into place. She slid a steel vambrace around her right arm and fastened the clasps.

Walker gazed upon her with an expression that was like sadness as she put her armor on piece by piece. Arya's hands shook in nervous agitation, though she knew a profound calm. The duality of her feelings struck her as profoundly tragic and beautiful at the same time.

"Walker," Arya said, looking away. "Tell me something."

"Perhaps." The voice was cold.

"Will there ever be peace ... for us?"

"Peace," Walker mused. "When the last one falls, will I find peace?"

Arya would not relent, though. "When this is finished—when I've found the missing couriers and you've killed enough men—did you mean what you said ... about dying? Or ..." She bit her lip. "Or can I see you again?"

Silence for a moment. Then she heard Walker's voice, and it was miraculously unbroken. "You would want that?" he asked, almost in a whisper.

Arya's heart cracked.

She whirled on Walker, about to continue, but an arrow whizzed past her ear and bloomed from his shoulder.

"No!" she gasped as Walker fell backward from the impact. "Gods, *no!*"

She threw herself down and snatched her sword from its scabbard. An arrow drove into her side, through the plate, and she screamed at the sudden flame that swept through her. Had she been unarmored, the shot would have been fatal.

"Arya ... run ..." Walker gasped against the pain. He reached down and grasped his sword. "They come ... for me ..."

She caught his hand and held it tight. He looked up, and the resolute fire they had known was in her eyes now. She stood and towered over his prostrate form.

"Let them come," said Arya, her voice cutting like a knife.

Half a dozen dark figures stalked out of the trees, steel glittering in their hands. Arya—sword and shield ready—rose alone to meet them.

CHAPTER 15

29 Tarsakh

Six rangers, two with drawn bows, stepped out of the forest. They wore the uniforms of Quaervarr watchmen but Arya was not fooled. The four in front pulled aside forest green cloaks to reveal drawn weapons. Their eyes shouted that she was hopelessly outnumbered and that she should surrender.

But Arya was one of the legendary Knights in Silver, and she knew nothing of surrender.

As she walked, Arya drew her sword up vertically before her, saluting them, and broke into a run, resembling a mounted knight charging with her lance ready.

So controlled and smooth was her run—despite the arrow standing out of her side—that the sword-wielding rangers hesitated as she came.

The bowmen, however, did not. They fired, one after the other.

Arya caught one arrow with her shield and the other jarred off her shoulder armor with enough force to make her flinch but not enough to slow her charge. She spun the blade back and over and slashed down at the first ranger—a wiry blond she mentally labeled Thin-Man—with an overhead chop, even as she brought her shield up to ward off the second, a cruel-looking veteran she decided to think of as One-Eye for his most dominant facial feature.

Recovering from the strike, Arya feinted at One-Eye and attacked Thin-Man with all of her strength. Both underestimated her speed. Thin-Man crossed sword and dagger to block the blow, but Arya had put all of her weight behind it. The resulting force crushed him down, but his parry held.

"Bane's boot!" he cursed.

Appropriately, Arya's boot slammed into his chest below the locked blades, knocking him to the ground. His parry came apart as he fell, and Arya spun, bashing him again with the shield before coming around to face the others, bringing her blade in line to parry a strike.

One-Eye was there, his twin short swords darting in for Arya's life. She swatted one away, but the other slipped under her guard and struck a glancing blow off her armored shoulder. Arya hissed a quick thanks to Torm that it was not her arrow-stung shoulder.

That reminded her, and she cast her eyes back to the archers. They had arrows nocked but held. Apparently, neither was thrilled at the prospect of firing into a melee.

The other two rangers with blades drawn charged, seeking to get at Arya's flanks, and the knight backpedaled smartly and bashed One-Eye back with her shield, keeping the rangers in front of her. One—the bulky ranger she had mentally dubbed Tough-Face—wielded a two-handed axe on her left and the other—a quick half-elf with a quicker rapier she called Red-Hair for his scarlet locks—came at her from the right. Ducking and weaving, Arya worked her blade and shield furiously to pick off their blows as she strove against her three opponents.

A few moments after the first blades clashed, the battle was caught in a high-energy holding pattern in which Arya could size up her opponents. Her advantages—greater skill and speed and higher quality weapons and armor—did not outweigh theirs—numerical superiority and an arrow in her side.

Remembering the latter, Arya bit back the pain and fought off the haze that gripped her brain. The rangers did not seem to have received orders to take her alive; indeed, half their slashes could have been fatal had Arya not deflected them. If they got behind her, Arya knew she would be done for. If not, then it did not matter. Soon, she would tire and they would have her, advantages or no.

Then she heard Thin-Man groan behind her. Apparently, her kick and shield bash had not put him out of the battle for good. As soon as he got into the melee, she would be surrounded.

She could not win unless Tymora smiled, and perhaps not even then.

Thus, she decided, it was time to indulge in what Derst called "calculated recklessness" and Bars called "prayer."

One-Eye stabbed one of his swords at her, but she smashed it left with her shield, causing Tough-Face to start back with a curse as the blade almost struck him. The brief opening she left was enough to tempt Red-Hair into thrusting his rapier in, just as Arya had hoped. She also prayed he would miss. She leaned forward, letting the thin blade shoot under her sword arm. Lady Luck did smile, it seemed, and the blade scraped off steel and went past her back.

Before Red-Hair could pull back his rapier, she gritted her teeth and snapped her arm forward. The steel screamed against her hard metal gauntlet and vambrace, and she felt a biting pain as the blade tore from Red-Hair's hand and slapped against her body. It fell to the ground and was quickly trampled into the ground.

Suddenly without a weapon, Red-Hair ducked Arya's wild slash and leaped back from the battle, heading for the south side of the grove. Arya followed, startling her other opponents, who both stopped short. She sidestepped away from them, keeping her shield up to ward off their blows. Even though they took the opportunity to attack, their blades bounced off her shield, leaving only tiny dents. Meanwhile, the Nightingale of Everlund bore down on her only unarmed opponent with fiery eyes.

"Shoot her! Darthan! Gieves! Damn it!" the unarmed Red-Hair screamed in vain as she pressed on him, her blade slashing and weaving.

He need not have been so terrified. Arya's code of honor would not allow her to strike an unarmed man, and her pursuit was a ruse. Another prayer passed her lips. As Red-Hair stumbled into the brush, she feinted an overhead slash, then threw her full weight back on her shield, reversing her movement.

Her pursuing attackers were caught entirely off guard by her sudden backward rush. One-Eye managed to dodge but Tough-Face was not so lucky. He went down under Arya's press, tripping over a root. Arya could not finish him, though, for One-Eye pressed her still. The knight dealt Tough-Face a furious kick, knocking his weapon away, and focused on driving One-Eye back toward the center of the grove. Overmatched, the ranger drew back, weaving his swords back and forth to ward her off.

She could have had him any number of times, but if she ran him through the archers would have a clear shot and she could not slap away arrows as easily as blades. She worked her blade to keep One-Eye on the defensive. If Tymora allowed it, she could play this battle her way, keeping her opponents alive, until she had an opportunity to . . .

An arrow slammed into her thigh, piercing the metal wrapping it. She screamed in sudden agony and followed it up with a curse as the limb went numb. A lucky shot, but that was all it took. Arya fell.

One-Eye, still up, immediately took advantage of the situation and leaped onto the prone Arya, blades raised high. The knight braced herself for the killing blow.

Sure enough, blood splattered her face, and Arya wondered

that she did not feel the sword that must be standing in her chest or forehead. Perhaps this was death.

Then she heard a bubbling groan and her eyes snapped open.

A black throwing knife in his remaining eye, the ranger sank to the ground. His short swords tumbled from his limp hands.

Arrows protruding from his shoulder and chest, Walker stood over her, his mithral shatterspike knocking one arrow from the air even as another nicked his shoulder. Red-Hair—a pair of daggers in his hands—Tough-Face, and Thin-Man were rushing toward them, murder in their eyes.

"Strong as steel!" he rasped.

Arya raised her brow, but she understood his extended hand.

"Up!" Walker shouted, just in case she hadn't. Arya was not about to argue.

Her armor weighed her down and her leg protested, but she managed to stand with his aid. Pressing her back to Walker's, she lifted her sword and shield and awaited the three rangers stalking in from all sides.

"Turn into a ghost!" commanded Arya. "Flee!"

"Not without you," Walker said through gritted teeth.

The rangers pulled up short, granting the two a wide berth. Walker's cloak of grim resolution intimidated them, and they came no closer. Instead, Red-Hair reversed his daggers for throwing, and the others pulled light crossbows from their belts. Thin-Man even produced a slender white wand and pointed it at them—the crystal at the end crackling with electricity. Darthan and Gieves came to join them, pointing their arrows at the two resolute warriors.

"Lower your blade," said Walker.

"What?" Arya could not believe her ears.

"No choice." The point of his shatterspike dipped toward the ground, and he dropped the throwing dagger in his left hand.

Hesitantly, Arya lowered her sword as well, though the shield was still strapped to her arm. If they fired at them, she could step in front of Walker and protect both of them. Perhaps. If she knew Tymora's favor.

"Smile on us, Lady Luck," whispered Arya.

As though they heard an unspoken command, the line of rangers with projectile weapons parted and another man stepped through. With dusky flesh made penumbral at night and curly hair the color of soot, he seemed made of darkness—a darkness he usually kept caged in white hunting leathers. Not now, however: now he wore black.

"Meris," growled Arya. "Bastard."

"Indeed," the wild scout laughed. "How nice to see you again, beautiful cousin. You spurned my well-meant advances before, but I assure you that you won't this time."

"Nothing from you is ever 'well-meant,' Meris." Arya took the smallest step in front of Walker, and all the arrows and bolts shifted to her.

Meris ignored his rangers. Instead, he turned his gaze to Walker. "I see your affections have found somewhere else to rest," he said.

"Leave him out of this," said Arya. "I'm the one you want—take me and let him go!"

"Actually, I'm here for him," replied Meris. "You're just an added bonus. I've always looked forward to getting you alone, but I thought I'd missed my chance. Tymora must be smiling on both of us."

The knight might have winced at the irony, but she was too confused. "You didn't know I was here?" Arya looked at him incredulously.

"Oh, I'd guessed he'd use you and leave you dead in the forest somewhere," Meris said. "He's a dangerous man, that Walker." He stepped toward them, his hand dropping to his axe.

Arya stepped in front of Walker and lifted her blade, warding him off. "Take another step and I attack," she warned.

Meris looked at the rangers on his left and right. "Oh, that's reasonable," he smirked. "Really, Cousin—"

"If I attack, you'll have to kill me, and you'll lose your 'added bonus.'"

Meris laughed. "Irrelevant," he rasped, mimicking Walker's broken voice. "I could just shoot both of you right now."

"But if I come with you willingly," Arya said. "You don't lose it."

"You would come with me willingly?" Meris's face was calm, but she could tell he was intrigued. Then his eyes narrowed. "How do I know you'll keep your word?"

"I am a Knight in Silver. I always keep my word."

"What do you ask in return? For this . . . accommodation?"

Arya bristled at his words but refused to let him see her discomfort. "Walker goes free."

"Of course," said Meris. "I might have guessed."

He pondered the agreement, crossing his arms before him. Arya could feel Walker's eyes on the back of her head, but she refused to flinch.

"Done," Meris said finally, a bemused smile on his face.

"Your word?"

"I swear on my sword." Meris extended his hand toward Arya.

Arya raised her brow. It had not escaped her notice that he carried no sword. "Have your men lower their bows first."

"You don't trust me?" Meris shrugged. "Well, believe it or not, I am a man of my word." He signaled, and the other rangers lowered their bows and put the arrows away. At the same time, Arya sheathed her sword and turned to the ghostwalker with tears in her eyes.

"Run away, Walker," said Arya. "I'm not going to lose you. Not now."

"We will meet again," Walker assured her softly.

Meris reached out and took Arya's arm, pulling her away.

❧ ❧ ❧ ❧ ❧

True to her word, Arya followed. The rangers dispersed, though they continued to watch Walker warily.

After handing Arya by the arm to Darthan, who dis-armed her, Meris turned back and strode toward Walker. He approached peacefully and unarmed. Walker kept his sword point down and stood calmly, awaiting the dusky scout's arrival.

It pained the ghostwalker to surrender. He knew what was coming next, but there was no other way he could save Arya. This simply had to be done.

When Meris stood within a pace of Walker, he stopped and stared him in the eye. Even this was more than the other rangers were willing to do, but Meris's hate overwhelmed any fear.

"I have been eager for this meeting since you humiliated me not once, not twice, but thrice, Walker," said Meris. "Now I'm going to set you free." He sighed. "Pity. I always hoped I'd get to cross swords with you."

Walker eyed Meris's black leathers. "Black covers all things—blood and hate, sins and lies—does it not?"

"What was that?" snapped Meris, thrusting his face next to Walker's.

Walker seemed not to hear him. "I have read the eyes of many men, most of them dying," he said. "And I have never seen so much hate as in yours."

"Look deep, Walker," Meris said. "Perhaps you'll see me laughing back."

A memory came unbidden into his mind.

The boy's eyes filled with fire . . . Rage? Anger? At the world or at himself?

Meris saw the look of recognition, and his eyes narrowed. "You know me," he said, almost intrigued, almost. . . .

"I remember your eyes," Walker said. "Eyes of anger, eyes of pain, eyes of fear. You were afraid, that night."

"Am I afraid now?" Meris asked through his hard grin, his hands trembling.

There was a moment of silence. Walker thought he could see the spirit of Tarm Thardeyn standing to the side, look-ing at him sadly. Then Walker smiled.

"You will always be afraid."

In a blur of motion, Meris seized the shatterspike from Walker's hand, whirled in a circle, and slashed the ghostwalker across the chest. Blood sprayed and Arya screamed. Even though his body lit with fire, Walker fell without a sound.

"No!" screamed Arya. The knight started forward, but one of the rangers cuffed her on the side of the head, stunning her. She slumped in their hands, helpless.

"How does it feel to be set free?" Meris asked.

Walker could not respond through the blood bubbling up in his throat.

"Still alive, eh?" Meris kicked Walker up to a kneeling position and stepped on his right hand. "No wolf's head ring keeping you that way. What, did you lose it somewhere? You know, the ring you always wear on this hand?"

Walker could only moan.

"Or did you give it to her?" Meris said, pointing the bloody shatterspike at Arya, who glared at him. He stomped over to the knight and slapped her across the face.

As Walker watched, he roughly tore off Arya's gauntlets to search for a ring, and then her breastplate, in case she wore it on a chain around her neck.

"The ring's not there," Meris shouted. "You must have lost it. Poor, poor Walker—the one time you break your routine is the one time it counts!"

The ghostwalker could not stop himself. He wheezed.

Sneering, Meris turned back to the Arya. His eyes were burning, but it was not merely anger this time. He smiled and turned back to Walker.

"I hope you live long enough to see this," he snarled to Walker, who could do nothing but twitch in reply. "I've waited for this a long time as well."

He gestured to his men, and they began pulling off the rest of Arya's armor. At first, the knight struggled, kicked, and screamed, but Darthan slapped her on the side of the head and she lay there, dazed, stunned, and helpless once more. Meris, standing over her, untied his cloak and began unbuckling his leather cuirass.

Walker tried to rise, but he could not. His strength literally bleeding away with his life, he, too, was helpless. The wild scout finished with the hauberk, looked down at Arya, and turned to grin at Walker one last time.

A whistling alerted Meris just in time to jerk aside as a throwing knife darted for his face. As it was, the projectile lodged itself in his shoulder. Roaring in pain, he dropped to the forest floor. Two of his rangers fell: Tough-Face cursed the blade in his arm and Thin-Man tried to breathe around the one in his throat.

Red-Hair turned in time to meet a huge man who leaped from the brush with a pair of maces.

"Forth the Nightingale!" the big man screamed, and his maces whirred in reply. They took the blades from Red-Hair's hands before the ranger could react. Then the wielder spun, and the first mace crashed into Red-Hair's chest with bone-crunching force. As the ranger started, the second mace slammed into his back, crushing his body between the two weapons. Red-Hair collapsed to the ground.

"A mighty blow, Sir Hartwine!" a weasel-like voice said.

"I wasn't the one who took down three in one breath!" Bars shouted back as he swung his twin maces around to knock an axe away and lunged, driving Tough-Face back a step.

Bars might have pursued, but he threw himself onto his back to avoid an arrow from Gieves that cut a red line across his shoulder. With the momentary respite, Tough-Face pulled his light crossbow from his belt and trained it on a spot in the brush.

"I suppose no one's perfect," replied Derst as he stood from that spot, letting fly with two more knives. "Except me."

One of the blades neatly cut Gieves's bowstring and the other slashed across Tough-Face's forearm, ruining his aim. The ranger fired anyway, and the bolt drove into a tree a hand's breadth from Derst's head.

Bars roared and slugged Tough-Face in the stomach with

a mace, knocking the bulky man back. The paladin pushed himself to his feet, only to find that he had to roll away again to avoid more weapons.

Disbelieving, Derst blinked at the quivering bolt for a moment. Then the wiry knight saw Darthan aiming a short-bow at him, holding it horizontally like a crossbow.

Derst leaped out of the brush, hooked his chain-dagger about Darthan's bow, and ripped it from the man's hand. Unarmed, the ranger reached down for a short sword but instead found a dagger sticking out of his side. The man went down swearing and Derst jumped over his head to engage Tough-Face, who bellowed in anger and slashed his war axe at the wiry man.

Derst dived under the slash and rolled back to avoid the next, overextending Tough-Face's reach. The man staggered and caught himself just in time to avoid landing on his face at Derst's feet. The short man looked down at his chain-and-dagger, then at Tough-Face's war axe, then up at Tough-Face sheepishly. Derst backpedaled, dodging slash after slash and seeking some respite to plan an offensive.

Meanwhile, Gieves drew a short sword and lunged at Bars, who barely had time enough to stand before he had to defend himself. Darthan rose, despite the pain in his bowels, and attacked Bars's flank with a pair of hand axes. Outnumbered, the paladin backed away to keep both opponents in his field of vision, but the rangers were too well trained to allow him to escape. His maces working independently, Bars fended off their attacks with a dizzying display of skill, but all three men knew it was of limited duration—he would tire before they did.

"Come play like a man, rat-boy," Tough-Face growled to Derst.

"What sense does that make?" Derst wondered aloud. "The very point of your threat is that men don't play, and yet you want me to 'play' like a man?"

Tough-Face snarled in frustration as Derst dodged and his axe took off a huge chunk of duskwood bark. "Well, fight like a man, then!"

"I'd rather not," Derst said as he hopped over a low slash

and slapped Tough-Face's cheek with the chain of his dagger to little visible effect. "People get killed that way." Another slash claimed a sizeable portion of Derst's forest cloak. He gulped.

Then Derst feigned a stumble. Tough-Face roared in pain and rage, bringing the axe from on high to split the quick knight in half, but Derst slid between his legs and slashed the back of Tough-Face's leg with the chain-dagger. Hamstrung, Tough-Face screamed and plunged to the ground.

"How does that—" Derst began, but stopped as he sensed a blade flashing toward his head. With a tiny gasp, he threw himself away from it and felt fiery pain rip through his shoulder. He rolled to feet and touched his wounded shoulder.

His attacker, holding Walker's gleaming shatterspike and a wicked hand axe, grinned at him.

"Come, goblin," said Meris. "Let us see how you fight your betters."

In the middle of the clearing, they circled one another, Derst with a chain-dagger whirling around his wrist and a worried look on his face. Meris's smile was a cruel one.

The scout launched an attack so fast that Derst barely registered it in time to block. The hand axe slashed open the leather covering his hip and the shatterspike tore his cloak in two. Derst tried to parry, but ended up having to dodge instead. Meris was by far the superior duelist, with strength and magic—in the form of Walker's sword—on his side. This would be quick.

Bars saw Derst's dilemma and howled in fury. "Meris!" he shouted. Pumping his arms as fast as he could, he swatted blades aside on both of his flanks and ran toward Meris's back.

Though his posture said he was oblivious to the paladin's rush, Meris winked at Derst.

"Bars, no!" Derst yelled, but it was too late.

Meris spun and the shatterspike flashed. It intercepted both of Bars's maces and cleaved both stout pieces of steel as though they were warm cheese. The paladin stumbled to a halt, looking at his destroyed maces, and Meris seized the opportunity to step inside his reach and slam a knee between his legs. The bearlike man dropped to the ground, curling up and moaning.

"Pathetic, for a 'Knight in Silver,'" Meris spat. He raised the hand axe in his left hand to deal a killing blow to Bars's unprotected neck.

Then the axe would not obey Meris's commands. It even pulled him back a step.

He looked and found Derst at the other end of the chain-dagger, straining to hold back Meris's axe—trying anything to keep the man from killing his friend.

"How noble," Meris sneered. He brought the shatterspike around in a dazzling arc and cut the chain holding his axe.

It snapped like thin twine and, because the opposite force had disappeared, Derst fell back a step. Meris took advantage of the misstep, continued his whirl, and hooked the axe around Derst's leg. He swept the man off his feet and dropped the axe. He raised the sword in both hands.

"No!" Bars managed to shout.

Weak, Bars kicked Meris in the shin, hardly enough to injure him, but enough to ensure that the killing blow was not true. The blade drove into Derst's shoulder. The wiry knight's scream was lost in pain. After an agonizingly silent moment, his body fell back and he lay still.

Still, Derst's chest rose and fell.

With a little smile, Bars did not even resist as Meris's men hauled him to his feet. They made to slit his throat, but Meris waved them off.

"No," he said. "He's earned life for him and his friend, for now." He flicked blood off the sword. "Not sure why you prefer death by torture, knight, but you'll have your choice."

Bars smiled grimly.

The scout slapped him across the face, wiping that smile away. "Back to Quaervarr," he said. "And the knight carries his wounded friend."

"I won't carry him back to be tortured," said the paladin. "Kill me if you want. I did everything I could."

Meris clutched at his chest in mock horror. "Oh no, I'm crushed," he said. "Stubborn knightly honor, eh? Well, if you're both going to die, the girl might as well die too." He nodded to Darthan, who drew his blade and started toward where Arya lay senseless. "A pity, really. She was quite lovely—"

"Stop!" shouted Bars, panic in his voice. Darthan stopped and Meris looked at the paladin with a raised eyebrow. Bars cast his eyes down. "I'll go. Just don't harm her."

Meris smiled. "I am a man of my word, after all." He waved Darthan off and the rangers came forward to bind Bars's wrists.

The paladin crossed over to Derst and put his hands on Derst's temples. "Sorry, old friend," he said. "We have no choice."

The healing power of Torm, his patron deity, flooded through his hands and pulled Derst back from death's door. The wiry knight's face was still sallow and wan, but it was something. As soon as Bars had lifted Derst, the rangers prodded him with their blades and they began to move toward Quaervarr.

❧ ❧ ❧ ❧ ❧

Meris went to stand over Walker, whose breath still came in ragged gasps. Meris contemplated him curiously, amazed that he still lived. Never had he met a man who clung to life so tenaciously—especially considering he was a man who seemed to have so embraced death.

He held up the mithral shatterspike and admired its almost translucent gleam in the moonlight. The blade seemed to have cleaned itself. Blood ran like water from its keen edge and he saw no dents or nicks. The blade looked as though it had never been used.

"This is a beautiful sword, Walker," said Meris. He bent low and repeated himself, so the ghostwalker could hear.

Walker, twitching, looked up at him without understanding.

Darthan appeared at Meris's shoulder. He pointed a thumb at Arya. "You still want to have a little fun, my lord?" he asked.

Meris regarded Darthan's lewd sneer. Apparently, he was not the only one who had taken an interest in Arya. It reminded him how far he had sunk, to share base desires with common rabble. The thought caused bile to rise in his gorge.

"No," he said. "Take her with us." Darthan's eyes lit up and Meris added, "But I carry her. You carry her armor. It'll fetch a fine price."

"As you wish, my lord." Darthan bowed, looking more than a little disappointed.

"Three of our men are dead—take their weapons and equipment," said Meris. "Leave the bodies for the crows. Inform the injured that they will walk back to Quaervarr or they will be left behind."

Darthan nodded, though he balked a bit at the harsh commands. He walked away.

"Oh, and Darthan."

The ranger turned back and looked at Meris. Meris was running a finger along Walker's cheek, contemplating where he had seen those sapphire eyes before.

No matter.

The dusky scout spun, brought the shatterspike high, and plunged it into Walker's chest. The ghostwalker shook once then lay still.

"Start digging," said Meris. "Burning is too good for this one. Let the worms eat his corpse. And make it deep." He wiped the blade off then indicated Walker with it. "Just in case he decides to come back, there won't be much he can do under the ground."

He looked back at Walker's body. "So ends the reign of the Ghost Murderer," he said.

As Meris scooped up Arya's limp form, Darthan shuddered and pulled his field shovel out of his pack.

CHAPTER 16

30 Tarsakh

Meris and the Greyt family rangers stalked back into town. The sun was rising but no one could see it through the clouds. It would be a wretched, overcast day, but Meris's smile was not diminished. In fact, nothing could dampen his spirits.

Meris waved off the guardsmen at the gate—different guardsmen, since the ones of the previous day had not reported to their posts. These guards proved no obstacle to entering Quaervarr, even with an unconscious woman in his arms and Bars and Derst in tow. Now Meris was glad of the uncomfortable uniforms they all wore and that the captives were hooded. It would not do to have to "take care of" another pair of soldiers.

Meris and his group had just barely made it inside when a rider in a forest cloak burst out of the gates, riding south fast. The wild scout narrowed his eyes, but shrugged. Nothing to do with him.

As soon as they were inside the city, he had the knights clapped in manacles and escorted to a certain Pitek's general store. Grossly fat Pitek, a loyal Quaervarr businessman, had expressed little hesitation about allowing the Lord Singer to use his store as the secret entrance to his dungeons. Pitek had no choice, after all, since the very reason Greyt kept his business in existence was to conceal the secret entrance, and as death would be the consequence of betrayal. There were two other tunnels as well: one to Greyt's personal wine cellar, and a final one from the ninth cell to Meris's servant's chambers in Greyt Manor.

Prisoners kept in the ninth cell rarely survived long.

Meris enjoyed the dungeons. Dark and dank as dungeons should be, hollowed out from preexisting caverns, they lay not directly beneath the manor but beneath the main plaza, deep enough that prisoners would not be heard. Light was nonexistent save for the candles kept lit in the guardroom—darkness was as much a torture as lack of food or drink.

Meris was glad and disappointed at the same time to see that the little pest Derst had survived the journey: on the one hand, he appreciated the chance to torture Derst, though on the other he did not look forward to hearing the man's snide commentary. Perhaps his tongue would be the first thing to go.

As for Bars ... The paladin's healing touch had ensured the wiry knight's survival in the forest. Meris made a mental note to break or remove Bars's fingers.

Regarding Arya, Meris had not yet decided what to do, though he relished a few torments he had dreamed up, most of which he had not tried for lack of a suitably beautiful female subject.

First, however, it was time for rest. After seeing the knights locked away in the dungeon, he made his way through the third secret door, back up to his chambers. As he went, he stripped off his black watchman armor and discarded it, only vaguely aware of its sweaty stench.

For the moment, though, he cared little as he thought about nodding off in the copper bathtub in his rooms. He had left orders to have it filled for him when he returned at dawn, and he was right on time. Meris stretched his back as he walked through the tunnel. The sweat felt cool on his bare skin and the packed earth around him smelled moist and almost metallic. The smell of blood did not dissipate in this place.

A good scent to end a good night, and this had truly been a good night: the courier taken care of, the knights captured, Walker slain ... What more could Meris ask for?

The question was answered for him when he found Greyt waiting for him in his bedchamber. The Lord Singer had not even been facing the door—he had been waiting for Meris to come out of the servant's quarters.

"A productive morning, son?" asked Greyt.

Meris swore inwardly. Apparently, he was not the only one who knew about the third secret passage. "Yes," he said. "I've killed Walker—oh, I forgot his head. It's buried in the Moonwood somewhere. But I've brought you three other presents, who wait down below."

The Lord Singer was pleased, but Meris hardly noticed.

"As for me," said the scout. "It's time for a bath."

The tub had been filled, as ordered, and steam rose from its surface. Meris stripped off his breeches, heedless of his bare body, and picked up a towel from the dresser.

"Not as such, I'm afraid," Greyt said.

"Excuse me, father? I don't think I heard you correctly," Meris said dismissively as he tested the water with his finger. It was nice and warm.

"I wouldn't do that," said Greyt with a wave of his hand.

"Do what?" He clutched the edges of the tub and jumped into the water.

Or rather, Meris jumped *onto* the water with a painful thud and immediately clutched at his smarting bottom. His flesh was cold where it touched the water, water that was now ice.

"Impressive, father," spat Meris as he snatched up the towel to gird himself.

"There are consequences when you ignore me," Greyt said with ice in his voice.

"I never thought you much of a wizard, father," said Meris. "It seems you've abandoned the man's sword for the little boy's Art."

"How little you know," replied Greyt. "In fact, the tub is not my doing." Meris raised an eyebrow, now curious. "I would not have shown you this—yet, anyway—but I have run out of time and it has become necessary. Talthaliel!"

A cloaked and cowled figure stepped out of thin air beside Greyt. Meris gave a shout and reached for the discarded shatterspike, but he found the handle burning hot to the touch. Cursing, he let the blade lie and turned to face his father and the mage.

"Rest easy, Wayfarer," said the cloaked figure. Talthaliel stood tall and gaunt, even for a moon elf. "The time has not yet come for violence."

"A secret wizard, father?" Meris asked, the approbation in his voice mocking. "I never would have guessed." Privately, he thought about all the mysteries that explained.

"You have your secrets, I have mine," Greyt said. "And now let me share another secret, which is neither of ours. A second courier has been dispatched, who rode from Oak House. She left not long ago and cannot be far yet. I knew the druids could not be trusted." He growled under his breath. "Unddreth sent this message, but don't worry—I dispatched Bilgren and six of my best rangers to handle the good Captain."

"And what does any of this have to do with me?" asked Meris, though he already knew the answer.

"Talthaliel will transport you by magic to the edge of the forest, where you will intercept this courier at all costs," said Greyt. "My spies report that she carries a document damning and condemning me as the source of the murders and attacks."

"That's not true, is it?" Meris could not resist.

The Lord Singer growled. "Of course not, but there are certain other activities we do not want Stonar or the Silver Marches investigating, right?"

Meris shrugged. "Do your own dirty work for a change, old man," he said. He wiped at his eyes. "I have spent a day and a night running errands for you—I'm tired. Send another."

"No one else can be . . . trusted with this," said Greyt.

He was hiding something, which made Meris more wary.

"Your pet wizard then," snapped Meris. He had expected to see Talthaliel bristle at the insult, but all he could see on the moon elf's face was resignation.

"I . . . cannot," Greyt replied, shooting Talthaliel a look.

"Why 'cannot?' " pressed Meris.

Greyt stared at him for a long moment, perhaps fighting the urge to lash out, perhaps worried. Had Meris just found a sensitive point? The dusky scout filed the emotional response away for future use.

"Go yourself, then," Meris said. "Or must the high-and-honored hero Dharan Greyt, Lord Singer of Quaervarr, keep his yarting fingers dry of blood?"

Greyt took a step toward Meris as though to strike but stopped, as though realizing something. The Lord Singer took a moment to compose himself, then stared murder at Meris.

"You are my pup. You do as I command," snapped the Lord Singer. "You leave shortly. Ready your gear." He waved and Talthaliel disappeared. Greyt opened Meris's door to leave. "For now, I shall go open those presents you brought me."

"Careful not to open them too much," said Meris, his tone evoking a wince from Greyt. "Leave some of the fun for me."

❧ ❧ ❧ ❧ ❧

The first sensation she knew was shivering chill. It was dark and bitterly cold, and she found that she was too weak even to huddle into a ball. Manacles encircled her ankles and held her wrists behind her back. Her throat was parched. She could see nothing but blackness. In the distance, she heard something dripping. She hoped it was only water.

Arya found that her captors had stripped her armor and left her in a torn tunic and breeches. Fortunately, she was not damaged beyond rough handling, and for that Arya thanked Torm and Tymora. With her toe, she felt along the wall until she had traced a rough mental sketch of her enclosure. Small and cramped, the room possessed only one entrance: a cell door with thick bars.

A dungeon cell, then.

Ignoring the wet, slipperiness of the stone floor, Arya sat and waited.

Then, after a long time—she couldn't see the sun, but it felt like half a day—Arya heard a door open with a long, rusty rattle. It slammed shut a moment later. Arya flinched at the bang and her head exploded in sharp aches. An involuntary gasp escaped her lips.

There were footsteps in the dark, and she became aware of a tiny spot of light slowly approaching as though down a long hallway. Arya had no choice but to stay still and try not to suffer any more pain until the light arrived.

When it finally did, she looked up to see a dim lantern held by a gaunt man in Greyt family livery. Arya's heart fell further when the man swung the lantern a little to the side and illuminated another familiar face, this one wearing a cruel smile.

"Ah, my darling niece," Lord Greyt said. He turned to the lantern holder. "This is the one, Claudir." He took the lantern and waved the steward away. Claudir padded off. If the butler felt any unease about wandering back through the lightless tunnels, he did not express it.

Arya scooted away from the cell door as Greyt opened it. She huddled back into the farthest corner of her cell, ignoring the damp and sticky feel of the wall behind her. She tried to scream at him to leave her alone, but her tongue felt thick and dry. Instead, she extended her feet to ward him off, though she realized she probably could not have injured him with a kick in her weakened state.

"Now, now," said Greyt. "What kind of monster do you take me for? You are my niece, after all." He reached into the folds of his robes and Arya's eyes widened. Then, to her vast relief, Greyt withdrew a skin and uncorked it. He held it out to her.

Arya looked at him suspiciously, but Greyt only smiled. Hesitantly, she edged closer to him, keeping her eyes locked on his face. When he had not moved, she brought herself into a kneeling position and looked up. He tipped the waterskin and cool water rushed into Arya's mouth. She drank frantically. To her parched throat, it tasted like the nectar of the gods. She could not catch all the water and a great deal splashed over her dusty face and undertunic.

"I'm so glad you could rejoin us, little Nightingale," said Greyt as he took the waterskin away. "We have so much to discuss, you and I."

"What do you want from me?" she asked coldly.

"Merely to explain myself," he said. "And it seemed meet to tell you of your defeat. Walker is dead. Amra and Unddreth are gone. Stonar is alienated. I win, little knight."

Arya looked up at him. "You wish to gloat over me?" she asked. "Save your breath, Lord Singer. I am a Knight in Silver. More than that, I have justice on my side." She set her mouth into a wry, bitter line. "And more than that, I'm a stubborn, defiant daughter. You think my father could break me, much less you? You will not vanquish me until the last breath leaves my body."

Greyt smiled at her jest. "Humor in the face of certain death? I respect such courage," he said. "Until you breathe your last, eh? Such could be arranged, even 'ere you be hanged . . ." He reached for the dagger at his belt.

She did not flinch, even chained and helpless before him. She may as well have been standing over him with a drawn sword for the look in her eyes.

"You won't do that," she said. "You can't."

"Is that so?" he snapped. He bent down, putting his face not a hand's breadth from hers. He drew his knife and pressed it against her cheek. "You know me so well, little wench? Then you must know that I am a hero—"

"Not a hero," she said.

"A villain, then!" Greyt roared in her face. "Bane of all that draws breath! Nothing but pain and death!"

"No." Arya prepared herself, body and mind. "A coward. You are nothing but a coward."

As she had expected, Greyt's face twisted in anger. He drew the knife up and back. . . .

"Get away from her!" came a shout from outside the cell door.

Greyt was startled, distracted for just an instant. But that instant was enough for Arya to attack with the only weapon she had left—the one atop her shoulders. She slammed her forehead into his face with all the force she could muster, and the Lord Singer staggered back, his nose shattered.

Her world spinning, Arya managed to make out a huge body moving in another cell across the hallway. A man banging meaty fists against thick cell bars.

Cell bars . . .

"Bars!" she shouted.

"Me too, lass!" came Derst's weak voice. The short knight stood at the hulking paladin's side and shouted at the Lord Singer. "Stay away from her, Greyt! Attacking helpless, bound women—some hero you are, Quickwidower!"

Greyt whirled at the mocking nickname. With his nose splattered across his face, his graying hair disheveled, and his eyes burning, he looked more a monster than a man.

"Hero?" he snapped. "Hero?" He grabbed Arya by the hair and threw her aside like a sack of flour. The knight slammed into the cell wall and lay stunned. "There is no such thing!"

Arya had just managed to raise her head when Greyt lifted her again and stared into her face. She prepared for another attack, but this time he merely shook her and shouted.

"How can you believe in heroism?" screamed Greyt. "How can you believe in heroism, when the heroes you worship are murderers such as your beloved Walker, men who seek vengeance over justice, violence over peace, death over life?"

Arya struggled to respond, but he was choking the retort out of her. Then he released her, and she fell gasping to the ground.

Greyt paid her no mind as he stood over her shivering body and roared at Bars and Derst. "The closest thing this world knows to a hero is the one I'm sending to murder that courier!" His voice grew quiet. "Meris, my son."

There was a chilling silence.

"Greyt," asked Arya in one last entreaty. "Why are you doing this? You play hero for these people—why can you not *be* one?"

Greyt's delicate façade broke and he lashed out, slapping her across the face with the back of his hand.

"Me? A hero?" he growled at Arya. "If these fools believe that, in spite of what I did to *her*, who am I to break them of that illusion?"

" 'Her?' " mused Derst under his breath. "Who's 'her?' "

Arya, reeling, could say nothing.

Greyt spent a moment recovering his self-control before he addressed her again. He was rubbing his gold ring. Then he lifted Arya's chin and examined her. "I could take you out of these chains, you know. You and I—"

"I'll never touch you," Arya said, staring into his eyes, "except with a sword."

Greyt smiled. He let her head fall again and turned away. At the cell door, he paused.

"As you will," he said. "You've had your chance to do your prancing, now your feet will do the dancing ... under the gallows."

CHAPTER 17

30 Tarsakh

As the clouds obscuring the morning sun grew darker and denser, a single rider galloped hard along the road to Silverymoon. Keeping a hood pulled low, the rider urged the steed on in the secret tongue of the druids. A forest green cloak whipped in the wind like the wings of a griffon flying low to the ground. Lightning cracked and flashed, but the rider paid it no mind, driving the horse on and on.

Camouflaged and invisible in one of his hiding places—he did not claim the Moonwood as his home ground for nothing—Meris hid a mocking smile inside his black cowl as he drew a bead with his light crossbow.

This courier would be the last victim of the "Ghost Murderer."

When the druid galloped within range, Meris almost lazily let the crossbow bolt fly.

The bolt took the druid in the face, blooming from the right eye socket. A hand clutching at the shaft, the druid went limp. The steed whinnied and bucked, and after a few steps the rider slumped off. Seeing its rider lying unmoving on the ground, the horse panicked and bolted down the trail toward Silverymoon.

Meris sighed. How disappointing. His aim had been too good. He had really been hoping for the chance to inflict some good old-fashioned terror and pain.

Well, he might as well go down and make sure the courier was dead.

He slid down the shadowtop trunk and landed deftly on both feet. Hooking his crossbow back on his belt, he drew his trusty hand axe. He had lost his old long sword in the forest, but he had Walker's shatterspike to replace it. He kept the fabulous weapon—spoils of war, he figured—sheathed at his belt. He would not need both weapons to handle a weak and helpless druid who was probably already dead.

The druid lay like a discarded doll, legs grotesquely bent. The quarrel, standing out from the druid's face, pointed straight up at the sky. Sighing at his own perfect aim, Meris raised his axe high and bent low to pull the hood aside.

When he did, he found Amra Clearwater's very alive eyes staring at him. She had been holding the quarrel up to her face, but now moved it aside and smiled at him.

"Well met, Meris Wayfarer," she said with a wink.

"Bane's blood!" Meris shouted.

He swung the hand axe down at that smile, but Amra caught it. The blade made not the slightest nick in her palm and Meris felt as though he had swung at solid rock. What was more, reddish magic flowed from Amra's palm and traced its way along the axe blade. Meris watched, horror-stricken, as the fine steel rusted over, corroded, and fell apart in his hand.

Suddenly unarmed, he leaped back and reached for the shatterspike. He was too slow, for Amra extended her hand toward him and a lightning bolt shot from the sky to strike at his feet, throwing him to the ground. Shivering with electricity, Meris tried to scream but found he did not have the breath. His legs, however, still worked, and he took full advantage of them to remove himself from the druid's presence.

As he ran, Amra rose up into the air, borne aloft by roiling lightning and wind. "You will pay for slaying Peletara, bastard!" she shouted.

"Everyone calls me that," muttered Meris as he hurled a dagger at the floating druid.

The tiny blade, flashing through the air, seemed inconsequential compared to the fury of nature's power coursing through his opponent. Sure enough, the dagger skipped off her shoulder.

Stifling a curse, Meris beat a hasty retreat to the cover of the trees and yanked the light crossbow free of his belt. Hands still twitching, he fought to load a quarrel into the weapon.

"You cannot run!" Amra shouted. "You cannot escape!" Words of power flowed from her mouth like a torrent of rain as she cast another spell.

At first, nothing happened. Then the trees behind which Meris hid twisted and curled, reaching gnarled branches toward him. Cursing, the wild scout struggled and squirmed free before they could grasp him.

"Beastlord's breath!" he growled as he fumbled at his belt pouch, staggering away.

He possessed a valuable—and expensive—item for just such an occasion: a last stand against a spell hurler. Normally, he never would have considered wasting such power for Greyt's sake—he would have preferred to run and leave the task incomplete. How, though, could he escape a woman at whose command the trees bowed and the very weather served? The choice was between much wealth and his life, and Meris was a survivor.

Even as Amra glided through the swaying, animate trees, lightning sparking from her eyes, Meris pulled the cloudy gray stone out of his pouch. It was plain and without ornament—it could have been any river-smoothed cat's eye, seemingly worthless. Within it, however, pulsed the spark of antimagic—a power he needed desperately.

As Meris leaped aside, narrowly dodging a bolt of lightning, he crushed the stone in two and hurled the pieces back. Not watching where he ran, he tripped over a slithering tree root and fell away from Amra. Even as he went down, he turned in the direction of his enemy, watching the stone's pieces fly toward her.

An aura of golden energy, pulsing with red sparks, burst from the broken stone in the air and struck Amra like a shock-wave. She started and collapsed to her knees as Silvanus's divine power abruptly left her and her magical protections dropped for an instant. She looked up at Meris in shock and incomprehension . . .

Right down the length of a loaded crossbow.

Even as he fell backward, Meris fired and the druid threw herself aside. The bolt grazed the side of Amra's head, sending a small splash of blood on to her light tunic. With a gasp, she collapsed, moaning, to the ground. At the same instant, Meris slammed into the turf with numbing force, and shivers of pain ran through his right leg.

After a long, agony-filled moment, the scout drew himself up. His leg was not broken, but it certainly did not appreciate being moved. Biting his lip against the pain, he dragged himself over to where Amra lay. The antimagic field had faded by now—the stone only dispelled all magic for a short breath—but the damage had been done. Amra lay squirming and gasping, clutching at the side of her face where the crossbow bolt had struck her.

Perhaps she was still protected by her accursed skin of stone, but Meris wondered if her magic would stop Walker's shatterspike sword. If it did, there was always smothering.

"Now, you little half-breed strumpet," spat Meris. The shatterspike came out of its scabbard and Meris admired the gleam along the mithral blade. "You've given me enough trouble, and it's time to—"

Too late, he caught sight of her eyes. Where they were usually soft blue, now they were stormy, and he thought he caught sight of tiny flickers of lightning.

Too late, he understood their significance. Too late, he heard the thunder overhead.

Too late, he realized that his antimagic stone had only suppressed, not dispelled, her connection with the lightning storm.

Amra shouted a word in Elvish and pointed. In reply to her call, a crack of lightning struck Meris full in the chest.

The cry blown from his lungs, the dusky youth tumbled, limp and senseless, back through the air to land, spread-eagled, with a bone-crunching smack against a wide shadowtop. He slid limply to the ground. Lightning coursed through his body, causing his limbs to spasm, then he lay still, thin vapors of smoke rising from his inert body. His eyes were wide and staring but saw nothing. The shatter-spike fell from his nerveless hand.

The world existed in a cacophony of ringing agony for a long moment before blissful darkness surrounded him.

❂ ❂ ❂ ❂ ❂

Panting, it was a while before Amra could stand. The bolt's impact—grazing her temple—had thrown her from her feet. Her shocked body refused to obey her commands. Nothing had hurt so badly in all her life. If the shot's angle had been just a few degrees steeper . . . Well, Amra thanked Silvanus, Mielikki, Tymora, and whatever other gods may have been responsible that it had not been.

Finally, she mustered the courage and energy to rise to her knees with a hand on the hilt of her belt dagger. It was dangerous, for she could not manage the concentration for a spell, and if Meris had been ready with his crossbow, she would have been done for. Fortunately, no lancing death came from any side. Scanning around quickly, Amra decided she was in no immediate danger.

Meris still lay where she had blasted him against a tree, unmoving. At first, his open eyes startled her and she drew her dagger, uttering a prayer to Silvanus. Meris did not move, so Amra felt it was safe to kneel beside him. Using techniques perfected by many years as Quaervarr's chief doctor and midwife, she inspected the young man. His breathing was shallow and his heartbeat faint. Even with the burn on his chest and back, he was not dead. He was, however, far from conscious.

Amra contemplated pulling her dagger across his throat. She had never killed anyone in cold blood, but the scout certainly deserved it for the murder of Peletara and the other couriers. Amra suspected that the arrogant and violent Meris was also guilty of plenty of other crimes she could hardly imagine. Few would miss him, and those who might—Lord Singer Dharan Greyt, just as conceited and foul a man as his son—did not warrant Amra's mercy.

All these things passed through the druid's head—and, more to the point, her heart—and she knew she could not pass that kind of judgment. If she let her personal distaste for Meris prompt her knife, that made her no better than him.

Instead, assuring herself that he slumbered soundly, she chanted the words to a simple spell. Vines sprouted from the undergrowth surrounding Meris's limp form and wrapped themselves around his body. Since he was not awake to struggle, they found a perfect grip that did not constrict or cause harm. Thus entangled, he would not be able to move if he woke. She even cast a spell of healing to stabilize his body until she could return to claim him. It would stave off death, but he would probably never walk again, not with the way his spine had cracked against the tree.

Amra considered that fitting justice for the atrocities he had committed.

She stood up and almost fell. The blow to her head left her dizzy and sick to her stomach. Struggling not to gag or deposit her breakfast in the helmthorn, the druid steadied herself against a nearby tree trunk. The forest spun crazily and the colors blurred.

Amra felt at her satchel for the scroll written in her own hand—under Unddreth's dictation—signed and sealed by the captain of the guard, which she would deliver into the hands of Geth Stonar or, failing that, those of Lady Alustriel herself. She called weakly for her horse. The noble animal neighed in reply from the path where it waited.

The message bore urgent news: Unddreth and his soldiers could not overwhelm Lord Greyt's forces and they needed aid. The Captain of the watch was probably dead or in Greyt's dungeons even now, and Amra said a prayer that her apprentices at the Oak House had escaped Greyt's long arm as well. The druids could defend themselves, she hoped, until she could return.

As Amra put her hand on her horse's neck, she became aware of another sensation, one that did not have its source in her muddy head.

Even as she shivered with a nameless fear, she felt everything around her grow cold and empty. It was as though the very life she held sacred bled slowly out of the forest. Ferns seemed to shrivel and die as trees rotted and petrified from the inside. A quick, bewildered look confirmed that none of the surrounding plants had changed—her connection with the life around her was what was under attack. Silvanus's power faded and died, as though nature itself had choked to death in the space of a few breaths.

"Oakfather help me." Amra stammered. The plea came out in a wisp of mist. Her steed whinnied and threw its head in terror, eyes rolling.

Pretender, a ghostly whisper accused in her mind. *Weakling. Disgrace.*

Amra whirled, but she couldn't see anyone there. She staggered back from the horse which, unattended, bolted in panic. With the horse gone, Amra could see a gray mist flow up from where it had stood. In that mist, gold and crimson mingled in a pair of burning eyes that bored into Amra's soul.

"Wh-who are you?" the half-elf druid asked. She tried to draw her dagger, but her hand shook too violently.

One who knows the power you spend your meager life seeking, the mist said to her without speaking. *One who knows you for the destroying scourge you are, you and your human blood. One who knows your heart and the deception there, lies told to the very nature you pretend to serve.*

"Stay away from me," Amra stammered. She tripped and crawled away, keeping her eyes fixed on those burning points.

I am your power and your purification, your doom and your redemption, your darkness and your spirit. The mist swept closer. Tiny winds snapped at Amra's hair and pulled her toward the burning eyes. *I am your enemy and your only hope.*

Then recognition dawned upon her. "Gods," Amra stammered. "But the Order—they turned you away a century ago! They destroyed you!"

The ghostly whisper became a horrible laugh that left Amra screaming soundlessly and clutching at her ears in vain. Her mind felt as though it were bleeding.

I am a force of nature, Gylther'yel said in Amra's mind. *I cannot be destroyed. Not until I rid the world of every last one of your wretched human kin.*

Amra felt cool earth swallowing her, but it was unlike any druidic spell she had ever felt—rather, this was the power of the ghostly itself, as much the power of unlife as her power was of life. She could not muster the power to fight against it except to cry out vainly to her god, Silvanus the Oakfather.

Then darkness took her, cutting off her scream.

❧　❧　❧　❧　❧

Gylther'yel stretched, causing a ripple through the Ethereal. The shadowy trees bowed in her presence and spirits ran from her, terrified. A warm, yellow-orange life beat before her, that of the half-breed she had just defeated and imprisoned.

The ghost druid's eyes narrowed. She hated nothing more than humans except two things: their crimes against nature and those humans who pretended to worship the natural order. Amra Clearwater, with her elf heritage and her faith, was both. Even so, the ghost druid hesitated to kill her. She did not wish to wet her hands with the blood of the true people, even when it came from a half-breed—a half-human—such as Amra Clearwater.

Gylther'yel decided to keep the druid alive for the time being. Perhaps she would find a more suitable use for her in the future.

Then she became aware of a second, fainter life beating beneath a shadowy tree a ways from where she stood.

Gylther'yel stepped fully into the Material. Colors became more vibrant and the shadows disappeared. The glare made her squint, but only for a moment. Smells and the sounds of birdsong returned, but Gylther'yel paid them no mind. Instead, she crossed over the soft forest turf toward the faint pulse of life.

"Ah, my poor little Wayfarer. You've wandered too far." She smiled.

Meris, wrapped in vines, made for a helpless target. His body did not move, but the Ghostly Lady could tell that he yet lived. She wondered if either of those observations would change if she drew on more of her ghostly power and lit those vines with shadowy flame.

She reached one lithe, deceptively delicate hand down to pour her power into the vines that entangled Meris's chest. . . .

Even as she was about to do it, the ghost druid thought better of burning the boy alive. Instead, she drew herself up and craned a pointed ear. Something caught her and she turned away from Meris, threw her gray cloak wide around her thin gold body, and shifted into a ghostly raven. The bird leaped into the air and took wing into the gathering storm.

If Meris had been awake, he might have heard a lonely wolf's howl.

CHAPTER 18

30 Tarsakh

Lightning cracked and torrential rain tore the grassy earth to muddy ruin. It was noon, but it might as well have been midnight for all the hidden sun's power to pierce the thick storm clouds. A lonely, unmarked grave stood in the center of Walker's grove. The blood had finally run out of the stream, but pockmarks filled with crimson fluid remained, and scars from blades and scrambling footfalls rent the earth, turning the peaceful glade into a battlefield. Three bodies—one crushed and the other two dead of wounds from which the knives had been removed—lay twisted and staring at nothing.

A terrible silence gripped the grove. The doe and fawns that often visited the tranquil glade were nowhere to be found. The birds and even the crickets had ceased their singing. Occasional peals of thunder rent the deathly stillness, but there was not a sound of life to be heard.

A lone spirit—that of Tarm Thardeyn—haunted the grove. He paced a circle around the grave, silent as always, pacing as he had for half a day. Finally, he looked up to the heavens, as though he heard a ghostly voice from on high. He knelt, threw his arms wide, and turned his face upward, letting the rain fall through his spectral body.

Perhaps he was praying to the god of justice he had served in life. Perhaps he was locked in a moment of silent, necessarily private thought.

Or perhaps he was merely waiting.

Then a rare smile brightened his middle-aged features and he mouthed a word of thanks. Tarm put his hand down toward the earth, as though reaching to help someone up.

A single sound answered: a lone wolf's howl, a sound of despair, anger, loss, and . . .

Vengeance.

❧ ❧ ❧ ❧ ❧

A left hand burst from the ground, its clawlike fingers covered in a mixture of blood and clay. The muck obscured even the silver ring on the fourth finger, but not the single sapphire that burned brightly in the storm light. It met Tarm's outstretched hand and paused for a moment, as though it felt the spectral flesh.

Then, passing through it, the hand scrabbled along the ground. It achieved a hold. Corded muscles wrenched an arm encircled by a dull steel bracer up out of the loose earth. Then another hand joined the first, then another arm. Together, the arms strained and pulled.

Into the rain and death, Walker hauled himself from the grave. His tunic hung in tatters around his pale shoulders and chest, where a long puffy ridge and mouthlike scars had joined the others. His sword belt hung around his waist but his sword was gone, as were his throwing knives. His hair lay matted with blood and his face was stained with tears, filth, and gore, but his eyes burned as fiercely as his ring's eye shone. Lightning cracked.

Walker pushed himself to his feet, clutching his arms around himself, and took a tentative step toward the tiny waterfall on the north end of the grove. He fell immediately, slamming his face into the dirt. Rain pounded his back and tore at his hair, even as his body shook with a coughing fit that threatened to tear him apart. He waited long, agonizing moments as the retching passed.

Then, when his coughing was done, Walker looked up. The spirit of Tarm Thardeyn stood on high, reaching down as though to lift him up. The old spirit's face was encouraging. Walker reached up for his hand—a hand he knew he could not touch. He thought he felt something, though—something of Tarm's spirit, a gift from beyond the veil.·

It was a touch that gave him strength.

In firm silence, Walker levered himself up again, only to fall a second time after two steps. Stoically, burning with resolve, he rose and fell a third time, then a fourth, and a fifth, covering about twelve steps. The sixth time he stood, his legs finally fully supported him and he managed to limp toward the fallen shadowtop that made a natural waterfall in the creek.

When he arrived, he sank down beside the small pond and reached a shaking hand toward the water, as though to splash his face. He plunged his hand and arm into the freezing water and searched the bottom of the pool for a moment. His fingers closed on something hard and he pulled it up and out of the water. It was a simple wood box sealed with wax to render it waterproof. With a grimace, Walker broke the seal and pulled it open. Eight throwing knives gleamed up at him.

Loading them into wrist, belt, and boot sheathes, Walker gazed about the grove. His eyes lit upon Thin-Man's corpse. He hobbled over to it and gestured to the air.

A mortal observer would have thought him mad, but only because he lacked Walker's ghostsight. In truth,

Thin-Man's spirit lingered over the corpse, caught in a state of confusion.

"Be free," said Walker. "Free as the wind through the glittering aspen leaves."

Thin-Man gave him a smile and dissipated like mist caught in a stray sunbeam.

Rain dripping from his nose, Walker inspected the body, but not for weapons or armor, which he knew would be gone. He did not even notice the stench of a body dead for half a day. He appraised Thin-Man's shoulders and chest and shook his head. Too small.

He moved on to One-Eye's corpse, dismissed that spirit in similar fashion, then scanned the man's huge body. He frowned. Too large.

"What are you doing?" came a sonorous voice from behind him.

Walker closed his eyes but did not turn. "Making ready," he said.

"Why? Where are you going?"

"To Quaervarr." He removed One-Eye's eye patch but otherwise left the body alone. He rose and went to Red-Hair.

"Why?" Gylther'yel asked. "You are not recovered enough yet to go, and it would not matter. I have planted the seeds that will lead to Greyt's downfall. Your revenge will happen anyway. All is done."

"Revenge is not why I go."

When Gylther'yel did not reply, Walker turned to look at her. In her shadowy gown, untouched by the rain that drenched Walker, the sun elf looked radiant in the half light—a creature of beauty that did not belong in a scene of such misery and destruction.

He noticed that, surprisingly, the spirit of Tarm Thardeyn had not fled at her approach. Instead, his father stood calmly next to his grave, saying nothing. Walker took strength from his courage.

"You would not understand," said Walker. "I will go." He started toward Red-Hair.

With a growl, Gylther'yel caught Walker's arm and held it with the strength of an enraged grizzly bear.

"You will not," she said, her face drawn in rage and her eyes glowing crimson in the storm's light.

The ghostwalker looked back at her, his eyes wide with surprise. Since when had she touched him? To his knowledge, she never had.

He felt visions coming to him, flowing from her touch. Her psychic resonance, showing him her memories...

A dark night, laughter—the night of his death. Words... "Whether you will or no."

As though remembering herself, she released Walker's arm and backed away. Her face was calm, but her eyes remained furious.

"I forbid you to go."

What vision had he seen?

"You have no control over me any more," said Walker without emotion.

"I am your master and you are my champion," argued Gylther'yel with steel in her voice.

"You sent killers after me, and you yet believe that?" Walker's voice seemed to cut Gylther'yel like a knife, but the ghost druid regained control in an instant.

"I sent them to kill that little harlot of a knight, not you, of course," said Gylther'yel with a dismissive wave. "It was for your own good—she was leading you astray, diverting you from your path. I am not about to throw away the fifteen years of work I spent on you, training and arming you, teaching you the powers you and I alone share—"

"But do you love me, Gylther'yel?"

The question set her back on her heels. For the first time Walker could remember, the ghost druid was speechless. Gylther'yel mouthed words, but no sound came out. She looked at Walker as though at a maddened animal.

Walker nodded sadly. "As I thought." He walked toward Red-Hair's corpse.

"You turn your back on me, on everything I have taught

you, on the years we have spent together, running the forest as mother and son, all because you feel neglected? Oh I'm sorry, you spoiled child!" Gylther'yel spat. "Love is not of nature, but is human artifice! You are better without it! The way I made you!"

Walker did not look at her. "Farewell, Gylther'yel," he said. Walker arrived at Red-Hair's corpse, sent the man's spirit away, and nodded, finding this one to his liking. He crouched down and began pulling off the man's clothes.

The ghost druid stared at him in shock.

"After all I have done for you. Even after I forgave you the female...."

With a grimace, Walker tore away the tattered remains of his tunic and slipped the Quaervarr watch uniform over his head. Then he strapped the sword belt around his waist.

Understanding seemed to dawn on Gylther'yel, and she stepped in Walker's way as he turned.

"Then she is what this is all about!" she said. "Do not bother. Meris and his men probably dispatched her quickly, as soon as they had enjoyed her to the fullest. Your heroism is amusing, but there is no one left to save."

"She lives." It was a statement of fact.

"How can you know that?"

"Her spirit is not here with me," said Walker with a shrug. "So she has not died."

Gylther'yel looked around then eyed him curiously.

"Why do you expect her spirit to be with you?" the ghost druid asked.

Walker looked at her. "She loves me," he stated. "And I love her."

Gylther'yel had no reply except to stare at him in shock.

Gliding around her, Walker crossed to the patch of grass where he and Arya had lain together and pulled something from a low fir branch. With a flourish, he threw his black cloak over his shoulder and stepped into the shadows, only to vanish as though he had never been there.

◈ ◈ ◈ ◈ ◈

The rain dissipated and the lightning stopped.

Gylther'yel stared at the shadow into which Walker had disappeared. They had never spoken to each other so bitterly as long as he had been in her keeping—and none of the bitterness had come from Walker.

A memory of long ago flashed into Gylther'yel's mind—the most painful she possessed. It was a day not unlike this one, with angry clouds overhead, and a conversation not unlike the one she had just shared. It was the day that marked the dawn of her hatred of the humans.

It was the day her sister Wyel'thya had told her she was going to the fledgling town of Quaervarr on an overture of peace from the druids of the Moonwood. She taught them the ways of the druids, of coexisting with nature—the ways of peace. Then a lover had come, and a child: Lyetha Elfsdaughter.

The ghost druid, betrayed, had never forgiven Wyel'thya, refused even to see her when she sought out Gylther'yel's aid. Then Wyel'thya had grown sick, deathly ill . . .

It had been a human disease.

The sun elf had lost control of herself for the first time in her long life. Much of Quaervarr had burned that day, but the fledgling druids of Wyel'thya's order repelled Gylther'yel, the golden angel of the Dark Wood.

Alone, left for dead in the forest, she had learned of a new power, borne of her hatred of the humans and all life. She had become the Ghostly Lady.

Gylther'yel's eyes turned back to the shadows. A tear slid down her cheek.

"I loved my sister," she said. "But I never got her back, did I?"

Then the ghost druid let out a keening shriek that pierced both the Ethereal and Material and collapsed to her knees. The spirits remaining in the grove started and sped away as fast as they could manage from the enraged ghost druid. The force of that shriek caused all the songbirds and animals in the trees to shudder and die, their life-force wrenched from them.

All was silent except for Gylther'yel, who wept bitterly into the mud, screaming in rage and frustration.

Finally, Gylther'yel sniffed and wiped her tears away with the fringe of her cloak. There was one card left to play, and play it she would. Her face still red, she rose.

"Forgive me, Wyel'thya," she said. "Forgive me for prolonging his suffering. And forgive me now for what I must do to the last of our blood."

Spreading her arms like wings, Gylther'yel leaped into the air and blinked out of the physical realms, turning into a ghostly raven. Riding the winds left spinning by the storm, she soared to a little grove near the edge of the forest, where she had left that last card slumbering.

CHAPTER 19

30 Tarsakh

The guards at Quaervarr's only gate had seen many strange comings and goings in the past few days, but none quite so strange as this.

The storm had passed but the sky was far from clear. A gray sheet of clouds still obscured the sky. The air hung thick and heavy, and a lingering tension caused more than a few watchmen to shift uneasily.

Both did a double take when a figure—a watchman by his garb—appeared some distance away, seemingly out of the very shadow of one of the great firs that flanked the road. In that silence, they should have heard him coming almost a mile distant. The man took a few zigzagging steps toward them, lurched, and fell.

They ran to him. Clad in the ring mail of a watchman, the man lay on his back in the mud. His face and tangled hair were plastered with mud and gore, obscuring his features except for a black leather eye patch that covered his right eye.

"Aye, Belk, it be one-eyed Tamel, eh?" said one guard, a hefty man named Mart.

"What's 'e doin' in one o' our tunics? In't 'e one of the rangers?" the pock-faced Belk replied. Mart shrugged, but his eyes flashed with worry. Unddreth would have both their commissions if he found out they were more loyal to Greyt than Quaervarr. Though Unddreth seemed to have disappeared, it was better not to take chances.

Belk checked the man for a pulse and breath, but neither were there to be found. His flesh felt like ice.

"Beshaba's bosom, he's dead! And 'e looks like he's been dead days!"

"What? What do we do?" asked Mart in a panic.

"Let's get 'im inside quick, afore someone sees 'im!" Belk hoisted the man's arms and Mart took his legs. Together, they carried the body inside and carted him over to an alley, where they dumped him.

"Where do we take 'im?" Belk's eyes darted this way and that, as though seeing spies hiding in every shadow. "Not to them druids, nor to Greyt's manor."

"We gotta think o' something—"

"But I don't know—"

"Silent as mist."

Belk looked at Mart.

"Aye? What was that?"

"I didn't say nothing," denied Mart.

" 'Anything.' You didn't say 'anything,' you halfwit. Gods, I'm soundin' like one o' the druids, wit' their grammar-ical lessons. An' you did say something, something about—"

"Still as death."

"No, it wasn't nothing like that," argued Belk. "Something about mist—"

Mart opened his mouth to protest then yelped when something grabbed his ankle. Belk's eyes went wide. As one, they looked down, only to be yanked from their feet.

Their heads struck the hard cobblestones and unconsciousness took them.

❀ ❀ ❀ ❀ ❀

Shaking off the last influence of his deathlike sleep, Walker wiped his face clean with the fat guard's cloak and stripped the Quaervarr tabard from his chest and the borrowed eye patch from his face. Dressed once again in his comfortable black, he sheathed one of the long swords at his belt. He would carry the other. Lastly, he opened his satchel and pulled out his thick black cape, which he draped around his shoulders. Walker stood, throwing his cloak wide and adjusting the high collar.

He looked over at the spirit of Tarm Thardeyn and nodded. The spirit did not respond, of course, but Walker thought he could feel grim pride resonating from Tarm.

After steadying himself, Walker padded over to the lip of the alley, bracing himself against a rough oak wall. Walker had not yet fully healed—not by his ring or by absorbing the energies of Shadow—but he had no time for weakness. When he reached the main street, he crouched and peered around the edge.

The street lay deserted, but Walker could hear shouts from a mass of people gathered in the main square of Quaervarr, farther up. Flitting between the shadows along the street was a simple matter and, indeed, hardly necessary—no eyes came upon him.

In the plaza, most of Quaervarr's population shouted for the Lord Singer. Guardsmen stood at the edges of the crowd, weapons drawn as though to ward off attackers, but their attention was just as fixed upon Greyt's door as were the eyes of the gathered hunters, trappers, traders, and families. Walker could see three dressed in the robes of druids wearing expressions of worry and undisguised anger. Walker noted the distinct absence of Captain Unddreth and Amra

Clearwater. He wondered what had become of them. Perhaps Greyt had removed them, for they were well-known as his enemies.

Then the doors to Greyt's manor opened and Walker's thoughts flew away in a wave of overwhelming hatred.

Resplendent in a full suit of golden mail, with a deep purple cape billowing out behind him and golden hair falling to his shoulders, Lord Singer Dharan Greyt stepped out beaming. His skin seemed to glow and the gray in his hair had disappeared. His golden yarting sang under his talented fingers, projecting chords of triumph and magic over the crowd.

Much of the crowd was stunned at his glorious appearance, and all—even the druids who looked at him with suspicion—fell silent.

"Welcome, friends!" shouted Greyt. His voice was loud and booming, and carried over the crowd to where Walker stood in the shadows. "You have come to my door questioning and concerned, but you will leave with answers well earned!"

Walker felt bardic magic resonate from the yarting and the Lord Singer's voice, Walker fought, exerting his will against Greyt's own, to keep the image of Greyt—his most hated foe—as the monster he had seen little but knew too well. The Dharan Greyt Walker knew was not the bold, self-assured hero standing before the crowd, but a weak, aging coward.

In the end, Walker was not fooled by Greyt's magic.

"Today dawns a new day in the history of our fair town, here in the frontier of the Moonwood," continued Greyt. "Or, should I say, today marks the end of an era. For too long, a dark scourge has haunted these woods and our fair streets, a scourge that walks without sound and wields merciless steel—a scourge some call Walker, and some the Ghost Murderer." There were grumbles in the crowd. "Well, no longer! Today, my son Meris and I have brought to an end the terrible reign of the Ghost Murderer!"

Cheers greeted this. Walker—standing there, listening

to the announcement of his own death—might have smiled were he not overcome with enmity for the man speaking.

Greyt waited for the cheering to die down before continuing. "This very last eve, my son slew him, with the help of several of my servants." With this, he indicated the gathered rangers. Gieves and Darthan nodded shortly. "We have also apprehended the Ghost Murderer's accomplices—three renegade knights from Silverymoon."

Gasps sounded from the crowd. Walker's brow furrowed.

"Surely you recall three strangers who came into town, led by a woman, asking questions? Lady Arya Venkyr, who came to Quaervarr on a mission to investigate missing couriers—couriers she and the Ghost Murderer slew! Along with her two companions, they sought to find what we knew of the ghastly crimes, so they could continue them at will!"

There were a few murmurs among the crowd refuting this. Some called for proof, others for motive.

Greyt had the perfect answer.

"She is a Malarite spy! See for yourselves!" With a flourish, he produced a small, carved claw on a leather thong, old bloodstains decorating its fingers. Startled cries ran through the crowd as many recognized the dreaded holy symbol of the beast god of the Black Blood. "This was found around Lady Venkyr's neck—it provides all the evidence we need, even if her damnable actions were not known!"

The crowd erupted in cries of terror and beseeching calls. They begged Greyt, their great champion, to defend them. A few even cried for Arya's death.

Walker gritted his teeth and tightened his grasp on the sword he held beneath his cloak. He had to exert all his terrible will to keep from striding forward to confront Greyt.

He caught a flash of a grin across Greyt's face, but no one else seemed to notice. "Fear not, friends of Quaervarr!" he called. "These vandals and thieves will not go free. The Ghost Murderer has already paid the penalty for his abominable crimes, but the traitor knights will also be punished. This eve, at sunset, the three shall hang in this very plaza, where all of you may bear witness to the consequences that await traitors and servants of darkness."

Silence gripped the plaza. Few remembered such brutal justice being meted out, even in this frontier town. Even those who had called out for executions were struck by the realization that it might actually happen. Then, slowly, several men in the crowd—men Greyt had planted, Walker thought—began to clap. The applause picked up, louder and louder, until cheers sounded from the crowd. In moments, the name of "Dharan Greyt" and "Quickfinger" were the dominant calls.

Walker had taken it all in stride, but he could listen no longer. Arya! The name resounded in his mind, followed by an image of the knight's face.

He could not allow this. This was wrong, and not only because the one he loved faced execution. This was wrong because three innocent people would pay for Greyt's crimes, three innocents who fought against those crimes. What was more, this monster undermined the town's stability—questioning its leaders and stirring up popular opinion against good, just people. More than just three knights would die in the chaos. Death was the only outcome of such madness.

Walker did not know where this sense of justice came from—perhaps from the same center that made him feel a twinge of sorrow over every man he killed unnecessarily, over every guard, every ranger, and every man or woman manipulated by the words or actions of one of the monsters he hated so much.

Feelings of justice, long forgotten and buried beneath years of pain, flooded back to him—values he must have held before his death at the hands of Greyt and his cruel fellows.

The spirit of Tarm knelt at Walker's side and grasped at his hand. Walker, surprised, looked at Tarm in shock. The spirit was trying to communicate with him, but Walker felt nothing but a long string of conflicting emotions from the spirit: joy, love, agitation, fear, and anger. Walker had never seen his father act this way and it caught him off guard.

Remembering the terrible purpose that had brought him here, Walker scowled.

"Why do you not speak to me, Tarm Thardeyn?" he demanded. "Are you not my father? Am I not your son? Speak to me!"

The spirit, shocked by the words, just stared, unmoving, and Walker felt nothing emanating from the spirit but sadness.

Then he heard another shout to the Lord Singer from the courtyard, followed by applause, and he turned to fix the hated Lord Greyt's features with his withering gaze. He felt the cold power of his ghostly rage beating within, waiting to take control.

Seething at the injustices perpetuated by Dharan Greyt, this hypocrite who so casually claimed the love and adoration of Quaervarr while he stabbed her people in the back, Walker made to step out into the open. He could picture the effect his appearance would have upon the assembled. The crowd would run in panic, scattering like flies before his cracked bellow of Greyt's name. Striding forward, sword pointed toward the Lord Singer, he would cut down any guardsmen who attacked him. He would swat aside the rangers like locusts. Even the towering Bilgren would fall under his blade. Finally, all his defenses gone, Greyt would cower, helpless before Walker and his sword—his avenging, just sword.

The Spirit of Vengeance would have his due.

That would have occurred, perhaps, except for the hand that reached out of the shadows of the alley behind him and cupped itself around his mouth.

❧   ❧   ❧   ❧   ❧

Chased back into his manor by cheers, shouts, and tangible adoration, Dharan Greyt shook his fists in triumph even as he fought against the ironic laughter that threatened to bubble up out of his throat. Claudir was a silent, lingering specter at his side. Greyt clapped the steward on the back, nearly knocking him down, and took the bottle of elverquisst he offered. In his triumph, Greyt almost forgot how to operate the corkscrew.

The greatest performance of his life! They had drunk up every word, even without his enthralling magic! He had but to beam at them, and these foolish sheep adored him.

Never had the stakes been higher, but never had his accomplishments been greater. Greyt loved the gamble—the risk that the townsfolk would see through the web he had woven, or the intrigues that won him their hearts—but he loved winning it even more. Secretly, quietly, he had removed Stonar's greatest supporters. Captain Unddreth, Amra Clearwater, and several local businessmen had met with "accidents" or had mysteriously disappeared in the last few tendays.

Now he was in the perfect position to seize his heroic title, and he had done it—and with what form! If he wanted to rule the town, he had but to breathe the suggestion and they would crown him Lord of Quaervarr. If he wanted to sweep the Moonwood and dispose of whatever remained of that annoying Jarthon and the Black Blood once and for all, he had hundreds of willing suicide fighters. Even if he desired to march against Silverymoon, he had no doubt these poor commoners would bring out their hatchets and saws to aid his cause.

Lord Singer Dharan Greyt felt a warm swell in his chest. So this was how it felt to be a hero at last—he hardly even remembered all the men and women he had slain to make it this far. They did not matter, for they had made *him!* A noble sacrifice, indeed.

The farther he walked into his manor, though, the quicker the warm feeling faded, only to be replaced with a familiar lingering emptiness, the same feeling that had come upon him when Lyetha had denied his heroism, ironic as it was, and when Meris had. . . .

Greyt growled to no one in particular. Was there no one who shared his vision of heroism? Would he be doomed to a lonely existence as a hero forever?

Well, Meris wasn't a concern any longer. Greyt could always have another son. How many women of Quaervarr were fighting over him even now?

He took a swig of the elverquisst and the hearty wine banished the feeling of emptiness in his stomach.

"So be it, then!" he shouted to no one in particular. He rubbed his gold ring. "If I must be a lone wolf, then so be it!"

The rangers outside his door cast quick glances as he came, then snapped back to attention. Any other day, their behavior might have struck Greyt as odd. At the moment though, still feeling enthusiasm pulse through his body, the Lord Singer thought nothing of it. He opened the door to his study, laughing at his own joke, and shuffled inside. Shutting the portal behind him, Greyt breathed a great sigh then turned toward his desk with a smile.

What he saw wiped the grin right off his face.

"Hail, Hero-Father."

❦   ❦   ❦   ❦   ❦

Walker spun, breaking the grip around his mouth, and held up the guard's sword to threaten his attacker. He opened his mouth but words would not come to his tongue. He faltered, drew his blade away, and took a step back.

His attacker—a golden-haired woman—stepped from the shadows. "I know why you have come," she said.

At first, Walker heard Gylther'yel in her voice, but this woman was taller and fuller-bodied than any elf, even though she was thin—gaunt almost. The years had done their work on her features, but Walker could see the beauty in her face.

Walker felt an overwhelming wave of emotion wash over him, a sensation of bittersweet love from the spirit of Tarm Thardeyn. Too stunned to address the spirit—and not about to turn away—he felt his fingers tingling on his sword hilt.

"Who are you?" Walker rasped. He felt oddly embarrassed by his broken voice.

"I am Lyetha Elfsdaughter, the wife of the Lord Singer, the last descendent of Wyel'thya, and the Daughter of the Sun," Lyetha said. "You are the one they call Walker. And you have come to murder my husband." Her eyes were sad.

"What do you want?" asked the ghostwalker.

"I ask for mercy—for my lord." Lyetha's face was smooth and her eyes were damp.

Walker bristled. "Dharan Greyt is a monster." His unshakable self-confidence was not there, though, and he wondered why this woman made him so uneasy. "I must destroy him, for what he did to me . . ."

Moisture flared in Lyetha's eyes, and those eyes seemed to glaze over.

"I cannot stop you, so you must kill me as well," Lyetha said, "for I cannot live without him." She pulled her dress up around her knees, knelt down, and bowed her head. She even shifted the gold mane off her pale neck.

Startled, Walker took a step back but kept a firm grip on his blade. "What?"

A tear dripped down Lyetha's cheek.

"I have not wept—not like this—since my Tarm died," she said softly, not wiping it away. "I live only for Dharan, for he was the only one who comforted me, but . . ." Then she looked up at Walker with tearful eyes. "But I have not wanted to live since my son died. Not truly." Then she bowed her head.

Walker became very cold. He drew the blade back and up.

Another tear fell from Lyetha's eye.

"Goodbye, Rhyn, if you yet live."

CHAPTER 20

30 Tarsakh

Walker's sword banged off a thick oak wall and clattered to the ground.

Lyetha looked up, startled, and Walker was on his knees before her. Having thrown his sword aside, he had pulled off his gloves and now clutched her face softly between his hands, though he knew without his power. Knew, but denied it, until . . .

Shuddering at his cold touch, Lyetha stared into his bright sapphire eyes.

Her eyes.

"Rhyn?" she asked, almost in a whisper. "Can—can it be?"

Lips trembling, unable to speak, Walker slowly nodded. He knew it was the truth.

Lyetha's arms slid around him and she held him fiercely.

"Oh, Rhyn!" she sobbed. "I never dared hope you were alive!"

The ghostwalker's eyes were almost soft. "Mother," he whispered.

His rasping voice, however, jarred him back to reality. Walker pulled his arms from around his mother and tore himself free with a cry. He half-crawled, half-fell backward, slamming into the alley wall, but he hardly felt the impact. Uncalled emotions flowed up in an overwhelming torrent. He clutched his arms around his head in a vain attempt to keep them in.

"Is this the secret you've kept from me all these years, Father?" cried Walker, as though it were a curse. "Is this what you could not tell me?"

As always, Tarm Thardeyn was silent. The spirit just stood there, watching, though when he looked upon Lyetha, his gaze was filled with love. Walker screamed soundlessly.

After a moment, a gentle hand touched his shoulder.

"What's wrong?" Lyetha asked.

He shrugged off her hand. Walker looked at her but found there was little anger in him. He turned his eyes to his bare hands, covered with scars and dirt as they were. They were the hands of a warrior, the hands of an avenger, the hands of a murderer.

"These hands are too bloody to touch yours," Walker rasped.

"What are you talking about?" Lyetha asked. She moved around in front of him and gazed at him. "We're together again. We can run from here, go to Silverymoon—beyond! We can leave here for—"

"You can suggest such a thing?" he asked. "After all I have done, all I have become ... All he did to me?"

"We can leave him behind. This is finished for us."

"Not for me," Walker said, shaking his head. "Not after what he has done. Greyt made me who I am, and he is the last." He stood and turned away. "He will be the last."

"No! You can't kill him!" Lyetha protested, clutching the fringe of his cloak.

"Why?" he snapped as he rounded on her. "Why? He has

taken everything from us, ruined our lives. Why cannot I kill him?"

"There is something you need to know about Dharan," Lyetha said. Walker watched her levelly, even as she struggled to get the words out. "You, ah . . . your—your ring."

"My ring?" He held up the wolf's head ring.

"The lone wolf is . . . it's Dharan's family crest. . . ."

"I know. He put it on me just before he killed me, so I would live through their blows," said Walker. Slowly, purposefully, he wound strips of watchman tabard around his hands, so that he did not have to look at them any more. "So I would be in pain to the last, until he removed it, and its protections with it. He lost it that night, and I found it. His old ring, from his adventuring days." His gaze turned cold.

Lyetha opened her mouth to protest, but the words would not come.

"What is it?" Walker asked, anger in his voice.

"When Dharan was just a boy, he grew up on tales of heroes," Lyetha said. "He . . . he always wanted to become one himself, to . . . to impress me, when we were young . . . but he . . . he. . . ." Her voice grew soft. "In all of his eagerness to be a hero, he forgot that a hero must sometimes give up his dreams in order to do what is right. For Dharan, self-sacrifice is simply not possible."

Walker was impassive.

"I loved him once . . . before I loved Tarm . . . and then . . . I . . . you . . ." Then she trailed off, unable to speak.

The spirit of Tarm looked tragic at that moment, as though she had slapped him. He clearly understood what she was saying.

Walker did not.

"Why does that matter?" he demanded.

Lyetha looked back at him with bleary eyes and managed a little smile. "I . . . I guess . . ." She looked down. "I guess 'tis easier to destroy than to create."

They were silent for a moment. Then Walker sniffed.

"Yes," he said. "Yes, it is."

With his toe, he flipped the sword off the ground into his hand. "Go home, Lyetha. I shall remember what you have said this day, and my vengeance will pass you by."

Lyetha reached out to embrace Walker, but he stepped out of her reach.

"I am lost to you, Mother," he said. "I did not see the truth, and now it is too late. Forgive me for what I have done, and for what I must do."

The spirit of Tarm Thardeyn looked at him and cast a wistful glance at Lyetha, who could neither see him nor feel his loving caress.

Walker left his mother weeping in the alley and stepped out into the street toward the house of Lord Singer Dharan Greyt.

Murderous eyes, a war cry, a sword, and a flail were there to greet him.

❦ ❦ ❦ ❦ ❦

"You've come back . . . so soon," said Greyt, startled but thinking fast.

"Surprised to see me, Father?" asked Meris, spinning the shatterspike so that it clicked against the fine oak of the desk. His hand axe lay imbedded in two volumes of Waterdhavian history that Greyt had left stacked there. " 'Tis no matter. I think we both know why I am here." Meris's voice was slurred, as though his tongue were swollen or he were in his cups.

Against his polished white leather, Meris's dusky features seemed especially exotic, and for a moment, Greyt had not recognized him as his son.

Coolly, the Lord Singer crossed to the sideboard and took two glasses, into which he poured the remainder of the elverquisst he carried.

"Talthaliel told me you would come," Greyt said. "That my son would come to kill me, but that he wouldn't defeat my mage."

"Did he?" Meris asked. He hefted the ghostly shatterspike and his hand axe. "Sorry, but he's indisposed at the moment. Outside. Fighting Rhyn—er, I mean Walker."

Eyes widening, Greyt tipped over the glass in surprise. He barely managed to throw his aging body out of the way to dodge Meris's thrust.

"Traitor elf!" he shouted as he whipped his golden rapier out of its scabbard and fell into a fencing stance almost as though it were second nature. His old muscles protested, but he was glad—for the first time—that he had continued sparring practice.

Standing a few paces away, Meris laughed and waved the shatterspike mockingly.

"Wonderful scheme, father," he said. "You were to become the hero of Quaervarr—a fifth time over? Gods! How much do you have to do? Has any level of brainless worship ever been enough for you? Who are you trying to convince—them, or yourself?"

"Bastard!" Greyt shrieked. He lunged at Meris.

The dusky scout casually parried his sword aside. "Indeed, but that's beside the point," replied Meris. "The point is, when I go outside next, they will all hear how I killed Walker, how I killed the renegade knights, and how I killed the 'mad Lord Singer.' I will be their hero, not you. You're just a murderer, and a mad one at that."

"You treacherous little bastard," spat Greyt.

"You keep calling me that. Sounds more like an insult to you than to me." Then he laughed. "Amazing how history repeats itself—this reminds me of fifteen years ago when you killed your own 'mad' father."

"You knew about that—you were with me the night Rhyn Thardeyn died, the night we murdered your grandfather and the others!" protested Greyt. "Rhyn—you killed him! You took the ring off, in your youthful ignorance—"

"No, Father," said Meris. "Purpose. I hated him and I wanted him dead. And I did it. Perhaps I didn't understand at the time, but I do now, and I don't regret it."

Greyt was horrified. He remembered that night, when he had taken Rhyn into the forest to frighten him, to chase him away. To have Lyetha to himself, to remove any reminder of Tarm Thardeyn, the priest he had killed years before. Meris had removed the healing ring before Greyt's scarring blow, and Greyt's wolf's head ring had been lost in the following argument.

And now . . . now he knew it had been no accident. Meris had been murderous even then.

"Foul creature!" he shouted. "How can Quaervarr accept you, once they know that you are just as great a monster as I?"

The Lord Singer thrust at his son again, but Meris was ready. He knocked the blow aside with his hand axe and lashed out with the shatterspike, tearing a neat red line down Greyt's left arm. The Lord Singer gasped and fell back, though he kept the golden rapier up.

"Correction, father," Meris said with a grin. "I am a greater monster than you will ever be. And, as for Quaervarr—well, who will believe you, a madman?"

"Spoiled brat, I am their hero!" Greyt asserted. "They will believe me, and my magic will persuade them even if they do not!"

Meris shrugged. "Then I guess I'll have to ensure that you don't live to persuade them."

With that, the wild scout charged in, launching a reckless offensive with his two weapons whirling, and Greyt pumped his arms, desperately fending off the attacks.

❧ ❧ ❧ ❧ ❧

Outside, in Quaervarr's main plaza, where the crowd had dispersed in terror at the battle unfolding, Walker struggled with his own attacker.

Attackers, actually, for there were two: the raging barbarian Bilgren, his gyrspike whirling like a zephyr of blade and flail, and a dark-robed mage floating far above, weaving threads of magic into deadly bolts of fire and lightning. Walker prayed Lyetha had fled, so at least he would have only his own safety to worry about.

It would be quite enough.

"Ye escaped me once, with the aid o' thy little fox," spat Bilgren, his mouth foaming in his rage. "Not again—this time, ye're mine. All mine!"

"Romantic," mused Walker. He realized with a start that it was something Arya might have muttered in this situation. The thought brought a twinge of anger. He had to get to her!

Walker parried blows from the gyrspike, swatting away the flail like a ball and slapping the blade wide so that it would not find his flesh, all the while dodging bolts of power the mage rained down upon him.

Bellowing, Bilgren swept the flail at Walker's legs, but the ghostwalker leaped over the blow, kicked off Bilgren's chest and rolled away, just in time to evade a bolt of lightning that slammed into the earth between them. Momentarily stunned by the blast, Bilgren staggered back, howling like a wounded animal.

"Talthaliel, watch where ye be aiming, ye lout!" shouted the big man.

Walker seized the opportunity to hurl two of the daggers from his belt at the barbarian. Bilgren caught one with the shaft of his gyrspike, but the other buried itself to the hilt in his thick stomach. The hulking man took one look at the tiny fang in his flesh and roared, more in anger than in pain. He ignored the blood that began to leak down his rothé hide armor.

Meanwhile, Talthaliel completed another spell and sent down a volley of magical bolts. Rolling, Walker dodged to the side, but the projectiles veered even as they were about to meet the ground and struck him instead, slamming into him with incredible force. Walker gritted his teeth but kept moving.

Bilgren was back, running at Walker with the gyrspike

spinning over his head. The ghostwalker ran as well, toward a bakery at the edge of the plaza, keeping the distance equal between himself and Bilgren. As he ran, he tossed two daggers up at the wizard, but Talthaliel waved them aside like irritating gnats.

Walker did not have to look to know that Bilgren was almost upon him. Running full out toward the wall, Walker leaped, kicked off the log wall at chest height, and flew backward. Bilgren's flail exploded into the wall, sending a shower of wood chips flying, just missing Walker's toes. The ghostwalker flipped over the barbarian's head, landed behind him, and slashed Bilgren across the back.

The cut might have been deeper but for the thick rothé hide. The guard's sword was too dull to penetrate fully, but it was enough to drive the barbarian deeper into his berserker frenzy.

The gyrspike came around in a withering slash, as though it possessed a mind of its own. Walker ducked the high flail and parried the sword blade, but the force of Bilgren's swing spun him around. Disoriented for a moment, he managed to duck the flail coming from behind him, and threw himself into a tumble to avoid a burning ray, which cut a precise line along the ground where his head had been a breath before.

He turned back to Bilgren and had to twist to the left as the gyrspike sword swept up. The flail followed it, and Walker twisted to the right to avoid it. Plying his skill with the curious weapon, Bilgren ducked forward and brought the gyrspike spinning over his shoulders. Walker ducked to avoid being beheaded, and parried the flail as it swept lower. The chain wrapped around his sword, and Bilgren howled in joy, ripping it from Walker's hand. The blade skittered among a pile of crates.

Walker did not, however, stand shocked as the barbarian disarmed him. Slipping a dagger into his hand, he thrust with all his strength, stabbing the tiny blade deep into Bilgren's thigh. The barbarian roared in pain and kicked Walker's midsection, sending him tumbling away. His flying body splintered the crates and he slammed against the store wall, only to slump down.

By coincidence, he landed near his fallen sword, but Walker did not pause to thank the gods. He snapped mental commands at his aching body, forcing it to move after such a hit. Groaning, it did. He rose, wincing, scooped up the blade, and forced his legs to run from the rampaging barbarian, whose smash destroyed another crate.

Walker paid little attention to Bilgren as he continued to leap and dodge blasts, his cape slashed and cut by magic strikes, but he knew he could not keep it up forever. Every now and then he had to turn and parry, riposte, and flee again. If his two opponents kept pressing, not allowing Walker to land a solid blow, it was only a matter of....

The flail of Bilgren's gyrspike slammed into Walker's shoulder as he turned, sending him flying like a petulantly hurled doll.

The ghostwalker sailed through the air to crash into the statue of dancing nymphs that stood in the center of Quaervarr's plaza fountain. He slumped down into the water with a splash and fought against the spinning haze coming over his vision. Walker felt the water around him grow leaden and sluggish, spurred by Talthaliel's magic to freeze and trap him, even as he lay dazed within the pool.

"I'll grind thy bones an' tear thy flesh with me teeth!" Bilgren roared.

A spiked flail blotted out the sun as it swung up over his head.

❧ ❧ ❧ ❧ ❧

Greyt spun right as the shatterspike hacked down, splintering a bookshelf and sending tomes sliding down onto him. He parried Meris's seeking axe on the other side and lashed out with his fist, catching the wild scout in the chest. Meris staggered back, but was quick to knock aside Greyt's riposte.

Backpedaling around the desk, Greyt warded off Meris's attacks with the golden blade. The Lord Singer was the greater swordsman, but Greyt was twice his son's age. How long would it be before Greyt tired and Meris's steel found his flesh?

The hand axe shot in again, and Greyt caught and pulled it wide. Too late, as the axe hooked and held his rapier blade down on the table, he saw the feint for what it was. The shatterspike came slashing in from the other side, and Greyt struggled to put a book in its path. The tome exploded as the steel struck it, sending illustrated pages floating everywhere.

"One of Volo's guides," cursed Greyt. He threw a second book in Meris's face, thwarting the next attack. "Not much more than pictures, but still worth coin—you'll pay for that!"

"I don't think I'll be interested—" said Meris as the sword flashed out again only for Greyt to swat it aside, "—in replacing the library. I was never much of a reader, after all."

Greyt scowled as he pressed the advantage back against Meris. Seizing a daggerlike letter opener he had left idle on the desk, he stabbed out with lightning quickness over the next parry, tearing open Meris's forearm. The youth cursed and slashed the shatterspike between them. Greyt blinked as he watched his favorite letter opener fall in two.

"Typical," said Greyt.

He lunged in, but Meris was ready. The scout sidestepped at the last instant, letting the rapier cut along between his arm and torso. Then Meris hooked the hand axe around Greyt's leg and yanked the Lord Singer from his feet, following the attack with a thrust, meaning to end the fight.

Greyt, though, was prepared. A blade sprouted from the bracer adorning his right arm, and he knocked the shatterspike aside with a scrape. Sparks flew, and he plunged the blade up into Meris's belly. The wild scout cursed and clutched at himself, bent over in pain. The hand axe fell to the ground and the shatterspike dipped. The Lord Singer swatted a blow across Meris's chin, sending the scout staggering back.

Then the Lord Singer stood, limping slightly from his bruised legs and backside. When Meris made no move to strike, Greyt straightened his collar and cuffs, holding the golden rapier between his legs. Supporting himself on the sword, Meris coughed and gagged. A trickle of blood ran from his mouth. Greyt smiled and walked toward him, stretching his arms and holding the rapier horizontally behind his head.

"Well, my boy," Greyt said. "It's been a good couple two and a half decades. I always admired your knack for promoting yourself higher in my esteem—and your dashing looks." He held up the golden rapier and inspected the tip. Giving it a snap, the metal vibrated back and forth. "I always saw such potential in you, but I see I was doomed to disappointment."

Meris moaned, his tongue still thick. Greyt tapped Meris on the cheek with the rapier.

"What a shame—I see so much of that Amnian strumpet in you, too. Poor girl, killed by beasts in the woods. An 'accident.' " Something dawned on him and Greyt smiled. "Ah yes, thank you for reminding me—I had almost forgotten her fate."

Meris's only reply was to stifle a cough. Blood ran through his fingers.

Greyt grimaced. Meris was bleeding all over the carpet, creating stains that would take tendays to get out. No sense making Claudir do extra work.

He drew the rapier back.

❧　❧　❧　❧　❧

I'll grind his bones an' tear his flesh with me teeth!
The words cut to Walker soul and, once there, made it hard and cold as ice. Screaming power filled his body, imbuing him with fifteen years of hatred and pain.

Walker leaped, stepped on the dagger in Bilgren's thigh, kicked off the one in his stomach, and flew over the barbarian's head, turning a forward somersault but flying backward, as though borne aloft on the wind of ghosts.

Barely nicking his trailing cloak, the flail came down and splashed into the water. There it stuck, much to Bilgren's surprise. The big man roared and strained, but he could not pull out the flail—the water had turned to ice around the spiked ball, thanks to Talthaliel's magic and Walker's timing.

Bilgren looked at the gyrspike in shock, then up at Walker, perched atop the fountain, his cloak billowing around him in the wind.

"Ye little rat, I'll be killin' ye!" slobbered the barbarian.

"And I'll be remembering you," said Walker, feeling at his chest. There was steel in his voice, and resolve shone so coldly from his eyes that Bilgren shivered despite himself.

As Bilgren strained to wrench the gyrspike free, Walker pounced, head over heels, his cloak flying. The chain on the flail snapped, Bilgren lurched forward, reversed, and brought the sword down as the ghostwalker landed behind him.

Walker parried the blow and threw Bilgren back as though the barbarian possessed all the strength of a child. Walker strolled a little ways away and beckoned the barbarian to attack. Bilgren slashed again, but again Walker parried, pushing the blade up and over, creating an opening for him to stick a third dagger in the barbarian's torso.

Bilgren blinked, his berserk fury shaken, then roared all the louder. With both hands on the gyrspike's handle, he slashed the blade at Walker as though it were a two-handed sword, but the ghostwalker dodged or parried each attack, slashing Bilgren slightly here and there, wearing him down. As the barbarian lost more and more blood, his fury increased to greater and greater heights. Regardless, though, of how much strength Bilgren gained from pumping adrenaline, Walker always slipped, snakelike, in and out of his reach, knocking the broken gyrspike aside with no more than a scratch on his cloak to show for it.

Finally, as Bilgren foamed and raved beyond the realm of sanity, Walker staggered back over a rock, bending down. The barbarian roared, thinking his triumph coming, and hammered his sword down, once, twice, then up on Walker's blade. The final blow tore the sword from Walker's hand and sent it flying away, and the ghostwalker spun to the right with the force.

Bilgren lifted his blade high, salivating at the thought of the death to come. . . .

Then he blinked down at the long sword jammed through his ribs. Facing away, Walker had drawn his second sword from under his cloak during the turn, and jabbed it backward. Bilgren had never had a chance to parry.

The barbarian tried to bring the gyrspike down anyway, but his limbs would not obey his mind's commands. With agonizing slowness, he sank, limp, to the ground.

"Rest, peaceful as the grass in the meadow, my murderer," Walker whispered over his shoulder as he drew the sword out from between the barbarian's ribs. He recovered his throwing knives, wiped them on Bilgren's hide armor, and slid them into their sheathes.

Only one murderer left—one last haunting face that chilled him at night, one last sword to face, one last heart to still.

Then a sphere of cold energy crackled around him, and Walker froze.

The black-cloaked Talthaliel descended before Walker's eyes and smiled at him. Memories of pain and hatred fled from the ghostwalker, replaced by an oath for being distracted, and he realized that the one who killed him did not have to be one of his hated enemies.

"We meet, Spirit of Vengeance," said the moon elf. "For the first—and last—time."

CHAPTER 21

30 Tarsakh

Walker hacked his borrowed long sword into the bubble of force that contained him—a slash that would have split Talthaliel's head—but the barrier held firm. The throwing knife he had palmed fell, bouncing off the crackling sphere and sliding down to Walker's feet as though down the inside of a bowl.

In the face of this black-cloaked mage, Walker's supernatural determination vanished and he felt his strength and endurance fleeing. This was not one of his enemies, and that left him at a severe disadvantage. He chopped and slashed at the bubble again and again, but the sword rebounded from the force each time and vibrated in his hand enough to numb his entire arm. He saw the spirit of Tarm outside the bubble, but he knew calling to the spirit would do no good.

"Do not trouble yourself, Rhyn Thardeyn," came a voice from outside the bubble. "My magic is quite impenetrable."

The ghostwalker lowered the battered sword, and stared into Talthaliel's eyes.

"Interesting," the seer said, as though he had just observed something and was probing to see if Walker had as well. "Ah, well. It is not relevant." The diviner shrugged. He continued, putting aside whatever he had found interesting. "I regret interfering with your quest, Spirit of Vengeance. You have fought valiantly, as befits your training and skill, but your fight against the Lord Singer is over."

"Your master deserves death," Walker said. "Release me."

"Please; the Lord Singer is not my master." The tiniest flash of irritation crossed his face, but Talthaliel's words remained even and solid. Walker felt a tiny chill—he had rarely met one who could suppress his emotions so forcefully. "Regardless, you are right. But, for the moment, I do his bidding, and that bidding means your defeat."

"Then you have me," said Walker. "My quest is at an end." He lowered his head. "Kill me then—if you serve such a villain."

Talthaliel didn't flinch.

"Actually, I have a different plan for you."

Walker met the elf's gaze, his eyes confused.

Talthaliel shrugged. "All is occurring as I have foreseen. I have but to borrow a few moments of your evanescent time, then we will escape the Lord Singer's clutches together, though we shall never meet again in this world."

Walker furrowed his brow, but accepted without fully understanding. He felt, rather than saw, that the diviner meant him no harm—even encouraged his quest.

Hope flickered, but not at the thought he might defeat Greyt. Rather, this meant he might see Arya again....

Sitting, Walker folded his legs beneath him and closed his eyes.

"In the next moments, would you like me to tell you of

your past life? What I have seen and you cannot remember?" asked Talthaliel. "This may be your only chance."

After a long moment, Walker shook his head. "Rhyn Thardeyn died fifteen years ago," he said. "Whatever you would tell me of the past would mean nothing to me now."

Talthaliel nodded.

"One thing only," he said.

Walker inclined his head to hear.

"Your voice was beautiful," the seer said. "For that of a human."

Walker almost smiled.

❂   ❂   ❂   ❂   ❂

Greyt thrust at his son, but Meris stood with a flourish, brought the shatterspike from right to left, and cut the golden blade neatly in two.

Greyt watched, stunned, as Meris continued into a spin and brought the blade snaking around, only to plunge the point between the Lord Singer's ribs.

When Greyt looked at his son in shock, the wild scout spat out a chicken heart and a small flow of blood trickled down his chin. That was why his voice had seemed odd. Greyt's bracer knife had merely pierced flesh—no vital organs.

"I have learned many habits from you," said Meris. "Gloating is not one of them."

Fighting the agony, Greyt tried to stab at Meris with the blade in his gauntlet, but the scout slapped it aside with his axe. Then he twisted the sword, wrenching a gasp from the Lord Singer. The shatterspike burst from Greyt's back.

Greyt slumped to his knees, the blade through his body, and fiery pain spread through him. Words came from his lips, along with a trickle of blood.

"Meris, please," he croaked. "Lyetha ... tell her I ... I am sorry. I killed Tarm and little Rhyn ... all those years ago. I alone! Tell her—I'm sorry."

Meris laughed at him.

"Lies to the last, eh, Father?" he asked. "I suppose it's close enough to true—true enough to keep me Quaervarr's hero." He smiled.

Greyt choked. Then he tried to speak again. "Talthaliel ... you lied to me ... you said you would fight ... and defeat ... my son ... you lied ..." With one shaking hand, he clutched the amber amulet that hung around his throat.

Then a boot fell upon his hand and Meris held him down.

The dusky youth grinned hideously. It was time for the final act of revenge.

"No, no he didn't, Father," he laughed. "He kept his promise. He has fought and defeated your son." Then he pushed with his foot, pulling the sword out, and the Lord Singer fell over.

Awash in a sea of pain, Greyt's face was wracked with both agony and confusion. Then, understanding came upon him, and his eyes softened.

"Lyetha ... why didn't ... didn't you tell me?" He gasped one last time. "Beloved ... forgive me ... for ... what I did not see ..."

As the room faded to black, he imagined that he saw a laughing face before his eyes. It was a young Rhyn—*his* Rhyn—and his dazzling blue eyes, so like those of his beautiful Lyetha, gleamed in the lamplight.

He heard Rhyn running toward him, but from so far away. He would never arrive in time, Greyt knew. Rhyn and Lyetha had never been his, and he had hurt them so much, he was almost glad they would never be his now.

"We will meet again," he whispered, almost fondly. "In a world free ... of hate and pain."

For the first and last time in his life, Greyt felt regret.

Then he felt nothing at all.

❂ ❂ ❂ ❂ ❂

Talthaliel's mouth curled up at the edges. "Ah," was all he said. Then he vanished.

As he went, the shimmering sphere around Walker disappeared. Tarm, his father, was at his side, silent as always, urging him to stand.

And stand Walker did.

Walker ran for Greyt's manor. Lightning crashed overhead, threatening fierce rain as before, but nothing came down.

In the courtyard, the cherry trees—imported from far south—were just beginning to blossom, showing white and pink all around him. The cobblestone path running from the gate to the front door seemed impossibly long and Walker ran for all he was worth, his cape billowing behind him black against a sea of beauty.

Once through the front portal he slowed, watching every shadow for hidden attackers. He stalked through halls he did not know but remembered, somehow, as though he had walked them before—a memory washed away with his own blood that night fifteen years ago.

After his meeting with Lyetha, he found his memories creeping back, as though his shattered mind had pulled itself back together. Now he regretted turning her away, refusing to hear what she might tell him. His anger had blinded him, and now he wondered.

There were, after all, the mysterious memories of Greyt's manor that crept into his mind.

There was something eerily familiar about this building he had avoided studiously for the last fifteen years, lest his thirst for revenge get the better of him. That wall hanging there, that end table . . . The layout of the corridors, the design of the carpet . . . Walker could have sworn he could say where each and every door led, as though. . . .

Even as he ran through the halls of his greatest enemy, Walker felt the cruel sensation of coming home.

"Empty as the darkness," he said under his breath, washing his mind of the memories. With the words, Walker pushed the painful, bittersweet sensation out of his mind, much as one would ignore a moment of déjà vu. It was difficult, but he did it.

Then he heard cruel laughter from ahead and knew his destination: Greyt's study.

❧   ❧   ❧   ❧   ❧

After running a hand through his black curls, Meris took his time wiping the blade with a kerchief from his pocket. Then he slid the shatterspike back into its scabbard and dropped the bloody cloth on his father's corpse. Absently picking at the blood spatters on his white leather armor, he paused to consider the fallen man. Greyt's face knew an almost peaceful expression, but there was sadness there also—a duality of emotion.

By contrast, Meris felt nothing.

That only made him smile.

His smile faded as the lithe Talthaliel stepped out of the air next to Greyt's body. Meris dropped his hands to his weapons.

The black-robed diviner ignored him entirely. Talthaliel knelt over the Lord Singer's body.

"I am to assume that Walker has been dealt with, then?" snapped Meris. "Did you kill the wretch? Where is Bilgren?"

"Yes, no, and dead," Talthaliel replied absently.

"What? Make sense, elf!" shouted Meris. "You were my father's slave, and he's dead, so you are mine now! Speak!"

Talthaliel looked at him with an expression Meris might have called amusement. He pulled an amber amulet from Greyt's dead hand and admired it.

"I serve no man," said the seer, "unless he holds this."

Meris looked at the amber without comprehension. Then he thought he saw a tiny gleam. "And what is that, your life-force? Your soul, or whatever you rat-faced elves have instead?"

"My daughter," said Talthaliel. He stood, and Meris watched as the amulet vanished into his robes. "But to answer your question, the Spirit of Vengeance has been defeated, once, but I have not slain him. He comes for you even now, and I do not have to see the future to know the violence he will bring."

"You fish-skinned, tree-kissing, elf bastard," growled Meris. "You get back there and—"

Talthaliel vanished as though he had never been.

Meris's frown deepened. Walker? Coming here?

Then it seemed obvious. The fool was trying to rescue Arya. Meris could ambush Walker and rid himself of the ghost at last—the shatterspike should do the trick.

First things first, though.

"Guard!" he called.

The door opened and one of the Greyt family rangers looked in. From his face, he did not find the carnage surprising.

"Too many liabilities," Meris said. "See that that wench Venkyr and the others have accidents in their cells. Immediately. When they are dead, post six men there. I want anyone who comes looking for them killed just as quickly, no matter who it is." The man nodded, then Meris continued. "And gather all the other rangers in the courtyard. I am coming soon."

"As you command, Lord Greyt-Wayfarer," the scout said. Then he disappeared out the door. Out in the hallway, Meris could hear voices as the two guards left.

"Lord Greyt-Wayfarer," murmured the scout. He enjoyed the sound of that.

After a moment, Meris bent over Greyt's body and seized the left hand. The gold wolf's head ring—the Greyt family crest—sparkled from the fourth finger. Meris wrenched it free, let Greyt's arm fall with a satisfying thump, and slid it on. It was too big.

"Once, I would have given anything to have your name," said Meris. He cradled his father's head in his hands. "I would have done anything to be worthy—anything to make you love me."

Then he dropped the head and rose, drawing away from the corpse. When he had gained his feet again, he slipped the ring off and admired it.

"It seems, however, that all I had to do for your name," said Meris, "was kill you."

He turned and started for the door.

But it was only to stop. He had noticed something new about the ring—something he had not seen before. Meris squinted to see. There was tiny lettering on the inside, elegant letters scripted in Elvish.

" 'It is easier to destroy than to create,' " he read aloud. He touched his stubbly chin as though in thought. "Stupid sentiment. Why create when others will do it for you?"

With a derisive laugh that echoed through the halls, Meris walked away from the corpse of his father, toward the door. As he opened the door, he slipped the ring on. Then he stepped out.

Lancing from the shadows, a blade bit through the white leather and into his stomach.

❧ ❧ ❧ ❧ ❧

In the darkness of her prison cell, Arya could see a light approaching down the dungeon corridor, and a feeling of foreboding hit her such as she had never known before. So the great and mighty Lord Greyt had finally ordered her murdered. She would almost welcome death to free her of the pain of watching Walker die, of sending her dearest friends to their deaths, and of knowing that such a twisted lunatic as the Lord Singer was soon to be the most vaunted hero in the land.

Almost.

The knightly oaths that bound her, however, would not allow Arya to give up. Even if it was hopeless—even if everything else was gone—at least she could try.

She swore. This perverted peace, even if Greyt brought it about, would inevitably fail. The Lord Singer was no friend of Alustriel or the Silver Marches. The rebellion of Quaervarr would bring war—innocents would suffer and die for nothing, all so his mad heroism could hold true, a version of heroism he himself admitted to be false!

Burning with resolve, Arya strained at her bonds, her mind racing to formulate an escape plan. She tried to call for Bars and Derst, but the two slept soundly across the way, and her gag allowed only muffled grunts. Arya knew she was alone. Perhaps, if the guards were to come close, she could trip one and get her manacles around a throat. . . .

But then she heard startled gasps from down the hall and the light vanished. Straining her eyes, Arya looked out but could see only darkness. Everything was silent and absolutely still. She could not be sure why, but she felt that a battle was going on, albeit a short one, though she could not hear the screams of either men or steel.

"*Illynthas, shara'tem,*" came a whisper, and a light the size of a torch flame gleamed into existence inside her cell, a man's length from her.

It was an eerie, blue-green light that shone from a crystal high overhead. Arya looked up at it, then allowed her eyes to slide down, along a long staff of black wood, down to a thin hand that held it aloft. That hand extended from black robes that swathed a gaunt figure, a figure with glowing green eyes that seemed to bore into Arya's very soul.

The dark figure made a little gesture, but it was not an attack. Her bonds crumbled and fell away, passing into nothingness before they touched the floor. Arya blinked in disbelief.

"I offer freedom, Nightingale," said the mage. "And a warning: you are his only hope."

Arya's brow furrowed. "What? What do you mean? Who are you?" she asked.

"Someone who is doing what he should have done long ago," the mage replied. He extended his hand as though to help her up.

Still wary, Arya took that hand and, with the mage's help, got to her feet.

"What—" she started, but he was gone. Where her hand had held his, there was only a sword: *her* sword.

The knight looked around in wonder, but the mage had vanished as quickly as he had come, and there was no sign of his passing, except for the open cell door.

And that terrible omen: "You are his only hope."

Heart pounding, sword in hand, Arya rushed out to release her companions.

❂ ❂ ❂ ❂ ❂

In another corridor, not so far away, Meris's eyes slid from the dagger stabbing into his belly to the hands holding it. Then they traveled up the slim arms to his attacker's face to see furious sapphire eyes glaring at him with all the fury and hatred of the Nine Hells.

But they were not the eyes of Walker.

Angry tears streaming down her cheeks, Lyetha pushed with all her strength, driving the dagger through Meris's white leather armor and into the tough flesh beneath. She had stabbed near the spot Greyt's knife had found, but her blade followed an angle that cut deep into his bowels.

Their gazes locked for a moment, and the two shared a terrible understanding. Meris saw in Lyetha's beautiful eyes the final cruelty, the last crime that could be committed against her.

He saw the death of her love.

Never had Meris seen something that stunned him—or frightened him—as much as the fury in those eyes.

"For my husband," she said, steel on her tongue. "And for my son."

Meris blinked in reply.

Only when the darkness down the hall swirled and Walker materialized did Meris awaken and realize where he was and what had happened. With a flourish, he dropped his hand to the shatterspike's hilt.

"No!" shouted Walker, leaping forward.

It was too late, though, for Meris drew the blade out and across Lyetha's chest, sending blood sailing. Slowly, as though time itself stood still, the beautiful half-elf fell back into Walker's arms. The ghostwalker, panic and wrenching pain on his face, gazed into her eyes.

Meris, who had never seen Walker express emotion, blinked in stunned silence at the depth of the ghostwalker's mourning, and it sent a pang through his heart. He did not even think of attacking, though Walker was defenseless.

Lyetha looked up at Walker as though she did not recognize him, for a long, agonizing breath. Then her brows rose and a soft smile creased her face where only a pained grimace had been before. She gripped his hand with renewed strength, as though finally understanding a secret only the two of them knew. Held in Walker's arms, Lyetha drifted into death as Meris watched. At last, her eyes shifted past Walker's shoulder, and her lips moved.

"Well met again, Tarm," she said.

Then Lyetha died, a peaceful smile on her face.

Though Meris knew he should have attacked, should have sent his blade screaming for Walker's head in the man's moment of vulnerability, he could not. Some part of him caught the sight of something greater than himself—for the first time in his life—and it stayed his hand. Or perhaps it was his fear of the unknown. He did not understand—indeed, he could not begin to fathom—the emotional depth of the scene before him, and confusion ran through him and with it, terror.

Meris knew then, for the first time, the full measure of his foe, and he was terrified.

❧ ❧ ❧ ❧ ❧

Even as he watched her spirit fade away, embracing that of Tarm Thardeyn, Walker gently laid his dead mother on the soft carpet and rose to face Meris, who still stood, apparently dumbfounded. Reaching down to his belt, Walker slowly drew out the guardsman's sword and pointed it across the short distance that separated him from Meris. The wild scout responded by raising his own weapon—Walker's shatterspike—and pointing it at the ghostwalker. The points of the blades almost touched.

Meris calmly pulled the knife out of his belly, grimacing as blood leaked out. Not taking his eyes from the ghostwalker, Meris dropped a hand to his belt, drew out a steel-encased potion, and quaffed it.

Walker watched as the blood flowing down the white leather slowed to a trickle, then stopped entirely. His eyes darted into the study, and he saw Greyt's corpse. Somehow, even knowing that his vengeance was done did not calm the rage that boiled within his heart.

"This will be our final duel," Walker assured him. "You will pay for all you have done."

"I'm sure I will," Meris replied. "We've looked forward to this duel—you and I both." He rolled the sword over in the air, and its mithral surface glinted almost gold in the torchlight. "But I have the advantage, my friend."

In response, Walker held up his bandaged left hand, upon the fourth finger of which gleamed his silver wolf ring. Its single sapphire eye sparkled.

Meris shrugged, conceding the point.

"I'll just have to make sure I cut your hand off before I kill you this time," he mocked.

Now it was Walker's turn to shrug, but he did not move a muscle. His focus remained upon Meris, this man who had taken all Walker valued in life—things he had never known, and things he had thought lost before but had only truly gone now.

Such was his focus upon Meris that Walker was completely surprised when the door behind him shook under a mighty blow and muffled shouts penetrated the wood. He lunged, startled, but Meris batted his sword out of the way and leaped to the side.

The scout slashed out with a counter—a blow Walker dodged—and his wince of pain told Walker that the healing potion had not taken full effect yet. Walker took full advantage, slamming his sword into the shatterspike with a ringing blow. The long sword snapped against the shatterspike's edge, sheering off with a scream, but the damage had been done. With a curse, Meris let the mithral blade fall from his shaking fingers. The scout dived for it, but Walker flung the broken blade at him, and it sank into the carpet a pace from Meris's hand. Scrambling away from the weapons, Meris fled down the hallway, shouting for the guards as he went.

Walker slipped a dagger out into his hand and pulled back, but another blow on the door jarred his focus and the blade ended up in a wall a foot from Meris's fleeing head. Before the ghostwalker could draw another knife, the scout vanished around a corner toward the door to Greyt's manor.

Stifling a curse, Walker turned back to the vibrating door. The sounds of fierce fighting came from behind the locked portal, deep within the manor. A blunt object pounded upon the locked portal, and a long crack had appeared through the door. Taking up the shatterspike, Walker readied his lunge.

The door splintered, cracked, and flew off its hinges. Walker leaped out . . .

And stopped. His mouth dropped open and his sword point fell with it.

"I told you I could have picked the. . . ." Derst was saying. Then he saw the ghostwalker. "Oh."

"Walker!" shouted Arya as she threw herself into his arms.

The ghostwalker was dumbfounded and his mind blanked for the next few moments. All he knew was that he was holding Arya and kissing her and, somehow, that was all that mattered.

Bars and Derst tried to fill the silence with chat.

"You know, Bars," said Derst, who hovered at the paladin's side, picking at his light tunic. "I'll be we could have found and donned our armor in the time it takes the two of them to say 'well met.' "

"Speak for yourself, Sir Goldtook," Bars replied. "You're the one who wears hunting leathers. I'm the one with the metal plates. Perhaps if you were my acting squire—"

"Forget it!" spat Derst. "You remember the first and last time I helped you put on your armor. Never again!"

" 'Never again?' Why so?"

"You almost crushed me when you needed a chair!" argued Derst.

"Squires often do much in the line of duty," shrugged Bars.

"I suppose sponge bathes, for example?"

"Only if you're a lass in mail—er, sorry Arya," Bars mumbled, his face turning bright red.

But the lady knight had not even noticed. Instead, she was holding Walker as though he might slip away at any moment.

"Ahem," Derst said, clearing his throat. "We're still here."

Walker and Arya, remembering themselves at last, pulled apart and turned. Though she had moved to the side, Arya still held his hand tightly, a warm touch that threatened to swallow Walker's focus.

The sounds of battle were still coming from beneath the manor. Bars and Derst had freed the other prisoners, who even now fought Greyt family rangers underground.

The three knights were covered with sweat and grime, clad in simple tunics and leggings rather than armor, and speckled here and there with blood—none of it apparently theirs. Their borrowed and improvised weapons (Derst's being a dagger, leather thong, and flask) were in sorry need of repair. All three seemed tired, weak, and totally unprepared for a fight except for the grim expressions they wore—looks that would cause the most hardened warrior to wince.

In perfect shape to wade into battle.

Walker nodded. "Well met," he said.

"Well met indeed," said Bars, extending his hand. "Arya's told us much about you. Well, not really that much ... Well, aye, nothing. Um ... Well met." He trailed off and left his arm out for Walker to take.

Walker looked down at the extended arm and took it, to his great surprise.

Derst shook Walker hand. "I thought you'd be taller," he mumbled.

"I'm glad you got to meet," said Arya. "Especially since we're probably all going to meet Kelemvor in his underworld soon."

Walker needed no words to explain what they were about to do. He merely pointed.

"Bah!" exclaimed Derst. "You're always the pessimist, Arya."

"Aye, how many rangers can Meris have?" rumbled Bars. "A dozen? Two? Babe's play!"

"Easier than poking a chest full of goblins with a rapier," agreed Derst. "And besides—are they the legendary Knights in Silver? No. We are." He paused. "The legendary."

"Right," agreed Bars. "The Knights in Silver have never been defeated on the field of battle, and for good reason. Each of us is worth twenty of them!"

Arya, none-too-confident, looked at Walker for support, but the ghostwalker only smiled. She rolled her eyes.

"Men," she said.

"Aye," agreed Derst. Then, after a pause, he looked at Walker. "So—what's our plan?"

Walker turned and looked down the darkened hallway. He bent and slowly retrieved the discarded shatterspike sword.

"The front entrance?" Bars said, bemused. "Smells like an ambush."

"Bah! Meris would never expect us to be so stupid as to go out the front!" put in Derst with a laugh.

Then, when no one laughed along with him, his face grew serious once more.

"We're not, are we?" he asked, looking to each one for a reply.

None were forthcoming.

The ghostwalker peered at each of the knights. Then, without a word, he began walking resolutely down the hallway.

A smile lit on Bars's face.

"I like that plan!" he said. He hurried behind Walker.

Derst and Arya looked at each other, both equally stumped.

"Well, I suppose there's always my foolproof backup plan," said Derst. Arya arched an eyebrow.

"Proof against you, you mean?" Arya asked.

"You know me," Derst said with a shrug. He indicated the hallway with an open hand, and followed Arya when she ran after Walker.

When they arrived at the closed double doors, Walker held up a hand to stop them. He turned to address the three knights, who shared his determination. They drew steel.

"We do not know how many rangers await," said Walker. "I will go first."

"Suit yourself," Derst whistled. He hid behind a small table. "I'm comfortable, being alive and everything."

Bars nodded, pressing himself into the corner between the door and the wall.

Arya was not as yielding. She stood next to Walker, stubbornly clinging to his arm. When he looked over at her, her eyes were firm. "I'm coming with you," she said.

"This is the only way," Walker replied calmly but firmly.

"But, Walker, I have to tell you—"

His steely gaze cut her off and told her Walker would brook no argument.

Biting her lip, Arya took Walker's hand and squeezed it.

"Be wary," she said.

Walker nodded, squeezing her hand back to show he understood. Then Arya took up her place opposite Bars.

The ghostwalker closed his eyes, breathing in deeply. His focus returned, dampening the hot rage to a cool fury, shuffling it behind icy walls of control. Deep in his dark resolve once more, Walker opened his eyes, prepared.

Sheathing the shatterspike, Walker stepped to the doors, pulled them open, and walked out, arms wide open ...

Into a hail of arrows.

CHAPTER 22

30 Tarsakh

Arrows from two dozen bows shot for him, arrows seeking to turn Walker into a human forest. The ambushing rangers were fully confident the battle was over before it had begun, for there was no way Walker could dodge or deflect so many arrows. The arrows shot right through him and slammed into the open doors, carpeted floor, and walls inside Greyt's manor, and more than a few bristled from the end table behind which Derst hid. Arya stifled a scream, covering her mouth. Bars and Derst looked at one another, shocked.

Walker just shook his head. It was all just as he had expected.

As the rangers, standing in a rough line in the middle of the plaza, looked down at their bows as though the weapons had betrayed them somehow, Walker raised his head and continued to stride forward. As he came, they realized they could see through his body; he was translucent, like a ghost.

More than a few of the twenty-four rangers gasped in terror, seeing the vengeful spirit of folk legend, and their limbs shook. The others, old and hardened veterans all, gazed at Walker in doubt and disbelief.

The two dozen men stood in front of the Whistling Stag, which rested across the way from Greyt's manor. Walker nodded. That must have been where Meris had fled.

"I am the Spirit of Vengeance," said Walker. His matter-of-fact words were soft, but they projected throughout the square loudly enough to reach all their ears. "I am the son of the Ghostly Lady of the Dark Woods, who brought the fires of heaven upon Quaervarr a century past. I was born and live in darkness, I breathe retribution, and I sleep to the screams of the damned. I fear no living thing, man or woman."

He paused, waiting while all that sank into his foes, but he need not have bothered. The rangers were trembling.

"I have slain your champions, and one alone awaits me," he continued. "My fight is with Meris Wayfarer, not with you. I offer you this one chance to throw down your weapons and to quit Quaervarr and the Moonwood forever."

Many of the guardsmen looked hesitant and afraid, but the reminder of Meris, their new lord, seemed to snap them out of it. Not that they knew loyalty, but as much as they feared the black specter before them, they feared the cruelty of Meris Wayfarer more. After all, one man could not defeat two dozen men, no matter his power. No ranger threw down his arms—indeed, many fitted more arrows to the string or drew swords.

"Then it seems I have no choice," said Walker, slowly drawing the shatterspike and continuing to walk toward them, "but to kill you all."

Half the rangers replied by aiming for Walker once more, and half tightened their grip on their weapons.

The ghostwalker made no sign of changing his calm walk

until the first ranger, two short swords in his hands, lunged at him, screaming the name of the late Lord Singer.

Walker whirled, his blade out and dancing in the breeze. It cleaved one sword in two then snapped against the man's arm, sending him away screaming. A second ranger thrust a long sword at Walker from the other side, a blow that was deflected with perfect timing. The ghostwalker brought the sword up high, then threw the ranger off and continued walking, as though the man had never attacked. This ranger looked at his sword, saw that it was still whole, and swung at Walker's back. At the same moment, the dozen rangers with bows drawn fired upon the ghostwalker.

Unfortunately for the rangers flanking Walker, the arrows passed through the ghostwalker's head and chest as through mist and found resting spots in their bodies.

Screaming, the rangers tumbled down, even as Walker broke into a run toward the bowmen, who now scrambled to set arrows to bowstrings. As he went, he leaped bodily through a ranger who chopped two axes down through nothing and ended up on the ground, confused.

"He's an illusion!" shouted one of the rangers. "He's not even really—"

Then Walker brought his blade down into the man's mocking smile and ended his words.

Even as the rangers milled around in confusion and terror, Walker flew into a dance of death, his sword weaving back and forth, deflecting and shattering weapons even as arrows and swords passed through him. Though his body had no substance, his shatterspike—shimmering and almost translucent—still cut with just as much deadliness as it always had. Only his blade could bridge the gap between worlds and inflict pain in either.

Ironically, Walker carried the only weapon in the plaza that could touch him as a ghost.

Rarely did the shatterspike cleave flesh, though—most of the wounds that set rangers grunting, cursing, or falling were the result of the rangers' own weapons. Arrows flew through the battle without guidance, sailing through Walker's ghostly form to find ranger flesh instead.

Walker brought the shatterspike whirling in a glittering semicircle, shearing two raised blades in half and cutting a bowstring neatly on the back swing. Before the bowman could even drop his ruined weapon, Walker slashed him across the face and sent him down into the mud. It was only his second kill.

As though at random, Walker danced through the crowd, leaping around and through rangers, his shatterspike flashing, dropping weapons and men. He cut bowstrings, cleaved apart bows, and sliced quivers in two.

After a few moments, when the rangers were largely panicked, mostly disarmed, and completely disorganized, Walker smiled. "Go forth," he whispered on the wind, even as he sheathed his blade.

With that, he turned and ran toward the Whistling Stag. Many turned to give chase, hefting what weapons they could—belt daggers, hatchets, and the like—but then they heard new shouts.

"Forth the Nightingale!" came a mighty cry, shared by three throats, from behind them.

Most of the rangers turned, just in time to see three Knights in Silver, stripped to gray tunics and breeches, charge into the fray, weapons hungry for Greyt ranger blood. And the rangers had no bows or swords with which to cut them down.

Meanwhile, Walker sprang toward the Stag and vanished through the closed door, passing through the wood like a ghost.

❧ ❧ ❧ ❧ ❧

The three Knights in Silver swept upon the confused rangers like a trio of giants, hacking and crushing left and right. Four rangers went down in the initial rush—Bars having taken down two himself—and the knights' courage did much to shake the rangers' crumbling resolve.

In the first confused moments of battle, Derst disarmed

two men of their backup weapons and was dancing around a third, his improvised chain-dagger creating havoc for the ranger as he tried to cleave the wiry knight in two with a mighty war axe. An overhead chop was sidestepped, a withering cross ducked, and a reversal hit nothing but air as Derst rolled and stuck the dagger in the man's side. The man yelped and staggered forward, but the dagger was firmly lodged between ribs and brigandine plating. The ranger turned, but his motion only pulled Derst to the side—in time to dodge the falling axe.

Meanwhile, Bars worked furiously to hold off four rangers, his mismatched maces dancing and flashing like lightning. Though he could not launch a counter, the huge paladin put up a stunning defense, where he picked off every thrust, slash, and jab his opponents launched. Every time, they recoiled from the attack shaking their sword arms, which rung with the force of Bars's parries. Growling, Bars kept his duel at a standstill.

Fighting three men, Arya, not as nimble or as strong as her respective companions, more than made up for it in ferocity and cunning. She parried aside one ranger and immediately shield rushed the second, catching him off guard. She discarded her shield, which she had only held, not strapped on, and he had to fumble it out of the way with a clumsy downward cross of his two short swords.

The Nightingale shield fell to the dust, but Arya followed through and slammed her left fist then her left elbow into his face. The man staggered and collapsed backward, and Arya brought her sword back around just in time to parry the attack of a third ranger. She locked blades with him, then hooked a foot around his ankle and sent him staggering into the man she had left behind.

With a shout to the Lord Singer, the man on the ground slashed her across the front of the shin with his blade, but it was a weak blow, driven mostly by panic and not by skill.

Arya gritted her teeth against the pain and brought her sword plunging down into his chest. The man screamed and lay still.

"No mercy!" she shouted, slashing back around to deflect another seeking sword. The feral rage in her scream sent two rangers staggering back, doubtful looks on their faces.

By this time, two other rangers had closed on Derst's duel and were slashing and thrusting, but they only nearly hit the axe-wielder. The roguish knight kept dodging their blows, running in two low circles around the ranger with the axe, weaving the lanyard of his makeshift chain-dagger as he went. Finally, with the man fully wrapped, Derst slid past one of the swordsmen, put both hands on the thick lanyard, and yanked for all he was worth. The lanyard pulled tight around the man's legs, ruining his balance, and one ranger staggered into the other, sending both down in a jumble of limbs.

"Hail, lass!" shouted Derst as he leaped over another thrust, freed his lanyard, and kicked out, catching the ranger in the face.

"'Arya,' Derst!" the lady knight snapped back. She parried a slash and punched the man in the face as though with a shield. Her fist had much less effect, but it was enough to send him reeling back. "It's Arya! You want to be 'lad?'"

"Oh, never that!" replied Derst. "Sorry! I was going to ask—" he parried a seeking blade with his dagger, hooked his lanyard around the weapon, and ripped it out of the man's hands, "—whether you think a—" he dodged another swipe, "—promotion's on the horizon?"

"I concur!" rumbled Bars as he swatted a ranger aside like an insect. He faced four more, but they looked more afraid of him than he of them. "'Tis not every day you fight almost a score of men with just your two friends!"

"Dashing friends," corrected Derst as he parried a sword and gave the man a quick kick to the shin, putting him down.

"'Tis not every day you win!" replied Arya as she narrowly deflected another slash. "Fight now, talk later!"

Even with that chastening remark—or perhaps because of it—Derst continued right on chattering.

"They might even make you a Knight Protector for this!"

he said. Then his brows knitted and he addressed his current opponent, blocking and parrying between each word. "What's that, eh, chap? Equivalent to Captain? Colonel? General? No, surely not that high."

He paused, expecting an answer. When nothing but another slash was forthcoming, which he dodged, Derst shrugged.

"Not sure, eh? Well, I guess I'll just have to find out."

The man bellowed and thrust again, but Derst leaped high into the air, kicked off the man's arm, flipped over his head, and come down slashing from behind. The ranger went down.

One of Bars's opponents finally made the mistake of planting his feet incorrectly on the thrust, leaving an opening as he stumbled back—an opening Bars took. With a bellow to Torm, the paladin leaped at him, working his maces independently to knock the man's sword aside. Bars thundered over the hapless ranger, knocked him flat to the ground, kicked his sword aside, and brought down both maces on the head of a fifth man who had been seeking to maneuver around Arya. With two foes down, Bars landed back on the ground and continued his defense.

With a glare, Arya lunged at the two hesitating rangers. They fell back into defensive stances, unwilling to approach the fierce woman. She was thankful for the reprieve, since pain was lancing up her leg, even as she bit her lip to ignore it.

The momentary lapse in her duel allowed Arya a moment to glance after Walker, at the Whistling Stag. She could hear nothing from within, and that did nothing to calm her nerves. It was only a momentary glance, though, then the ranger was back, sword lancing for her heart.

Her heart . . .

"You are his only hope," had been the wizard's words.

Arya slapped it aside and growled her frustration.

❧ ❧ ❧ ❧ ❧

Meris ran into the Whistling Stag's common room only to find it deserted except for the innkeep Garion and a few regulars drinking at the bar. At the sight of the bloodied Meris, carrying a drawn axe, bursting through the door, all eyes turned.

"Oi, lad, wha' be the—" Garion began.

Running across the room, Meris slapped him across the face, silencing his next few words. Stunned, the big man staggered back and knocked a few tankards over—including the ale of a wizened old man who kept right on drinking air without noticing.

Wearing a haggard and hunted look, Meris grabbed up one of the drinkers—a drunken rake with long brown hair and a half-beard—and held the drunkard's body before him like a shield.

"Now, wait jes' a moment—" stammered Morgan.

"Silence!" shouted the wild scout. "Malar's claws!"

He held the rake up between himself and the door, as though expecting a blade to come lancing for his heart at any moment.

Then a fist came out of the darkness behind him and struck the back of his head.

Meris staggered and fell, shoving Morgan away. He drew the main gauche from the rake's belt, though, and turned with the blade slashing, but there was no one to attack. There were only the other Whistling Stag patrons, who were even now fleeing up the stairs, with a surprisingly sober Morgan following them.

"Meris Wayfarer," a haunting, ghostly voice called.

"Face me like a man, damned creature!" challenged Meris.

Walker appeared in a dark corner of the room before him, and Meris let fly with the main gauche. It stabbed into the wood wall and wobbled there.

"Dark as shadow," intoned Walker. His voice, from no visible source, echoed around the room eerily.

Meris drew a throwing knife from his belt and looked around, but no one was there.

"You will die, Meris Wayfarer, Meris the bastard," Walker promised. As he spoke, he stalked Meris around the room, passing between the shadows, always just on the verge of material presence. The drawn shatterspike glittered, as did the sapphire eye of his wolf ring, spectral as both were. "For crimes against my family, for crimes against those I love, for crimes against the people of Quaervarr and the people of the Silver Marches."

Walker stepped across a pool of light, and Meris threw the knife. It passed through the intangible ghostwalker and thunked into the closed door.

Walker continued. "I am the silence of the grave, the shock of lightning. My passing is rain upon the mountains and wind through the plains. My rage burns in the Hells, and I will bring you to those Hells. I, the spirit of vengeance, promise you death."

"Stay away from me!" shouted Meris, his expression terrified beyond belief. "Away! Take anything you want! Leave me be!"

"Tempt not the spirit of vengeance," came the voice. Walker materialized right before him, his pointing finger but a hand's breadth from the scout's face. "He comes for you."

Then Meris's expression changed and his feigned terror vanished. "Perhaps not, Rhyn," came the searing reply.

◉ ◉ ◉ ◉ ◉

No matter how fierce and skilled the three knights were, they knew it was only a matter of time before the rangers realized they outnumbered the knights. With renewed vigor—aided by simple assessment of the enemy forces—the Greyt family rangers fought back with greater confidence, with multiple men going to attack each of the knights in a coordinated fashion.

"It's about time for that backup plan, Derst!" Arya shouted, parrying and running, keeping the four rangers that were now her opponents from surrounding her.

Several more were moving her way, though—maneuvering to get at her flanks. Without armor or a shield, Arya would not be able to fend off more than one or two attackers.

"Backup plan?" Derst asked dubiously, evading a swipe,

rolling under the man's arm and gouging him in the thigh with his dagger. A ranger cut along his back, leaving a long red line, but Derst only grimaced, dodged, and fought on.

"You used to be a thief!" roared Bars. "You always have a backup plan!" A pair of daggers shot in, seeking his flesh. He batted one aside, and the hand that went with it, but accepted a stab from the other. A knife wound for a broken hand would be more than a fair trade—under other circumstances. "And it's about time for that plan!"

"You know," panted Derst, even as he snagged a sword with his chain-dagger, only to have the thick leather snap in two. The cutting blade nearly sliced his arm in two, and it was only Derst's reflexes that pulled it out of the way. Frowning at the destroyed weapon as he dodged and eluded his attackers, Derst finished the sentence. "I think you're right."

The door of Greyt's manor burst open and a score of men—some watchmen, some businessmen, even a couple noble dandies—with the gigantic Unddreth at their head, burst out, captured swords and daggers in their hands. With cries of "Quaervarr!" and "The Stag!" they rushed to join in the fray.

Derst had always had a talent for opening locks—and more than enough experience with cell doors.

"How's that for a backup plan, lass?" shouted Derst. Then he dived away from a frightened ranger and corrected himself. "Sorry—Arya. How about this development, eh?"

There was no reply.

"Arya?" he asked again.

❧ ❧ ❧ ❧ ❧

The ghostwalker gave Meris a bittersweet smile in reply. "Rhyn Thardeyn died long ago," Walker said. "That name holds no power over me."

"No, no it doesn't," Meris said. "But your true name does, doesn't it, Rhyn Greyt?"

Walker hesitated, shock spreading over his face, and his

body wrenched fully into the physical world. Immediately, Meris slashed his axe at the ghostwalker.

Stunned, Walker managed to deflect the axe, but it hooked around the shatterspike. Meris ripped the weapon from Walker's hand, spun it, caught the sword's hilt, and turned it into a stab. With his bracer, Walker managed to turn the killing thrust into his shoulder. The hand axe darted low and hooked around Walker's leg. Blinded by the pain in his shoulder, Walker couldn't resist as Meris yanked him from his feet. Walker's head slammed into the hard floorboards and the air fled from his heaving lungs.

"Your mystery is your power, Rhyn Greyt," said Meris, "is it not? Your betrayer told me this. Not so confident without your secret, are you? You didn't even know, did you?"

Walker was speechless.

"Oh yes, brother," Meris said over him, spinning the shatterspike in his hand. "Lyetha loved our father first—before Thardeyn, the old priest. When Greyt wouldn't marry her, Lyetha turned to Thardeyn to hide you. And to think, all that time pretending that you were Thardeyn's—all for naught. I always suspected, but I didn't know. Until now."

How did he know this? Who could have told him? Lyetha? She would never have ...

"Why?" Walker managed to croak through the lights dancing across his eyes. He felt so weak, so unsure, so unfocused.

A memory flashed through his head, a memory of Meris: *The boy stood over him. The look in his eyes; no anger, no passion, no sadness, no softness. Not even pity. Only hate.*

Meris pulled the shatterspike out of Walker's shoulder and looked at its sparkle.

"How poetic, an avenger killed with his own sword," he said. "What do you say to that, Walker? You're a poet, right? Or perhaps it is really my sword, eh?"

Walker stared up at him defiantly.

"Rhyn, you've been deceived," said Meris as he held the sword between his legs and buckled the axe to his belt. His hands freed, he stripped his gauntlets so that he could kill Walker barehanded. "I did what I did fifteen years ago for my own gain and, well, because I've always hated you. You inherited all our father's qualities—singing, courage, charisma—and I took all his faults—ambition, violence and, well, madness."

Meris shared a private laugh with himself. No one joined him.

"And you probably would have taken his wealth when you came of age. The truth would have come out, I knew—somehow." He growled. "And that's 'why,' really. My father would've spared you in the forest—the coward. He just wanted to frighten you, but I took the healing ring off your finger." He trailed off with a smile. "You were the first sibling I killed, even if I didn't know it at the time. Now you will be the last as well."

Flashes of the forest swam in his mind—the rapier that rammed through his chest, that cut his throat and ruined his voice. Greyt's sword. But the healing ring . . .

The boy with eyes filled with hate loomed over him. The wolf's head ring sparkled in his hand. "Let's hear you sing now," he said as his father's sword descended.

A tear slid down Walker's cheek. How could Meris have known this? Walker had not even known. Who knew Walker's name? Who knew what only Lyetha could know? Who could have betrayed him?

Walker did not know, and now it was too late.

Meris laughed. "And here, look at me, gloating over my victory like my old man!" A chuckle. "Can't forget that ring—my father's ring." Meris knelt and pulled the wolf's head ring from Walker's finger, tearing away much of the improvised covering as he did so. Then he leaned over and ran a finger along Walker's cheek.

The touch of death.

"Well, Rhyn, let's hear you sing now," Meris said as he raised the sword over his head.

❧ ❧ ❧ ❧ ❧

In a distant grove, among verdant trees that seemed to weep in the winter's breeze, a ghostly golden figure stood atop a huge, overturned boulder and looked into the sinking sun.

"It is done," Gylther'yel said with a sigh.

❖ ❖ ❖ ❖ ❖

"Meris!" came a shout.

The wild scout hesitated and looked. Wild-eyed, Arya stood across the room, sword in hand. She wore almost as much blood as cloth—not all of it her own—and her hair blazed in the lamplight.

"Arya," Walker managed. "No. . . ."

The lady knight bent her knees and held the blade low.

"Come, bastard," she growled. "We are not done yet, you and I. We have had this dance waiting from the beginning."

Meris sneered. "You should've killed me while my back was turned, while you had the chance."

"Knights do not stab enemies in the back," Arya said.

Meris gave her a mock salute and chuckled. Then he charged, shatterspike and axe held out to his sides. Arya ran at him, sword held low.

They met in the center of the common room, blades whirring and sparks flying. Arya slashed in high, and Meris picked off the attack with shatterspike and axe then spun, bringing the weapons around at her head. Arya ducked the shatterspike and parried the axe, sending the axe back and shooting in a fist to pound Meris's chest through the opening he left. Her punch hardly affected the man through his thick leather armor, and he pushed her back with a lunge. The two separated for a moment.

"Oh, yes, wench, that's right," laughed Meris, beckoning her with his axe. "A valiant stand, as useless as valor itself!"

The knight fought silently, though her shoulders heaved from the exertion of battle. Weariness shuddered through her body, threatening to slow her blade. Arya reasoned that perhaps she should just run—she could never defeat Meris alone, even if she were fresh, fully armed, and fully armored. His skill was beyond hers. What was she doing here? Letting Walker see her one last time, only to see her killed?

She could not run, though. A Knight in Silver never ran, and never abandoned her friends and those she loved. She would fight Meris to the death—likely her death, but at least she would not die a coward, as he was.

Then Arya saw something out of the corner of her eye, and hope glimmered in her heart.

"For the Marches!" she cried, throwing herself forward in a desperate lunge.

Meris, momentarily caught off guard by the wild thrust, brought the shatterspike around to parry her sword high, even as he swung in low with the axe to trip her. Then the blade twisted in Arya's hand—a rolling of the wrist that reduced her grip almost to nothing—and her long sword went under the shatterspike, deflecting it wide. The notched steel sheared off against the shatterspike and she dropped the broken hilt. Her left hand shot in and seized the throwing dagger at Meris's belt even as her sword hand grasped his wrist with as much strength as she could muster. The axe, ignored, hooked around her knee to pull her down.

"What are you—" Meris started even as he pulled with his axe.

"A trick I learned from Walker!" Arya snapped.

Then Meris screamed in pain as Arya drove the tiny blade into his unarmored wrist.

The shatterspike tumbled from Meris's nerveless hand even as he yanked Arya to the ground. Since she was still holding his arm, he fell with her. As she fell, she caught the ghostly blade in her free hand—by luck not shearing off her fingers—and held it between them, its hilt against the floorboards. As Meris fell, his weight drove the blade through his left side.

The two of them stayed there for a moment, Arya holding herself up under the impaled Meris, who rested on his knees. Blood leaked from his mouth and he looked at the knight without comprehension.

Then madness returned to his eyes and, with it, rage. Meris spat blood on Arya's face, causing her to wince. Then, his hand scrabbled across the floor and seized her fallen, splinted sword. He slammed the hilt into Arya's forehead, knocking her back, stunned. As he rose, Meris didn't seem to notice the sword running through his side. He turned the splintered sword in his hands and loomed over Arya, ready to deliver the killing stroke.

Then he stopped as a chilling melody came from behind.

❀　❀　❀　❀　❀

Meris turned.

Walker, standing again, sang a song of dark beauty, a lullaby to lead a sleeper into the endless night, a song of velvet softness and nameless fear. The words in lyrical Elvish, it was a song of mourning, begging for forgiveness, and promising vengeance.

Stunned, Meris looked at Walker for a moment, his eyes wide and staring. Then he came back to his senses and slashed the broken sword at Walker's head. The dark warrior ducked smoothly and reached out with both hands. He pulled the blade from Meris's side and stabbed it back into the dusky youth's chest.

Meris looked down at the sword and gave a weak gasp. The scout's limbs went limp and he sagged, but Walker caught his body and held his face up.

"Who?" he demanded. "Tell me. Who?"

He did not truly need to ask, for Meris had torn the bandage free of his left hand and he felt the truth keenly through his bare skin, in ghostly resonance, from the shatterspike. But some part of him had to be sure.

Meris smiled almost wistfully. "The Ghostly Lady," he said.

It seemed to Walker that he should be surprised, hurt, or frightened, but he felt nothing. Nothing but cold.

Then Meris's eyes slid closed for the last time.

Walker held the cooling body for a moment, looking into

the face he had hated so much, the last of his tormentors and the one who had taken his dream from him.

Somehow, he felt no anger. Only sadness.

"How?" Arya asked as he helped her to her feet. "How did you do it? The name. I thought your name had destroyed you."

"Rhyn Thardeyn will always be my name," the ghost-walker said. "Never Rhyn Greyt."

Before they left the Whistling Stag, Walker looked back at Meris's body.

"Farewell, my brother," he murmured.

CHAPTER 23

30 Tarsakh

As the sun set, Walker stood in the center of Quaervarr's main plaza, his cloak billowing out behind him in the wind. The rain had passed and the clouds were clearing, but the fearsome wind still blew, threatening to rip cloaks from the backs of any foolish enough to go outside. Despite this, hundreds milled about the square, voices chattering and shouting. Though the place was abuzz with activity, Walker's silent and unmoving form went largely unnoticed.

The watch, with Captain Unddreth restored to command, had taken control of the courtyard quickly and was even now sorting out the prisoners. The surviving rangers—all fifteen of them, several too injured to move without assistance—were shuttled into the Quaervarr jail and, when that was full, to the very dungeons that had until recently housed Unddreth and others loyal to Geth Stonar.

The rangers would be held until such time as their ultimate fate could be decided, but Arya had dissuaded Unddreth from calling for the noose. Loyal men should not be punished so severely for defending their master, especially when they thought him to be a noble and virtuous hero, she had convinced him.

A courier had been dispatched to fetch Speaker Stonar back from Silverymoon, along with a cadre of watchmen for protection. They also sought to ascertain the fate of Clearwater and the other riders. One of the druids went along as well—the Oak House simply couldn't ignore the disappearance of two of their own, one their mistress.

In Quaervarr's main plaza, a crowd had gathered to listen as Arya and her companions explained the events of the last few days. Under the watchful and approving eye of the stony-faced Unddreth, the knights spoke of Greyt's plots, kidnappings, and murders, as well as the atrocities committed by Meris and his cronies. The town had been thrown into disarray, with the late Lord Singer's charismatic bravado pressing against the firm, peaceful rule of Geth Stonar. With the recounting of the day's bloody events and the revealing of the truth, however, most of the citizenship had grown disillusioned with the legend of Greyt and turned back to those civil leaders they could trust: Stonar and Unddreth.

Mercifully, Arya chose to remain silent about the events of fifteen years previous—Walker did not think he could stomach a retelling of his murder. In addition, he lived, once again, in mystery—a mystery that kept all the citizens, except for the most inquisitive (and foolish) children, away from him as he rested and healed. The silver wolf's head ring was back around his finger, helping his wounds re-knit and his scars disappear, a process that Walker had gone through so many times he hardly even felt the itchy tingling running through his body.

Hardly, that is to say, except for four particular wounds. With the deaths of Greyt and Meris, the flesh they had broken could finally heal. Though he would carry the scars, and speak in a whisper to the end of his days, Walker felt nearly whole.

Then a pain seized him and Walker's tranquil frown dipped.

That was when he knew he was not fully whole. He had one task still to complete, one last wrong to set right, one last crime to avenge. He had one last life to take.

Shifting into his ghostsight, Walker turned to the side, expecting to see the spirit of Tarm Thardeyn, who had always given him silent guidance. But there was no spirit there.

Walker smiled. He remembered watching the spirits of Tarm and Lyetha fade, reunited at last in death. He also remembered the gentle, sweet emotion that had swept through him at the time—love, the kind of feeling Walker knew when he looked upon Arya Venkyr.

Arya.

Walker looked over at her as she addressed a body of gathered citizens, much as Lord Greyt had done in the past. She had cleaned her hair and wounds after the battle, and Bars had applied his healing touch to her as well. The knight was radiant in the fading sunlight that filtered through the clouds, the silver of her armor gleaming and her hair burning. As though she noticed him watching, she drew herself up straighter and tiny spots of red bloomed in her cheeks.

How could she ever understand what he had to do? How could he explain it to her?

Walker decided he could not. He simply had to do it.

With a sigh—a gesture that would have seemed foreign to him a few days ago—he pulled his cloak around his shoulders and walked away.

❖ ❖ ❖ ❖ ❖

Smiling broadly at the shouts of support, Arya turned away from the crowd and massaged her throat. Shouting for such a long time had worn out her voice, but it had been worth it. Her mission was accomplished: the threat to stability in the Silver Marches removed. Finally, she could relax.

A strand of auburn hair blew in her face, and she brushed

it aside. As soon as she had done so, though, she realized something was amiss.

Walker was not there.

Gripped by sudden, unreasoning panic, Arya scanned the plaza. She caught sight of him at last, striding toward the main street of the town, as though to leave.

"Walker!" she called, breaking into a run. At the sound of her voice, he stopped and let her hurry to his side. She put gauntleted fingers on his arm. "You're going?"

Rather than looking at her, Walker's eyes were far away.

"All my scars are healed, all my enemies dead," he said. "All but one." He put his hand over his heart.

Confused, Arya covered that hand with her own. Walker smiled at the touch.

"I don't understand," she said. "Who else is there?"

"My teacher," replied Walker. "She who taught me my powers. She who betrayed me." He paused, as though digesting that. When he spoke again, his voice was soft and sad. "Gylther'yel, the Ghostly Lady."

"The spirit of the Dark Woods?" asked Arya. "The folk legend? She actually exists?"

Walker nodded. "And she is powerful," he added, "much more powerful than any foe either of us has faced, able to level armies with a sweep of her fingers."

"Armies?" she mouthed. Walker moved to go, but Arya held his arm tighter. "You can't go now—wait until there are more of us! Wait until we find Clearwater and can muster up a score of warriors, Legionnaires, Knights in Silver, wizards of the Spellguard—"

"No," said Walker. "This is my fight, and my fight alone. No man or woman will die in my place."

His fatalistic tone made Arya's heart race. "Wait, at least, until you are fully rested—"

"If I do not confront her now, I will never find her," replied Walker. "Her spies are even now on the wing, going to tell her all that has transpired today. I must fight her now." Arya frowned, but Walker was firm. "I will heal as I walk."

The knight did not understand, and she bit her lip.

He took another step, but still Arya held him back. He turned to her, his eyes cold and hard, and Arya swallowed. She had meant to argue, but the determination she saw in those eyes told her that it would be no use. She closed her eyes, fighting within herself for words, and when they finally came, she fixed him with a gaze as full of resolve as his own.

"Then I am coming with you," she said.

"You are not. . . ." Walker started to argue, but then he trailed off. He did not need to look into her steely eyes to know argument was useless. "As you will. But if you are to come—" With a twist, he removed the wolf ring and offered it to her. "You will need protection."

"But—but you need healing," she protested.

"The shadows will provide," said Walker.

Though she did not understand, Arya found herself trusting him. She slid the ring onto the fourth finger of her left hand. It felt heavy, but she took reassurance in its weight. She nodded then took a step away, meaning to call for her horse.

This time, it was Walker's turn to grasp her arm and stop her.

"You will need no horse for this journey," he said.

Arya slid out of his grasp and eyed him. "How do we journey, then?" she asked, hesitant to be away from Swiftfall and her trusty lance.

"The only way Gylther'yel will not hear us coming—along the most silent of paths." He extended a hand silently to her. "The Shadow."

Arya shivered. "Can she not see ghosts, if she is a ghost?" asked Arya.

"Not the Ethereal. The Shadow," he said. "This is the only way."

The others in the plaza had observed the two by now, and Bars and Derst were walking over, wearing questioning looks.

"Take my hand," said Walker, his eyes gleaming.

Arya gnawed on her lip, indecisive. Though she wanted to

delay, to explain to her brother knights the reason she had to go, or even ask them to accompany her, she felt Walker's need for haste.

"The grove!" she called out to Unddreth, Bars, and Derst. Then she stepped into Walker's reach and clutched his outstretched hand.

Instantly, shadows surrounded them and the world seemed to turn black. Walker wrapped his billowing cloak around her and took her firmly in his embrace.

"We walk the shadowy realm beyond the Border Ethereal—the Shadow Fringe—where our travel will be quickened," explained Walker. "Whatever you may see, whatever you may feel—remember that I am with you. Whatever else speaks, do not reply. Cling tightly to me—I will not forsake you."

Arya nodded.

Then, as Walker took a step forward, she followed him into the shadows.

❖ ❖ ❖ ❖ ❖

Arya felt her lungs fill with smoke, and she could not breathe. As they stepped between worlds, all the colors of Quaervarr and even the sun seemed to fade to a dull, bleak haze. She felt a tug, as though the very darkness pulled her in. Her gorge rose and her stomach danced. The afternoon sunlight became muddy, as though the sun were but a smoldering torch behind thick spider webs.

Surrounding her were a multitude of moving figures, all engaged in different activities, from pacing back and forth, to acting out duels, to mumbling or shouting incoherently. Their faces were blurry, obscured as though by a hand that had smudged their very being and wiped their features from sight. She started, seeing the men and women who had been in the square as mere blobs of light, and she became aware of the heat flowing from them like water.

This is the ghost world, she thought. From here, we step into Shadow.

An ephemeral man lunged at her out of the darkness, so violently and with such rage burning from him that Arya screamed and clutched at Walker. At the same time, a wave of panic washed over her.

"I am here," came a voice, a deep and resonating voice, along with a wave of comfort. The angry spirit spun past her and continued on its way, jabbering about orc chieftains it had faced.

A wave of sadness not of her own making swept through her.

"Gharask is an old spirit—the father of Dharan Greyt. He has haunted Quaervarr for fifteen years," said the voice. "Kept there by anger, rage, and helplessness. Perhaps tonight we will set him to rest."

Caught up in Walker's arms, Arya felt herself borne away on wings of shadow. The angry spirit, and the gathered multitude vanished, along with the darkened buildings of Quaervarr. Soon, Arya found herself in the woods, where Walker continued his slow steps, each of them covering dozens of paces.

Then there came a scream, jolting Arya's attention to a spirit who ran beside them. Her face was blurred, but when Arya focused upon her features, they shifted and cleared. She was a comely woman, younger than Arya, but her features were lined with wrinkles of madness and her eyes burned with impotent wrath. There was a bloody wound in her breast.

"Why? Why? Why?" she asked, repeating the word again and again, building in volume until it was so loud that it stung Arya's ears. The spirit wept black tears, which disintegrated in the smoky air.

"Chandra Stardown?" asked Arya, as she recognized the spirit. She had known Chandra in Silverymoon—both had served under Sernius Alathar as cadets, but Arya had not seen her since her promotion into the order.

Chandra's spirit seemed stunned for a moment. Then she burst back into her demands, reaching for Arya.

"Why! Why! Why!"

Startled, Arya cried, "I know not!"

At this, Chandra paused again, but then gave a wrenching scream, stunning Arya to silence, and reached at her with fingernails grown into claws. The knight gasped and reached for her sword, but a warning hand clamped down upon her wrist.

"Whatever you see, do not reply!" repeated Walker. "I am here—I am the only one here!"

Arya started to argue, but then the spirit gave a gasp and vanished, as though it had suddenly fallen from a galloping horse they rode. Chastened, Arya clung to Walker, her only protection in this strange and fearful place. They continued their trek through the Shadow.

For the longest time, Arya did not dare to look up at Walker. Fear and horror surrounded her like the very air, and it was only through Walker's soothing presence that she was able to keep her sanity in the darkness.

"Walker?" Arya finally asked, trembling. "Tell me something?"

"Perhaps."

"Do you live . . . all your life like this?" she asked.

"Always in darkness," was Walker's only reply, a reply that sent a chill of fear down Arya's spine. If her ghostly, shadow body had a spine, that is.

As if in response, a wave of adoration came over her, then sympathy for her fear. With a start, Arya realized she could feel his emotions, rather than just hear his voice. For the first time, Arya mustered the courage to look up. She caught her breath.

Walker's darkness was gone. In its place, his skin was golden and his hair glowing. His body seemed built of light and his life-force warm. He had spoken true of healing, for his body seemed to be siphoning energy from the shadow and turning it into light. In the world of the dead, Walker shone bright and alive, a shining beacon among the shadows.

"Walker, you . . . you're so different," said Arya. "So . . . bright."

A wave of confusion came to her then, and when she explained, she felt his disbelief.

"You must be mistaken," Walker explained. "You glow brightly to me, a creature of life. I should not shine brightly, for I am a creature of shadow—I dwell always in darkness."

"I only describe what I see," said Arya.

Walker inclined his head, which registered to Arya as a blur of light.

"Perhaps," he allowed. Then he stopped walking and clutched her hand. A wave of trepidation came from him, and Arya realized she had never known Walker to be afraid.

"What is the matter?" asked Arya, worried. She could see no attackers, no spirits at all. Even the trees seemed to have vanished.

"We have arrived."

CHAPTER 24

30 Tarsakh

Pulling Arya with him, Walker stepped from the Shadow Fringe into the center of his grove and the Material. He quickly became aware of two things that had changed since his last visit. The three bodies of the Greyt family rangers were gone, and the body of an unknown woman lay entwined in vines not far to the north.

"Druid Clearwater?" asked Arya wonderingly. She ran toward her.

"No, wait!" Walker shouted, but it was too late to stop the knight.

Arya knelt beside Clearwater and felt at her throat. Even as Arya confirmed that the druid rested in a magical slumber, the vines that held the druid prisoner began to twitch and sway, as though with an eerie mind of their own. Arya gasped and scrambled back from the vines that reached, fingerlike, to ensnare her arms and legs. Despite her struggling, they caught her, pulled, and dragged her to her knees.

Walker sprang to her side, the shatterspike whistling through the air as he sliced low and then high, horizontally over Arya's head, severing two thick tendrils of vines that held the knight fast. Freed for a moment, Arya managed to draw her sword and hack away at a vine that had caught her left arm. After two swings, it ripped apart and whipped through the air like a snake, recoiling from the knight.

"Back!" Walker commanded, and Arya staggered away, leaving him next to the enwrapped Amra Clearwater.

The entangling vines did not attack the ghostwalker, however—almost as though he were not there. Instead, the vines coiled snugly around Clearwater's limp form, awaiting their next target.

"Are you amused, Gylther'yel?" he called, his voice rolling across the grove. "Are you watching us from hiding, awaiting the time to strike us down?"

There came no response. Arya looked at Walker, but he waved to the knight, reassuring her.

"Have you become a watcher once more, apart from the affairs of humans?" he asked.

The grove was silent.

"Or are you afraid?" he pressed. "Afraid to show yourself, because I remind you so keenly of your failure?"

The Ghostly Lady appeared, rising from the ground in a mist, her ghostly body as insubstantial as the spirits Walker saw every moment. *Afraid?* she asked, her voice sounding in Walker's mind. *I fear nothing.*

"I have left the ghostly realm," said Walker. "Face me upon the ground of mortals."

Why, when the two of us should be gods? Gylther'yel asked in reply. When Walker said nothing, she laughed. *Very well.* Then her form became substantial. Arya, who had never seen her, was stunned at her golden beauty in the fading sunlight.

"You pick a fitting time to come against me, Rhyn Greyt,"

she said in Elvish. "When the sun of life sets and Selûne rises, bringing the night in her wake. The night is our ally, a friend to all of us who dwell in darkness."

"I have come to destroy you," Walker said in the Common tongue.

Gylther'yel merely laughed. "The prodigal son has lost his way, and returns with helpless dreams of violence," she replied in kind. "You have no inkling of my power."

"Nevertheless, I have come to sweep your perversion from the face of Faerûn," said Walker, drawing his sword.

"My perversion?" asked Gylther'yel. Both humans could hear the anger in her voice, anger hidden carefully behind a mask of ice. "*My* perversion? Have you forgotten that it was I who taught you your own perverse powers? I who returned you to life when you should be dead? If anything, we share the same corruption."

She waved at Arya, where she stood at Walker's side with her sword and shield up, but Gylther'yel addressed Walker.

"You favor the living, though you and I belong in the cult of the dead. Rhyn, you disappoint me. I had thought your mind broader than that of a mere human."

"This is my choice," said Walker.

"You merely confirm my overestimation of your intellect," said Gylther'yel. "Humans cannot choose. Lyetha could not choose between Dharan Greyt and Tarm Thardeyn until circumstance forced her hand. Dharan Greyt could not choose between weeping for the love he had lost and vengeance against the man—and the boy—who had stolen her, until I called to him fifteen years ago. Meris Wayfarer could not choose between fear of his father and vengeance, until I ordered him to slay his father . . . and you, his brother."

She laughed. "Even your little pet there, Arya Venkyr, cannot choose between justice and her heart." She turned her attention on the knight, who bristled at her words. "How do you justify yourself, Nightingale of Everlund, loving a man who espouses the very darkness and murder you deny? Walker, the avenger, the assassin? Vengeance is not justice, and Walker is nothing if not a vengeful god."

Arya's mouth moved, as though to argue with the ghost druid, but she found she could not. She turned her head, shamed.

Gylther'yel smiled. Then she turned back to Walker.

"And you cannot choose between loyalties," she said. "Loyalty to she who raised you from a child, and loyalty to she who would carry your child, she whom you love." The ghost druid spat the last word.

There it was. Walker knew the words to be true. His resolution wavered and faltered, stolen by the damning accusation. Desperately, Walker opened his mouth to argue.

"Do not attempt to deny it," she added, interrupting Walker's words. "I sense the conflict within you, the struggle to raise your blade. You cannot choose. You claim to dwell in darkness, Rhyn Greyt, you claim resolve and unwavering resolution, but you dwell in ambivalence only."

"You betrayed me," said Walker as he lifted the shatterspike and pointed it toward the ghost druid. His resolution had wavered, but now anger replaced it—a long—simmering rage that had been galvanized by the sound of his blood name. "I was your guardian—and you betrayed me. I have no choice but to—"

Gylther'yel laughed aloud. "And so you allow me to make your choice for you, once again," she said. "Young fool. You have never 'chosen,' all your life—all has been as I have directed, all as I have planned. I created your vengeance, so that you would wipe the truth away. I delayed you these fifteen years so that your foes would not recognize you as the boy they had killed and reveal the truth. The weak-willed Meris was the final test—of your abilities and your loyalties—and you have passed that test. I have made you my willing tool, my dark falcon, my hunting wolf, who claims independence and cannot sense the leash that binds him to me."

It sounded so preposterous—had not Gylther'yel been the one stopping his vengeance? Had not she tried to kill him with Meris, first in the forest, then in Quaervarr? But something inside Walker, something buried in the depths of his heart, knew—hoped—it to be true.

"Why? How could you do this to me?" asked Walker through clenched teeth.

Gylther'yel assumed a hurt expression.

"Everything I have done, I have done for love of you," she said. "To strengthen you. To raise the god of ghosts you have become, Son."

"Son?" asked Walker in complete astonishment. In his heart, though, he felt that she spoke the truth. Or, rather, he prayed with every fiber of his being that she spoke the truth.

The shatterspike shook in his trembling hand and he fell to his knees. The emotions he had kept long suppressed were surfacing with terrible force. Gylther'yel was right—even as she had betrayed him, he had known that his reins belonged to her. As he thought back to every argument, he realized that she had manipulated him into his course. Gylther'yel, the stern, distant mother, controlled his every action with an iron hand and velvet words.

"Walker?" Arya asked, reaching out to comfort him. Gylther'yel's eyes flicked to her, and she extended a clawed hand toward the knight.

Sudden tremors tore through the grove and threw Arya to the ground. A hulking claw of earth erupted from the ground and caught her between its five fingers. The knight screamed and struggled, but the fingers—each as thick as her body—were too strong. The claw closed around her and held her aloft, even as Gylther'yel closed her hand halfway and smiled.

The ghostwalker, stunned at the ghost druid's attack, had just leaped to his feet when a ring of fire surrounded him, cutting him off from Arya. He slashed at the flames with his shatterspike, and the tip of the blade glowed red with heat.

"Walker!" screamed Arya. "Don't give up! Don't give in to—" Her words were cut off in a screech of pain as Gylther'yel closed her hand tighter and the claws closed around Arya's body. The vines that bound the unconscious Amra Clearwater reached up and began whipping at the knight, tearing at her metal armor and exposed skin.

Walker instantly retreated into etherealness, meaning to leap through the flames and attack, but Gylther'yel's fire burned just as brightly there. Walker cursed himself for a fool—of course the ghost druid's magic pierced the veil between worlds. Such was the nature of the netherworld powers they shared.

Fighting the helpless rage that clawed at his heart, Walker turned back to Gylther'yel and held his sword low to the ground.

Why? he asked, and the words flowed from his mind, but, in his sinking heart, he knew the answer. She had lied. This was an attempt to delay him, not to express any real love. Gylther'yel had indeed sent Meris to kill him. Her words had startled him, and he had fallen into her trap.

Gylther'yel wove her hands in another casting, and the wall of fire began to close around Walker. *Once again, and for the last time, I make your choice for you,* she said in his head. *You have the choice to die, the choice I denied you fifteen years ago, and I choose that you will take it now.*

He had been a fool to trust in Gylther'yel, a fool to listen to her coaxing words. Meris had not been a test—he had been Gylther'yel's attempt to slay her errant guardian. It had all been a trick, a trap designed to stab at his deepest desire—the desire for another.

It was so welcoming, so easy to fall into the embrace of a mother, or a father, or even a lover, and to let his choices be determined by another. So easy. . . .

And now he would pay the price for his dependence, his lack of self-worth, a fault that had been buried beneath years of darkness, vengeance, and hatred. All of his life was coming to an end, all of his strength was unraveling.

The ghostwalker knew himself defeated.

❀ ❀ ❀ ❀ ❀

Wriggling, ignoring the crushing pain that threatened to shatter her limbs, Arya finally managed to pull her blade free. She brought the borrowed Quaervarr steel down on the earthen hand, sending sparks and shards flying. Though her arm soon went numb from the ringing vibrations her swings caused, she sent a spider web of cracks across the thumb of the hand.

Suddenly a soul-wrenching cry that broke into a high-pitched wail shattered her concentration. The scream split the boundaries of life and death and jarred her very soul.

Walker's scream.

Panicked, Arya looked over at the ghost druid and ghost-walker and her breath caught. Walker had vanished, but somehow she could feel him there. Even now, she knew he fought beyond her physical sight, but not beyond the range of her heart.

Nor, she realized, beyond the range of her voice.

Though she could not see him, his ghostsight would allow him to see—and more importantly hear—her.

"Rhyn Thardeyn!" she cried. "Rhyn Thardeyn! I believe in you, Rhyn! I believe in you!"

As she shouted those words, words that did not even break Gylther'yel's concentration, she brought her sword down on the stone finger with one last mighty blow. The blade was terribly notched and bent but it held for this one last swing. Cracked beyond endurance, the stone split apart with a scream—a scream that matched Gylther'yel's own scream. Arya looked to see blood gushing from the torn thumb of the ghost druid's right hand.

Gylther'yel turned to Arya with murder in her eyes. With a snap of her fingers, Arya's bent sword suddenly glowed white hot and tumbled from her hand. Even as Arya cursed and drew her belt dagger to throw, Gylther'yel brought down the fires of nature upon the knight.

And Arya screamed as she had never screamed before.

I believe in you!

In the depths of a shaking Ethereal, Arya's face flashed across his vision, vision that was blurred between the two worlds. At once he saw her body writhing in agony—gripped by the hand of earth, slashed by animate thorn vines, and illumined in a column of fire. Her spirit was screaming one thing: his name. He could feel the pain and terror rippling through the shadowy half-world, but also love—love that burned more brightly than the flames that tore at it.

His first real choice—the choice that brought him from Gylther'yel's clutches—had been made in Arya's arms. Arya had become the source of his strength and resolve; in her arms, he knew a stronger power, a greater determination than anything rage or hatred could muster.

He would not give up. He would not yield to Gylther'yel's lies and deceit.

Then a memory, a memory not of love but of horrible pain, flashed across his mind. A memory long buried in his mind but uncovered in Gylther'yel's words, the walls chipped away by the chisel of Walker's love for Arya.

"Greyt could not choose until I sent him. . . ." she had said.

Through newly opened ears, he heard again the ghost druid's subtle admission that she had met Greyt fifteen years previous.

Suddenly, spirits surrounded him, the spirits of his attackers, speaking again the words he remembered, the words by which he had condemned them. He did not hear them, though.

There was only one cold, familiar voice.

Whether you will or no.

Two spirits appeared over him, those of Lyetha and Tarm. They looked down at him sadly, but he could see the light of hope on their faces—tragic, resigned hope, but hope nonetheless.

And, suddenly, Walker knew what must be done.

Forgive me, Arya, he said to his beloved knight on the

ethereal winds. *I must pay for my sins. My vengeance must be complete. It has to end.*

Walker? came her startled reply. He did not know how she, in the Material world, had even heard, nor how she replied. Then a swell of love, so tragic it tore his cold heart asunder, threatened to overwhelm Walker. He had to let it flow past him. *Walker!*

You are my perfect melody, he said to Arya, *and I shall sing of you forever. The song of the Nightingale—the lay of the ghost she taught to love.*

Walker, what are you doing? asked Arya. Then she felt his emotions resonating through the shadows and she knew. He felt her terror, and knew that she realized his desperate plan. *Walker, no! Please! Don't—*

But Walker did not reply. Instead, he tore himself out of the Ethereal. The shades vanished from around him as he emerged into the physical world of torment and agony. Outside the ghost world, he knew he could feel physical pain, ansd he wore no healing ring to save him after this. This was the end.

Black hides blood. Black shrouds pain.

Gylther'yel's fire was stripping the flesh from his bones, but slowly, agonizingly, so that he could feel every tiny bit of his death. He had to feel it in order for this to work, though—he had to feel enough pain to push him to the breaking point, then. . . .

Perhaps she would not realize what she was doing until it was too late.

"Hurt me, false mother!" he called through the inferno. "Punish me, burn me, attack me!"

Gylther'yel looked at him and laughed. The fire did not intensify.

"Your entire life has been a lie!" he shouted. "The love you taught me to ignore, the good of humanity . . . I found it, but you never did. You cannot!"

She turned furious eyes upon him.

"What?" she snapped, her voice as thunder.

"You always tried . . . to be a mother to me . . . but you failed," said Walker. His words were broken with gasps of agony, but he could not succumb. Not yet. Not while this final task had to be done. "I watched my mother die . . . you could never . . . understand . . . love. . . ."

Gylther'yel screamed with laughter.

"Then teach me, 'Son!' " Throwing her hands up, she brought down a column of flame upon his head. "Whether you will it or no!"

As the agony gripped Walker with a viselike hold, he felt cold, terrible power fill his body. Though she had spoken his birth name—Rhyn Greyt—she denied his true name, the name that would take away his powers. Some men are born to a name, some men are given a name, and some men name themselves.

Rhyn Thardeyn was one of the last.

In an instant, his mind flashed back fifteen years to that terrible night when the men had killed him. His eyes saw again that terrible scene as through a red lens, blurred by the blood that had burned like fire. He heard again the taunts that had brought his memory back.

Then he saw, in his mind, something he had never remembered until now.

◈ ◈ ◈ ◈ ◈

He was lying on his back, choking but alive, and staring upward when he heard a soft voice, speaking to Greyt from the trees.

"I must have that boy," said Gylther'yel. "The agreement, Greyt."

"Damned if you will have this boy!" Greyt shouted. "I deny you!"

A rapier drove through Rhyn's throat, cutting off his breath.

"Let's hear you sing now," Meris whispered.

Rhyn Thardeyn opened his mouth but only a bloody rattle emerged.

The ghost druid smiled. "Whether you will it or no," she said. Then she turned away.

❧ ❧ ❧ ❧ ❧

Awake again, Walker turned burning eyes on Gylther'yel, eyes empty of anger, pain, rage, or love.

Eyes that knew only vengeance.

"I remember you," he said simply. The shatterspike glowed white hot in his burning hands but he felt no pain. "You were there. You let them kill me. You made them kill me."

The ghostwalker vanished out of the column of fire. Back in the Ethereal, he ran through the flames, his cold anger ignoring the agony, toward the shadowy storm that was Gylther'yel, the only mother he had ever known.

Walker! came a despairing voice. *No!*

Farewell, Arya. A smile spread across the ghostwalker's face. *Farewell, my love.*

Then he burst through Gylther'yel's ghostly halo of flame and brought his shatterspike down and through the sun elf's spectral body. The ghost druid gave a scream that tore the veil between worlds and fire exploded forth.

Spectral hands spread to welcome him, those of Lyetha and Tarm, his true mother and father. Smiling, Rhyn reached out.

All went white.

Greengrass, The Year of Lightning Storms
(1374 DR)

When Arya awoke, what could have been days later but was merely nightfall, she could see nothing through the darkness that surrounded her.

She did not need her sight, though, for she keenly remembered that haunting scream and the terrible flash of light that went with it. Gripping the grass in front of her, Arya pulled herself hand over hand, toward where she had seen Gylther'yel fall. She did not have far to go.

The grass receded as she reached a scarred swath of land, and Arya knew that she had found where Gylther'yel had died—died in a great explosion nothing could have survived.

Why, then, was Arya alive? Why had she. . . .

Then Arya felt the surprisingly cool metal around her finger, and she knew.

The wolf's head ring! The damnable ring had

kept her alive! Alive, on the very spot....

Had he known it would end this way? Had he known that one of them would die, and chosen to save her? Had he known, all along?

With a moan, Arya felt around blindly. Long, agonizing moments passed before she realized there was nothing there to find. Walker and Gylther'yel had both vanished.

A wave of love, undying love, washed over her, and Arya wept in agony, great sobs welling up from her aching, torn body. The sound attracted someone else from nearby, who came to her side. Arya felt a momentary swell of hope, that perhaps it was Walker, but even her blurry vision could tell her it was not.

"There, there," a feminine voice whispered in her ear. Tender arms hugged her. "My name's Amra Clearwater. You're safe now."

"Wh-where is he?" Arya asked in agony, only part of it physical. "Wh-where. . .?"

"Who?" Amra asked. "There is no one here but you and me. The Ghostly Lady's gone. There was no one else."

"He's gone," said Arya, her heart sinking. "Gone without me. . . ."

But then there was another sound, cutting her off. Even as Selûne ushered in the dawn of spring, rising silver and full, a lonely wolf howled.

"Seek your redemption," Arya whispered to the wind, tears sliding down her cheeks. "And if—when—you find it, I'll be waiting."

Arya smiled as darkness closed around her and she knew no more.

Amra Clearwater smiled sadly, thinking the now-slumbering knight spoke nonsense.

The wolf's song to the spring moon was at an end.

The Nightingale's Song

A cold hand touches my cheek, but it is only wind,
the breeze that caressed us as we lay
peaceful and warm among the shadows,
tangled together and guarded by stars.
In love—in a moment.

Now you walk one way and I the other,
but your voice lingers in my mind —
I hear its broken beauty shattering the stillness,
and I know I would throw my memories away
for just one moment more with you.

But all I can lose is your ring from my hand,
a kindness and a curse, and
all I have left of you to touch.
Though I walk lonely into the years,
I won't let go.

I could not save you, could not find your path.
Were you too lost for salvation?
Perhaps, you would say. But, perhaps
I was the one who lost the way,
And you saved me.

> —composed by Lady Arya Venkyr (1375 DR)
> Translated from the original Elvish

THE FIRST INTO BATTLE,
THEY HOLD THE LINE, THEY ARE...

THE FIGHTERS

MASTER OF CHAINS

Once he was a hero, but that was before he was nearly killed and
sold into slavery. Now he has nothing but hate and the chains of
his bondage: the only weapons he has with which to escape.

GHOSTWALKER

His first memories were of death. His second, of those who killed him.
Now he walks with specters, consumed by revenge.

SON OF THUNDER

Forgotten in a valley of the High Forest dwell the thunderbeasts,
kept secret by ancient and powerful magic. When the Zhentarim find
out about this magic, a young barbarian must defend his reptilian
brethren from those who would seize their power.

BLADESINGER

Corruption grips the heart of Rashemen in the one place they thought
it could not take root: the council of wise women who guide the people.
A half-elf bladesinger traveling north with his companions is the people's
only hope, but first, he must convince them to accept his help.

For more information visit **www.wizards.com**